SKIN AND BONES

Tom Bale has worked as a retail assistant, claims negotiator, office manager, business analyst, freelance consultant and househusband. He now writes full-time and lives with his family in Brighton. For more information, visit his website at www.tombale.net.

TOM BALE

SKIN AND BONES

arrow books

This paperback edition published by Arrow Books 2010

10 9 8 7 6 5 4 3 2

Copyright © Tom Bale 2008, 2010

Tom Bale has asserted his right to be identified as the author of this work under the
Copyright, Designs and Patents Act 1988

Lyrics on p1 reproduced by kind permission James and Blue Mountain Music Ltd

First published in Great Britain in 2008 by Preface Publishing

Arrow Books
20 Vauxhall Bridge Road
London SW1V 2SA

An imprint of The Random House Group

www.rbooks.co.uk

Addresses for companies within The Random House Group Limited
can be found at www.randomhouse.co.uk

The Random House Group Limited Reg. No. 954009

A CIP catalogue record for this book is available from the British Library

ISBN 978 1 84809 073 6

The Random House Group Limited supports The Forest Stewardship Council (FSC),
the leading international forest certification organisation. All our titles that are printed
on Greenpeace-approved FSC-certified paper carry the FSC logo. Our paper
procurement policy can be found at www.rbooks.co.uk/environment

Typeset in Electra LH Regular by Palimpsest Book Production Limited,
Grangemouth, Stirlingshire
Printed and bound in Great Britain by
CPI Bookmarque, Croydon CR0 4TD

For Niki

PART ONE

Come, dip on in
Leave your bones
Leave your skin
Leave your past
Leave your craft
Leave your suffering heart

James, 'Sound'

One

A glance to her left was all it took. A simple glance as she pushed open the door to the village shop. If she had kept her eyes straight ahead, or looked to the right instead, she might never have become involved. She might have been spared.

Her conscious mind, bruised by the experience of the past month, refused to believe what it had seen. But her subconscious knew and understood.

There was a dead man in the street.

It was the third Saturday of January, not quite eight in the morning. She parked outside her parents' cottage on the outskirts of the village and decided to delay the day's grim task by a few minutes. The store was no more than fifty or sixty yards away, tucked around a bend at the foot of the High Street: a ludicrous name for a place with only one shop and one pub.

Julia was thirty-one, a tall slender woman with dark shoulder-length hair. She taught at a junior school in Newhaven, and like the best teachers she had perfected a good-natured toughness that equipped her to cope with the worst that any ten-year-old could throw at her. In the past few weeks she had needed that resilience more than ever.

Her breath rose in clouds as she walked along the edge of the narrow road. A clean shimmer of frost lay over the grass verge. Roof tiles sparkled in the late Downland sunrise. The air tasted clean and sharp, and made her wish she was out jogging. Made her wish she had the day free to do as she chose.

It took her less than a minute to reach the shop. In that time she didn't see or hear another soul. No traffic, no tradesmen, no walkers or cyclists. But it was a Saturday, she reasoned. It was January. It was cold.

At the point where she glanced to her left, she had a clear view along the High Street, all the way to the Green Man pub at the north end of the village. There was a Royal Mail van parked at the kerb up by the church, facing towards her. She vaguely noticed the rear doors were open. If there was a body, it was lying in the road just beyond the van, only the feet visible.

Telling herself she must be mistaken, Julia entered the shop.

A bell rang as she stepped inside. The air was deliciously warm, with an aroma that always prompted a smile: a cosy blend of bread rolls, sliced ham, newsprint and mailbags. The kind of smell you'd like to bottle for nostalgia. *Essence of village store*.

The shopkeeper, Moira Beaumont, was a small twitchy woman in her fifties. She pulled her baggy cardigan together in response to the draught.

'Hello, love. You're an early bird. Don't tell me you stayed overnight?'

Julia's curt shake of her head disguised a shudder. 'I've just driven here,' she said, adding, 'I can't keep putting it off.'

Moira nodded sadly. 'It's Lewes where you live, isn't it?' She spoke as though the county town was some distant exotic locale, when in fact it was less than ten miles away. But then Chilton was the sort of place where people still returned from Brighton, outraged by beggars in the street and the brazen display of homosexual love.

Julia browsed the newspapers for a minute, aware of Moira's sly scrutiny. Trying to spot a crack in the facade. A couple of weeks ago it would have bothered her, but she was used to it by now. All things considered, she felt she was coping pretty well.

So why the body in the street? her subconscious piped up. Hallucinations were hardly a sign of robust mental health.

Pushing the thought aside, she picked up the *Guardian*, a carton of semi-skimmed milk and on impulse a packet of chocolate biscuits. She had a long and difficult day ahead: she deserved a treat.

When she reached the counter Moira leaned over and grasped her hand. Even before she spoke, Julia knew she was going to use the gentle hushed tone that people reserve for the recently bereaved.

'I just want to say, I'm dreadfully sorry for what happened. They were such a lovely couple.'

Julia swallowed and nodded tersely. She had learned just how easily such expressions of sympathy could unlock the grief.

'Is your brother not coming to help clear the house?' Moira asked, taking Julia's five-pound note and prodding at the till.

'He offered, but it seems ridiculous when he's up in Cheshire.'

'I suppose so. What a shame you and Peter aren't still together,' said Moira, blithely unaware of her tactlessness. 'I know your mother always thought you were made for each other.'

'So did I,' said Julia. *Another subject she was keen to avoid.*

'But you've a new feller now, haven't you? I can't remember his name . . .'

'Steve.'

'That's it. Steve.' Moira gave a rather disdainful sniff. Probably remembering Mum's verdict on him, Julia thought.

'I'm not sure it's got much future, to be honest,' she said.

Moira clicked her tongue. 'You've really been in the wars, haven't you?' There was a moment when Julia felt sure she was going to say something about bad news coming in threes, but perhaps thought better of it. Instead she puffed out a breath. 'I'd give you a hand myself, but Len's away to Leicester to watch the football. Time off for good behaviour,' she added wryly.

Julia grinned. 'I'll be fine. And if I don't get it finished today . . . well, there's no great hurry.'

'You'll feel better when it's done, believe me.' Moira pressed her hands together as if in prayer. 'In my experience, it's the most unexpected things that can catch you out. If they do, you know where to find me.'

'Thanks.' Julia propped the biscuits under her arm and picked up the milk. For the sake of conversation, she said, 'Quiet round here this morning.'

Moira took a moment to consider. 'I suppose it is. I had a couple of folk in when I opened at seven, Mrs Collins and Tom Bradbury with those ruddy dogs of his. But it's freezing out there. I bet everyone's decided to stay in bed, lucky beggars.'

'I expect that's it,' Julia agreed.

When she reached the door, Moira called, 'Keep in touch, won't you? Don't be a stranger!'

Julia trapped the door with her foot and turned back, smiling. At that moment, with her own heart weighing so heavily, she would never have believed Moira had less than twenty minutes to live.

Leaving the shop, her attention was caught by a poster in the window of the house opposite. Another of Philip Walker's campaigns, she guessed from the headline in bold four-inch letters. Because of what was to happen next, the words would be forever imprinted on her memory.

```
This is OUR village!
Don't let them DESTROY IT!!
```

She snorted. Walker was the outspoken leader of a group of local activists, waging a war against developers seeking to expand the village. Probably a futile endeavour, if history was any judge, but Julia had a sneaking sympathy for them. If nothing else, her parents had been enthusiastic supporters of the cause.

And then, unable to resist the nagging voice of her subconscious, she turned to look north once again. She had to know if she had imagined it.

There was still no sign of activity in the village. The Royal Mail van remained in place. The rear doors were definitely open. And the body still lay behind the van, feet angled up on the pavement.

Oh Christ.

Shielding her eyes against the low morning sun, she squinted and took a few paces forward. She could feel her mouth going dry, her heart speeding up. She pictured herself slowly climbing the stairs in her parents' cottage. She couldn't go through that again, couldn't expose herself to—

And you can't let him die, a stronger voice spoke up. *He might have had a heart attack or a stroke. He might be epileptic.* Her knowledge of first aid was only rudimentary, but she could at least raise the alarm and keep him warm.

Her confidence wavered as she drew near the van. It looked as though he'd collapsed and rolled partly beneath the rear doors. A bundle of letters lay in the gutter, the breeze not quite strong enough to tease them free of the rubber band that restrained them.

Maybe a hit-and-run, she wondered, steeling herself for an unpleasant sight.

But it was far worse than a hit-and-run. The postman had gunshot wounds to his head and chest. One eye was missing, and the other stared lifelessly at her, wide with surprise that this could happen in such a privileged enclave of Sussex. The van was splattered with blood and brain and skull fragments.

Julia gasped and dropped her milk. The carton split open and leaked across the pavement, mixing with the blood in the gutter.

Two

Must have been a robbery, she thought. She peered into the back of the van, but it told her nothing. There were several grey sacks of mail, but plenty of space where other sacks might have lain.

The blood on the road was fresh, glistening like resin in the sunshine. That meant it had happened recently. She hadn't seen or heard any vehicles, so the killer must have escaped on foot.

The implication of this wasn't lost on Julia. She turned slowly, searching for signs of anything else out of place.

The village was roughly rectangular, with the cottages she'd just passed forming the eastern flank from the shop up to the sturdy Norman church of St Mary. Next to the church was the Rectory, and then the Green Man, a handsome Tudor inn. Then Hurst Lane, a private road which ran north for half a mile to Chilton Manor and Hurst Farm.

On the other side of the lane was the Old Schoolhouse, home to NIMBY activist Philip Walker. After that came Arundel Crescent, a line of grand Georgian houses which ran down the western flank and gave way to another terrace of smaller homes, ending opposite the shop back at the southern tip.

Chilton's centrepiece was the village green, complete with pond and a magnificent yew tree said to be over six hundred years old. The pond was partially frozen, and a couple of seagulls paced the perimeter, jostling smaller birds like hooligans on a day trip. They were the only living things in sight.

It's too quiet, Julia thought. Eight o'clock on a Saturday, someone should be out here, walking their dog, going shopping, ferrying the kids to football. Her brother and his wife were like a full-time taxi service for their children at the weekend. And surely someone would have heard gunshots and come out to investigate?

Something's very wrong.

Because she'd only intended to pop to the shop, she had left her handbag and mobile phone in the car, along with the cardboard boxes and plastic sacks for packing up her parents' belongings. Not that her mobile would have helped, she remembered. The village action group had fought off plans for a phone mast. She would have to find a land-line.

Or you could walk away, a tiny, shameful voice spoke up. The postman's dead. You can't help him. Just turn round and go back to your car. It doesn't have to be your problem.

For a moment she might have succumbed. How wonderful to get in her Mini, start the engine and drive away. She'd been through enough trauma lately. Let someone else deal with this.

Then she imagined how her parents would have regarded such cowardice. She didn't really believe in an afterlife, but since their deaths she'd often envisaged them watching over her, judging her or passing comment on her choices and decisions. Now they would expect her to do whatever she could to help.

She ran on shaky legs to the nearest house, in the terrace next to the churchyard. The garden gate creaked as she opened it, under-scoring the oppressive silence of the morning. The front door was painted a cheery red, with a small handwritten sign at eye level: *Doorbell not working. Please knock.*

So she did. Leaning close to the door, she could hear music playing inside: something melodic, with a Sixties twang.

There was no response. She knocked again, thumping the door

hard enough to rattle the hinges. 'Please!' she called. 'It's an emergency!'

Her cry provoked mournful cawing from the rooks in the trees around the church. Julia felt her skin crawl and cast an anxious glance over her shoulder, suddenly convinced she was being watched. Had she sensed movement in Hurst Lane?

She waited a few more seconds, debating whether to run back to the shop. She knew Moira was a nervy creature, and certainly not the coolest of heads in a crisis. Besides, the postman might be a friend of hers. Better to spare her that if she could.

St Mary's was a safer bet. Someone was bound to be up and about by now. And if not, there might at least be a phone.

The churchyard was enclosed by a waist-high wall of Sussex flint. She passed through the lych gate and followed the gravel path to the entrance porch. Her route was lined by weathered gravestones, listing at drunken angles.

To her relief, one of the heavy oak doors was open. She stepped into the vestibule and saw another of Philip Walker's posters on the noticeboard, alongside lists of services, cleaning rotas, an advert for a jumble sale.

Pushing through a second set of doors, she entered the nave and immediately felt calmed by the soft light and atmosphere of peaceful reflection. The air smelled of dust and damp stone. And possibly something else, but she refused to acknowledge it.

A wave of dizziness swept over her. She grabbed the back of a pew and eased herself down. Leaning forward, she rested her head against the pew in front, her hair falling across her face like a fan. Slowly the other smell permeated her senses: something sharp and foul and metallic.

This is no good, she told herself. You have to find a phone.

She repressed an urge to vomit, made herself breathe through her mouth, slowly and deeply. It was at the mid-point, the breath suspended in her lungs, when she heard it.

A soft, scrabbling sound. Something moving on the ancient stone floor in front of the pews. Quiet, stealthy movement.

She sat upright, eyes locked on the point near the altar where the noise had originated. Every muscle was rigid with terror. She couldn't even release her breath.

If the killer was here, lying in wait, she would never outrun him. She would never get out in time.

It was a simple, inescapable fact. If he was inside the church, then she was already dead.

Three

She heard it again. A scraping noise, a heel scuffing over stone.

Then a man's voice. Very weak, barely intelligible.

He said: 'Please . . .'

Then: 'Uhh.'

It was such a distinct exhalation, Julia immediately understood what it meant. The man who made that noise had just lost his life, not twenty feet from where she was sitting, paralysed with fear. She had sat and heard a man die and done nothing.

She began to shake. She felt she might be going mad, and for a few seconds it was almost a temptation. In shedding her sanity she could shrug off all responsibility along with it.

Then the moment passed, and she rose to her feet and approached the front of the church. She tried not to remember how the postman had looked. Tried not to think about what she would see this time.

There were two bodies, lying several feet apart in the space between the front pew and the chancel. The vicar was curled in a foetal position, one hand reaching for the altar as though in a plea for clemency. He'd been shot several times in the stomach. There was a smear of blood on the floor where he had dragged himself towards the aisle.

His eyes were open, staring at Julia with sorrowful reproach. *You didn't help*, he might have been saying. *You heard me and you didn't help.*

A few feet beyond him was the body of a heavy grey-haired woman in sweat pants and a blue fleece. She'd been shot in the back of the head. The resulting debris lay around her like old porridge. A tin of Pledge rested at her side, a blood-speckled yellow duster still gripped in her hand.

Julia backed away. Her imagination hardly dared to conclude what was happening here. Paradoxically, the words that leapt into her head made no sense, and yet they made perfect sense.

This wasn't a robbery. It was a massacre.

Slowly she came back to the present, aware that a few minutes had passed. She had no recollection of returning to one of the pews, but that was where she found herself. She was shivering, clutching herself to try and stop the trembling.

Visions flooded her mind: a grisly panorama of the bodies she had seen, jumbled together with news footage of Hungerford, Port Arthur, Dunblane. The perpetrator invariably male, white, a troubled loner nursing real or imagined grievances in a cauldron of paranoia.

She imagined him walking from house to house, knocking quietly. The villagers readily opening their front doors, expecting to greet a neighbour or perhaps the postman with a parcel. And instead, he was killing them all. Wiping out an entire community.

Moira.

It was the jolt Julia needed, the adrenalin rush like a blow to the stomach. She jumped up and quickly checked the vestry, then a small office next to it, but there was no phone. She knew she couldn't remain in the church, but leaving by the main entrance was too risky.

Instead she made for the side door in the east chancel. It meant passing the bodies of the vicar and the cleaner, but she forced herself to do it. She had to keep moving, had to stay focused.

The heavy door creaked open, sounding horrifically loud. She stepped out, blinking in the bright sunshine, and followed the path diagonally across the churchyard. A gate in the wall led to a footpath that ran behind the cottages, parallel to the High Street.

She was level with the first house, the one she'd tried earlier, when she noticed the back door was ajar. She'd been intending to make straight for the shop, but now she stopped. She could phone the police from here.

There was a low fence at the back of the property, easily vaulted. The garden was a narrow strip of turf, strewn with partially deflated footballs and a plastic cricket set. There was a soiled cat litter tray by the door.

Julia could hear the radio playing in the kitchen, the mindless chatter of a DJ. She stepped inside and called, 'Hello? I need to use the phone. Is anyone there?'

No one answered, but the sound of shifting crockery made her jump.

The dishwasher. According to the display, it had eight minutes left to run. There was a mug of herbal tea on the worktop. Julia felt it with the back of her hand. Still warm.

Someone should be here.

She crept into the narrow hallway. The door to the living room was open. She spotted the phone and the bodies simultaneously.

A young woman in a towelling dressing gown was sprawled over her child, a small boy with glorious white-blond hair. Playmobil fire trucks and figures were scattered around them. There was blood everywhere. The woman had obviously tried to shield her son, and then covered his eyes with her hand. She couldn't stop him dying, but at least she could make sure he didn't see it happen.

Julia wobbled again. Felt she was breaking apart. *No one would blame me*, she thought.

Turning away, she snatched the phone from its perch on the wall. There was no dialling tone. She stabbed the call button. Listened. Stabbed it again. Nothing.

The phone was dead. It couldn't be coincidence. It was part of the plan.

Movement outside caught her attention. She took a cautious step towards the window. Across the green, a door had opened in Arundel Crescent, causing a flash of reflected sunlight. The man who emerged was short and stocky, with spiky straw-coloured hair, wearing a denim jacket and camouflage trousers. He held a pistol in one hand, and there was a shotgun slung over his shoulder.

He closed the door behind him, then stopped and slowly surveyed the scene. For a moment he seemed to be staring right at Julia. When he smiled, she thought her heart would stop beating.

Then she realised he was looking at the postman's body. Admiring his handiwork.

He strode away, disappearing behind the massive yew tree. The direction he was taking would lead him to the shop.

In desperation Julia tried the phone again, but she knew it was hopeless. The village was cut off from the rest of the world, just as the killer intended.

She was on her own.

She ran back through the kitchen. On the radio the Rolling Stones seemed to be mocking her: *You can't always get what you want.* The words echoed in her head as she retraced her steps through the garden. Again she thought of her parents. She hoped they would be proud of her for overcoming the urge to flee.

She sprinted towards the shop, praying she would make it in time. The path was a mixture of gravel, earth and weeds, and the crunch of her pounding feet seemed to reverberate around the village.

The shop backed on to a yard containing several wheelie bins, a stack of cardboard boxes and an old plastic crate. There were two small opaque windows, protected by metal grilles. The back door was solid timber and couldn't be opened from the outside.

Julia knocked as loudly as she dared. Another bout of giddiness made her sway on her feet. Black spots danced in front of her eyes. Her heart was thudding so loudly she thought it would explode from her chest.

Then a voice: 'Who's there?'

Julia forced herself upright. 'Moira, it's Julia Trent. Open the door.'

She feared Moira might argue, or tell her to come round the front, but she heard the thud of a bolt being drawn back. The door opened and Moira peered out, reacting with alarm at the sight of Julia's face.

'Oh my word. What's happened, love?'

Julia tried to speak but was overcome by a flood of nausea. Her chest heaved and she turned away, clutching her stomach and spitting bile on to the dusty cement.

'You poor dear,' Moira said. 'Come on, let's get you indoors.'

Julia nodded, turned back and stepped into the stockroom. Moira stroked her arm. 'You've had a shock. I told you it could happen, didn't I?'

Julia tried to put her right but could only stammer, 'No, I . . . I've g-got . . .'

Moira shushed her. 'Don't try and tell me yet. Just rest a minute.' There was a clipboard lying on an old chair in the corner of the room. Moira picked it up and dragged the chair towards Julia, causing a bell to ring from somewhere. A *eureka*! moment, Julia thought, and wondered if she had finally lost her mind.

Moira said, 'Here, sit yourself down while I pop the kettle on.'

Julia frowned. Why would moving a chair cause a bell to ring?

Then she understood, but panic overwhelmed her, short-circuiting her brain. She knew what she had to say and do, but her body wouldn't respond.

Some sort of noise must have emerged from her throat, for Moira turned towards her in a strange kind of slow motion. At the same time Julia had a clear line of sight through the shop. The man with spiky hair was walking towards the counter. She saw he was young, no more than mid-twenties. He had very pale eyes and an uneven growth of bristles on his chin.

He saw her and smiled. His teeth were yellow and crooked, with a distinctive left canine jutting out like a vampire's fang. He raised the gun and Julia noticed the thick cylinder attached to the barrel. A silencer. That's why no one had heard gunshots.

Moira was speaking again, making clucking noises of sympathy. She noticed Julia's terrified gaze and turned to see what had provoked it. There was a spitting noise and a spray of blood blew from her neck. Moira's eyes widened, her mouth a perfect circle of surprise as she toppled forward.

Another *phutt* and Julia felt the bullet brush past her hair, thudding into the doorframe behind her. Then there was a moment where Moira's falling body obscured her view of the killer. A third shot hit the shopkeeper as she fell, and by then Julia's survival instinct had kicked in.

She leapt out of the stockroom, dragging the door shut behind her. Grabbed one of the wheelie bins and pulled it across the door. It wasn't heavy enough to prevent him getting out, but it might gain her a few seconds. But which way should she go?

She had two options. Back up the lane towards the church, or along the alley by the side of the shop and rejoin the main road. That was the one she favoured. Once on the High Street she could make a run for her car. Fifty or sixty yards, she'd cover that in no time.

It was the wrong choice. She knew it when she heard the bell ring again, but by then it was too late. She was only yards from the main road, running too fast to stop. Her forward momentum sent her skidding on to the narrow pavement just as the killer emerged from the shop.

He had outguessed her. Then she registered his surprise and realised it was worse than that. He'd just been lucky. Sometimes that's all it came down to, she thought. He'd struck it lucky. She hadn't.

They stood a couple of feet apart, facing each other. There was no way she could escape. This was the end.

She stuck out her jaw and tried to look defiant. She wasn't going to beg for her life. In any case, she didn't trust herself to speak.

The killer made a dry snickering noise that brought to mind some half-remembered cartoon character. He examined her for a long second, his attention lingering on her body. Her jeans and jacket couldn't disguise the fact that she was tall, slim, shapely.

Finally he met her gaze, and seemed to come to a decision. His pale eyes gleamed. His smile hinted at the pleasures of anticipation, and she knew all too well what that meant. He liked what he saw. He wasn't going to kill her straight away.

She understood this perhaps half a second before he spoke.

A single word in a low, guttural whisper.

'Run.'

Four

She took his advice. It didn't matter that she was giving him what he wanted. It meant she had a chance. Every second she stayed alive was a tiny victory.

There was no point trying for her car. He'd never let her get close to it. She spun on her heels and ran back the way she'd come. Back on to the lane behind the cottages, back towards the church. It was a couple of seconds before she heard his feet on the gravel. He was deliberately giving her an advantage.

Remembering something she'd read, she began to weave from side to side, trying to present a more difficult target. The churchyard was only sixty or seventy yards away. She had maybe ten yards on the killer, and could probably extend that to twenty. But it wouldn't be enough.

The problem was the gate. The latch was heavy and cumbersome. If she stopped to open it, he would be on her in seconds. Game over.

She studied the gate, and the wall either side of it. Made some calculations. The wall was roughly three feet high, the gate an inch or two higher. She'd jumped taller obstacles in her life, but not since her schooldays. A good fifteen years or so.

But there was no choice. It was that or die.

No, she reminded herself. It was that or be raped, and then die.

She pumped her arms, measured her stride. She was aiming at a spot on the wall just to the left of the gate. She focused on timing the jump, thanking God she'd worn jeans and trainers today.

She almost made it. She launched herself into the air at exactly the right spot. Her leap was strong, her body lithe and primed by adrenalin and fear. Her feet lifted and curled to give her clearance, and as she started to descend she thought she was over. But then her left foot dropped, just a fraction, and caught on a lump of flint.

She pinwheeled, frantically trying to maintain her balance, but landed heavily on her right foot. A searing pain tore through her ankle. She fell sideways and rolled on the wet grass. Her knee scraped a gravestone, tearing her jeans, and there was a whoop of laughter from the path.

Well, fuck you, she thought. A surge of fury gave her the strength to get up. She risked a look back. The killer had reached the gate. He was smiling, as though he expected to chase her around the village for as long as it amused him, then finish her off.

There was an agonising jolt when she put her weight on her right foot. She took a few steps, hobbling at first, testing the ankle until she trusted it not to give way on her. Gritting her teeth against the pain.

She ignored the church. As a place of shelter it hadn't offered much protection to the vicar or the cleaner. Instead she cut across the grass, towards the lych gate. She didn't give any real thought to where she would go: all that mattered was putting some distance between her and the killer.

Disturbed by the commotion, the rooks flapped above the church-yard, their bleak throaty cries like a comment on her prospects. Julia reached the gate and wrenched it open. The houses in Arundel Crescent were bathed in sunlight, lending a honeyed tint to the white render. She wondered if any were unlocked.

She took another glance over her shoulder. The killer was trotting in her wake, a little faster now, and scowling, possibly beginning to regret giving her a head start. It made her feel absurdly pleased. He'd underestimated her.

But hitting tarmac increased the pain in her ankle. She realised she couldn't run for much longer. She had to find somewhere to hide.

She crossed the road a few feet from the mail van, disturbing a sleek black crow perched on the postman's chest. It turned its inky gaze upon her, decided she was no threat, then pecked lavishly at the dead man's face.

Shuddering with revulsion, she looked away and caught something far more significant: a woman's stricken face in an upstairs window in the crescent. A moment's guilty eye contact and then she was gone. If not for the curtain swaying in her wake, Julia might have believed she'd imagined it.

She increased her speed, wincing as her ankle protested. She clung to a vision of a front door opening, the woman beckoning her inside. If they timed it right, she could rush through and slam it shut before the gunman reacted. Then the two of them could barricade themselves in. Wait for help to arrive, or even find a weapon and fight back.

Julia was halfway across the green, still believing she could make it to safety, when the bullet brought her down.

She didn't hear it coming. Didn't even feel anything at first. Just a coldness on her skin, a disturbing friction, and she glanced down to find blood soaking through her jeans. The bullet had grazed her right calf, taking a sliver of flesh with it.

A moment later the pain hit and her leg seized up, slapping her to the ground. She landed awkwardly, one arm caught beneath her body, forcing the air from her lungs.

Bastard! she thought. *He's not playing fair.*

She twisted round and saw him, standing in front of the lych gate. He looked immensely satisfied, as if winging her had been precisely his intention. He was back in control. Now the real fun would begin.

Some primeval imperative refused to let her surrender. She struggled to her feet. Her right leg wouldn't bear her weight for more than a moment at a time. She saw she was only fifteen or twenty feet from the yew tree, and instinct propelled her towards it, even though her rational mind knew it was hopeless as a hiding place.

She took one difficult, lurching step. Then another. Turning away from the killer was the hardest part. Every nerve screamed with tension, expecting another bullet to strike. Probably he'd aim low again. He would want her conscious for what else he had in mind.

'You. Cowardly. Evil. Wretch.'

The voice came from nowhere. Not a shout but a determined growl, delivered slowly and through terrible pain. Julia and the killer reacted to it at the same time.

It was Philip Walker. He was a tall, thin man, perhaps seventy years old, with white hair and a face almost as pale. He was slumped in the doorway of the Old Schoolhouse, pressing a blood-soaked towel to his chest.

Julia heard the killer grunt, taken aback by this intervention. He'd obviously left Walker for dead. The old man caught her eye and gave an almost imperceptible nod: *get out of here*.

In her peripheral vision she saw the killer turn and approach the Old Schoolhouse. It should have given her renewed hope, but instead there was an awful temptation to collapse on the grass, just shut her eyes and let it happen: defilement, death, whatever he had planned for her.

Then she rebelled against the defeatism. But she also knew she'd never make it to the house in the crescent. In any case, there was no guarantee the woman would let her in. Her best chance was the yew tree.

She limped towards it, dragging her useless leg like a ball and chain. As she drew close she saw the tree comprised four massive trunks, creating a natural hollow in the middle. Moving around the base, she located a gap large enough to squeeze through.

Walker was speaking again, snarling at the killer, who laughed in response. Julia heard the creak of the garden gate, then footsteps on Walker's path. She concentrated on pushing herself into the centre of the tree, experiencing a burst of excitement as she realised she was now out of the killer's sight.

Then she heard the peculiar spitting sound of the silenced gun. Peeked out in time to see Philip Walker, shot twice at point blank range, drop at his killer's feet.

She ducked back, tears clouding her vision as it hit home that he'd sacrificed himself for her. She owed it to him not to waste this chance.

But what could she do? The only option was to climb the tree. If she could gain some height, she might be able to use the thick branches for concealment. Denied a clear shot, the killer would have to climb up after her. She might be able to fight him off, perhaps kick him or stamp on his fingers.

She grabbed the highest branch within reach, pressed her back against one of the trunks and began to lever herself up. Even with her bad leg, it was a surprisingly effective way to climb. The bark was cool to the touch and resembled sunburned skin, dry patches flaking away from the smoother surface beneath. The branches were thick and sinewy, like something from a fairy story. At any moment she expected one to curl around her waist and lift her to safety in the higher reaches of the tree.

She was seven or eight feet above the ground when she regained a view of the killer. He was walking away from the Old Schoolhouse, doing something with the pistol. Reloading, Julia guessed. She could see Walker's body crumpled in the doorway of his home.

The killer replaced the magazine, reached the green and stopped abruptly. He looked round, at first confused, then angry. Julia felt a savage exhilaration. *That's twice I've outwitted you.*

She continued to ascend. The short needles of the yew grew thickly around her, obscuring her from view. He would have to walk right up to the trunk to see her now. Another couple of feet and she could hide completely.

Now she had a real chance of surviving. After all, she reasoned, this nightmare can't go on for ever. Help must come eventually.

Something's got to happen, she told herself.

And then it did.

Five

He looked like something from a movie. A superhero, a Special Forces agent and James Bond all wrapped up in one.

Her saviour.

He was clad entirely in black leather: boots, trousers, jacket, gloves, like some sort of costume. He wore a black motorcycle helmet with a full-face visor. He burst into view from Hurst Lane and marched towards the killer. He didn't appear to be armed, but he showed no fear. He moved fast, his body confident and determined. It was the most thrilling sight Julia had ever seen.

He called out in a gruff voice. The killer heard it and spun round. His demeanour changed immediately. He seemed to shrink, bowing his head in deference to the man striding towards him.

'What the hell are you doing with that?' the man demanded. Julia's heart leapt with joy. Finally, someone with the moral and physical strength to confront the killer.

The man in black shook his head, as if disgusted, and raised his arm in the air. It looked like he was preparing to punch the killer in the face, and Julia willed him on, praying that the murdering bastard wouldn't read the blow in advance.

But it wasn't a punch.

It was a high five.

*   *   *

25

What shocked her most was that she'd been about to shout a warning. She saw the killer adjust his body to what the other man was doing. He's going to dodge it, Julia thought. And then he'll shoot you. And suddenly she couldn't bear to see this man, this wonderful brave man, become yet another victim. Her best hope of rescue wrenched from her grasp.

So she opened her mouth to scream a warning. Filled her lungs to fuel the words. Delayed half a second while she searched for the right phrase: *Be careful!* Or *Watch out!* Or *He's got a gun!*

And then the man in black slapped his hand against the killer's hand, and the killer grinned and whooped and nodded ferociously at something the stranger was saying. Talking in a low voice, their heads close together, the killer almost blushing with pride as the man in black spoke to him.

Congratulating him.

Julia's whole body spasmed with fear and despair. She threw both arms around the tree and clung to it until the feeling passed. Her left leg was wedged uncomfortably against the trunk, her injured leg dangling in the air as if it no longer belonged to her. Blood ran over her shoe and dripped on to the leaves below. The sight of it made her head swim. She gulped in fresh air and looked up instead. Saw aircraft trails criss-crossing a milky blue sky. It seemed incredible to think that beyond the village there was a whole world carrying on as normal.

And then she cocked her head. She could hear something. Faint and far away, but it was there.

A siren.

The killer's words floated up to her: 'I shot this bitch, but she got away.' Julia peered through the leaves and saw him gesturing towards the tree. The man in black also turned to look. The faceless visor sent a bolt of terror through her. He's Darth Vader, she thought. A dark angel of death.

'. . . hiding over there,' the killer was saying, his voice whiny and defensive.

The man in black leaned close and murmured something Julia couldn't hear. To her astonishment, the killer meekly handed the pistol to his partner, then slipped the shotgun off his shoulder.

Then both men froze. They could hear it too. Urgent pulses of sound, growing louder.

The man in black took a step away from his partner and pointed across the green. The killer swivelled his shotgun in the same direction. Julia almost went to look herself, but then had a flash of insight: *it's a bluff.*

She saw the gun coming up and instinctively shut her eyes. Remembered how the young mother had protected her son from the knowledge of his death.

Heard the familiar *phutt.*

She opened her eyes. Saw the killer falling, shot in the temple at point-blank range. Blood everywhere, all over him, all over the grass. A spray of it on the motorcycle leathers. The man in black stepping back, nodding to himself.

Julia made a noise, a little horrified yelp. She couldn't help it.

Then the branch cracked.

It didn't break. It didn't give way. It just dropped an inch or two and she dropped with it, scrabbling desperately with both hands to hang on. Her movement caused the tree to shake, the leaves whispering as they rubbed together. Telling on her.

The man in black whipped round and faced the tree. At the same time Julia realised the siren was fully audible. Perhaps on Chilton Way by now, she thought. A couple of minutes away, maybe less.

But still too late to save her.

She hung suspended in the tree as the man in black approached. At times his head seemed to be dipped, facing the ground. Julia was confused. Why look down?

27

Her trainer offered the answer. Blood. He was following the blood trail. It confirmed the noise in the tree wasn't from a crow, or a pigeon, or even a frightened cat.

Her bladder let go. Hot urine soaked through her jeans and ran down her legs. She barely noticed it.

Calmly, even casually, the man in black walked back to the body of his partner, then turned and fired a rapid burst of shots into the tree. Julia heard the bullets striking leaves and branches above her head, gouging out chunks of bark. The debris rained down on her, but she couldn't squirm away from it without revealing her position.

The next sweep was a couple of feet lower. She felt the bullets whipping past, the lethal *zing* of displaced air.

Bizarrely, she didn't feel the bullet that hit her.

The impact caused her to topple sideways, where she struck her forehead on a branch and then slithered and fell through the tree, taking a few smaller boughs with her, finally bouncing off the lowest branch and dropping cleanly the last four or five feet, landing face up on the grass with a dull thud.

The man in black waited a couple of seconds, watching her body for movement. The siren was very loud now, battering against the vivid peace of the morning. He couldn't fail to be aware of it.

With a last thoughtful look in Julia's direction, he placed the gun carefully by his partner's corpse and hurried back towards Hurst Lane. Then he vanished as if he'd never been here.

As if he had never existed at all.

Six

The first police car arrived twenty seconds later. It was an armed response vehicle with two male officers from the Tactical Firearms Unit, PCs Davies and Eade. They had been diverted from routine patrol in mid-Sussex following a report of an incident involving a firearm. A second ARV, from Brighton, was approximately fifteen minutes away. Two unarmed police vehicles and an ambulance were also en route, but wouldn't enter the village until the ARV gave clearance.

According to the control room, a householder in Chilton had witnessed the shooting of a Royal Mail driver. The 999 call had been logged at 8.09 a.m. It was now 8.22 a.m. If it had been an armed robbery, which seemed the likeliest explanation, the perpetrator would be long gone.

PC Davies, in the passenger seat, had checked the village's location and noted that it had only one access road. He'd warned his colleague of the possibility that they might encounter the getaway vehicle driving towards them along Chilton Way. He had also drawn his weapon, a Sig Sauer P226.

As it was, not a single vehicle passed them on the short journey from the B2112 to the village. This gave Davies a twinge of unease.

Rounding a bend close to the village shop, they saw the Royal Mail van parked at the kerb. As Eade reduced his speed, Davies killed the siren and began scanning the village for any visible threat. The passenger window was open, and he realised how quiet it was. Apart from the sound of their car, all he could hear was birdsong. There was no one in sight. Nothing moving.

Then he spotted a form on the green, maybe ten or fifteen yards away. At the same time PC Eade realised there was a body lying behind the van.

Both men exclaimed softly in unison. As the car pulled up, there was a moment when they exchanged a glance and understood they'd each reacted to something different.

As soon as he got out of the car, Davies saw the shotgun lying on the grass next to the body. The 999 call had described the suspect as carrying both a shotgun and a handgun. The description of his hair colour and jacket also matched the body lying on the grass.

'I think this could be our shooter,' he called to Eade, who had also drawn his weapon. Eade took aim at the body, providing cover while Davies made a cautious, circular approach, ensuring he didn't stray into his colleague's line of fire.

Another few feet and he could see enough to know the man was dead. A single shot to the temple from the handgun. Looked like a .22. Nevertheless he knelt down, careful not to disturb the scene, and checked for signs of life.

Then he stood up. Made a note of the time. Looked at PC Eade and pointed to the postman's body.

'Take that one. I'm going to have a look round.'

Even as he spoke he spotted the next victim, in a large house across the road. He had a direct line of sight along the garden path. There was an elderly man slumped by the front door.

Twenty past eight on a Saturday morning, in one of the smallest, sleepiest villages in the county. What the hell was going on?

He turned to Eade, who was standing by the postman. 'Dead?'

'Yep.'

'Hit the siren for a minute, will you?'

Eade frowned, but wasn't in the mood to argue. He returned to the car and activated the siren. The slow whoop sounded eerie as it echoed off the fine Georgian terrace. A flock of birds took flight from the trees around the church.

Davies raised his hand: that's enough. The silence returned so abruptly it made him shiver.

He resumed a slow 360-degree scan of the village, using his hand to shield his eyes from the sun.

Ten seconds. Nothing.

Twenty seconds. Nothing.

After half a minute he was convinced there would be no reaction. But then came the sound of a front door opening. One of the big Georgian houses on the far side of the green. A woman peeped out, face as white as snow, a slash of dark hair across her forehead.

She made eye contact and seemed to sag, like a punctured balloon. Davies broke into a run, skirting a large yew tree, and almost collided with a body. This one was a young woman, face up on the grass, covered in leaves and blood.

'Another victim here,' he yelled to his colleague, and hurried on. His priority was the living witness. He wanted to get to her before she fainted, or slammed the door on him.

'It's all right,' he called. 'It's all under control.'

She went on staring at him, her eyes haunted. She was going into shock.

'Are you okay?' he asked. 'Are you hurt?'

She managed the tiniest shake of her head.

'I'm PC Davies,' he said. 'Just relax now. We're going to take care of this. It'll be fine, okay?'

She laughed, and it made him flinch. It was the bitterest sound he'd ever heard.

'It's never going to be fine,' she said.

He glanced round, taking in the scene behind him. Eade was returning from the house where the man lay in the doorway. He made a thumbs-down gesture.

Davies turned back to the woman. He had to work hard to control his voice. 'What happened here? Where is everyone?'

The woman shut her eyes tightly, perhaps praying she was still asleep and this was just a dream. Then she opened them, settled her gaze on his and gave him the answer he was dreading.

'They're dead.'

He heard a shout from Eade and told the woman to go back inside. Someone would be with her very soon.

This time he gave the body by the tree a wide berth. Eade was almost hopping with impatience. 'What did she say?'

'Says they're dead. I don't know if she means the entire village, but it's not looking good, is it?' Although the adrenalin was pumping like crazy, he felt a wave of weariness at the thought of what lay ahead.

'What's the call, then?' Eade said.

'Got to be Major Incident,' said Davies. 'We'll have to seal the whole area. Search every house.' He sighed heavily. He was supposed to be off duty in a couple of hours. A tiny voice reminded him of his intended plans for the day: quick scoot round Homebase with the missus, doze in front of the telly, out with some friends for a few pints and a curry in the evening; then a lie-in and hopefully a legover Sunday morning.

All of it blasted away by some nutter.

Christ, he thought, if this is another Hungerford we'll never hear the end of it.

'The church door's open,' Eade said. 'I'm going to check it out.'

Davies nodded, still absorbed in his reverie as he reached for his Airwave radio. He wondered if Eade had considered the firestorm of activity about to descend on them.

Then he heard a groan, and nearly jumped out of his skin.

As he turned, he saw the woman's leg twitch. He knew that corpses sometimes made little movements, caused by stray electrical impulses running through the muscles. The process of dying could take hours beyond the actual moment of brain death.

But then her head moved, no more than half an inch. Bubbles of blood appeared on her lips.

Oh shitting hell. She's alive. She's alive and I ran right past her.

He fumbled with his radio and shouted: 'We have a Major Incident here. Repeat, this is a *Major Incident*. Three confirmed fatalities so far, plus one serious casualty. We need that ambulance ASAP. Hotel 900 too, if it's available.'

He dropped to his knees and checked her airway was clear. Felt for a pulse and found one. Very weak. There was so much blood that at first he couldn't work out where she'd been hit. Somewhere on her right side, he guessed, with various cuts and scratches adding to the confusion. If he didn't know better, he'd say she had fallen out of a tree.

He looked up in time to see Eade stumble out of the church. 'Two more in there,' he shouted. 'This is a fucking disaster.'

No, it's a massacre. 'This one's alive,' he shouted back. At the same time he was told Hotel 900, the police helicopter, could be there in ten minutes. The paramedic on board was being briefed about the situation.

Good luck to him, Davies thought. He took the woman's hand and squeezed it gently. It felt very cold. Her eyelids fluttered and he leaned close, urging her to focus on him.

'Hang on, love,' he said. 'Be strong for me. We'll have you in an ambulance in no time.'

He hoped he sounded more confident than he felt. He'd seen plenty of dead and dying bodies before, mostly from his time in Traffic. The woman lying here looked just as bad as any RTA victim. He wouldn't have given her more than a ten per cent chance of surviving, but he prayed she would prove him wrong. If she died, he'd always ask himself whether he could have made a difference if he'd noticed her sooner.

'Be strong,' he said again. Whether to her or to himself, he wasn't quite sure. 'Stay alive for me, love.'

Stay alive.

Seven

The killer ran along the narrow lane. His vision blurred. Despite the cold morning, it was hot inside the leathers. There was sweat rolling down his face, a stinging pain in his eyes. The helmet bumped against his shoulders and the visor entombed him, made him feel like an exhibit under glass. But he couldn't risk lifting it, not even for a single gulp of air. He had risked too much already.

The killer was scared. And he was angry. His meticulously planned operation had turned into an almighty fuck-up.

He pushed himself harder, faster. He was running for his life. There were sirens blaring in his head. He had no way of knowing if they were real or imagined. His heart thumped inside his chest and his boots pounded on the tarmac. His breath roared in the helmet.

No one saw me. He clung to that hope, repeated it to himself like a mantra. No one except the woman in the tree, of course. And she was dead. Almost certainly dead.

He rounded a curve in the road and saw the bike, partially concealed by the thick hedge that bordered Hurst Lane. He covered the distance like an Olympic sprinter. Like a hero.

Then he skidded to a stop, and saw how stupid he'd been.

He could be a hero. The man who stopped a killer. For half a second he saw himself in that role, paraded and garlanded and acclaimed by the nation. Pictured himself on TV and brought on stage at public events. Waving to the crowds like a Roman emperor.

Then he thought of the discrepancies. What was he doing there? How had he disarmed the killer and overpowered him without a struggle? Why did he shoot him at such close range?

It was a stupid idea, the product of a mind in panic. He wasn't thinking clearly. Besides, he had never craved the limelight. He belonged in the shadows.

He told himself to get a grip.

The bike was a Kawasaki KDX200, lightweight and fast, road legal but well equipped to handle rough farm tracks and fields. He'd bought it two months ago for eight hundred pounds in cash. Registered it in a false name, kept it garaged where no one knew him. He was especially glad of that caution now.

He gripped the handlebars and pulled the bike upright. Then he turned his head slowly, scanning in every direction. There was no movement, no sign of anyone. No birds singing. No engines. Just a tremendous crushing silence.

Then suddenly the whoop of a siren, not close but carrying well in the still morning air. The sound chilled the sweat on his face and made him shiver. He looked down at the bike and realised how lucky he was. The siren had saved him from another fuck-up.

The police were in the village, less than half a mile away. If he started the bike they'd hear it easily. Maybe they wouldn't think anything of it, but maybe they would. He couldn't take the chance.

He wheeled the bike as fast as he could, jogging beside it. He took the turning towards the farm, bouncing the Kawasaki along the beaten dirt track. Ice gleamed like broken glass in shallow ruts. His lungs burned and his muscles screamed, but he ignored them and allowed himself a little hope. You can still do this. You can still get away with it.

The farmhouse loomed into view beyond a line of beech trees. He shuddered. The farmhouse was where it had all gone wrong.

He saw the front door was open slightly. He thought he'd shut it, but couldn't remember for sure. He kept an eye on it as he passed, half expecting someone to spring out.

Beyond the farmhouse the lane twisted to the right, between a barn and a large corrugated-steel shed. It should be safe to ride from here. The buildings and trees would muffle the sound.

Mounting the bike, he raised the visor and wiped his face. As he glanced back, he caught a flash of light in the sky. A helicopter, no more than a speck against the Downs. The perspective made it appear to be gliding along the top of the hills. It was heading for the village.

For a second he was transfixed. The enormity of the event was starting to sink in. It wasn't just murder. It was fucking *slaughter*.

He imagined alarms sounding across a vast network. Emergency services descending on an enormous scale, the media hot on their heels. The impact reverberating around the whole world.

This realisation sent a bolt of adrenalin through him. With it came a peculiar spreading warmth in his chest. Gradually he recognised it as pride. He'd faced terrible obstacles, and against the odds he had come out on top.

The bike kick-started on the first attempt. He set off along the track, heading north of the farm. He looked back again, but couldn't see the helicopter. He forgot about it and accelerated, keeping a light grip on the handlebars as the bike juddered over the track.

He'd planned the route carefully. After half a mile he turned off the main track and cut through a gap in the hedgerow, joining a bridle path that took him north-west. He raced past winter fields of dark churned mud, glistening with frost like icing sugar on melted chocolate. Another mile, then left across a meadow of wild flowers.

He threaded through a knot of trees that marked the northern perimeter of the farm, then burst on to the road and sped away. And as he did, he allowed himself a brief scream of laughter. He had never in his life felt so vital, so extraordinary, so *complete*.

He had found his vocation.

Eight

The first media report was broadcast at 9 a.m., by a local independent radio station. The BBC picked it up shortly afterwards and prepared to insert a mention into the next round of headlines. At this stage it was merely a brief, unconfirmed report of a shooting in a small Sussex village. News producers monitored the situation before deciding whether to break into regular programming.

Craig didn't hear the first bulletin. He was watching *Spongebob Squarepants* and refereeing between his children. Usually good-natured and co-operative, this morning they seemed to have picked up on his irritable mood and were determined to push him over the edge.

Nina had gone to the office again. Christmas aside, she'd worked something like seven out of the past eight weekends. Usually Saturday mornings, but once or twice the whole day, and a couple of Sunday afternoons.

'I need to do it,' she had said. 'My career matters to me.'

'More than your family?' he'd retorted. He stopped short of saying, *More than your marriage*?

'No. And don't try emotional blackmail. Have I ever complained when work took you away for days or even weeks at a time?'

'That's why I went freelance, to have more control over my life.' But it was a valid point. 'Isn't it something you can do here?'

37

'I already work from home two days a week. I can hardly object to a few hours at the weekend.'

She left the house at eight. Her office was in the centre of Crawley, a ten-minute drive away. She gave him a perfunctory kiss on the cheek and promised to be back as soon as she could.

'Give me a rough idea,' he said as she opened the front door. Clad only in jogging trousers and a t-shirt, the freezing cold air was a pleasurable shock.

'I don't know. One o'clock. Two at the latest.'

'Two at the latest,' he repeated, as if her own words might bind her.

She nodded, unlocked the car and got in. There was something unreadable on her face as she backed off the driveway. A look he was seeing more and more frequently, and didn't like at all.

During the ad break he got up to make coffee and asked if the children wanted another drink.

'More juice, please,' said Maddie, thrusting her cup at him.

'Can we turn over?' said Tom. He reached for the remote control, only to find his sister snatching at it. In doing so she slopped the dregs of her orange juice over the sofa.

'Bloody hell!' Craig roared. Loud enough to make both children flinch. He was a big man, six feet tall and broad-shouldered, and often he was clumsy himself. Part of him knew he was overreacting even as he took the cup from her, but then Tom grabbed the remote control. 'You're not having that, either,' Craig said, and Tom, seeing the look on his face, meekly handed it over.

'Fetch a cloth to wipe this up,' he said. Maddie hurried from the room, bottom lip trembling. Craig felt the familiar pang of guilt that his anger had upset them, and made sure he thanked her when she returned with a hand towel. Not what he'd asked for, but it would do.

'Go and play upstairs,' he suggested. 'Better still, tidy your bedrooms.'

Alone in the room, he did some idle channel-hopping. On *News 24* a grim-faced presenter said, '. . . village of Chilton.' He'd already pressed the remote again, and had to wait for it to go back. This time he caught, 'More on that as soon as we have it.'

The newsreader went on to the next story. Craig sat forward, watching the ticker flow along the bottom of the screen: *Bush declares real improvements in Iraq.* Then, beneath the banner of BREAKING NEWS: *Reports of a serious shooting incident in a Sussex village. Emergency services are at the scene.*

At first the words didn't sink in. Chilton was practically the most sedate place he'd ever been. He could only imagine that someone had committed suicide with a shotgun.

There was a cordless phone on the unit next to the TV. He picked it up and pressed number four on the speed dial. Heard the rapid set of bleeps and then a moment's silence. Instead of a ringing sound, a recorded voice announced, 'Sorry, we have been unable to connect your call.'

He got a dialling tone and tried again. Same result. He tried dialling the number from memory, in case the programmed number was wrong. Same result.

It didn't mean anything, necessarily. Far too early to think the worst. But still he felt a shiver. A small but robust conviction that something was very, very wrong.

The phone book wasn't in any of its usual locations. He grew frantic, running around the house. He found it in Nina's office, hidden in a stack of paperwork beneath her desk. He knelt on the carpet and riffled through the pages. Stupidly, the name of the pub deserted him. Was it the Green Man or the Long Man?

It was the Green Man. He used the phone in Nina's office and rang the number. Got the same result: no connection possible.

He found a number for the village store and tried that. Same result. He stared at the phone book, then swiped it shut. This was absurd. Probably just a technical fault. And the TV must have the wrong place.

* * *

By the time he got downstairs, the situation had escalated. It was now the lead story. The background image was a distant shot of an idyllic rural village: red tile roofs and a church tower peeking from a stand of oaks. The news ticker read: SUSSEX SHOOTING: MAJOR INCIDENT DECLARED.

There were two presenters, a middle-aged man and a much younger woman. The man looked grey and tired. The woman was perky and over-made-up.

The man said, '. . . have now confirmed a serious shooting in the Sussex village of Chilton. As yet the extent of the casualties remains uncertain, but we do know that emergency services are at the scene in significant numbers, and the Major Incident Plan for Sussex has been initiated.' The words tumbled around inside Craig's head and finally made sense. He picked up the phone to try Dad again, then had a better idea. Abby.

The number he wanted was on his mobile, and that was in the kitchen. He discovered the kids had grown bored upstairs and were watching *High School Musical 2* on the little TV/DVD player.

'I'm hungry,' Maddie announced.

'Get yourself some sweets.'

She gave him a sharp look. Such instant capitulation was unheard of. It prompted a reminder from Tom: 'Mum says we're not allowed until after tea.'

'Is Mum here?' Craig said.

Tom shrugged. Good enough for him.

On TV the presenters were speaking to a retired chief constable. While they nudged him towards ever more newsworthy speculation, Craig listened to a phone ringing. And ringing.

Then a slightly peeved voice said, 'Craig? It's been a while.'

'Did I wake you?'

'Don't be silly. I have a living to earn.'

Now he made out the hum of traffic in the background. 'Where are you?'

A gentle laugh. 'Classified, my dear. I could tell you . . .'

'I'm watching *News 24*. Something about a shooting in Chilton.'

Her tone quickly changed. 'That's where I'm headed. What have you heard?'

'Nothing. I was hoping you'd know.'

'Sketchy, but the word is another Hungerford.'

There was a brief, blunt silence. Hungerford is a small market town in Berkshire. In 1987 a man named Michael Ryan had gone on the rampage, killing . . . how many?

Abby said, 'So what's your interest?'

He went to speak, but his tongue sat like a dry sock in his mouth. It was almost a surprise when he heard himself say, 'My dad lives there.'

Abby Clark was a journalist on *The Times*. Fifteen years ago she and Craig had started out together on a local paper in Hampshire. Contact had been pretty sporadic in the past few years, which was entirely Craig's fault. She had been greatly amused to hear of his move into features and sports writing, without knowing much about the reasons that lay behind it. 'Always in search of the easy life, eh?'

He hadn't taken offence. He never did with Abby. She could say the most outrageous things to him and get away with it. 'Because you've got a crush on me,' she'd once teased him, and she was probably right.

Now she sought to reassure him. 'I'm sure it's not on the scale of Hungerford at all. You know what the initial stage is like. All kinds of rumours buzzing around. Terrorism, accidents, organised crime.'

If that was supposed to allay his fears, it didn't succeed. 'I've tried phoning but the whole village seems to be cut off.'

'The police have probably taken the lines down. Or commandeered them for their own use.'

'Maybe,' he said. There was another reason why the police would cut off the phones, but neither of them said it aloud. A hostage situation.

'I'm sure he's fine,' Abby said. 'I'll call you the moment I hear anything. Okay?'

Despite everything, he smiled. Her concern was quite sincere, but this was also work. She couldn't afford to have her mobile tied up for too long on a personal call.

He tried his father's number again. No connection. On TV there was a link to a local correspondent in Lewes, standing outside police headquarters. The correspondent had been told unofficially that casualty numbers were believed to be 'significant'. The interview concluded and the presenter gave a brief, unnecessary recap, emphasising the words *significant* and *casualties* with particular relish.

'Quiet news day, was it?' Craig muttered. He could well imagine the excitement filtering through news agencies and TV stations across the country, perhaps even the world. Tragedy meant a story. It wasn't personal, and Craig knew that as well as anyone. He couldn't really blame them for sounding thrilled by what might transpire to be the death of his father.

It was the first time he'd admitted that possibility to himself, and it brought him up with a jolt. Although in his seventies, his father was still fit and active. After a long legal career as a QC, circuit judge and finally a spell as Attorney General on the island of Montserrat, in retirement he'd found a new lease of life as a dedicated guardian of the village he had made home. If Abby was right, and someone had gone on the rampage, there was very little chance that Dad would have settled for running or hiding. Whatever the risk, he would see it as his duty to confront the gunman.

Craig sighed. No point thinking the worst. He jabbed the remote control and the screen went blank. In the silence that followed he registered what he'd been hearing subliminally for some time, but had attributed to the TV.

Dropping the remote, he got up and left the room. He was aware of a breathlessness, his heart beating in peculiar rapid trills. When he opened the front door the sound grew louder and unmistakable. Sirens.

Goosebumps rose on his skin as he stood on the driveway and listened. The Maidenbower estate was situated on the south-eastern edge of Crawley, and the road in which he lived was less than half a mile from the M23 motorway. Sirens were simply part of the sound-track of their lives, barely noticeable any more, but Craig had never heard anything like this. The noise was so intense, so unwavering, it could only be a whole fleet of vehicles, speeding in convoy towards their destination.

And their destination was Chilton. Craig had no doubt about that.

Briefly the sirens were drowned out by the deep throbbing burr of a helicopter. It raced overhead, travelling south. A few seconds later another followed. When someone grabbed his leg, Craig gave a start. He looked down to see Maddie, gazing at him with a concerned expression. The sound of the helicopters subsided, allowing the wailing chorus of sirens to dominate again.

'Is that police cars, Daddy?'

'I think so, darling. Police or ambulance.'

'Or fire brigade.'

'Or fire brigade,' he conceded.

'There's lots of them. Has something really bad happened?'

Craig tried to look genuinely untroubled. Lying to his daughter had never been such a challenge.

'I don't know.'

Nine

Julia regained consciousness once on the way to hospital. At first she thought it was the man in black holding her down, and her relief at being alive was tempered by the knowledge that he had taken her prisoner. Terrified of being raped, she struggled against her restraints and tried to scream, but there was something blocking her mouth. As she thrashed in panic, she heard muffled voices, almost drowned out by a deafening clatter of engines. Someone shouted, 'Whoa! Careful!' and someone else said, 'Watch the IV. She'll pull it out.'

She was moving, but immobile. Strapped to a board, being man-handled into a vehicle of some sort. She tried to open her eyes but saw only blurs of light. Her senses were overloaded by noise and move-ment and a terrible threatened pain. She could feel it lurking deep within her, like a deadly animal barely held at bay. If it broke loose it could kill her, and with this knowledge came an understanding that she mustn't struggle. She must accept her fate.

She drifted away for a time, then opened her eyes again. Now it was a little clearer. She saw people huddled beside her and recog-nised them as paramedics. The terrible rhythmic noise increased, and a slice of blue sky shifted oddly downwards.

She was on a helicopter. She was being rescued, not captured.

Ten

George Matheson sat in the waiting room, his mind blank. It was an ability he had cultivated through years of interminable meetings and seminars and tours of inspection. Rather like being in the royal family, he imagined.

So he didn't think about Vanessa, or the prognosis. He didn't think about the business, or how it might be wrenched from his grasp. He didn't think about anything.

There were two other people in the room: the consultant's secretary and one other patient. He ignored them as studiously as they ignored him. There was an LCD television mounted on the wall above the secretary's desk, but it was switched off. The only sound was the occasional patter of keys from the secretary's laptop and the rustle of the other patient's *Telegraph*.

Into this silence, the ringing of his mobile phone seemed a tasteless intrusion. He'd neglected to switch it to vibrate. Cowed by a sudden aura of disapproval, he nodded an apology and examined the display. The number intrigued him, so he stood and walked to the door before answering.

George was a burly man in his mid-fifties, with a thick torso and hard, slightly rough features. He had been a keen amateur boxer in his youth, and continued to exercise hard until only a few years ago. The weight he'd gained recently had helped smooth out his appearance, giving him a more cultured look, befitting a man who had risen from nothing and built a billion-pound empire.

The caller was DI Terry Sullivan, a useful acquaintance of many years' standing. And in no mood for pleasantries, evidently.

'Where are you?'

The question disarmed him. He was on the second floor of a converted town house in Harley Street, in a waiting room whose low leather sofas, Persian rugs and mood lighting were in stark contrast to the consulting rooms beyond. *None of your business*, George thought.

'You're not in Sussex?' Sullivan added.

'No. We stayed in London last night.'

George heard a loud sigh. His frown deepened as he picked up other sounds in the background: raised voices, sirens, something that might have been a helicopter.

Sullivan said, 'There's been an incident in Chilton.'

'What do you mean?'

'Do you own a shotgun?'

George, startled, was about to repeat the detective's last word, but managed to stop himself in time. He squeezed the phone a little tighter and said, 'Yes, I do.'

He heard Sullivan mutter an expletive. Then: 'Is there a TV where you are?'

George glanced over his shoulder, saw both the receptionist and the other patient staring at him. 'Uh, yes.'

'Turn it on. I'll ring you again in a minute.' George heard someone shouting the policeman's name. 'If I can,' Sullivan added darkly. He ended the call.

George went on staring at the display for a moment, then he offered the secretary his most disarming smile.

'Would you mind putting the television on?'

There were four consulting rooms on the second floor, two each side of a central corridor. Lavatories were at one end of the corridor, and the waiting room at the other. Vanessa quietly closed the door to consulting room number three and entered the ladies' cloakroom.

The room was empty, thankfully. She had no need of the toilet, but a great need for solitude. Just for a minute or two. Long enough to compose her thoughts.

She stood in front of the sink. There was a shelf above it, containing a pretty little basket of soaps, each wrapped in shiny pink paper. Above the shelf was a mirror, and in the mirror was a monster. It was no one she recognised. She had given up on mirrors months ago, practically as soon as the chemotherapy began.

The pointless, futile chemotherapy.

The secretary was the usual formidable creature these places seemed to favour, but on this occasion she didn't say a word. She just did as she was asked, and in silence all three of them watched the screen swim into life, revealing a headline in bold red letters: SHOOTING IN SUSSEX VILLAGE.

There was a live camera feed from a helicopter, hovering somewhere above Chilton's southern perimeter. It showed the road into the village choked with emergency vehicles. Dark figures scurried in the neighbouring fields. There was an unfamiliar white square on the village green, and another on the road by the church. Forensic tents, George realised. His phone rang again.

'You watching it?'

'What's going on?'

'We've got a lad dead on the village green. Shot in the head with a Walther P22, complete with suppressor. There's also a Purdey shotgun by the body.'

'I don't understand. Who did it?'

'Looks like he topped himself. I need to know if the gun is yours.'

'It could be,' said George. 'Does that mean . . . the house?'

'We've not been there yet. Got more than enough to occupy us in the village. Communications are a bit of a bastard out here, but hopefully we'll have the landlines fixed soon.'

George's attention was distracted by the sound of a door opening, so he didn't quite catch what Sullivan said. Glancing round, he saw Vanessa emerge from the corridor. She was walking as if on tiptoe, every muscle tense but controlled. Her eyes met his for a moment, bright and cold. Betrayed. He looked away. What did Sullivan mean about fixing the landlines?

'There are other fatalities,' the policeman said.

'How many?'

'Dunno yet, but it's a lot.'

On screen the aerial image flickered and went black. They returned to the studio, where the presenter looked unprepared and slightly chastened. Apologising for the loss of picture, he briefly recapped the situation. A gunman was believed to have carried out a shooting spree in the Sussex village of Chilton.

He heard Vanessa gasp. She took a couple of steps forward and grasped the reception desk for support. George turned away from her. A buzzer sounded, and after a moment the secretary invited the other patient to go through. Sullivan had been interrupted again, but he came back on the line just as something else occurred to George.

'What about the farm?'

'What?'

'Hurst Farm. It's along the same road as the house. The Caplans live there, Laura and Keith, with their daughter.'

Another curse from Sullivan, as if an impossible job had just got harder still.

'We'll check it out.'

A hand touched his shoulder, and he heard Vanessa say, 'Can we go?'

He half turned, distracted and irritable, shrugging her off. Then he remembered why they were here. 'What did he say?'

Vanessa sniffed; her contempt quite expected, and quite deserved. 'It can wait.'

'I'm sorry.' He gestured at the television. 'You can see why . . .'

There was a brief report from outside Sussex Police HQ, then it was back to the aerial shot, this time a little further from the village. It showed a helicopter taking off, while another waited its turn to land.

He heard a sigh, then felt Vanessa move around him. She clearly intended to leave, no matter what he did. Reluctantly he followed her out to the lobby.

'Terry Sullivan rang me,' he told her. 'He was worried we might be there.'

'Do they know what happened?'

'Not really. Sounds like pandemonium at the moment. I just hope the Caplans are all right.'

Vanessa pressed the button to summon the elevator, then turned to face the doors.

George shook his head. 'Dreadful,' he muttered. Lost in thought, he went on staring at his phone. 'Absolutely dreadful.'

'Eight to ten weeks.'

'What's that?' George looked up, confused.

'Mr Templeton's prognosis.' She swallowed loudly, moistened her lips. 'I have two months to live. At best.'

Eleven

He'd been in Chilton less than an hour, but PC Davies was already exhausted. A second armed response vehicle had arrived at eight-forty, quickly followed by half a dozen patrol cars and the first contingent of CID. They were joined by fire and medical crews, and the arduous task of searching the entire village began.

The man lying dead on the green might well be the sole perpetrator, but the chief inspector who'd assumed the role of Silver Commander urged caution. So far the only witness was the woman from Arundel Crescent, and she was flaky to say the least. He wanted at least one armed officer assigned to each team, along with a paramedic and a couple of uniforms.

Everyone present knew this approach might well mean an injured victim died before medical assistance could reach them. It also meant forcing entry to homes and screaming at the occupants to get down, traumatising people who were already in a state of shock, and in some cases badly injured.

Once the first couple of survivors had confirmed the description of a single gunman, Davies began to take greater risks with his own safety, and he suspected his colleagues were doing the same. His team were the first to finish searching their allotted properties. He emerged from the village shop and left a uniformed colleague to supply the command post with details of the only occupant: a middle-aged woman in the stockroom, fatally wounded.

He stopped on the edge of the green and wiped his face. A passing paramedic offered him water and he took it gratefully. As he tipped the bottle up, he saw a helicopter descending into the field behind Arundel Crescent and recognised it as the one which had transported the female victim to hospital. He wondered if she'd made it there alive.

He heard a shout and looked round. A hugely overweight man with untidy grey hair was striding towards him. Davies vaguely recognised him, but had a look at his warrant card just the same: Detective Inspector Sullivan. 'We need to check out Hurst Lane,' he said, signalling to the paramedic who had given Davies the water. She was a short, plump woman who bore a disturbing resemblance to Ann Widdecombe.

The car groaned as Sullivan sank into the driver's seat. Davies caught a whiff of body odour, masked by a generous dose of after-shave. Sullivan drove one-handed, his arm held high and bent at the elbow, his belly wedged against the steering wheel. Alongside him, Davies had to lean against the door to avoid the risk of physical contact.

The village made a surreal backdrop, like a scene straight out of *MASH* or *Apocalypse Now*. Helicopters swooping in and out, fed with casualties by stretcher bearers running to and fro. Forensic teams in paper suits, swarming around the victims like white blood cells around a wound. The village was now so crowded that only ambulances were being permitted access to the High Street. Everyone else had to park on the approach road.

Weaving past a cluster of cars outside the church, Sullivan nearly collided with a SOCO taking photographs of the dead postman.

'Fucking nightmare,' he muttered.

'It's like a vision of hell,' the paramedic piped up from the back seat. After that, no one spoke till they reached the farmhouse.

*   *   *

The first thing Davies saw was the front door standing open. He felt a tingle of apprehension, and a heaviness in his gut. *No more*, he thought. *Don't let me find any more.*

But there would be more. He felt sure of that, as soon as he got out of the car. There was an unnatural quality to the silence. Even on an arable farm, people would be up and about by now. Someone who'd heard the sirens and the helicopters and come out to investigate.

'No one in there,' DI Sullivan said as he followed Davies towards the door. 'No one alive, anyway.'

From behind them, the paramedic said, 'We shouldn't give up hope.'

Davies nudged the door open with his foot. He peeked over the threshold and immediately caught the stench of blood and human waste.

He stepped inside. It was an old dwelling, with low ceilings and small rooms. The decor was tired, but efforts had been made to brighten it up with well-chosen lamps, mirrors and pictures. A woman's taste and ingenuity, trying to offset a man's reluctance to spend time or money on decoration.

The living room was dominated by a big old Philips TV with an equally ancient VCR. No DVDs or game consoles. The room opposite, next to the stairs, had a large oak dining table and looked like it was never used. By contrast, the kitchen was warm and cluttered and much more welcoming. It was here that he found them.

He was in the doorway, staring at the bodies, when Sullivan came in behind him. 'Clear?'

Davies shrugged. He hadn't checked upstairs yet, but it all seemed a bit academic now. He moved aside to let Sullivan see the room.

Like several other victims, the occupants of the farmhouse had been having breakfast when the killer struck. There were two plates on the pine table, one with a half-eaten pile of eggs, bacon, sausages and mushrooms; the other with poached eggs on toast, untouched.

The farmer was sprawled on the floor. He had been blasted in the stomach with a shotgun, but it hadn't killed him straight away. The blood and intestines covering his hands suggested he had literally tried to hold himself together.

The woman had also been killed with the shotgun, a blast to the head at close range. There was little of her face left, but they could tell she was fairly young, maybe early thirties, with a slim figure. Her jeans lay discarded on the floor. Her sweater and t-shirt had been hiked up, and her bra torn off. There were marks on her skin where she had been pawed by her killer. Her pubic hair was matted with blood.

Sullivan whistled. 'This is a bit different.'

'Rage,' Davies said. 'Sexual rage.'

'Seen any others where the shotgun was used?'

'Not yet.'

'Me neither.'

They both pondered for a moment. 'Wonder what it means,' Davies said.

'Doubt we'll ever know,' said Sullivan. 'Fucker took his secrets with him.'

There was a soft thud from overhead. Both men gave a start. Davies whipped round, bringing his gun up. The paramedic, waiting by the front door, threw up her hands in terror.

'Hey,' said Sullivan. 'Where's the kid? They've got a daughter.'

Davies took the stairs as lightly as he could. Reaching the top he sensed movement at the end of the landing, as if someone had ducked into the bedroom. His heart raced. If it was the girl, why had she run away from him?

Because she's bloody terrified. She probably saw her parents murdered.

'Armed police!' he shouted, trying to sound stern but not overly intimidating. 'Come out slowly. You're going to be all right.'

Silence. No reaction at all. What if it's not the girl? He knew it was unlikely, but the sexual assault on the woman had challenged his assumptions. There was something else going on here, and it unnerved him.

Maybe he should withdraw. Get a full team here to storm the house. But he'd never hear the last of it if there was only a little girl, too petrified to show herself.

'I'm a policeman,' he called, more softly this time. 'My name's Chris. Will you tell me your name?'

No answer. He sighed. Took a cautious step forward.

Then he heard it. A low, frightened mewling. He smiled, thanking God he hadn't called for back-up, and strode towards the end bedroom. Poised on the dressing table was a large black cat, regarding him with spectacular disdain.

'Have you found her?' Sullivan said.

Davies ignored him, turned and pushed open the door he'd just passed. A spare bedroom, with a single bed. But the duvet was rucked up, and there was a Tom Clancy paperback on the bedside table. A crumpled pair of jeans on the floor.

Next door was the bathroom, and the final room was a little girl's bedroom. The walls were painted a light purple, with a matching lightshade fringed with beads. Posters of Girls Aloud and Take That on the wall, and a row of Jacqueline Wilson books on a glass shelf.

The girl was in bed. At first glance she might have been asleep. Her pink duvet was drawn up to her chin, just as you would expect on a cold morning. She lay on her side, nothing visible except a pale sliver of cheek and a sweep of long brown hair. Only the pillow lying partly across her face gave any indication that things were not as they seemed.

'Up here,' he called. For the first time that day, he felt tears straining behind his eyes. He blinked rapidly and turned away.

Sullivan hurried into the room, followed by the paramedic. He took a brief look at the girl, then touched Davies's shoulder. 'You okay?'

'Fine.'

Sullivan grunted, as if he couldn't understand why Davies needed to maintain the pretence. There was a hushed exclamation from the paramedic. She had pulled back the duvet, and at first Davies imagined she was reacting to some terrible violation of the child's body. Then he registered the awe in her voice.

'I've found a pulse.'

Twelve

By the time Nina called, Craig was on the A23 in his VW Golf, heading south as fast as the Saturday morning traffic would allow. It was almost eleven o'clock and he was no closer to finding out if his father was safe.

'What's the matter?' she said. 'Are the kids all right?' She sounded different, somehow. Slightly flustered, slightly upset, but there was an aggressive edge to her voice.

'They're fine,' he said. 'Where are you? Why didn't you answer your mobile?'

'I switched it off. I always do when I need to concentrate.'

'I wasted ages trying to get hold of you. The guy on the switchboard couldn't find you anywhere.'

'The switchboard isn't manned on Saturday.'

'Well, someone answered. He said you weren't at your desk.'

A long, theatrical sigh. 'It was probably one of the lads on the ground floor. Maybe they looked in the wrong place. Maybe I'd popped out to the loo.'

'I had to take the kids to your mum's. She tried phoning you as well.'

'Why? What's happened?'

He fought back an impulse to shout: *How can you not know?* Instead he laughed. By ten o'clock both the BBC and ITV had broken into their normal schedule to bring live coverage, and there were constant updates on all the main radio stations. It was at his in-laws' house that he'd first heard the word 'massacre' used to describe the incident.

'You really don't know?'

'No.' Her voice wavered. 'What?'

'There's been a shooting. In Chilton.'

Her gasp was followed by a peculiar busy silence.

'Who are you with?'

'No one. Have you spoken to your dad?'

'I can't get through to him.'

His peripheral vision caught a flash of blue light in the rear-view mirror. He veered left, leaving the outside lane clear. A convoy of six vehicles sped past: police cars and scientific support vehicles. And there was a black Transit, whose purpose wasn't immediately obvious. Then he understood: it was a mortuary van.

'Craig? You're not going there, are you? Wouldn't it be better to call the police?'

He laughed again, and ended the call before he said something he might regret.

A travel update on the radio warned of long delays in the area. The A272 around Haywards Heath was singled out, as was the A273 towards Brighton. These were the main routes for casualties to be ferried to hospital, and for police and forensic vehicles to reach Chilton.

Craig stayed on the A23 until Albourne, which was slightly south of the village, but meant spending less time on slower, single-lane roads. It was heavy going through Hurstpierpoint, but when he reached the adjoining town of Hassocks he knew a couple of short-cuts that got him on to the B2112. He set off north, with the Downs behind him, and almost immediately joined a slow-moving line of traffic.

It took almost fifteen minutes to cover the next mile. There was virtually nothing coming the other way. Craig was sorely tempted to pull out and overtake, until the driver behind him tried just that, only to encounter an ambulance with a police escort.

He was about half a mile from the turn-off to Chilton when the queue came to an emphatic halt. Up ahead he could see cars pulling on to the grass verge. By now all the incidental traffic had given up and turned around. Those who remained had only one destination in mind.

It wasn't until he got out and approached on foot that Craig appreciated the scale of what was happening. The road ahead was a mass of people, abandoning their cars and trudging towards Chilton. It reminded him of big outdoor events, rock festivals or the South of England Show at nearby Ardingly, but with one major difference.

There was no jollity. No excitement or anticipation. Just an oppressive silence and an air of undisguised dread. Faces dull with shock and worry. Eye contact was made reluctantly, accompanied by embarrassed smiles. No one was about to ask why he had come, because no one wanted to be confronted with the answer. They were all here for the same reason.

They were here to find out if their loved ones were alive.

He crested a low hill and saw what had stopped the traffic. There was a roadblock just south of the turning to Chilton, and another to the north. The road in both directions was an identical scene of haphazardly parked cars and grim clusters of people making for the police cordon.

Next to the junction was a large grassy area, not quite big enough to be called a field. It was thronging with people, many in uniform, erecting tents and tables, setting up for a long operation. There was a catering van doing a brisk trade, and a lorry unloading portaloos.

An ambulance sped along Chilton Way and paused briefly at the junction. Police and civilian workers in orange tabards held back the crowd, some of whom screamed and wailed at the sight of the ambulance. One group of onlookers surged forward and began photographing both the ambulance and the emotional reaction to it.

Craig noticed TV vans parked on the verge, satellite dishes mounted on their roofs: the media were already here in force.

It struck him that Nina was right. He would be competing with dozens of equally concerned relatives for what meagre scraps of information were available. He knew how chaotic such operations were in the early stages. Keeping the public informed was a low priority, and the police knew better than to release information until it could be confirmed beyond any doubt.

Then someone from the crowd turned in his direction. A slim, elfin woman with short dark hair. Shielding her eyes from the sun, she peered at him and smiled. Abby.

'I thought you'd be here already,' she said as they hugged briefly.

'Nina's at work. I had to find someone to have the kids.'

She nodded, looked at him closely. 'I hate to say this, but it might be a wasted journey.'

'Are they in a mess?'

'Not too bad.' She indicated the tents behind them. 'This is the command post, which is as far as anyone gets. They're setting up a casualty bureau and a media-briefing room. They've got the fire brigade and civil defence volunteers trying to seal off the entire village.' She grinned. 'Breaking the cordon doesn't go down well, as some of my colleagues have discovered. One of them reckons he got chased away at gunpoint.'

Craig shook his head. They both turned and stared in the direction of the village. Fields and trees and bushes in a hundred shades of green, still sparkling with melted frost, and the grey church tower peeking above the treetops. It looked an idyllic scene, utterly benign. How could there be anything wrong here?

'Beautiful part of the world,' Abby murmured. When he didn't respond, she added, 'Your father was campaigning against development in the village, wasn't he?'

Craig nodded. He caught her use of the past tense. She coloured slightly.

'I'm sorry. I wasn't implying . . .'

'I know.' He stared at the trees. Until a breeze caused them to sway, he could almost believe they were false; painted scenery that might fall away and expose the horror of what had happened here.

'Makes me think of that John Wyndham story, *The Midwich Cuckoos*.'

Abby frowned. 'Was that the film with those creepy blond kids?'

He nodded. '*Village of the Damned*.'

Something in his voice must have affected her, for she reached out and patted his arm. Then she indicated a couple of officers sitting at folding metal tables, a large queue forming in front of them. 'That's where they're taking details of friends and family.'

There was a ripple of noise and movement from the crowd. They turned to see a car approaching at speed from the north, sounding its horn to clear pedestrians out of the way. It was a brand-new Jaguar XJR with tinted windows. Craig could just make out a man behind the wheel and a woman in the passenger seat.

A policeman stepped into the road and raised his hand. For a moment it looked as though the driver would ignore him. Onlookers gasped, fearing another tragedy, but the Jaguar braked sharply and stopped just in time. There were a few jeers, and shouts of, 'Send him back.'

The driver's window opened. The officer walked round and they conferred in low tones. The photographers moved closer, raising their cameras. Just before they blocked his view, Craig saw who was in the car.

'That's George Matheson.'

'Ah. I wondered if he'd be putting in an appearance.'

Craig was surprised she knew who he was, until he remembered her comment about his father's campaign.

'Lucky he wasn't here this morning.'

'Very lucky,' Abby echoed, with perhaps a trace of sarcasm. 'But then they have several homes. Villas in Nice and Antigua, and a town house in Knightsbridge, I believe?'

It sounded like she was fishing, but Craig wasn't going to bite. 'You know more about him than I do.'

The shouts from the crowd increased as the police officer stepped away and the Jaguar jerked forward, probing a path through the photographers. George Matheson's gaze was set straight ahead, while his wife, cloaked in sunglasses and a headscarf, raised a hand to cover her face. They turned into Chilton Way and increased speed.

'One rule for the rich . . .' Abby said, only partly in jest.

'Tell me something I don't know,' said Craig.

Thirteen

George Matheson had become a master at denial. Bit by bit his life was falling apart, yet here he was, still functioning. Still pretending none of it was happening. He stared through the windscreen and allowed his world to shrink to just the road ahead, but even his well-constructed emotional forcefield couldn't suppress a twinge of fear at the prospect of what he was driving into.

If Vanessa was troubled by the shouts and catcalls, she gave no sign of it. He couldn't even tell if her eyes were open. She had barely said a word on the drive from London, so maybe she was asleep. The medication often knocked her out.

He would never forget his first sight of the village. Normally so serene, it had been transformed into something resembling a war zone or a refugee camp after a huge natural disaster. What seemed like dozens of police cars and ambulances were parked along the High Street. Everywhere he looked he could see armed police, doctors and paramedics, grim-faced search teams and forensic officers in white suits.

There was another roadblock outside the village store. George gave his name and waited while the officer consulted a list on a clipboard. His eye was caught by a man unloading something from a van. Bodybags, made of heavy-duty vinyl, folded and stacked on the village green.

'They're waiting for you at the manor,' the officer said. 'Watch how you go.'

As he set off again he glanced at Vanessa, hoping she was asleep and wouldn't have to witness this. But she was staring, transfixed, her hand cupped over her mouth as if to hold in her shock. He wanted to offer some comfort, but had no idea what to say.

He drove slowly, stopping to let an ambulance get past a Royal Mail van. There was a tent set up behind the van; George glimpsed a man's leg and a pool of dried blood on the road. A group of emergency workers stood nearby, drinking from Styrofoam cups and stamping their feet to keep warm. They all turned and stared as the big Jaguar glided past, and something in their blank unwavering gazes seemed to transmit a sense of the carnage they had encountered. He shivered.

Hurst Lane provided a brief respite. For a few seconds it was almost possible to believe this was just a terrible dream. Then he reached the fork in the road and took the right-hand path, drawing down the blanket of denial over any speculation about the fate of the Caplans. He would know soon enough.

The gates to Chilton Manor were open, presumably a forced entry by the police. He drove along the wide gravel driveway and saw a black Vectra parked next to a patrol car. DI Sullivan was standing by the driver's door. He was wearing a heavy blue parka the size of a tent, along with grubby-looking jeans and trainers: weekend clothes. As he turned, George searched the detective's face for some tiny hint of reassurance. He got nothing.

They shook hands. Sullivan's was freezing cold, and the tip of his nose was red. George said, 'Did you check the farm?'

The policeman nodded, wiped his nose on his sleeve. 'We found the adults dead in the kitchen.'

George had been expecting it, virtually since he'd first spoken to Sullivan, but for a moment he felt utterly destabilised. He groped for the Jaguar behind him and half leaned, half sat on the bonnet.

'And their daughter?'

'Smothered with a pillow. She's been airlifted to the Royal Alex in Brighton. They don't expect her to survive.'

There was silence. Nothing to say to news like that. George realised the passenger door was opening, Vanessa slowly easing herself out of the car. Sullivan followed his gaze and said, 'It might be better if she waits here.'

George exchanged a glance with his wife. She glared at Sullivan and shut the door.

'I'm afraid the house will be out of bounds for a while,' Sullivan said. 'There's been a break-in. We think the killer did it.'

'The shotgun?'

'It's gone.' Sullivan was staring straight at George. 'Did you have any other firearms? Any handguns?'

'No. Absolutely not.'

Sullivan nodded, but looked no happier. 'What about the alarm system?'

'I set it myself yesterday morning. Why?'

'It's deactivated, and it doesn't appear to have been tampered with. Are you certain you set it?'

'I think so.' George faltered. 'It's such an automatic thing to do, I can't remember precisely, but I'm sure I would have . . .' He tailed off, aware of how feeble he must sound.

'There's no one else living here? No staff?'

'Not full-time. There are gardeners, and we use a cleaning company twice a week, but they don't have keys or the alarm code.'

Sullivan sighed. He rolled a bit of loose gravel back and forth beneath his shoe. 'You say you left here yesterday morning?'

'Yes.' George drew himself up, exploiting his height advantage over the detective. 'Am I suspected of something?'

'Don't be silly. We're just trying to build up a picture of what happened.'

Stung by the ridicule, George was silent for a moment. Then he said, 'May I see where he broke in?'

Sullivan nodded. 'Wait a second.'

He opened the Vectra and picked up a digital camera, which he slipped into the pocket of his coat without explanation. George saw Vanessa watching them and detoured to the car. He told her what Sullivan had said. She listened, lips pursed, and said, 'Be careful. He's an odious man.'

George grunted, concerned that Sullivan would hear her. 'We'll be better off in London anyway,' he said.

'What have they taken from the house?'

'Apart from the gun, I don't know.'

She gave a curt nod and turned away from him. Conversation over.

'One bit of advice,' Sullivan said as they followed the stone path around the perimeter of the house. 'Not a word to anyone about our past association or I'll be kicked off the case. And I'm no help to you then.'

'What makes you think I'm going to need your help?'

Sullivan didn't respond, but the way his breath whistled through his nostrils made him seem habitually scornful. He said, 'Take me through your itinerary yesterday.'

'We left here around ten o'clock. I was in meetings all afternoon. Vanessa had an appointment in Harley Street this morning, so we stayed up in town.'

'Nothing serious?'

George made an almost involuntary sound in his throat, but didn't answer the question. Instead he said, 'My shotgun. Was it used at the farm?'

Sullivan met his eye, and nodded. 'I'm afraid so.'

They reached the corner of the house. Wide lawns covered almost an acre, leading on to a tennis court, a Victorian walled garden and a small orchard. Beyond that, miles of open farmland: not a road or a building in sight.

Sullivan, gazing at the view, said, 'How long had you known the Caplans?'

'Oh, it must be at least six, seven years. Keith was a very capable farmer. They were nice people. I counted them as friends, not just employees.'

The detective nodded thoughtfully. They walked on in silence. The western side of the house had a ground-floor extension added in the late nineteenth century, and it was here that one of the windows had been smashed. A uniformed officer was standing guard on the path.

'Is there much damage inside?'

'Superficial. Cupboards and shelves emptied. I can't say whether any valuables have been taken, but it seems unlikely.' Sullivan looked to be fighting a smirk. 'He also took a dump on your dining-room table.'

George shuddered, then remembered what had occurred to him during the phone call. 'Do you think this was premeditated, or done on the spur of the moment?'

'Why do you ask?'

'The fact that he came here to steal my shotgun. How was he to know the place was empty?' He glanced in the direction of the village. 'If we'd been at home, perhaps none of this would have happened.'

'As far as we know he already had the pistol with him. He might have blasted in here, killed the two of you and taken the shotgun anyway.'

It was an odd sort of consolation to offer someone. Sullivan took the camera from his pocket and turned it over several times, pondering something.

'Right now, there's a lot we don't understand.' He glanced at the uniform, who read his expression and turned away as if rebuked. There was a whirring noise as the camera powered up.

'I reckon you might be able to help us,' he went on. 'Take a look at this.'

He held up the camera for George to see. There was a tiny screen on the back, no more than an inch or so square, but the image displayed on it was perfectly clear. It was a man's head, taken at close range but with part of it obscured, perhaps deliberately, by a sheet of paper. Concealing a wound, George guessed. But there was enough of the face visible for him to understand two things.

The man was dead. And he was familiar.

'That's Carl Forester.'

Sullivan's eyes widened. 'Who is he?'

'He used to work for me, some years ago. He helped out on the farm.' Remembering something else, George felt the blood drain from his face. Fortunately Sullivan had chosen that moment to switch the camera off, and by the time he looked up George had recovered.

He would have to tell the police at some point, of course. But not now.

'He lived locally, then?' Sullivan said.

'Falcombe, I think. He had a very disruptive home life. Father's long gone. Mother is an alcoholic. Carl himself was a bit of a tearaway, I believe.'

'So we'll find him in our records?'

'I imagine so. Motoring convictions. Petty theft, perhaps.'

'Any sex offences that you know of?'

George felt dizzy again. 'What?'

Sullivan shoved the camera back in his pocket and looked George squarely in the eye. 'Mrs Caplan was raped before she died.'

Fourteen

It was nearly two in the afternoon when Craig got home. He turned into the cul-de-sac and saw Nina's Citroën on the driveway. He remained in the car for a minute, not so much collecting his thoughts as dispersing them. His preoccupations felt like steel cables, coiled so tight they might suffocate him.

While Abby rejoined her colleagues in the media tent, he had stood in line at the grandly named Friends and Relatives Reception Centre. Eventually he spoke to a community support officer, who by now had been politely resisting demands for information for several hours and could reel off official platitudes while simultaneously filling out forms and keeping an alert eye on potential troublemakers further along the line.

Craig had envisaged that he would insist on learning his father's fate. Refusing to budge until he knew the facts. Probably everyone else in the queue thought the same. But when the moment came, faced with the implacable barriers of bureaucracy and innate polite-ness, almost everyone accepted they couldn't be told anything right now. The priority was to secure the scene and give help to the injured. To protest would be not only unseemly, but also an insult to the victims.

'Best thing is to go home,' the officer told him. 'Soon as we know something definite, we'll be in touch.'

Craig looked for Abby before he left, but couldn't find her. He had his press card and no doubt could have talked his way into the media tent, but it was bound to lead to trouble. He knew exactly the kind of morbid humour that journalists employed at times like this, and he'd just end up picking a fight with someone. He had no desire to mix with people for whom this was little more than a thrilling carnival.

Now he forced himself from his car, knowing he didn't really have the stomach for a fight with Nina either. It was tempting to turn around and drive away, except that he'd told the police he would be at home.

She opened the door while he was fumbling with his keys. She looked emotional, under strain, but also immaculate. He'd always marvelled at the way she could do a demanding job, bring up two children and still devote time to hair and clothes and make-up. Some of her friends teased her about it, calling her 'Superwoman', and although Craig joined in he was secretly proud. Today, though, it irked him. She had no right to look so good.

She stepped forward as if to embrace him, but perhaps sensing it wouldn't be welcome, settled for lightly caressing his arm. 'Is he all right?'

'No news yet. They said they'll let me know.' Again she reached out, but he brushed her off and made for the living room. He felt her freeze, slightly incredulous that she had been shunned. 'What are they saying on TV?'

'Mostly speculation,' she said, 'recycled over and over. Reporters interviewing each other because no one will speak to them.'

Craig grunted. He threw himself on to a sofa. *Sky News* was showing what appeared to be the same aerial footage from earlier. The voiceover said, '. . . now confirmed to be one of the worst spree killings in recent years.'

'Where are Tom and Maddie?'

'Still at Mum's. They can stay over, if need be. I thought it was best . . .'

Craig nodded, rested his head back and stared at the ceiling. He ran his hands through his hair and down around his neck, holding them there as if he wanted to throttle himself.

'Where were you this morning?'

Nina flinched, but hid it well. She turned to the armchair behind her and found some comics to tidy away before sitting down.

'I was at work,' she said, imbuing the words with a scorn that implied he had insulted her by asking.

'No you weren't. The guy I spoke to told me he'd looked everywhere. He said your PC was on standby, and your coat and bag were gone.'

The words tumbled into the room like grenades, turning their familiar living room into hazardous territory.

Nina's eyes sparkled with tears. She shook her head. 'Don't do this now.'

'What do you mean, *Don't do this now*? How can you say that?'

'I mean, let's have this conversation another time. When we know your dad is safe.'

He isn't safe, said a voice in his head. *He's dead*.

He sighed. She had as good as told him already, hadn't she?

'Who is it?'

'Craig, please. You're upset because of this, and we're still—'

'Who?'

'No. Listen to me.'

'Just tell me. Tell me his fucking name.'

She leaned forward, pressed her knees tight and hugged her arms together, as if making herself as small as possible. He looked away, disgusted with himself as much as with her.

She breathed in, held it, breathed out. Then she said, 'Bruce Abbott.'

She got up and left the room. He listened to her putting on shoes and a coat, pick up her keys and leave the house. She over-revved the Citroën and the wheels squealed as they fought for grip.

Six hours ago he'd been lying in bed, contemplating a weekend of relaxation and marital harmony. Now he might have lost both his father and his marriage. What was next?

He stood up. He knew exactly what was next.

As a rule they didn't keep much alcohol in the house. Red wine, mostly, which Nina drank, and sometimes a bottle of white. Beer was a no-no, and had been for more than four years. Four years, three months and ten days, in fact.

Spirits were also barred, but there was a bottle of good malt which Nina had won in a raffle at Christmas and not yet given away. That would do for starters.

Two cars tailed them back to London, and when they turned into Cadogan Place there was a TV van and a group of people waiting outside the house. George had expected as much. He wasn't a particularly high-profile figure, but from time to time he featured in the financial pages. For an event of this magnitude, that was probably more than sufficient to single him out for attention. Vanessa gave a cry of alarm when she spotted them.

'We won't stop,' he assured her. True to his word, he almost ploughed into them as he passed the house. Vanessa twisted away from the lenses, covering her face with her hands. He quite understood her reaction, but knew it would only encourage the use of the photos. It made them look guilty of something.

Oblivious to their own safety, the reporters pursued them along the street, hurling questions as they ran.

'What did you see in Chilton?'

'Will you give us your reaction to the massacre?'

'What did the police tell you, Mr Matheson?'

He ignored them all. Kept that same steely gaze and drove on until he found somewhere to park. He kept telling himself that later he would allow himself some time to reflect. He sensed that his life had changed beyond recognition: the ramifications of this were impossible to predict.

It came as a greater shock to realise, an hour or more after they were safely ensconced in their respective refuges – she in her bedroom, he in his study – that he had given no reaction, nor barely any thought, to Vanessa's news.

Weeks. She had only weeks to live.

Alone in his study, toying with a brandy, he tried to imagine himself a widower. He had known it would happen. The initial diagnosis had been about as bleak as they come. What he had never imagined was that he'd have to combine it with this . . . devastation.

People might look to him, he realised. Despite everything, it caused a tiny swelling in his heart. He might be called upon to give a lead.

Ironic, really, considering that until now he'd been depicted as the would-be destroyer of Chilton's perfection.

But it might take weeks, perhaps months for the dust to settle. And in the meantime . . . everything would be in limbo. His life would be in limbo.

The tears came without warning, a hot rush suddenly there on his cheeks, and a single deep sob that convulsed his chest. His life was over. Destroyed.

Afterwards he didn't feel better, as everyone always predicted if 'you just let it out'. He felt worse. Utterly wretched and exhausted, and wishing he could drop dead right there and be spared all the trials that now lay ahead of him, as unavoidable as night after day.

Starting now, he decided.

Starting with Kendrick.

The phone was picked up on the third ring. 'Yes?'

'It's George Matheson.'

'What a nice surprise.' The sly amusement made George furious. It was bad enough that he couldn't speak to Kendrick directly. Having to go through Vilner, of all people, was nothing short of humiliating.

'I assume you've seen the news?'

'Watching it now,' Vilner said. 'I told myself, someone had better have a bloody good reason to drag me away from it.' He laughed. 'I guess you qualify.'

'I need to see Kendrick as soon as possible. I'm sure he'll want to discuss the . . . implications.'

Another throaty laugh. 'Implications?' he repeated, as though it were an absurd euphemism.

'Yes,' said George firmly. 'If you let me have his number I'll call him myself.'

'I'm seeing him later. He'll get the message.'

'See that he does.'

Vilner's tone hardened. 'Toby all right these days?'

George grunted. That was the next call he had to make.

'So where does this leave the development?' Vilner went on. 'Seems to me it could go belly up.'

'Not necessarily. But it does seem prudent to consider all eventualities.'

'Yeah, you can spill out that bollocks till the cows come home. Just don't forget what you owe me. If I'm not getting the contract Toby promised, then I want the cash instead.'

George fought back his rage, and said quietly, 'You will get it.'

'When?'

'I can't possibly say.'

'Listen, George, I've been more than patient. I won't let anyone make a fool of me.'

'We'll talk again soon,' George said. His hand trembled as he dropped the phone in its cradle. Dealing with Vilner always left him feeling squalid.

He had intended to call Toby as well, warn him to keep his mouth shut, but he simply wasn't capable of it. Overcome by a craving for oblivion, he thought of Vanessa's painkillers. It really could be that easy.

'Oblivion,' he murmured, reaching for the brandy.

*   *   *

Craig was drunk when the doorbell rang. After years of abstinence the alcohol hit him like a train. He'd bypassed the pleasurable stage altogether and gone straight to hangover. Instead of giddy euphoria there was just disgust that he'd added weakness of character to his many other flaws.

He saw the police car draw up outside and was at the door before they rang the bell. There were two of them, both men: one uniformed and very young, the other CID and about Craig's age. It was almost fully dark outside, just a few streaks of purple and red in the western sky, the temperature probably below freezing.

Despite the cold an obnoxious neighbour was standing across the way, blatantly waiting to see what might happen. For that reason as much as anything Craig made an attempt at sobriety and ushered them inside. Stumbling in the doorway didn't help, but if they disapproved they gave no sign of it.

'Offer you a drink?' he said, trying hard not to slur.

'Good idea,' the detective said. 'My colleague will put the kettle on.'

Not hearing, Craig took a couple of steps towards the kitchen. The uniform waylaid him, directing him to a seat like an errant child.

'Is your wife here, Mr Walker?'

Craig shook his head. 'Left me,' he said.

'Oh.' The detective seemed flummoxed by this. Craig thought he should elaborate, then decided he lacked the energy. But he did need to sharpen up a bit.

He slapped his face a couple of times, the sound echoing in the quiet house. He was surprised to find moisture on his fingers. He touched his cheeks again, dabbing gently, like a man tracing a leak.

'I won't put you through any more agony,' the detective said. 'I'm afraid your father, Philip Anthony Walker, was a victim of the gunman in Chilton this morning.' He waited a second. 'He was fatally injured and died at the scene. I'm very sorry.'

Fifteen

James Vilner had come a long way in his thirty-eight years, both geographically and socially. He reflected on this as he drove his Range Rover into the basement car park of one of London's most exclusive hotels.

Born in Scarborough, his life had changed at the age of seven when his father died in an industrial accident. Denied compensation by a legal blunder, his mother moved to a poor district of Leeds, where financial hardship drove her to supplement social security benefits with prostitution. Young Jimmy quickly learned that to survive in this harsh new environment, he had to be financially independent.

He stole his first car stereo at the age of nine, and within two years had become a proficient thief. At twelve his mum kicked him out, and he was happy to go, happy to be away from her creepy punters and her violent new boyfriend. He slept on the back seat of stolen cars, camped out with friends whenever he could, and sometimes he slept rough, curling up in bus shelters or office doorways in the quiet streets around Park Row.

One night a fat, middle-aged businessman took him for a rent boy. Never one to miss an opportunity, Jimmy began to lure men into toilets on the promise of sex, then produce a Stanley knife and demand their money. It was a good earner, but several times he picked the wrong targets, and once he came close to being raped by two men.

Then, at fourteen, he lost control of a stolen XR2 on the Armley Interchange and flipped it, killing his passenger, a fellow thief. Jimmy was caught trying to flee the scene, despite a broken leg and half a dozen cracked ribs. He was in hospital for three weeks, and then a young offenders' institute for two years. It was like attending a crime academy, and when he graduated he immediately began putting his newly acquired skills to good use.

In 1989 his life went tits up again. He and two other men held up a sub-post office in Roundhay Road, but the Pakistani family who ran the store put up a fight. Jimmy discharged his shotgun during his escape, injuring the shopkeeper's daughter, and then fired blindly from the car while trying to shake off the police on the inner ring road. He was sent to Wakefield prison at the age of twenty-one and served just over six years.

It was a much smarter operator who emerged. Moving to London, he made use of prison contacts to find work as an enforcer, and within a few years he'd built enough of a reputation to set up on his own. With the approval of one of the big North London crime families, he carved himself a share in several clubs and restaurants, using the proceeds to set up similar, legitimate ventures. A small chain of video and DVD rental shops was particularly successful, and soon he was laundering money for others, before diversifying into money lending.

Now he had a four-bedroom home near Finsbury Park and a couple of cars each worth more than the houses he'd grown up in. By any measure he was a success, but somehow it wasn't enough. He was aware of a whole other league above him: people with so much money they didn't even *think* about money any more. That's what he wanted, and his aim was to get there by the time he was forty – the age at which his mum had died of a brain haemorrhage.

At first he had no idea how such a grand ambition would be realised, but he was a patient man, with an optimistic outlook. The right opportunity was out there somewhere. All he had to do was find it.

And then, one day, he did.

He found the Mathesons.

He was ten minutes early, but not from any desire to be here. He had no time for posh functions in posh hotels, and no idea why Kendrick had told him to attend. If it was about a show of strength, Kendrick had plenty of his own muscle. As soon as Vilner stepped out of the lift he saw two of them, stationed outside the Dorset Room. Gorillas in tuxedos.

One of them recognised him, nodded him past. He pushed through the double doors, into a room that was a little smaller than he'd expected, but beautifully laid out. A huge ice sculpture shaped like leaping dolphins formed the centrepiece of the buffet table, flanked by ice luges. The catering staff seemed to be exclusively female and stunningly attractive. A smart move, considering the majority of guests would be male and middle-aged.

There were none here yet, he noted. Just the waitresses buzzing around, and half a dozen of Kendrick's men eyeing them up. Then a door opened at the side of the room and Jacques emerged. He was a thin, dapper man with slicked-back hair, pale brown skin and very dark, almond-shaped eyes. Whereas the muscle was mostly locally recruited, Jacques had come from the Caribbean. It was clear he'd worked hard to install himself as Kendrick's right-hand man, and he was pathologically jealous of anyone who might threaten his status.

'You've left it too late,' the little man declared. He had a prissy voice that perfectly suited his pinched features.

'No, I haven't,' said Vilner evenly. 'I only need two minutes.'

'Well, you'd better hurry. The first guests will be here presently.'

Vilner strode away, not waiting to be dismissed. He went through the side door and found himself in a small, functional anteroom. Max Kendrick was sitting at the only table, tapping deftly on a laptop. There was a leather bag at his feet and a glass of water on the table next to him. He looked up as Vilner approached. Nodded and almost smiled. Almost, but not quite.

'With you in a moment,' he said.

'Okay.' It was only then that Vilner noticed the woman in the corner, sitting so still that she might have been part of the furniture. A young black girl, barely out of her teens, she was tall and willowy, wrapped up in a tight velvet dress like a gift too exqui-site to open. She had flawless skin and long, glossy hair. Vilner's stomach contracted at the sight of her. She risked only a single glance in his direction, then cast her eyes back to the floor. She had the nervy poise of a beauty contestant facing the flare of cameras for the first time, while a voice in her head screamed: *This is not me!*

With a pianist's flourish, Kendrick stopped typing and rested back in his chair. A year or two older than Vilner, he was a handsome man who also had a slightly disquieting appearance. His striking features were obviously the product of a confusing array of genes. From what Vilner had gleaned, Kendrick was from Trinidad, the son of a successful businessman with interests in the Caribbean ranging from leisure and tourism to insurance and oil. His father was a white Englishman, but his mother's heritage was a complicated mix of native Caribbean, Venezuelan, Indonesian and Dutch. Perhaps this explained the dark, wavy hair, flecked with grey, the coffee-and-cream complexion and brilliant blue eyes.

The unmistakable Caribbean lilt was equally disconcerting, mostly because of its similarity to the patois adopted by a generation of white kids who'd never travelled beyond the M25.

Kendrick said, 'Been quite a day, hasn't it?'

'I had a call from George Matheson.'

A thoughtful look warmed Kendrick's face. He stared at the laptop for a while, then leaned forward and snapped it closed. 'What did he say?'

'Not much. He'd like a meeting with you.'

78

Kendrick chuckled. 'Well, I guess I can spare some time next week. You heard anything more from the playboy?'

'Toby? No. He's on his best behaviour.' Vilner wanted to ask why Matheson hadn't been invited along today, but thought better of it. No doubt Kendrick had his reasons.

He said, 'I'm not sure why I'm wanted here, to be honest with you.'

'As a guest, James. This is a celebration of future success, and you're as entitled as anyone to share in that.'

'You don't think it'll seem insensitive, celebrating on a day like this?'

Kendrick nodded towards the function room, where the hum of conversation suggested his guests were arriving. 'You think these people care about anything except preserving their own pampered existence?' He chuckled, but there was no mistaking the contempt in his voice. 'You could wipe out half the population before this group took any notice.'

Vilner shrugged: if you say so. Kendrick put on his suit jacket, then reached into the leather bag and brought out a small black revolver. Noticing Vilner's frown, he held it out to him.

'Smith & Wesson 686, four-inch barrel. It's a beauty, isn't it?'

'What do you need it for?'

It was a gut response, and came out harsher than Vilner intended. Anger crossed Kendrick's eyes. He slipped the gun into his waistband and made sure it was concealed by his jacket. Checked his watch.

'You'll see,' he said.

Sixteen

Toby Harman had spent most of the day slumped on his long white sofa, skipping from one news channel to the next like a junkie chasing bigger and bigger hits. It was a grim lesson in the law of diminishing returns, but by now he was too lethargic to do anything else.

Toby was twenty-six years old, five feet ten and weighed a hundred and sixty pounds. He wasn't muscular and he wasn't flabby. He belonged to an expensive gym but rarely attended it, and although he liked to eat well in restaurants he was lazy about cooking at home. During periods of social inactivity he could subsist for days on cheese and Ritz crackers.

He wasn't particularly good-looking, but he wouldn't have changed a thing about his appearance. He had a long face, dark wavy hair and thick black eyebrows. His upper lip was slightly fuller than the lower, with pronounced crests that made him seem to be sneering, or about to blow a sarcastic kiss. Women were either entranced or they found him repulsive: he enjoyed both reactions equally, although the latter made for a more satisfying conquest.

When the phone rang, it sent a bolt of energy through him. About time.

'I thought I should warn you,' George said, 'the media are camped on my doorstep. They followed me back from Chilton.'

'You've been in Chilton? Today?' In fact Toby already knew this, because several channels had reported it, but he wasn't going to give George the satisfaction of letting on. He thought he might get more information if he played dumb.

'Terry Sullivan wanted me there. Ca— the killer apparently broke into the manor.'

Toby nearly dropped the phone. 'You know who it is. What did they tell you?'

George sighed. 'I'm not in the mood for this.'

'It'll come out soon enough. I don't see why you can't let me—'

'Christ, Toby. The Caplans were murdered today, along with God knows how many others.'

'The latest is twelve dead, according to the BBC. CNN say fourteen.'

A noise from George: a stifled groan.

'What about Philip Walker?' Toby said. 'Is he one of the victims?'

'I've no idea.' George seemed taken aback by the question, as though he hadn't considered it. *Surely you have,* Toby thought.

'If he is, then who knows what could happen?' he suggested. 'Let the dust settle for a few weeks. The protestors might not have the stomach for a fight.'

'Listen to me,' said George in a steely voice. 'If one whisper of what you've just said were to leak out, can you imagine the flak it would attract?'

'Calm down. I'm just thinking aloud.'

'It's bad enough that I still have to keep Vilner off our backs.'

Toby sighed. So that's what was really irking George. 'What's he saying?'

'If he doesn't get the contract you promised him, he'll want another instalment.'

'Tell him to piss off.'

'Don't lecture me,' George shouted. 'It's your bloody debts I'm sorting out, remember?'

Toby grunted. No point going down that route.

'Anyway,' he said, 'this affects my earnings as well. What if we do have to wait longer for a second application? How am I supposed to live in the meantime?'

For a second there was a silence so intense that Toby could imagine George vibrating with indignation.

'I'll pretend I didn't hear that,' said George quietly, and put the phone down.

Vilner didn't feel much like a guest. No one paid him any attention. No one tried to flatter him or talk to him. Kendrick ignored him completely, and so did Jacques. Even the catering staff were a bit slow to offer him their trays of champagne.

That suited him, he decided. He preferred Coke, anyway. Piling a plate from the buffet table, he found a chair on its own in the corner. He ate slowly, scanning the room, and wondered exactly what it was that Kendrick was trying to prove.

He didn't have to wait long to find out.

It was a select gathering, a couple of dozen people at most. Nearly all male. Everyone looked prosperous and smug. The ruling class. Until he'd moved to London, Vilner had been sceptical about the concept. He thought it was a cliché of the past, watered down if not washed away altogether. Yet here they were, all around him: florid cheeks and braying laughs, bred to give orders and recognise only their own kind. You could see it in the way they wafted drinks into their hands, as though the tray had floated up to them on strings.

Vilner couldn't distinguish much of what was said, but it did seem to him as though a low thrill passed through the crowd at each mention of the shooting in Chilton. An equally powerful thrill accompanied Kendrick's presence as he moved from group to group, skilfully working the room. At first Jacques followed, trying to join in with his boss's conversation, but gradually it sunk in that he wasn't welcome. He ended up standing by the wall opposite Vilner, gazing into his glass and pretending solitude was a deliberate choice.

It's like an old-time dance hall, Vilner thought. *And we're the boys who can't dance . . .*

Then Kendrick moved in front of the ice sculpture, and one of his men clapped his hands for silence. Kendrick began by grinning modestly.

'Thank you for coming, ladies and gentlemen. For those who don't know me so well, let me tell you a bit about myself. I was born in Trinidad, to an English father and Trinidadian mother.'

His audience were listening intently, but there were fixed smiles, and one or two quiet sniggers. Laughing at his accent, Vilner realised.

Kendrick sensed it, too. He hesitated, the grin still in place, and Vilner saw that dangerous look in his eye again. The moment passed and Kendrick spoke a little about his childhood. About his troubled teenage years and his time in the wilderness. His triumphant return to the family fold in his late twenties, and the decision to knuckle down and build on his father's legacy.

Now his voice wavered with emotion. 'I wish he had lived to see me now, on the brink of a whole new chapter. My mother, too. But I know how proud they would be. I didn't let them down.'

Vilner watched people grow fidgety; Kendrick was in danger of losing his audience, but now he ramped it up.

'I want to thank all of you,' he said. 'It's a thrilling journey we're embarking on together.'

His accent was momentarily stronger: *a trillin journey we're embarkin on* . . . Vilner had no doubt it was deliberate. He wanted them to think he was a country bumpkin, the God-fearing boy from the Third World.

'Some of you have already worked with me, here and back in the Caribbean. I'm hoping you all want to be on board as we grow and diversify in the UK, and I tell you now, I haven't come all this way just to start small and slow. I'm already in discussion to acquire a major business in the UK with interests in land, property, leisure and construction.'

That's why George Matheson wasn't invited, Vilner thought. His presence would have given the game away.

Kendrick acknowledged the exclamations of surprise and admiration. 'Your support is warmly appreciated,' he went on, 'but I need to know how far that support goes. Some of the places I've done business, the rule of law can't always be relied on, you understand?'

There were nods and grunts, but they sounded slightly confused. They sensed a subtle change in tone, and so did Vilner.

'Trust,' Kendrick declared. 'In business, it means everything. You agree with that, Maurice?'

His attention zeroed in on a short, overfed man with thinning ginger hair and a freckled scalp. He stared at Kendrick, red in the face and blinking furiously. His mouth dropped open, and when Vilner turned back to Kendrick he saw why.

Kendrick was holding the revolver. He opened the cylinder and displayed it to his audience. There were six chambers, five of them empty. Just a single, ominous round in the gun.

Kendrick spun the cylinder and slapped it back into place. 'Come here, Maurice,' he said.

There was silence in the room. Nobody moved. Vilner noticed the catering staff had made themselves scarce. The gorillas were standing in front of the doors, discreetly preventing entry or exit.

'Don't be scared, Maurice.'

Nudged by the man next to him, Maurice took a couple of reluctant steps towards Kendrick.

'Maurice here kindly lent his assistance on one of my last deals back in the Caribbean. Told me about a hotel in Jamaica, ripe for redevelopment. Promised he could get me the best price for it, and offered to act as go-between.'

Maurice was now only two feet away from Kendrick. There was sweat dribbling down his cheeks. Everyone else had shuffled as far back as they reasonably could without drawing attention to themselves. But nobody protested, Vilner noticed. Nobody put Maurice's well-being ahead of their own morbid curiosity.

Kendrick said, 'What I didn't know was that Maurice had a stake in the business, which someone else was already keen to buy. News of my interest sent the price much higher, which was his plan all along.'

Silence, except for Maurice's high, wheezing breath.

'Now I'm sure Maurice and his partners didn't intend me any harm. It was a tactic, that's all. Using me to make a little more money for themselves. And it didn't cost me much, financially. Some lawyers' fees. Including this lawyer right here.' He prodded Maurice in the belly with the Smith & Wesson. Maurice squealed and shut his eyes.

'But it cost me time,' Kendrick said, emphasising every word. 'And it damaged my reputation. Some people think I was beaten to a deal. Well, I can live with that, I guess. But others know I was set up.'

At this, Maurice finally seized the courage to protest, but Kendrick cut him off.

'Professional suicide,' he declared, raising the gun and jamming it against his own temple. 'That's what I'm talking about. Betraying trust is professional suicide.'

He squeezed the trigger. There was an audible click. A woman screamed. An elderly man sank to the floor, his face ashen.

Kendrick looked grimly satisfied. He hadn't even broken a sweat. He let the gun fall away, then pointed it at Maurice, holding it level with the man's face. 'Your turn.'

Maurice opened his mouth again, but couldn't speak. Someone behind him exclaimed and pointed at his legs. There was urine running off his shoes, pooling on the floor.

'Russian Roulette is a fool's game,' Kendrick said. 'I know you're not a fool, Maurice. None of you here are fools, are you?'

It took a second for the question to penetrate, then there was a chorus of overeager nods. No one was laughing at him now. Vilner even detected a certain loathing directed at Maurice for embroiling them in such an unsavoury scene.

'To succeed in life, it's essential to be lucky,' Kendrick concluded, tapping the gun against his chest. 'I guarantee my luck by careful preparation, and by working with people I can trust. I know none of you are going to let me down.'

More nodding. More keen murmurs of assent. It was a masterful performance, thought Vilner, and it worried him that Kendrick had wanted him to see it.

Did Kendrick suspect him of disloyalty, and if so, why?

Seventeen

The police were professional and sympathetic and practical. They encouraged him to drink two mugs of strong coffee, and by the time they left Craig felt almost sober.

It was seven o'clock, and he still hadn't heard from Nina. He had no idea where she was, or if she was coming back. The rest of the evening yawned ahead of him: he could either stay like this or get drunk all over again.

Before he could decide, the doorbell rang. He went to answer it, wondering if the police had forgotten to tell him something. But it was Abby Clark, looking tired but oddly exhilarated. She was holding a pizza box from a local takeaway.

'I know this is an imposition . . .'

'But?'

'Can I eat in here? I'm very cold and very hungry.' She moved closer, wafting melted cheese and pepperoni fumes under his nose. There was an audible growl from his stomach.

'Sounds like you could do with something.'

He shrugged. 'No appetite. The police have just left.'

'I know. I watched them go.'

He couldn't help smiling. 'So you waited just long enough . . . ?'

'Not too long. Pizza would have gone cold.' The twinkle in her eyes was like a laser, obliterating any resentment he might have felt.

She followed him into the hall and shrugged off her coat. 'Isn't Nina here?'

'No.' He paused on the threshold to the lounge. 'Do you want a plate? Cutlery?'

'Nah. And I insist on sharing.'

She sat beside him on the sofa, dragged the coffee table closer and opened the box. She tore out a thick cheesy wedge and thrust it at him. 'Eat.'

He took a desultory bite. Chewed, swallowed, winced. It felt like cardboard in his gullet, but at least it would help soak up the alcohol.

'Bad news, I take it?' Abby said, hooking a long strand of cheese from her chin.

He nodded. He went to tell her his father was dead and found himself speechless. He'd assembled all the right words in his head but his mouth just wouldn't let them out.

It should have been Nina who comforted him, not Abby, but right now that didn't matter. This was grief so raw and unexpected that it couldn't be suppressed. Its ferocity shocked him. He cried for practically the first time since his children were born, without once feeling self-conscious or stepping back to scrutinise his feelings in the way he was usually given to doing.

To her credit, Abby was up to the task. She didn't shirk from holding him close. Didn't complain when his tears ran down her neck and dampened her shirt. She smelt warm and wonderful, thrillingly unfamiliar, and when that thought filtered into his head he knew it was time to break apart.

'Sorry,' he said. 'And thank you.'

'You'd do the same for me. Albeit with an erection.'

It was such a frivolous comment, and yet so true, it surprised a laugh from him. He felt briefly guilty, then much better. Better than he'd felt all through this long and dreadful day.

'I'll warm the pizza up,' he said.

'Good idea. Cup of tea would be bliss.'

Accompanying him into the kitchen, she spent a few seconds admiring the units, and then said, 'So where's Nina?'

'No idea. She doesn't even know about Dad yet.' He stopped short, felt another pang of guilt. 'She's been seeing someone else, and today wasn't exactly the ideal time to find out.'

'You're kidding me?'

He shook his head.

'Is it serious?'

He dropped the pizza on to a baking tray and turned to face her. 'Does it matter?'

'Yes. It doesn't have to destroy your marriage. Not if you don't want it to.'

'Would you say that if Nigel slept around?'

'We split up last year.'

'Did you? Oh God, I didn't realise. Was there anyone else involved . . . ?'

'Sort of.' Now she blushed slightly, something he'd never seen her do.

'Are you with someone now?'

She nodded. Studied him and laughed. 'Don't look so disappointed.'

'I wasn't.'

She narrowed her eyes. 'I was just teasing.'

'I know.' He busied himself filling the kettle. After a respectable pause, he said, 'What's he like?'

'Very nice, thanks. Only it's a *she*.'

'Oh.' He was suitably gobsmacked.

'I don't broadcast it. Early days. But we're very happy.'

He nodded, thinking back over all the years he'd known her, wondering if she'd ever given any hint.

Reading his mind, she said, 'It was just about the last thing I expected. As much a surprise to me as anyone else.'

'How has Nigel reacted?'

A snort. 'He doesn't know whether to challenge her to a fight or suggest a threesome.'

They took the pizza back into the lounge, and he went over what the police had said. He'd been told to expect a long and detailed investigation, but off the record the facts were pretty clear: a young man had gone on a killing spree. In the next day or two he'd have to make a formal identification of his father's body. An inquest would be opened and adjourned, and the body released for burial. Every affected family had a police liaison officer assigned to them, available for information, guidance and support over the coming weeks.

Abby listened solemnly and then ran through her own experience. The police had held their first full press conference at two o'clock, hosted by the detective chief superintendent in overall command of the operation. By that time all the injured had been conveyed to hospital.

'How many victims in total?' he asked.

'Fourteen confirmed dead at the scene. Another four wounded, three of them seriously.'

Craig let out a breath he hadn't known he was holding. 'So the death toll might rise?'

She nodded. 'A girl from the farmhouse is in a coma. And there was the woman who fell out of a tree.'

'What?'

'I got that little nugget by chatting up one of the search team.' She winked; some of her natural exuberance leaking out at last. He couldn't reproach her for it. This was the type of event that could make a journalist's career.

'They think she was chased by the killer,' Abby went on. 'She must have tried to hide in the tree, but he shot her and she fell.'

'Will she live?'

'Anyone's guess at the moment,' Abby said. 'After going through that, I hope so.'

Another sigh from Craig. He cradled his mug in both hands and held it close, although it was virtually empty. 'What do you know about the killer?'

'Young. Male. Possibly local. That's all we've got.'

'Nothing on the grapevine?'

Abby shook her head, then grew pensive. 'Craig, I don't know how you'll feel about this, but I'd like to mention your dad in my article. He was obviously a high-profile figure in the village.'

Craig gave her a sidelong glance. 'So this wasn't just a social visit?' She looked suitably abashed, but before she responded he said, 'Don't worry. I don't blame you.'

'I've been looking at some of the local issues, and it's clear that Matheson's plan stirred up a lot of controversy. I thought it would make for an interesting background story. Your dad was leading the fight.'

'For all the good it did him.'

'But the proposal was rejected. Surely that's a victory?'

'They won the first skirmish, that's all. A man like George Matheson doesn't give up easily.' As he said it he was aware of an uneasy feeling that this wasn't the time to unburden himself of such thoughts.

Abby said, 'I can't see him trying anything now.'

'Who knows? Maybe it will help him.'

She was staring at him, desperately trying to conceal her excitement. Craig saw it, knew he should change the subject. But he couldn't resist.

'Maybe this just clears the path for him,' he said viciously. 'After all, who's left to fight him now?'

Eighteen

The killer powered up his laptop and opened Internet Explorer for the second time that evening. It was almost midnight. On TV a panel of worthies was debating the possible repercussions of what had already been dubbed 'The Chilton Massacre'.

He'd first logged on an hour or so before. He signed into Hotmail, using the email address and password he'd been sent four months ago, from someone he knew only as Decipio.

There was a new entry waiting for him in the Drafts folder. His finger poised over the mousepad for a few seconds. He took a deep breath and clicked it open.

```
Was I supposed to be impressed by that? If
anything, you've made the situation worse.
You failed in your main objective.
She's still alive.
```

He had stared at the message for a long time, feeling sick and furious and most of all despairing. He felt like a marathon runner who turns what he thinks is the last corner and instead sees a vast unforgiving road stretching to the horizon.

Then he deleted the message and composed a reply.

```
I don't know why he ignored my orders. He
knew exactly what he was supposed to do,
but he went berserk. I stopped him as soon
as I could, at great risk to me.
Are you sure about the survivor? I dealt
with her myself.
```

He saved the draft, then logged off. Decipio had instructed him to keep the language vague, but this was really an unnecessary precaution. By sharing the log-on and using only the draft function, they ensured the messages were never transmitted, and thus couldn't be eavesdropped. It was the same method by which some of the 7 July London bombers had communicated.

Then he'd gone back to the TV, and listened to a rentaquote MP assert that further restrictions on firearms might be necessary. A senior churchman wanted greater moral leadership in society, and a psychologist argued there was inadequate screening or support for the kind of unstable men who are driven to commit such atrocities. The government representative, a junior Home Office minister, seemed on the brink of tears.

The killer muted the TV and opened Hotmail again. Read the new message that had taken the place of his own in the Drafts folder.

```
Quite sure. You failed.
Try again. This time get it right.
No loose ends.
```

He snarled at the screen, feeling a resentment familiar to footsoldiers everywhere. All very easy to dish out orders from a comfortable office somewhere; not quite so simple to accomplish on the ground. And where was the recognition of what he had achieved?

He felt disgusted. On the verge of refusing. But he knew he

wouldn't. There was too much at stake. He had no choice but to carry on.

Like the message said, he would have to try again. And this time, make sure he killed her.

No loose ends.

Nineteen

In the dreams she always died.

In the dreams she was chased, hunted, caught and killed. Each time she died she found herself back in the darkness, her pursuer hot on her trail, and the whole terrible story played out again. The dreams went on in another world, where fears could not be rationalised, reflected on, dismissed.

A world with no escape.

Then, quite abruptly, she found herself in a room flooded with light. At first she didn't know who she was, but that lasted only an instant. With identity came one startling recollection: her parents were dead.

The grief was suffocating. She wanted to believe it was part of the nightmare, but when she searched her memory the details came too clearly and rapidly to be anything other than genuine.

It was mid-December, a squally evening. Both she and her brother, Neil, had spent the day trying to reach them by phone, and finally Julia agreed to drive over after work.

Pulling up outside the terrace in her red Mini Cooper, she had noticed the house was completely dark. For a minute she remained in the car, gathering her nerve. Rain pounded on the roof, making her feel cocooned and yet vulnerable at the same time.

She knew something was wrong as soon as she unlocked the front door. A wave of cloying heat was sucked into the storm, leaving an imprint of the stillness which had preceded it, like the after-image of a flashbulb. There was something else, too. An ominous quality to the silence that ran like a cold finger along her spine. She felt an over-whelming urge to turn and flee.

She stepped inside and turned on the light. Once she'd filtered out the muted howl of the wind, she began to identify sounds from inside: the sombre ticking of a carriage clock, the staccato buzz of the fridge, the roaring boiler.

Already the heat was building again. It felt sinister and out of place. Her father was notorious for his thrift. When she and Neil were kids he'd always been turning off lights in their wake. He wouldn't go out and leave the heating on at this level.

Which suggested that they hadn't gone out. They were here. In the dark.

'Mum! Dad!' she cried. 'Are you there?'

No answer. She could see all the downstairs rooms were unlit, but there was still a chance they were in one of the bedrooms.

It was a forlorn hope, she knew as she climbed the stairs. With each step her legs seemed to grow heavier and more reluctant. Reaching the landing, she experienced a little pitch of nausea and had to grab the handrail.

There were no lights on upstairs.

'Mum?' she called again, and paused, stalled by dread. 'Dad?'

She faced her parents' bedroom and slowly eased the door open. Her hand trembled as she reached for the light switch. Despite the gloom she could just make out the twin shapes beneath the lilac M&S duvet. It brought back a long-forgotten memory of childhood, one Sunday morning, giggling with her brother on the landing while strange gasps and moans emanated from the bedroom. Then, as now, she'd felt she was intruding on something she didn't understand.

But she couldn't turn back. She had to know.

She switched on the light, offering a desperate prayer: *Let them be asleep*.

And just for a moment, until she saw their faces, it seemed that they were.

Her parents were dead, and she had found the bodies. But where was she now? Had she suffered a breakdown as a result of the trauma? Was she confined to a mental hospital?

Desperate to stay away from the dark world of her dreams, she clung to the memory of that night in December. She would force herself to relive the experience, and perhaps by doing that she could find a path back to the present day.

They had looked as if they'd just come in from one of Dad's route marches over the Downs. Lying snugly beneath the duvet with the rosy glow of obscene good health, she had almost expected her father to rear up in bed and berate her. 'Turn the bloody light off, Julia. Your mother and I fancied an early night.'

But he wasn't going to do that. Not tonight or any other. They were dead. And in an instant several things had made sense: their complexions, the stifling heat, Julia's vague headache and nausea. The sort of thing you hear on the news: a dreadful but essentially mundane tragedy that always happens to someone else.

Until it happens to you.

She lunged for the window and threw it open. Dashed downstairs and into the kitchen, knocking a picture from the wall in her haste. The boiler hung in the corner like a malevolent caged dragon, breathing death into the house. She shut it down, grabbed her parents' cordless phone and ran into the garden. Now the wind and rain were a kind of salvation.

She dialled 999 and explained in a shaky voice what she suspected. The operator ran her through a sequence of questions so smoothly that she had no choice but to reply calmly, without panic. It was a form of hypnosis, she realised much later. He told her the emergency services were on their way, and asked if she felt all right. Was there a friend or neighbour who could wait with her?

She mumbled something about going next door and ended the call. Almost immediately the whole thing seemed unreal. What if she had imagined it, or been mistaken? She'd look such a fool. Surely she ought to go back in and check?

She got as far as the door before an immobilising terror stopped her in her tracks. Of course she hadn't imagined anything. They were dead.

She thought about Neil. He was four or five hours away. But she could feel her throat closing even as she imagined trying to tell him.

Then the phone rang, making her jump. She pressed the Talk button, expecting to hear the 999 operator.

'Can I speak to Jules?' a voice shouted.

'It's me, Steve.'

'I couldn't get you on your mobile.'

'There's no signal here,' she said, noticing for the first time how abnormal her voice sounded. But if it was apparent to Steve, he gave no sign. Earlier he had derided her concerns and refused to accompany her, preferring to play squash instead. *It's obvious they don't like me*, he had said. *I don't wanna go and see them.*

Well now you won't have to, she thought. You'll never have to.

'It took me bloody ages to find your mum's number,' he said. 'When are you gonna be home? I was thinking I could drop by after the pub. Bring a takeaway, bottle of vino?'

'No, Steve. I can't.'

'Don't give me that. We might as well be an old married couple for the sex life we've had lately. Fucking non-existent . . .' His grumbled complaints tailed off, and she spoke into the sullen silence.

'My mum and dad are dead,' she told him. 'I'm in their garden, waiting for the police, so I'm not really in the mood tonight. In fact, I'd like you to piss off. Can you do that for me, Steve? Can you piss off?'

*   *   *

Her awareness now extended to an array of equipment around her bed. There were tubes tethered to her body; machines that hummed and bleeped in response to her gradual healing. It made her sickly aware of her own heartbeat, her breathing. It hurt when she breathed, she realised. Lots of vague, generalised pain that managed to be intense and yet muffled at the same time.

She was in hospital, then. But not a psychiatric ward. She was recovering from some sort of physical injury. An accident? That seemed plausible. In the aftermath of losing her parents, she wouldn't have been thinking clearly. Perhaps her concentration had lapsed while driving.

Then an abhorrent thought: perhaps she had tried to commit suicide?

Fire officers with breathing apparatus had entered the house first and declared it safe. Julia was ushered into the kitchen by a police officer, who set about making tea. Shortly afterwards another officer returned from upstairs, nodded grimly at her colleague and addressed Julia: 'They're both dead. I'm very sorry.'

After that, time passed in a blur. Julia had little clear recollection of how long she sat in the kitchen, while various people trooped up and down the stairs. Some introduced themselves, some did not. Most lingered in the doorway for a few seconds, looking at her with a vague professional curiosity, as though they might have welcomed a dramatic reaction. Something to make the evening memorable for them.

Eventually she summoned the courage to phone her brother. She expected him to ask lots of questions, but instead he absorbed the news in a dull, shocked silence. She was still waiting for a coherent response when his wife Donna took the phone. It was as if they'd already known, she told Julia. As if they'd known all day.

Unable to sleep on such news, they arranged for Donna's parents to come over and look after the children. Then they packed a suit-case and left Knutsford in the early hours, arriving at Julia's flat just after dawn.

The sight of Neil as he stumbled from the car – pale, red-eyed, faltering – brought home to her the enormity of their loss. It was just the two of them now, brother and sister. Orphans.

Now there were voices. Sometimes distant and vaguely soothing, like running water. Sometimes loud and brash. Her senses felt cruelly heightened, overwhelming her, threatening to send her back to that other world. The world where he waited, again and again, to complete his task.

But who was he? Why did he want to kill her?

She continued tiptoeing cautiously through her memory of the days that followed. The post mortems confirmed that Bernard and Lisa Trent died from carbon monoxide poisoning. The local authority arranged for the central heating system to be examined by an engineer, who concluded that the boiler had been poorly maintained. In addition, a crucial vent had been blocked, possibly to prevent a draught. Julia felt sure her parents would have had it serviced, but a search of the house revealed no paperwork to corroborate that. She'd even contacted some local plumbers, but none recalled working on it.

The family liaison officer explained that an inquest would be held. It would be for the coroner to determine the ultimate cause, but the likelihood was either accidental death or an open verdict. The sheer senselessness of it was one of the hardest things for Julia to bear. The thought that two lives had been lost for the price of a routine service.

A week or more had passed in a dull haze of grief. She was too numb to be affected by the funeral, and suffered a delayed reaction that hit at the worst possible time: just as she sat down to Christmas dinner with her brother and his family in Knutsford. Like the rest of the adults, she'd been determined to make an effort at normality for the sake of the children, but she found herself weeping so helplessly that in the end even her four-year-old nephew decided it was impolite to stare. Neil virtually had to carry her from the room.

The solicitor had made it clear there was no hurry to do anything with the cottage. Julia and her brother were sole beneficiaries, and there was no mortgage. But they both agreed there was no question of keeping the house. It had never been a family home, and now it would only ever be associated with tragedy.

Simple geography dictated that Julia would take care of clearing out the furniture and sorting through a lifetime's accumulation of belongings. Once she'd started back at school and had the first couple of weeks under her belt, she finally steeled herself to get on with it.

I can't keep putting it off. That's what she had told someone. In a shop. An old-fashioned village store.

She remembered a cold, sunny morning. A deep frost on the grass and the tiled roofs. It was a Saturday, very early. No one around.

It was Chilton, she realised. Whatever it was, it had happened in Chilton.

'Is there any improvement?'

She recognised the voice as her brother's. Neil was here, at her bedside. She could even smell his aftershave. Hugo Boss. It was what she usually bought him for Christmas.

In reply, a man with a soft Indian accent said, 'She's definitely on the mend. We're reducing the sedatives, so she should be back with us quite soon.'

From her brother, a heartfelt rush of breath: pure relief. She felt touched, but also scared.

'She was very fortunate,' the other man said. 'The bullet could have done a lot more damage.'

She was hiding in the tree, but he knew she was there. A man in black motorcycle leathers.

Oh God. No.

'It's the psychological effect that worries me,' her brother said.

'I quite understand, but let's concern ourselves with that at the appropriate time. For now, we should be thankful she survived at all. So many did not.'

'I know.' A hand took hold of hers, and she knew it was Neil. 'She's a real fighter, aren't you, love?'

This was addressed to Julia, and she longed to answer, longed to reassure him she was all right, but nothing would work, not her mouth or throat, her arms or legs, everything comfortable but locked in place, as though she were immersed in some kind of thick resin. As a child playing hide-and-seek she had crawled into her parents' wardrobe and piled all the winter coats on top of her until she could barely move. It was the same warm safe weight lying on her now: she was powerless against it.

Just as she had been powerless to stop the bullets strafing the tree.

She felt the draw of the other world and tried desperately to resist, but of course it was hopeless. The machines dutifully recorded her panic, but no one came to her aid.

This time, she knew who was waiting.

Twenty

Sullivan chose a little pub up the hill from the station. Brighton wasn't his manor, but he knew it was a lively place, and Thursday night practically counted as the weekend. He wanted somewhere quiet and discreet, somewhere they were unlikely to be noticed.

The pub was in a terrace of Victorian homes, no bigger than a front room, with too many tables squashed into the space each side of the bar. At eight o'clock it wasn't busy: a bunch of students clearly intending to move on somewhere more exciting, and a few late commuters in shirts and ties, sipping pints and reading the *Argus*. Sullivan had once been the same, knackered after a day's work but reluctant to go home and face the missus. Now she was long gone, and it made no difference to him whether he went out or stayed in. Either way he drank alone and pleased himself.

Not tonight, though. He was halfway through his Guinness when the door opened and Craig Walker came in. He had the same anger, the same glowering intensity as the last time they'd met. That had to be four or five years ago at least, but he seemed to have barely aged at all. Pity I can't say the same for myself, Sullivan thought ruefully.

Craig didn't bother disguising his reaction. 'You look even worse than you did on TV.'

'They must have got my good side.'

'What happened? Were you locked in a bakery for five years?'

'Yeah, I wish. It's called getting older. What can you do about it?'

'Exercise?' Craig snapped back. 'Eat well? Drink less?'

Sullivan raised his glass with perfect timing. 'Another Guinness, cheers. And get me some peanuts.'

Craig glared at him, but turned to the bar without a protest. Whatever it is, he must want it badly, Sullivan thought.

He was contemplating what it might be when a bag of dry roasted plopped into his lap. Cursing, he looked up and noticed Craig slopping beer from each glass as he set them down. Now Sullivan took in the trembling hands, the red-rimmed eyes. 'Looks like you're a fine one to give advice on healthy living.'

Craig just smiled. Gripped his glass with a real effort and raised it in a toast.

Sullivan finished the dregs of his first pint, smacking his lips noisily. 'So how come you're not putting the world to rights any more? From what I hear, you're interviewing C-listers and reporting on the sports events no one else wants to go to.'

'I moved on.' He stared at Sullivan. 'Got tired of dealing with all the lying, cheating scum.'

'I know that feeling. That's why I do my best to put 'em behind bars, where they belong.'

'What about Chief Inspector Kennedy? Did he end up where he belongs?'

Sullivan chuckled. 'He's got a very nice place in Malaga.'

Craig laughed with him, but there was a bitter edge to it. 'Along with the rest of the villains. You still see him, do you?'

'Been out there once or twice. Too hot for me, but he's a changed man. Really taken to retirement.'

'You won't be following him over there, then?'

'Nah. It's Bournemouth for me.'

'It'll be a wooden box if you don't get your act together.'

'Nice of you to worry.' Sullivan picked up the Guinness, drained a third of the pint and wiped the foam from his lips. 'Kennedy's old news. And I had no idea he was bent.'

He tore savagely at the bag of peanuts and it split open, spilling half a dozen on the table. He tipped the bag up and poured them into his mouth, part of him relishing Craig's disgust.

'You covered for him. And I fell for it.'

Sullivan chewed, swallowed, but still sprayed a few fragments as he answered. 'I was a lowly fucking DS. All I did was give him the benefit of the doubt, and I asked you to do the same. End of story. Now tell me what you want or piss off.'

Craig settled back in his seat, apparently pleased that he'd provoked a reaction. 'I hear you're part of the Chilton investigation.'

Sullivan nodded. Deciding it was time to cool the atmosphere, he said, 'I'm sorry about your old man.'

He waited, watching Craig assess the sincerity of his comment. He wondered if Craig was aware of his connection to George Matheson.

'I want to know what happened,' Craig said.

'Carl Forester went on the rampage.'

'That's really all it was?'

Sullivan didn't answer. He thought about the scene at the farmhouse. The woman assaulted. The dying husband forced to watch.

'What do you reckon it was?' he said.

'I think there's a connection to George Matheson. You must know that everyone in the village was opposed to his plans.'

Sullivan was careful not to react. He shook his head slowly. 'You're barking up the wrong tree.' Then he laughed.

'What?'

'You know about the woman who fell out of the tree?'

'I heard about her. Julia Trent.'

'That's right. We still haven't been able to speak to her yet, but from what we've pieced together, it looks like Carl chased her on to the village green. Somehow she managed to climb the tree, even though he would have been hot on her heels.'

Sullivan paused, waiting to see if Craig had caught his emphasis. 'Somehow?'

'Did they tell you your dad was shot twice?'

'Two bullets, you mean?'

Sullivan shook his head. 'Two separate occasions.'

The colour drained from Craig's face. He sat forward, gripping the sides of his chair as if he feared being hurled into space. 'What?'

'The first one was a chest wound. Serious, maybe even fatal. But not necessarily.' He waited again, let the words sink in.

'You mean Carl went back to him . . . ?' Craig faltered. 'But why?'

'Maybe because of the woman. It's only speculation, but it looks like your dad opened his front door and tried to intervene. Carl made a detour to shoot him before he dealt with Trent.'

'So he could have stayed inside? And he might have survived?'

'Yep.' Sullivan also leaned forward, putting on his best 'straight talking' demeanour. 'I'm telling you this because I want you to understand it was just an act of random craziness. If you want to start blaming people, fine. But in that case Julia Trent got your dad killed, as much as anyone else. There was no grand plan, and certainly nothing that involved George Matheson. If he'd been in Chilton that day, he would have been one of the victims, I'm sure of that.'

Craig was quiet for a moment. When he spoke he sounded much calmer than Sullivan expected, his tone measured and oddly respectful.

'You say you haven't interviewed her yet? When you do, will you tell me what she says? And before you say it, I'm not going to threaten you. But if you're honest with yourself, and you truly didn't know Kennedy was on the take, then you'll agree you still owe me a favour or two.'

'How do you work that out?'

'Because if I hadn't kept my mouth shut, all kinds of shit would have been thrown at him, and at you, and I'm willing to bet that some of it would have stuck.'

Craig stood up, bumping the table and almost knocking the glasses over. Sullivan instinctively grabbed his pint. Craig gave him a thin smile.

'Go on,' he said. 'Surprise yourself. Do the right thing.'

Twenty-One

Friday. She had to keep telling herself it was Friday. It mattered a lot, that she could keep track of the date, just as it bothered her that three days had effectively vanished. A trivial thing to be concerned about, compared to everything else, but it produced a strange disorientation. It felt like it should be Tuesday.

Julia thought about her class, probably still lethargic after the Christmas break. January was a tough month to get their enthusiasm stoked up. Still, she'd give anything now to be standing in front of them, suffering any number of bad jokes and impressions from TV shows they shouldn't even have been watching. *Little Britain* had been like a curse on teachers: just how many times could you hear a prancing child declare, *'I'm a laydee!'* and not want to commit murder?

Her thoughts hit a brick wall. Shouldn't have used the M word.

The memories of what happened had returned, not gradually but in a rush. Finding the postman dead behind his van, trying to save Moira, the chase, seeing the first killer shot. Then the second killer, staring at the grass, knowing he had guessed where she was. The gun coming up . . .

The doctor had explained that amnesia was quite normal after such a period of unconsciousness, but equally that she might be completely unaffected. So far she had been cagey about what she told them, and no one had pushed her on it. Yet.

Her brother had been delighted by her recovery. Tears rolled down his face the first time he spoke to her. Once again she'd felt a stab in her heart, realising it was because their parents were gone. Neil had been terrified of losing her as well.

After chatting for a few minutes, he asked, 'How much of it do you remember?'

'Enough,' she said, a cue that she wasn't yet ready to discuss it.

But he had taken her hand in his, and said, 'They've identified the gunman. A local man, Carl Forester. The typical oddball. He killed himself . . . afterwards.'

For the briefest moment she was exultant. Her eyes must have lit up, for her brother smiled and said, 'They found his body on the green. I thought you'd want to know he's dead.' He squeezed her hand. 'He can't hurt you any more.'

She smiled back, managed a nod. He meant the first gunman. Not the man in black.

She opened her mouth to tell him, but fear and confusion held her back. She knew he'd watched it on TV, read the newspapers, perhaps even spoken to officers directly involved in the case. And if he believed there was only one killer . . .

So did everyone else.

The cold, clear spell had given way to milder weather, a succession of low pressure systems trudging along the south coast, bringing rain and wind and heavy skies. Even at midday most of the traffic on the main road had their headlights on, and in the roads around the hospital some of the street lights were still illuminated.

Parking close to the hospital was virtually impossible, but he had expected that. He found a space half a mile away. He was driving a ten-year-old Ford Escort, bought in Milton Keynes three days ago. Same routine as with the Kawasaki: private sale, cash purchase, false details.

He wore jeans and trainers and a hooded top. He knew there would be CCTV everywhere, but he also knew the images were frequently useless. Eyewitnesses would notice only what he wanted them to notice: the slicked-back hair, the goatee beard, the tinted contact lenses.

He walked briskly and confidently on to the hospital site. Took out his mobile phone and dipped his head as he passed the cameras above the main doors. Once inside, he slipped the phone into his pocket and concentrated on looking as though he knew exactly where he was going.

Her consultant was Mr Chapman, a rotund man in his fifties who reminded her of a badger. Black and white hair, big bushy eyebrows, more hair sprouting from his ears and nose, and a solemn but sprightly manner. It had fallen to him to describe the emergency laparotomy to establish the extent of the damage, and the subsequent three-hour operation to repair it.

'The bullet was lodged in retroperitoneal tissue between your right kidney and the inferior vena cava, which brings blood from the lower part of the body to your heart. There was slight damage to the pancreas, but not the main pancreatic duct. In many ways, you were extremely fortunate.' He smiled, acknowledging that she might not feel that way. 'The bullet was a .22, low velocity, fired from some distance. A larger calibre or a shot fired at closer range would have carried far more destructive force.'

In addition, she had sustained dozens of minor lacerations and widespread bruising from the fall. She also had a badly sprained ankle and a laceration to her leg that differed in nature from the others.

'Another bullet,' she'd said, and Mr Chapman had nodded to himself, as if he'd suspected as much. She could see him regarding her with a mixture of pity and horrified fascination. It was her first experience of feeling like a circus exhibit, and she knew it would get much worse when she told them what really happened.

Maybe it would be better to say nothing at all.

*   *   *

He had allowed himself one reconnaissance mission, the day before. He had wandered the corridors, taking note of the myriad signs and instructions, trying to calculate the risks involved and weigh them against the potential benefits. Then he sat in the cafeteria, sipping a coffee and relishing the knowledge that she was very close now. Almost in his grasp.

He took the elevator to Level Eight and stepped out into an empty corridor. Turned towards a set of green double doors with three porthole windows arranged vertically on each door. As he pushed through them he saw a nurse at the far end of the corridor, but she was standing with her back to him.

Perfect.

In the days after the shooting, media interest in the survivors had been predictably intense. The hospital was besieged with reporters, who had to settle for regular updates, when what they really craved was access to the patients themselves. This interest subsided when some of the survivors came forward to recount their experiences, but in Julia's case it was judged that a general ward wasn't sufficiently secure. After being discharged from Intensive Care, she was moved to a side room on her own.

Julia knew very little about the media coverage. She hadn't once switched on the TV in her room, and her brother's offer to bring in newspapers had been politely declined. He'd visited this morning, bringing some toiletries and a couple of books from her flat. He told her that Donna and the children couldn't wait until she was well enough to come up and stay.

She had smiled, recalling the disastrous Christmas dinner, but said nothing. Soon afterwards she felt herself getting dozy, and he had kissed her forehead and quietly left the room. The consultant had told her that daytime naps should be a feature of her recuperation for several weeks at least. Another reason she wouldn't be able to take up Neil's offer: no chance of sleeping with three boisterous children in the house.

She woke quickly, at some kind of disturbance. A noise outside the door.

She rubbed her eyes and looked at the clock on the unit beside her bed. It was just after midday. The door opened slightly and one of the nurses, Shauna, peeked into the room. She was a chatty young Irish woman, very friendly but with a tendency to outstay her welcome. On occasions Julia had faked sleep to end a conversation.

'Oh good, you're awake,' Shauna said. 'Someone here to see you. He says he'll not stop long if you don't feel up to it.' She glanced back over her shoulder, then mouthed at Julia: 'He's police!'

Julia frowned. All visitors were supposed to be cleared by her consultant.

Then something else occurred to her. It hit her like a thunderbolt.

The second killer might come after her. She had no idea what he looked like. No idea who he was. What if he had heard she was still alive, and tried—

'I can't reach Mr Chapman,' Shauna chattered on, 'but you're making such good progress, I thought if you're all right to see him . . .'

She stepped into the room, and Julia saw the man was right behind her. He was in his early forties, quite tall, with neat dark hair and a serious face. He didn't look like a killer, but then he didn't look like a policeman either. He met her gaze and gave an uncertain smile.

'I don't think . . .' Julia began, but it was too late. The man stepped around the nurse and began to produce something from inside his jacket. The gesture took her right back to the green, to the moment the second killer had brought the gun up and aimed it at her hiding place.

He had found her. And this time she had nowhere to hide.

Twenty-Two

The door had a porthole window at eye level. He could see her lying in bed, surrounded by the equipment that had saved her life. Little good that would do her now.

His hand was on the door when a voice called out, 'Help you?'

He looked round and saw a policeman ambling towards him, holding a steaming cup of coffee in one hand and clutching several chocolate bars in the other. He was tall but paunchy, with a swarthy complexion and suspiciously dark hair. He looked the way Elvis might have done had he made it to his fifties with no great modifications in his lifestyle.

He could probably be overcome, the killer thought. He looked fat, lazy, probably marking time till retirement. It wasn't until the policeman came a bit closer that he saw the hard edge in his eyes. Maybe not such a pushover.

The policeman was shaking his head. 'You fellers disappoint me, you know.'

The killer frowned. Waited for him to elaborate.

'Fair enough, you have to earn a living, but trying to sneak a picture of a nine-year-old girl lying in a coma.' He tutted, then took a slurp of coffee. 'Poor little mite doesn't deserve that.'

The killer shrugged. 'Yeah, well, I got an editor on my back. Thought it was worth a punt.'

'I'm gonna let it go this time. Try it again and I'll have you up the station, explaining yourself to my sergeant. You get me?'

The killer nodded ruefully and turned away. He heard the rustle of chocolate wrappers. 'Oy!' the policeman called, and his heart skipped a beat.

He looked back. The policeman was jabbing a Mars bar at him.

'And I haven't forgiven you lot for Princess Di, either.'

Leaving the hospital, he reflected that it wasn't all bad news. He'd verified that the girl was still in a coma, nearly a week after she'd been smothered. There must be a good chance that she would never wake up. And if the policeman was only there to protect her from the media, it meant they didn't anticipate any other kind of threat.

The one potential danger to him was the woman in the tree. But he knew from the newspapers that she'd now regained consciousness, and since there hadn't been any suggestion of a second gunman in the media, he was guessing she probably had amnesia – in which case he was safe.

Relatively safe, at least.

Suddenly the room was full of people. The nurse was shouting, and a doctor shouldered his way through. Julia was dimly aware that she was hanging half off the bed. The man who had caused the panic was trying, haplessly, to lift her back into position. There was a woman in police uniform just behind him, looking very upset.

Above the shouts and running footsteps she could hear an awful keening noise. It sounded inhuman, like something from her nightmares. Gradually she realised it was coming from her. Then she realised the distress on everyone's faces was only mirroring her own distress.

They gave her a sedative. Slowly the noise drifted away, and she felt herself sinking into warm sand. She recalled wanting to talk to the police, wanting to give them her side of the story, but that didn't matter any more. Nothing mattered any more.

Twenty-Three

On Friday there were several reporters camped outside the house. It wasn't the first time this week, but today Craig decided he couldn't face them. He ignored the doorbell and kept his phone off the hook all morning, which meant he didn't find out why they were there until Nina returned from shopping in Crawley.

He was in the kitchen, cradling a coffee and brooding on last night's meeting with DI Sullivan. When he'd first spotted the detective in a TV news bulletin, it had seemed like a good idea to try and call in a favour, but now he wasn't so sure. The revelation that his father had been shot twice was a terrible blow, and one that he wasn't yet ready to discuss with anyone.

Nina came in, holding a newspaper open to the middle pages. She let it slide on to the worktop in front of him. 'That's your friend, isn't it?'

He glanced at the byline, saw Abby's name. 'Yeah.'

'You might want to read it,' Nina said, then turned and left the room.

It had been like that all week: an uneasy truce. She'd returned late on Saturday night and found Craig dozing on the couch, the pizza box and empty bottle of Scotch lying on the floor. When she woke him, he groped his way upstairs and collapsed on the spare bed.

The next morning she brought him coffee and offered to talk. He gave her a brief account of what he knew, and he mentioned seeing

Abby, without divulging that she'd been here and shared the pizza with him. Didn't want to risk conceding some moral high ground, maybe.

Nina was keen to explain the affair, but he couldn't listen. He was afraid he wouldn't be able to hold his temper in check. Instead he went out and was gone all day, drifting from pub to pub, drinking alone. Dozing in a park in the January cold like a tramp. He thought seriously about never going back, and then saw what a remarkably easy process it was, how from a single tragic event you could fall through the cracks. He woke drunk and frozen on a bench and had a vision of himself in five years, wild-eyed and ranting in some shopping precinct, not even his own children able to recognise him.

So he went home, resolving to lay off the booze. At first the kids were delighted to see him, then quickly mystified by the peculiar atmosphere in the house. They'd never experienced this sort of tension before, and the false bonhomie which he and Nina displayed in their presence wouldn't have fooled anyone.

Now Maddie was throwing tantrums at every little disappointment and refusing to go to school. Tom was wetting the bed. And Craig's abstinence had lasted only until Monday afternoon, when he was driven to Brighton mortuary to identify his father's body. Since then he'd managed to sustain a permanent state of semi-intoxication. It made sharing the house with Nina slightly more bearable, while simultaneously adding to the strain on their relationship.

He sat and waited a moment, listening to Nina's footsteps on the stairs, and then read the article. It was a long, reflective piece, the kind of writing Abby excelled at. She had the tone exactly right, judging that by now the horror at what happened, while still fresh, wouldn't feel quite so raw. The first scabs were forming, and here she was to gently pick at them. She said some nice things about his father, but left the controversy until last:

    At the moment the consensus is that the
    massacre has finished off George Matheson's

plans for a large housing development in
Chilton. But others aren't so sure. 'Maybe
it'll clear the way,' says Craig Walker,
son of murdered campaigner Philip. 'After
all, who's left to fight him now?'

'Oh, Abby,' he said. He tried to think himself back to Saturday night. He thought she had quoted him pretty accurately, maybe even word for word.

Perhaps, he thought bitterly, she had recorded the whole thing.

It was Friday afternoon before Kendrick deigned to see George Matheson. For some reason he suggested they meet in Brighton, on the roof of the multi-storey car park in the Marina. George understood the other man's desire for anonymity, but surely there were better venues he could have chosen.

Kendrick's Jeep Grand Cherokee was parked at the far end of the roof, well away from the exit ramps. There were only a handful of other cars up here, and no one else in sight. George parked his Jaguar and got out, buttoned up his overcoat and shivered.

It was a dismal day, low cloud clinging to the hills above the city, reducing the horizon to no more than a mile or two. Seagulls hung and drifted in a blustery wind, and the grey-green water seethed like something alive.

As George walked towards the Jeep, the front passenger door opened and Kendrick got out. There were two other men in the car, but they stayed in place.

George offered his hand. Kendrick held it a few seconds longer than necessary, staring deep into George's eyes. It was all he could do not to step back and wrench his hand free. This was only the third time he'd met Kendrick in person, and he knew that he hadn't yet got the measure of the man.

'I had some business down this way. Hope you don't mind.'

'I'm honoured,' said George drily. 'I did wonder if I'd be seeing Vilner instead.'

Kendrick grinned as if he appreciated the joke, but his eyes said he didn't. 'We're busy men. Sometimes we have to delegate.'

'It's to whom we delegate that concerns me.'

'Vilner's a bit rough and ready, but you wouldn't deny he's useful.'

George grunted. 'I don't appreciate the way he's become your emissary. It certainly wasn't my idea to have him involved in my organisation.'

'No. Another of Toby's messes?'

George wasn't going to answer that. He turned away, stared at Brighton Pier, ghosting from the gloom, its multicoloured lights smeared on the water. Kendrick stood alongside him, hands thrust in his pockets. A picture of relaxation.

'I came to England once before, when I was ten years old. I couldn't believe how people could live somewhere so cold and grey.'

'Hard to believe this is a top tourist destination, isn't it?'

'Oh, it's got a certain charm. As it happens, Trinidad is mainly geared around industry. Much better beaches on some of the other islands.'

George nodded. 'I have a villa in Antigua. Don't get so much time to spend out there these days.'

'Maybe you will soon, eh?'

'You tell me.'

'What happened Saturday makes a big difference. From now on there's going to be a lot more scrutiny.'

George said nothing. He'd heard enough opening gambits in his time to know what was coming.

'That has to affect the value of the business, wouldn't you say?'

'Not necessarily,' George said. 'I agree it's very sensitive at the moment, but things change. People have short memories.'

'So you will be looking to make another application?'

'It depends on the timescale. But if you acquire the land along with the business, I don't see why it couldn't be pursued.'

Kendrick chuckled. 'You mean I take on the headache of getting planning approval?'

'It might not be a headache. As I say, attitudes change.'

'Philip Walker's son made just the same point in *The Times* this morning. You've seen that?'

'Yes. A vindictive little piece.'

'But maybe he's right. Not a lot of opposition left.'

'An ironic charge, given that he seems intent on taking up the baton.'

'Still,' said Kendrick. 'Quite a few empty properties in Chilton at the moment. And maybe some survivors who decide they can't face living there any more.'

'I'm aware of the potential. It's in hand.' George turned, wandered towards the northern perimeter wall. 'The last few months you've given some very conflicting signals. I'd like to know if you're in or out.'

'Do you have other buyers beating down your door?'

'You don't expect me to answer that question?'

'George, you don't need to.' Kendrick clapped him on the back as if they were friends. 'I think we can work something out. Let's watch how the dust settles, then discuss what adjustments are needed.'

George gave him a sidelong glance. 'Adjustments?'

'To the deal, as a whole. To the price.'

George snorted. He stared at the cliffs that ran behind the marina. Brilliant white from a distance, at closer range he could see the chalk was studded with flint, as well as clumps of mud and weeds. A catch fence had been bolted in place to prevent rockfalls.

Kendrick leaned his hands on the wall and looked over at the drop. He spotted a pebble at his feet, picked it up and placed it on the wall. He toyed with it for a moment, then flicked it over the edge.

'I threw someone off a roof once,' he said in a matter-of-fact tone. 'Only four floors up. Or maybe five.' He shrugged. 'It's not a pretty sight.'

Twenty-Four

Craig tried to phone Abby, but got her voicemail. He thought about emailing her, and while he considered what to say he scanned the rest of the paper.

There were more stories about the gunman, Carl Forester, whose upbringing had been mercilessly scrutinised. The usual debate had taken place: at what point does personal responsibility overcome the effects of an abusive childhood? His widowed mother, Peggy, had been arrested late on Saturday, after attacking one of the officers sent to take her into protective custody. Now, at her own insistence, she was being released. A tabloid had captured a shot of her being escorted from the station, thrashing beneath the blanket that was supposed to safeguard her privacy. THE MOST HATED WOMAN IN BRITAIN, the headline raged.

Another article confirmed what Sullivan had said, that the police were still waiting to interview Julia Trent. Under the title DOUBLE TRAGEDY OF CHILTON VICTIM, it disclosed that Julia's parents had died shortly before Christmas, as a result of carbon monoxide poisoning, and quoted an unnamed 'friend' who raised fears about her mental stability. An invented quote to give the story a little more punch, Craig guessed.

He heard movement in the hall and the door opened. Nina.

'They're still out there,' she said. 'What am I going to do about collecting Tom and Maddie from school?'

Craig sighed. 'Do you want me to go?'

'No. I don't want the children getting dragged into this.'

She was right, but the vehemence of her tone stung him. 'When it's time, I'll go out and keep them busy,' he said. 'You can slip past while I'm talking to them.'

Nina nodded, but remained in the doorway. 'Did Abby make it up? Or did you really say that?'

'I wasn't thinking clearly. I was angry, upset.'

'Drunk?'

'It was stupid. I know that.'

She didn't contradict him. 'It's awful having people try to photograph you every time you step out the door.'

'We're not exactly Brad and Angelina, for Christ's sake.'

She folded her arms, resolute. 'Maybe not, but I think . . . well, perhaps one of us should move out.'

Craig took a moment to reply. He could see Nina was having the same fight to keep her emotions in check. This wasn't just about Abby's story.

'Yeah, I've been thinking the same thing. Maybe I'll go and stay at Dad's for a while.'

Nina looked surprised. 'You don't want to live there, do you?'

'I can't avoid the place for ever. And at least it draws the media attention away from here.' He was going to add that it would only be a temporary move, but decided to wait and see if Nina said it.

Instead there was an awkward silence. Then she nodded. 'Well, it's probably for the best.'

Returning to their cars, Kendrick said, 'How are you going to respond to Craig Walker's comment?'

'I won't, publicly. That's not how I conduct my affairs.'

'Glad to hear it.' They were nearly at the Jeep. The man behind the wheel snapped to attention as his boss came into view.

'And Toby?' Kendrick said. 'He still doesn't know about the deal?'

'No.'

'Good. I want it kept secret until it's signed and sealed. He doesn't strike me as reliable.' He added, 'How do you think Toby will react when he finds out?'

'I don't particularly care. It's time he made his own way in the world.'

'So why let him work for you?'

'He's Vanessa's nephew. She argued that he should have a role, and at the time I couldn't see a reason to object.'

'Blood is thicker than water.'

'Exactly.' George felt uncomfortable. Something about the way Kendrick's lilting tone played with the word *blood*. 'Anyway, he won't be destitute.'

'He will if he goes on throwing his money away in casinos. And borrowing from men like Vilner.'

George gave him a sharp look. 'I don't see that this needs to concern you.'

'What about your wife?' Kendrick went on, as if George hadn't spoken. 'How will she take it?'

'Vanessa won't—' He stopped, registering Kendrick's expression. 'You know, don't you?'

'I do my homework, George. It's how I guarantee my good fortune.' A malicious light danced in his eyes. 'I know all about you.'

His hand shot out as if to punch George, slowed at the last moment and clasped his shoulder instead. He got into the Jeep. The engine fired up and it reversed sharply, pulling away with a squeal of tyres. George watched it descend the exit ramp and disappear.

He stood in the car park, Kendrick's parting shot still ringing in his ears.

I know all about you.

Twenty-Five

Craig moved out on Sunday afternoon, after a long and heated discussion. Nina had assured him the affair with Bruce was over, but she wouldn't countenance changing her job. That meant she would still be working with him, sometimes closely, sometimes going away together to visit clients or attend conferences.

'So it's over till the next time you're in a hotel, and you've had a few drinks, and you're lonely?'

She shrugged. 'If you can't trust me, say so. We'll make this separation permanent.'

They were alone in the kitchen, while Tom and Maddie played upstairs. The children had been told that Craig had to go and live in Granddad's house for a while, and would keep coming back to see them. Tom seemed happy with that explanation, but when it was time to leave Maddie clung to him and howled.

'I don't want you to go. Please, Daddy.'

His voice choking, Craig said, 'It won't be long. Just until I've sorted everything out.' He glanced at Nina, who looked away.

'But Granddad died there,' Maddie said. She clung to him, pressing so tightly against his chest that her next words were too muffled to hear.

Craig lifted her, bringing her face up to his. 'What is it, darling?'

'I'm scared, Daddy,' she said. 'What if you die there, too?'

* * *

Her question played on his mind as he drove to Chilton. He already had misgivings about taking up residence, but he was facing an uncertain future, and with his freelance career on hold he couldn't justify booking into a hotel when the house was standing empty.

His foreboding intensified as he turned off the B2112. There was a single police van parked on the corner of Chilton Way, the grass around it trampled into wet mud. There were cars parked all along the approach road, and at the foot of the High Street he was forced to stop for a coach as it laboriously negotiated the corner. It was packed with people, and the driver looked disgruntled. What the hell was going on?

The answer was clear as he drew alongside the shop. The village was swarming with tourists, staring and pointing at the cottages, the church, the pub. A large cluster stood around the tree, peering at something on the ground. For a terrible second Craig wondered if something had been overlooked during the police investigation: a splash of blood, a fragment of bone. Then he realised they were looking at bouquets of flowers, left there by well wishers.

He drove on, forced down to walking pace by people who strolled across his path as if he wasn't there. Everyone had cameras, and many had video cameras as well. He saw a couple struggling to flatten out the pages of a newspaper, trying to compare a photograph of the village with the real thing.

Incredibly, there was another coach parked outside the church, and more visitors wandering along Hurst Lane, as dumb and unresponsive as cattle. His father's house was on the corner, with a garage at the back, accessible from the lane. Before he could put the car on the drive, he glimpsed movement behind the hedge to his left.

There was someone in the front garden.

He jammed on the brakes and jumped out of the car, attracting some mild curiosity from people nearby. His father's garden gate was open. There was a man on the path, short and thickset, taking photographs of the front door with a neat little digital camera.

'What are you doing?' Craig said, with a calmness that surprised him.

The man ignored him until he'd taken his photo, then he turned. He was perhaps sixty, with lank grey hair and bad teeth. He didn't look fazed by Craig's challenge.

'One of 'em died right there, in the doorway,' he confided.

'Is that right?'

'Shame there's no blood, but I can soon fix that.' The man winked. 'Photoshop. They fetch more that way.'

'You'll sell the pictures?'

'Limited-edition prints, in sets of ten,' he said proudly. 'Great market for this stuff on the net.'

Craig nodded as if impressed. 'I'll bear that in mind. Maybe I'll cut up the hall carpet and sell it in chunks.'

The man's eager expression was quickly overtaken by a frown. 'Was this . . . ?'

'My father lived here,' Craig said. 'Now get the fuck off my property.'

The man flinched. 'All right, chum. No need to be like that.'

'No?' As the man edged past, Craig grabbed the camera and wrenched it from his grasp. He strode across the road and hurled the camera into the air. It sailed over the heads of the tourists by the tree and landed in the pond.

'Hey, now that's not on—' the man began. Craig whirled round and glared at him. The man took one look at his face and stomped away, grumbling to himself.

Craig realised that most of the tourists on the green were now staring at him, and his fury redoubled.

'What are you looking at?' he shouted. 'Is this not enough for you? You want a floorshow as well, do you?'

There were a few tuts, a few shrugs. Most just stood and gaped, blinking impassively. They reminded him of Nick Park's plasticine animals in *Creature Comforts*.

'People died here,' he said, lowering his tone a little. 'This isn't a fucking theme park. We're not selling tea towels and commemorative plates. People *died*. And they deserve respect.'

More mumbling. A few people shifted their weight from foot to foot, signalling their discomfort.

'You should be ashamed of yourselves,' Craig said. 'Get back on your bus and leave us alone.'

There were a few muttered comments. Some of the tourists had the good grace to turn and amble in the direction of the coach, but even as they went they continued snapping away at the cottages, the church, the green, the flowers.

And if they could, Craig had no doubt, they would photograph the bodies, the blood, the pain, the loss.

Twenty-Six

The killer felt he'd justified what had happened at the hospital, but Decipio clearly didn't agree.

```
Don't dress this is up as anything other
than failure. She's still alive, and there-
fore still a threat. You'd better pray she
doesn't wake up.
```

His email had also made oblique reference to the campaigner's son, Craig Walker. He'd warned that if something wasn't done, people might start to make a connection between the massacre and the planning application. Despite raising a valid concern, his instructions were merely to keep an eye on Walker: nothing more. The message had ended with:

```
Remember: this is your neck on the line.
Not mine.
```

He stared at the screen until every word was burned into his memory. *No loose ends*, the previous message had said. Well, there *were* loose ends. There was the girl. There was the woman in the tree. And then it struck him: from Decipio's point of view, of course, there was potentially one other loose end.

Him.

He saw how easily he could be offered up, like a sacrificial lamb. He was in a very precarious position. While he had his suspicions, he still didn't know for certain who Decipio was. The name sounded like something out of Shakespeare. When he'd looked it up, he discovered it was Latin. It meant *ensnare, deceive, trap*.

Very appropriate. And perhaps another hint at the fate that awaited him.

But not if he fought back. Got in a pre-emptive strike.

Certainly it was time he stopped taking instructions. From now on he would act as he saw best. Protect his own interests, and no one else's. If that meant eliminating anyone who posed a threat, so be it.

PART TWO

Twenty-Seven

February brought a spell of clear days with light winds and enough warmth to tease the early spring flowers into bloom. Perfect walking conditions, and the vast empty beach at Camber Sands was ideal terrain on which Julia could exercise, gradually building her strength.

Most of the time she felt surprisingly optimistic. She had been incredibly lucky. That was how she had to view it. And not just in the past tense: she *was* incredibly lucky. With each day she grew a little stronger, a little more confident; another step closer to resuming her life.

Until the day she saw him.

The old town of Rye is a charming warren of ancient buildings and narrow lanes, perched on a hill overlooking the river Rother and the Romney Marshes. The most picturesque area, known as the Citadel, is at the top of the hill, where apart from the ever-present cars and road signs, the streets around the twelfth-century church have barely changed since the days when the likes of Henry James resided here.

After finding Lamb House, once home not just to James but to E F Benson and Rumer Godden, and now owned by the National Trust, she was disappointed to learn it was only open to the public from March to October. After resting for a few minutes, she decided to return to the High Street and find a café. It had been a slow, punishing climb from the bus stop, and the descent, on wet cobblestones, would be almost as taxing.

Thankfully she was past the stage where every movement had to be carefully planned in advance, but still her limitations came as a fresh shock every time her brain sent a signal that her limbs couldn't instantly obey. Despite this, she refused to be defined by her physical condition.

She moved at the pace of a much older woman, in short, shuffling steps, grateful for the walking stick she'd been bullied into taking with her. She wore a long coat and a fabric baker's cap that offered both warmth and protection. Although she still attracted plenty of glances, because of her obvious frailty, she hadn't been recognised.

Yet.

It was as she walked along the High Street that she became aware of a man on the opposite pavement keeping track with her, pausing each time she stopped to examine a window display. She turned and stared at a collection of watercolours in a gallery window, and in the reflection she saw him hesitate, then dart inside a newsagent's.

For a moment she felt nothing but an all-consuming panic. Not only were the events of 19 January flooding back, but the thought of being stalked evoked memories of a much older scare. Every instinct told her to run, to get away quickly, but that was the one thing she couldn't do.

She thought about stopping a passerby. Grab someone who looked trustworthy and plead for their help. Then the sense of panic abated. The quickest route back to the bus stop was down another steep hill, but it wasn't far to go. The man hadn't yet emerged from the newsagent's. She still had a chance.

She crossed the road, gesturing with her stick to acknowledge a motorist who'd braked to avoid her. Focusing on the path ahead, she started her descent, her feet and stick clacking on the pavement in a little three-note rhythm. She wasn't going fast by any means, but a cold sweat broke out on her skin. Her ankle throbbed and in her abdomen she felt an unnatural tightness. In her head she could hear the smooth professional tones of her consultant, setting out the many potential risks and complications of an inadequate recuperation. Two words in particular had summoned a ghastly vision of a sudden, unforeseen collapse: internal bleeding.

Several times she glanced back, and once thought she saw the man duck out of sight. At the bottom she rested for a few seconds, panting like a dog. An elderly woman touched her arm and asked if she was all right.

'Fine,' Julia gasped. She managed a smile, but the woman looked horrified.

'Oh, my dear,' she said. 'I thought you were—'

Julia didn't wait to hear what the woman thought. She rammed the stick down and used it to propel herself forward, once again crossing the road with little thought for the traffic. She suspected part of her didn't care much if she was knocked down and killed.

A bus pulled in as she reached the stop. She was relieved to see plenty of passengers, offering safety in numbers. She got on and settled on a seat halfway back. Conscious of a few curious gazes, she turned towards the window, resting her cheek against the cool glass. The gruff diesel engine seemed to vibrate at the same frequency as her nerves. At last the doors closed with a whoosh and the bus pulled out. She turned and saw no sign of her pursuer.

She let out a breath. Shut her eyes and she was back in Chilton, watching the gun swing round in her direction. She captured an image of the man in black, picturing his height, his build, and compared it to the man she had just seen. She asked herself: could he fit?

In her nightmares, she never saw his face. Even when he stood over her, pumping bullets into her body, his face was always covered by the visor.

He didn't exist. He was a figment of her imagination, a manifestation of her psychosis, brought on by extreme trauma. That's what the police had told her, and during the day she could almost believe it.

But at night, awake or asleep, he was always there, a menacing shadow in the background. She would picture him lying awake somewhere, thinking about her just as she was thinking about him. A little bit of unfinished business.

You're stalling, she told herself. Answer the question.

But she already knew the answer.

The answer was *yes*. He could fit.

It was just over a week since she'd left hospital, and more than two weeks since the police had first tried to speak to her. That disastrous attempt had provoked a furious altercation between her consultant and the detective. It was also the last Julia saw of the Irish nurse.

Negotiations between the police and her doctors had taken several days. The police were under intense pressure to complete their investigation, while the medical team had a responsibility to protect their patient, whose mental state was judged to be extremely precarious. Eventually it was Julia who insisted on consenting to an interview, against her consultant's advice. Afterwards she wished she'd listened to him.

Perhaps she was too tearful and inarticulate to be taken seriously. Perhaps the detectives – a woman chief inspector and a young male sergeant – had arrived with too many preconceptions. Or perhaps they were exhausted and simply wanted to put a gruelling investigation to bed. Whatever the reason, it was no less of a disaster than the first attempt.

Almost from the start, her memory refused to co-operate. Had she seen the postman's body before she went into the shop, or afterwards? Had she tried to get help from the cottage or did she run straight to the church? Had Carl really invited her to run before giving chase? Every attempt to describe her ordeal gave her the shakes. Her throat constricted and made it physically impossible to speak.

She would never forget the reaction when she first mentioned the second killer. They might as well have terminated the interview there and then. She read it in the glance they exchanged. She heard it in the scrape of chair legs on the vinyl floor: an unconscious attempt to distance themselves from her.

After that, the questions took on a weary, half-hearted tone. On the surface they remained polite but sceptical, creating a vicious circle that she recognised but couldn't break. Their refusal to listen made her increasingly upset, and the more distressed she became, the more it reinforced their opinion that she was unstable. A basket case, raving about a man in black leathers who killed Carl Forester and then turned his gun on her.

At the end, the sergeant left the room first. The DCI was a kind, matronly woman, but with a certain severe intelligence that warned against taking her lightly. She reminded Julia of a head teacher she had once worked with: steel wrapped in cotton wool.

'I know this has been dreadful for you,' she said. 'You're obviously still very confused and upset. In time I think you'll realise your memory is playing tricks, and hopefully then you can put this behind you and move on with your life.'

Julia nodded, as though these platitudes meant something. By now all she wanted was to be left alone.

'I must offer you one bit of advice,' the DCI went on. 'However much you're tempted, don't breathe a word of this to the newspapers. Whether they believed you or not, they'd eat you alive.'

Afterwards Julia spent a lot of time reflecting on that advice. She didn't doubt its wisdom, but saw that it had one very serious consequence. If she kept her mouth shut, it meant she was completely on her own, with the killer still out there. Still a threat. And perhaps one day he would decide to conclude his unfinished business.

Perhaps today.

Twenty-Eight

The land east of Rye is unlike anywhere else in Sussex. The bus trundled over marshland and fields of winter crops where an occasional tractor went about its solitary work. Electricity pylons marched across the landscape in mighty columns, like a robot army hatched from the great brooding power station at Dungeness. In winter it was a bleak, cold, unforgiving place. Until today, she had thought it was perfect.

She was staying at a private hotel called Bayside; the result of another compromise with her consultant. He had strongly recommended a nursing home that specialised in convalescent care. Appalled by the thought of what she saw as confinement in an establishment better suited to geriatrics, she had gratefully leapt at an alternative suggestion from the DCI. Bayside had just a dozen rooms, and it specialised in a women-only clientele. The proprietor, Kate, was a former police officer, and the hotel was sometimes used to accommodate vulnerable prosecution witnesses.

Now, as she grew calmer, Julia began to consider the other possibilities. Maybe the man she'd seen hadn't been following her at all. At worst, maybe he was a journalist. To avoid media attention, she had left the Royal Sussex County late at night, via a back entrance, and her brother had driven her to Camber Sands. Very few people knew she was here – her only visitors so far had been a couple of old friends and the head teacher at her school – but there was always a chance someone had talked. She felt sickened to think someone she knew and trusted might have leaked her whereabouts in return for money.

The hotel occupied a substantial plot of land right on the coast, with a golf course on one side and a scattering of large private homes on the other. The upper floor offered spectacular views of the bay and the wide expanse of sand that gave the area its name.

As a precaution she stayed on the bus until it had gone past the hotel, then got off at the next stop. None of the passing traffic aroused any suspicion. She walked along to the hotel and checked the car park for unfamiliar vehicles. There was a laundry van backed up to the entrance. The driver slammed the rear doors and nodded at her as she passed.

Kate was behind the reception counter, talking on the phone. She was a tall, striking woman in her early fifties, with long white hair pulled back in a ponytail. Seeing Julia, she quickly finished the call and gave her a stern look.

'I told you it was too soon to be venturing out.'

'What?'

'You look shattered. If you're not careful, you'll end up back in hospital.'

'I'm okay. Just need a lie-down.'

'You need to start listening to good advice, that's what you need.' Kate tutted, then looked regretful. 'There was someone here this morning, asking for you.'

Julia clasped a hand to her chest. 'When?'

'About half ten. Not long after you left. I said I'd never heard of you.'

'What did he look like?'

Kate thought about it. 'I'd say mid-thirties. Slim, dark hair. Wearing black jeans and a blue tailored jacket.'

Julia nodded, struggling to keep her panic in check. 'Journalist?'

'I think so. I acted dumb, so hopefully he's long gone.'

'No. He was following me in Rye.'

'Oh, bugger.' Kate turned towards the door as if expecting him to burst inside. 'What do you want to do?'

'Nothing. Just let me know if he comes back.'

The stairs seemed twice as steep as usual, and each one brought another twinge of pain. Hauling herself up, Julia felt drained of hope as well as energy. If one journalist had found her, soon there would be more. Either she would have to give them what they wanted, or else move on to the next hideaway, the next sanctuary. And what kind of life was that?

Her room was at the end of the corridor on the first floor. It was a good size, clean and nicely decorated in neutral tones, but it wasn't home. She'd brought a single suitcase, packed by her brother on her instructions, but after a week she'd hardly unpacked, almost as though unconsciously she'd been preparing for sudden flight.

She propped the walking stick by the door and shrugged off her coat. The room felt a little stuffy, but as she went to open the window she stopped in her tracks.

The tide was a long way out. The distant sea looked glassy and unreal. A thin haze of cloud diffused the sunlight, giving the air a strange vanilla glow. Fishing boats bobbed in the distance, and sea-gulls dipped and swooped over the beach. The sand lay flat and damp and brown beneath her, and there wasn't a soul in sight except for one man.

He was about a hundred yards away, standing perfectly still, feet set apart, arms crossed. Patient and resolute. He was staring in her direction, but with the light reflecting off the glass she had no idea if he could see her.

He must have come straight here, she realised. He knew her destination, and if he had a car he would have beaten her by ten minutes or more. All that effort to evade him, the risks she'd taken with her health, all for nothing.

There was a stick lying at his feet, probably driftwood. From this distance it looked like a small dark snake. She understood what it was only a second before she registered what it had been used for.

Just behind him, in letters six feet high, he had etched a single word. SORRY.

There was a knock on the door. She jumped, aware that she had been caught in a daze. She couldn't even recall what she'd been thinking. The man on the beach was still there, still staring at the hotel.

Kate had brought her a tuna sandwich and a glass of cranberry juice. When Julia protested, she said, 'You're meant to eat regularly, and you'll forget otherwise.'

Julia nodded. Thanked her, and then said, 'Come and see this.'

Kate stepped past her and stood at the window, her head slightly tilted and her arms crossed in a pose that exactly mirrored the man she was looking at.

'That's the guy from this morning,' she said. 'What's he sorry for? Hassling you?'

'I suppose so,' Julia said, keeping her voice neutral.

'Very polite, for a hack.' Kate studied him for a long moment. 'Still, I wouldn't kick him out of bed.'

Julia snorted. 'Perhaps I should find out what he wants?'

'Don't do anything hasty. Have your lunch first, at least.'

She left the room, shutting the door gently behind her. Julia took a bite of her sandwich and sat down on the bed. The angle was tight, but she could still just about see him. After a minute or two he stretched and turned round, examining the message he'd written. She caught a definite air of despondency in his posture.

He turned back, lifting one hand to shield his eyes. Without quite knowing why, Julia stood up and stepped to the window, moving her face to the glass. Seeing her, he gave a small, hesitant wave. He picked up the stick, moved to a clean spot of sand and began inscribing a new message.

Julia tutted, not sure whether to be amused or alarmed. She waited for the words to form and tried not to second-guess, but found herself doing so anyway.

I'M

I'm sorry? she wondered.

I'M NOT

I'm not a journalist? Not a sleaze ball? Not here to cause more pain?

But the message, when he stood clear to reveal it, was something far more shocking. She nearly choked on her sandwich.

I'M NOT HIM.

Twenty-Nine

He knows, she thought. He knows there was a second killer. He's trying to reassure me.

Then she thought: *How can he know?* She hadn't told anyone, other than the police. And they hadn't believed a word of it.

She went on staring. The man dropped the stick and approached the hotel, coming right up to the back fence. He bent over and retrieved a black laptop bag. Delved inside it and produced a thick brown envelope, which he raised for her to see. He inclined his head, as if to say, *May I?*

Be careful, a voice in her head warned. It could be some type of trap.

But she didn't think so. Her instinct was telling her he had something important to say, and while she might not be ready to trust him, she knew there was no way she could ignore him.

The lobby was empty when she got downstairs. Kate was probably in the kitchen, or maybe her private quarters. Julia walked gingerly over to the main door and waited, leaning against the wall. The pose gave a sense of exaggerated nonchalance, but it was actually because she'd succumbed to vanity and left the walking stick in her room.

A minute later the man jogged into view. He was taller than Julia expected, around six feet, with the sort of lean, triangular frame that suggested a swimmer's physique beneath the jacket. His thick brown hair was in need of a trim, and as he reached the steps she could see a torment in his face as acute as anything she'd suffered in the past few weeks.

She opened the door but blocked the entrance, making it clear he wasn't welcome to come any further. He stopped and gave her an uncertain smile. His eyes were a rich dark brown, deep and liquid and full of hurt.

Before he had a chance to speak, Julia said, 'If you're a journalist, you're wasting your time.'

The smile turned ironic. 'I am, actually. Freelance sports and features, but that's not why I'm here.' He stuck out his hand. 'Craig Walker.'

'Craig . . . ?'

'Philip Walker's son.'

Julia clutched the door for support. It took her a moment to regain her composure. She shook his hand and said, 'He saved my life.'

'I know,' he said, and she wasn't sure if there was a slight coldness in his voice. There was no trace of it when he added, 'Sorry about earlier, in Rye. I wasn't sure how best to approach you.'

'How did you find me? No one's meant to know I'm here.'

'I have a contact in the police.'

'And he leaked the information?'

'He didn't have much choice.' Seeing her frown, he said, 'It's a long story, and now's probably not the right time.' He offered her the envelope. 'He also gave me this. The preliminary report into the massacre. I'd like you to read it and then discuss it with me.'

She hesitated, a little riled by his tone: it was more of a demand than a request. But she took the envelope, unaware that she was trembling until it rattled in her hands. She clutched it tight to her chest.

'What did you mean, *I'm not him?*'

Craig looked taken aback. 'You know, don't you?'

'Do I?'

'Carl Forester didn't dream up that massacre on his own. Someone put the idea into his head, and that person is just as guilty.'

Julia said nothing for a moment. She tapped the envelope. 'Is that what it says in here?'

'No. But I don't believe that,' he said simply. 'I believe you.'

He told her he was going for a walk on the beach. Said he would wait as long as it took. He shook her hand again and thanked her for listening to him. Again she caught a brusque note in his voice.

She returned to her room and sat down on the bed. As she peeled the envelope open she was conscious of her thudding heart, and told herself not to be so ridiculous. It was an official document, and nothing more. Just words on paper.

After everything she'd been through, what harm could it do her?

Thirty

SHOOTING INCIDENT AT CHILTON, EAST SUSSEX
ON 19 JANUARY 2008
PRELIMINARY REPORT PREPARED BY CHIEF SUPT
MALCOLM ELLIS
FOR THE CHIEF CONSTABLE
8 FEBRUARY 2008

INTRODUCTION

On Saturday, 19 January 2008 a series of shootings occurred in and around the village of Chilton, resulting in the deaths of fourteen people and injuries to a further four. This report has been prepared with the agreement of the Chief Constable of Sussex to cover all the events of 19 January. Certain inquiries are ongoing and will be covered in more detail in the final report, due for completion on 1 May 2008.

CHILTON

The hamlet of Chilton is situated ten miles
north-west of Lewes. It lies approximately
one mile along Chilton Way, a no-through-
road which provides the only vehicular access.
An unadopted access road, Hurst Lane, runs
north from the village to Chilton Manor and
the neighbouring farm.

Prior to January 2008, the population of
Chilton was sixty-three people, including
fifteen children, resident in twenty-eight
properties. Most of the buildings are Georgian
or Victorian, with a handful of Tudor cottages
and a twelfth-century Norman church.

Chilton's residents work hard to maintain
the village's unspoilt appearance, and to
this end they have fought many campaigns
against local development, recently defeating
a proposal to build several hundred homes on
adjacent farmland. They also successfully
opposed plans to site a mobile-phone mast on
the tower of St Mary's church, a move which
had significant implications on 19 January.

There are few local services other than
the church, the Green Man public house and
one shop. Responsibility for policing lies
with Burgess Hill police station, approximately four miles away, but historically
crime in Chilton has been practically non-
existent.

CARL FORESTER

Carl Brian Forester, aged twenty-five, had lived all his life in the neighbouring village of Falcombe. An only child, Carl lived with his mother, Peggy, aged fifty-three. His father, Albert, walked out on the family when Carl was five and had no further contact with his son. Inquiries revealed that he died of a heart attack in 2001.

Forester's mother is a chronic alcoholic with a long record of public-order offences. She served several prison sentences, during which time her son was placed in care. The family was well known to social services, and Forester was a persistent truant from the age of seven.

Leaving school with no qualifications, Forester's most stable period of employment began at the age of nineteen, working as a groundsman for George Matheson at Chilton Manor. His duties included assisting with pheasant shoots, and it is thought his fascination with firearms stems from this period. He also helped out on a seasonal basis at Hurst Farm, owned by Matheson but managed by Mr Keith Caplan.

His employment was terminated two years ago, following an alleged assault on Mrs Laura Caplan. According to George Matheson, Forester had been spying on Mrs Caplan, as well as stealing her underwear and other personal items. Forester entered the house by stealth and exposed himself to Mrs Caplan in the presence of her daughter, Megan, then aged seven. After that, Forester did no further work for Matheson, although the incident was not reported to the police.

It is believed Forester subsequently nursed a grudge against both the Mathesons and the Caplans. Whilst it cannot be stated with certainty that this led directly to the events of 19 January, it must be considered an important factor.

Inquiries have revealed no close friends, but there were a number of individuals with whom Forester drank on a regular basis, usually in the King's Head public house in Falcombe. Most have alcohol and/or drug dependency issues. They all describe Forester as a loner, incapable of forming proper relationships. His drunken approaches to women frequently saw him ejected from the King's Head, and as a result he was regarded as a rather pathetic figure

During our inquiries, however, two of the females from this group made allegations against Forester, ranging from indecent exposure to attempted rape. Once again, these offences were never reported at the time, possibly because of the aforementioned drug use.

There was unanimous agreement that Forester was terrified of his mother, and frequently beaten during his childhood, an allegation that met with frankly unconvincing denials from Peggy Forester. During the police investigation, Mrs Forester was often violent towards the officers interviewing her, and on one occasion stabbed a female officer with a kitchen knife.

Even allowing for her heightened emotional state following her son's death, it suggests Forester grew up in a volatile environment. He had a number of criminal convictions, mostly relating to minor acts of vandalism and theft, as well as a range of vehicle offences, but prior to 19 January Forester's potential for violent or sexual assault was unknown to the authorities.

FIREARMS

The principal firearm was a Walther P22 semi-automatic pistol, fitted with a suppressor and firing .22 subsonic ammunition. Indications are that it was part of a small consignment of arms smuggled into the UK in 2003 by individuals with links to Russian organised crime. Despite extensive inquiries, it has not yet been established how or where Forester made the sort of connections necessary to source such a weapon.

The other firearm was a Purdey double-barrel twelve-bore shotgun, used for two killings. This was a legally held weapon, purchased by George Matheson from a registered firearms dealer. Matheson holds a valid shotgun licence, and the weapon was stored in an approved gun safe.

The following section covers the events
of 19 January in more detail.

Julia threw the report aside and got to her feet. She felt dizzy and
nauseous. She opened the window and took a huge gulp of air. On the
beach a woman in a green puffy anorak was walking her Labrador.
There was no sign of Craig.

However much she dreaded it, she knew she had to read on. But
first she opened her suitcase and rooted around in it. When he'd
dropped her off at the hotel, her brother had presented her with a
couple of small gifts: a CD and a half-bottle of brandy.

She poured a small measure and took a sip. It was her first taste of
alcohol since before the massacre, and its burning warmth felt comforting
in her stomach. A little rush of courage.

She would need it.

Thirty-One

EVENTS OF 19 JANUARY
It must be stated that there is a considerable degree of conjecture in the sequence of events stated here. Immediately after the incident, a team of twenty-four detectives and almost fifty other officers was employed to conduct the most thorough possible investigation. However, the lack of eyewitness evidence means that in some cases it was necessary to make educated guesses about Forester's movements.

We know Forester rose early, at around 0530, in the house in Falcombe where he lived with his mother. She estimates he left the house at approximately 0600. He was dressed in camouflage trousers and a blue denim jacket, and armed with a crowbar purchased from a builder's merchants in Burgess Hill on 15 January. It is believed he also had the Walther P22 in his possession at this time.

From Falcombe he made his way on foot to Chilton Manor, approximately two miles away, gaining access to the house by breaking a ground-floor window. The owners, George and Vanessa Matheson, were at their London home, and appear not to have set the alarm the day before. There is no evidence that Forester had any knowledge of the security codes or could have disabled the alarm.

Forester used the crowbar to break into Matheson's gun cabinet and removed the Purdey shotgun. He also ransacked the house and defecated on a dining table, before moving on to Hurst Farm. Keith and Laura Caplan were eating breakfast in the kitchen, but it appears their nine-year-old daughter, Megan, was still in bed.

It is thought Mrs Caplan answered the door and was led back to the kitchen at gunpoint. Mr Caplan rose from his chair and was shot in the stomach with the shotgun. It is likely he was forced to watch as his wife was stripped and subjected to a savage sexual assault, and at some point he died from his injuries. Mrs Caplan was also shot and killed with the shotgun. Forester then went upstairs and attempted to smother Megan with a pillow. She suffered serious oxygen deprivation, and as of the date of this report remains in a coma.

Forester left the farmhouse at approximately 0720, heading along Hurst Lane towards Chilton. As he passed the Green

Man public house he saw the publican, Mr Barry Johnson, attending to his pet rabbits in the garden. Mr Johnson appears to have been running for shelter when he was shot three times and killed.

Telecommunications in Chilton are routed via a BT cabinet 'green box' situated on the corner of Hurst Lane. Forester forced entry to the box and severed the wires at 0733, rendering the village without landline communication. As previously mentioned, Chilton does not have mobile-phone coverage.

Forester then approached the Old Schoolhouse, the residence of seventy-two-year-old widower Philip Walker. Mr Walker was shot in the chest and left for dead in the hallway of his home.

It appears Forester crossed Hurst Lane again and made for St Mary's church. Here he found the vicar, the Reverend Mark Armitage, and a Mrs Dorothy Poplett, aged sixty-three, who was employed as a cleaner. Both were shot several times. Mrs Poplett died immediately, but Rev. Armitage appears to have lived for another twenty-five minutes, and was possibly still alive when one of the few surviving witnesses, Ms Julia Trent, sought help in the church at approximately 0800.

Forester moved on to the terraced cottages south of St Mary's. At No. 18 High Street he killed Ms Samantha Todd, aged thirty-four, and her six-year-old son, Frankie.

The occupants of number 16 were away, so Forester went to number 14, where he killed the only resident, eighty-one-year-old Audrey Wheeler.

At number 12 he killed Mr Geoffrey McBride, fifty, and then stopped to reload. His wife, Rose McBride, fifty-two, managed to warn her two children, who were able to hide. Forester shot and wounded Mrs McBride as she fled upstairs, then moved on to number 10, where he shot and injured Mrs Doreen Collins in the hallway of her home. Mrs Collins, seventy-seven, survived the incident but was left paralysed from the waist down.

Forester then retraced his steps, possibly in response to the appearance of a Royal Mail van driven by Mr Trevor Fox, aged thirty-seven. Mr Fox had opened the rear doors of the van when Forester appeared from his left and shot him twice in the face.

The murder was witnessed by Mr Ian Sorrill, at number 5 Arundel Crescent. Mr Sorrill shouted to his wife and children to get up and called 999. Finding the landline dead, he attempted to call on his mobile phone but without success. He then led his family through their back garden and across farmland for approximately one mile, until they reached the main road. Eventually Mr Sorrill got a signal and made an emergency call at 0809.

Gaining entry to number 1 Arundel Crescent, Forester killed fifty-nine-year-old Tom Bradbury and his wife Mavis, fifty-eight, who had just sat down to breakfast. He also killed their dogs, two red setters, then remained in the home for some ten or fifteen minutes, eating their breakfast.

At this point, around 0800, Julia Trent discovered the body of Trevor Fox and went into St Mary's church to raise the alarm, only to find the Reverend Armitage and Mrs Poplett. She made her way to the footpath that runs parallel to the High Street and entered number 18, where she discovered the bodies of Ms Todd and her son.

Meanwhile, at 2 Arundel Crescent, Mrs Alice Jones had also witnessed the murder of Trevor Fox. She bolted her front door and went upstairs with her three young children, where they barricaded themselves in the master bedroom. Mrs Jones focused on keeping the children calm and quiet, but occasionally looked out. At approximately 0813 she glimpsed Julia Trent running on to the green with Forester in pursuit.

From the living room of number 18 High Street, Ms Trent saw Forester emerge from number 1 Arundel Crescent and walk towards number 2. Receiving no answer there, he moved on to number 3, whose occupants, Mr and Mrs Granger, had been to a party until the early hours. Mr Granger believes he was vaguely aware of the doorbell, but decided to ignore it. He and his wife continued to sleep through the incident, and did not stir until wakened by the noise of the police helicopter at 0840.

It is thought Forester may have grown frustrated by the lack of response, for he ignored the remaining houses and instead made for the village store. Unfortunately, Forester entered the shop and killed the proprietor, fifty-seven-year-old Mrs Moira Beaumont, before Ms Trent could alert her to the danger. Forester then pursued Ms Trent back along the path to the church. Her recollection is somewhat unreliable, as will be noted later, but she alleges Forester engaged in this chase for his own amusement.

Trent fled through the churchyard and on to the green, as confirmed by Alice Jones, and was brought down by a long-range shot which grazed her leg. At this point, Ms Trent's life was saved by the intervention of Philip Walker. Despite being severely wounded, Mr Walker distracted Forester, who returned to the Old Schoolhouse and shot him dead. Ms Trent used this diversion to reach the yew tree on the green, which she managed to climb to a height of approximately ten or eleven feet.

It is thought Forester returned to the green and discovered the trail of blood leading to Ms Trent's hiding place. Possibly by now he could hear the first police siren. In any event, he raked the tree with fire from the pistol, hitting Trent in the side and causing her unconscious body to fall from the tree.

Finally, Carl Forester took his own life, with a shot to the temple. It is thought he died just a minute or two before the first police officers arrived on the scene, at 0822.

Thirty-Two

The report became progressively harder to read. Without knowing it, she began muttering, 'No . . . No . . .' A cry to ward off the horrors of that day, but also a protest at the report's conclusion.

Carl Forester took his own life. There was the confirmation, in stark black print, that she was on her own.

She quickly scanned the next section. Under the heading 'Police Response', it detailed the actions taken by the emergency services to secure the scene and provide aid to the victims, including Julia. It went on to give a summary of the huge investigation launched on that morning, and then touched on the country's reaction to the tragedy, including a visit by the Home Secretary on the Monday.

Julia went on reading, but at some point stopped taking it in. All she could see was that one dreadful sentence. The official verdict.

Carl Forester took his own life.

Carl Forester killed himself.

End of story.

She hadn't realised she was crying, or that it was loud enough to be heard in the corridor. Gradually she became aware of a tapping on the door, Kate asking if she was all right.

Wiping her cheeks, Julia got up and opened the door.

'I'm okay,' she said. 'Really.'

'You don't look it.' Kate hesitated, then said, 'I don't know if I should tell you this . . .'

'It's all right. I've already spoken to him.'

Kate's gaze shifted from Julia to the bed, where the report still lay open, then back to Julia. She was bursting with questions, but to her credit all she said was: 'He's in the car park.'

He was waiting in a black VW Golf. Julia felt slightly irritated to see him sitting there, as if he had known she would have to seek him out, but there seemed little point in snubbing him. He might just come back tomorrow or, worse still, leak her whereabouts to the media.

This time she'd brought the walking stick with her. She was reluctant because she didn't like the assumptions people made when they saw it. But he'd already seen her using it in Rye, and more importantly a voice of caution warned against getting into his car.

He opened his window, his smile fading as he registered her sombre expression.

'There's a café just down the road,' she said. 'Shall we go there?'

'Fine.' He went to put his seatbelt on.

'I'd prefer to walk.'

'Sure?' He glanced at the walking stick. 'Wouldn't it be easier by car?'

'Maybe. But I'd like to walk.'

He gave her a look, as though he might object, then thought better of it. 'Sure.'

Bringing the laptop bag with him, he followed Julia out of the car park. It was a short journey on level ground, and with the aid of the stick she was able to keep up a fairly brisk pace. She didn't want him feeling he had to dawdle for her sake.

The pavement was narrow, with a covering of sand deposited by winter storms, and once or twice his arm brushed against hers as they walked. Remembering her earlier panic in Rye, she was impressed that it didn't make her flinch.

The café was a grim single-storey building on the edge of a large car park serving the beach. Next to it were a couple of shops selling beachware and tourist tat, but they were locked up and shuttered for the winter. Inside the café there was only one table occupied, an elderly couple quietly bickering in the corner. Julia and Craig sat down in the opposite corner and ordered coffees from a surly teenage girl.

Julia had brought the report with her, and the envelope now lay on the table between them.

'It must have been painful to read,' Craig said.

She was tempted to answer glibly: *Not as painful as living it.* But she wasn't entirely sure that was true. She tore open a sachet of sugar, poured it into her coffee and stirred for longer than was necessary.

'That last section must have really pissed you off.'

She frowned. 'Actually, I didn't . . . By then I was just skimming it.'

He upended the envelope and the report slid on to the table. Julia had to struggle not to recoil from it. She watched him flick through the pages. His hands were large but smooth, the nails neatly trimmed except for those on his thumbs, which were bitten ragged.

'Here it is,' he said, tapping the relevant paragraphs.

```
It was nearly two weeks before detectives
were permitted to question the last of
Forester's victims, Julia Trent. During
interviews she was highly emotional and
her recollection was often flawed and in-
consistent. Fortunately her description of
Forester's pursuit on to the village green
can be partially corroborated by Alice Jones,
who was the last witness to see Forester
alive.
```

However, Trent also made a number of allegations about the involvement of another
person in the shootings. No evidence could
be found to support these allegations, either
in terms of forensic evidence at the scene
or from witnesses such as Alice Jones or
the other surviving residents of the village.
In addition to her ordeal on 19 January,
it must be remembered that Ms Trent suffered
the loss of her parents in a domestic accident in December 2007, and this no doubt
contributed to her fragile mental state.

It is therefore the conclusion of the senior
investigating officer that Carl Forester,
acting alone and for reasons known only to
him, attacked a total of eighteen people,
killing fourteen and injuring four, before
taking his own life.

'There you go, then,' Julia said. 'It's a wonder they didn't just cart
me off to the nuthouse.'

Craig looked away, developing a tactful fascination with his own
drink. 'Maybe this is too soon,' he said.

Julia put her coffee down and dug in her bag for a tissue. She blew
her nose loudly, then let out a long sigh.

'I don't know what to think any more. By the time the interview
finished, they almost had me believing I was a madwoman.'

'What did you tell them, exactly?'

Julia looked at him. He was leaning forward, close enough for her
to catch the smell of mints on his breath. It made her conscious that
she'd eaten a tuna sandwich. She leaned back in her seat, giving the
impression she was much more relaxed than she felt.

'Do you really want to know?'

SKIN AND BONES

He nodded. Quite vehement. She thought again of the detective's warning: *Don't breathe a word of this.*

She glanced at the report. *During interviews she was highly emotional and her recollection was often flawed and inconsistent.*

Fuck you, she thought.

So she told him.

Thirty-Three

Toby Harman owned a BMW M6, courtesy of his uncle. The journey to Sussex was a perfect opportunity to open it up, but today he just couldn't summon the kind of carefree attitude the drive required. George had sounded troubled on the phone. He wouldn't say why he wanted to see Toby, but it was unlikely to be good news.

After education at a minor public school in West Sussex, Toby had gone to Durham University and scraped a 2:2 in Ancient History. Almost immediately he'd been set to work in his uncle's organisation, embarking on an individually tailored training scheme that would see him move between different companies and departments over a period of years, in order to fully understand and gain experience of working at every level, before taking his place amongst the senior management team.

In practice, it hadn't quite worked out like that. For one thing, Toby was easily bored or distracted, and the training role wasn't sufficiently challenging to hold his interest. There were other problems as well, often involving female colleagues. Getting caught having sex in the boardroom didn't go down terribly well with his uncle.

Then there were the issues with timekeeping. He saw no good reason to adhere to the nine-to-five rigidity imposed on the rest of the workforce. Everyone knew he was different, and there was no point pretending otherwise. If he wanted to come in at eleven after a particularly late night at a casino, why shouldn't he?

His finances were another constant source of tension. On one occasion, after he'd persistently siphoned the petty cash at a manufacturing firm, George had threatened not just to sack him, but to prosecute him for theft.

From that point, Toby agreed to mend his ways, in return for a higher degree of involvement. He was given a couple of directorships, and allowed to concentrate his energies on the one area that truly interested him: property development. So far it had been a mixed success, complicated by the fact that he'd been unable to kick the gambling habit. He fully expected today's meeting to involve yet another reading of the riot act.

He left the A23 at Hickstead, skirted around Burgess Hill and headed into the countryside of East Sussex. The Downs loomed over him, and the shadows of trees scurried across the windscreen. He always found the lush greenery faintly unsettling. He preferred a world of tarmac and concrete and steel.

As he drove through Chilton he caught a flash of light. For a moment it looked like the yew tree was on fire. With a start he realised it was sunlight reflecting on cellophane, wrapped around the dozens of bouquets and wreaths that had been left at the site. He kept his gaze on the road ahead, ignoring the sightseers who roamed the green. Worthless scum, the lot of them.

He turned into Hurst Lane, reaching for the remote-control key fob that opened the gates. He mistimed it slightly, and had to wait a few seconds, the car pulsing forward on the accelerator until the gap was wide enough. Then he gunned the engine and roared up the drive, spraying gravel in his wake.

George was waiting for him in front of the double doors. He was dressed in grey slacks and a blue jacket, his hand delving into one pocket in a faux-regal pose. He frowned as the BMW slewed to a halt, and when Toby got out of the car the first thing he said was: 'Show a little respect, would you?'

*   *   *

Despite protestations from Craig, Julia insisted on getting up to order more coffee. She wanted to prove she wasn't useless, that she could walk without the stick.

When she came back to the table Craig still looked stunned. She had watched his jaw drop with each new revelation. He hadn't interrupted or bombarded her with questions. Better still, he hadn't looked even slightly sceptical.

'I thought there was probably a conspiracy,' he said at last. 'But I hadn't dreamed it would be something like this. I can see why the police dismissed it.'

'Because it's so far-fetched?'

'No. Because it's untidy. According to my source, the only thing they can't figure out is where Carl got the pistol. Pretty soon they're just going to forget it. They want this wrapped up.'

'To be fair, I wasn't the most convincing of witnesses. And the way it happened, the second killer probably didn't leave any evidence.'

'Which means he's got away with it,' Craig said. 'He's out there somewhere now, walking around scot-free.'

Julia shivered. 'Don't remind me.'

'I couldn't understand why Carl stole the shotgun from Chilton Manor,' he said. 'If there were two men, that explains it.'

'But if he'd got one gun from the Russian mafia, or whoever it was, couldn't he have got two?'

Craig paused, then nodded reluctantly. 'True. There's still a lot that doesn't make sense.'

'Perhaps it's unrealistic to try. The actions of a man like Forester can't be analysed rationally.'

'If he'd acted alone, I'd agree with you. But he didn't, did he?' There was a challenge in his voice that she found disturbing.

'We don't know.'

'Well, it looks like—' He stopped abruptly. 'Tell me you're not doubting it?'

Julia felt herself blush. 'No. I just . . . I'm not sure what to make of your reaction.'

'What do you mean?'

'You've accepted it so readily.' She gestured at the report. 'I don't want to find you're one of those conspiracy theorists, obsessed with hidden meanings that aren't there. Someone who can't accept that, sometimes, bad things just happen for no reason.'

Unbidden, an image of her parents' bodies flashed through her mind.

'So because I believe you, that makes me a nut?' He laughed, but there was a bitter edge to it.

'Seeing it there in black and white, who's to say my memory is any more reliable than the official version?'

'Okay. Carl Forester killed himself. Simple as that.' He pulled the report away from her and picked it up. He looked as though he was going to storm out of the café, and Julia felt a surge of disappointment. She'd just alienated the only person who believed in her.

'But if that's the case,' he went on, 'why did you panic when you saw me in Rye?'

'You might have been a reporter.'

'Crap. You thought I was the other killer. That's why I wrote the message in the sand, and that's what persuaded you to talk to me.'

She cleared her throat. 'It wasn't just that. There was another reason why I reacted the way I did.' She hesitated again, aware that she didn't owe him an explanation. At the same time, she was reluctant to let him make a false assumption. 'I was attacked in the street when I was nineteen. Someone tried to rape me.'

Craig sat up with a jolt. 'Oh Christ. I'm sorry.'

'You weren't to know.'

'What happened?'

'I was out with friends in Brighton on New Year's Eve. I'd had quite a lot to drink, but it was one of those nights when the alcohol and the partying just weren't having an effect. You know how sometimes you just can't get into the mood?'

Craig smiled. 'Only too well.'

'This guy had hit on me at the bar. Rubbed himself against me and made a few obscene suggestions. I told him to get lost. A bit later I had a silly argument with one of my friends over something really trivial, so I decided to leave early and walk home. In those days my parents lived in Hove, less than a mile from the pub. It was about ten to midnight, and of course the streets were almost deserted. I didn't realise I was being followed until I heard footsteps. Someone grabbed me round the neck and pulled me into the gardens near Palmeira Square.'

'The man from the pub?'

'I think so. He wrestled me to the ground and started pulling at my clothes. He said he had a knife, and he'd kill me if I didn't lie still.'

Craig said nothing. Julia cleared her throat again.

'At first I froze. I was so terrified, I was all set to obey him, let him rape me. And then I heard a woman laughing, very close by, and I thought: This is crazy. How can he do this to me when there are people walking past, just a few feet away? So I screamed and kicked and fought him off.' She snorted. 'I think I caught him in the groin. He ran away and the people I'd heard found me and called the police.'

'Was he caught?'

She shook her head. 'I couldn't give a very detailed description. Even in the pub I hadn't really seen him properly. You know what it's like when you're all crushed together at the bar. And in those days there weren't CCTV cameras everywhere like there are now. But a year or two later I read about a man who'd been convicted of murdering his girlfriend, and when I saw his picture I was fairly sure it was him.'

'It's terrible that he wasn't brought to justice for your attack.'

'Me and God knows how many others.' She shrugged. 'Actually, at the time I was almost relieved. The idea of having to relive the experience under cross-examination seemed even worse than the original attack. But the key moment was when I went back to university. For a week or two I hardly left my room. I was a bundle of nerves, jumping out of my skin at every noise, every shadow.

'And then one day I came to my senses. I knew I had a simple choice. Either I was going to let this incident define me and destroy my life, or I was going to put it behind me and move on.'

Craig nodded. 'What doesn't kill you makes you stronger.'

'Exactly. So I started pushing myself to do things I wouldn't have done before the attack. I exercised a lot more, got in really good shape. Took a self-defence class. I went out on my own, even late at night, almost daring something to happen because this time I was going to prove I could handle it. I chose to be a survivor, and I'm convinced that's what helped me get through on 19 January.'

Craig chose his response carefully. 'I'm sure it did. But isn't that even more reason not to give up now?'

'I haven't given up. I was just pointing out that we're in a pretty hopeless position. We can't prove the police are wrong. We can't prove the second killer exists.'

Craig appeared to listen sympathetically, but there was a sly look on his face.

'Maybe we can.'

Thirty-Four

The two men climbed the stairs and entered George's office. Their footsteps echoed on the polished oak floorboards, emphasising the lack of life and spirit in the cavernous old house. As they reached the door, Toby thought he could make out the faintest strains of classical music from the far end of the hall.

'Is Vanessa here?'

'London,' said George.

Toby made no comment. He couldn't remember the last time he had seen his aunt, and he wasn't particularly sorry. He was the bastard son of Vanessa's younger sister, a drug-addled dropout who had died when Toby was seventeen, and as such he'd always carried with him the taint of failure and disgrace. Except on one notable occasion, Vanessa had always been careful to keep him at a distance.

The office was a large room with windows on two sides and floor-to-ceiling shelves on the other two. One end was dominated by George's desk and chair, both crafted to order from reclaimed timbers salvaged from a folly that had once stood in the manor grounds. George took his seat with all the satisfaction of a monarch settling on his throne.

Toby went straight for the Jura coffee machine and made himself an espresso with three sugars. Deciding that he didn't want to sit opposite George like some hapless candidate at a job interview, he sank on to one of the leather sofas at the other end of the room. He was surprised to see George had a glass of sherry on the go. The old man didn't usually drink during the day.

'Heard anything from your friend Vilner?' George began, speaking as if shouldering a heavy burden.

'Not lately. Why?'

'No reason. What about settling your debts? Any progress?'

'Look, I have every intention of getting my finances straight.' Toby gestured unhappily towards the tall sash windows and the land beyond. 'If this was cleared, it would all be resolved overnight.'

'What do you mean?'

'The plans for the village. We agreed I'd come in as an equity partner.'

George looked bemused. 'Funded by . . . ?'

'Well, it would have been funded by last year's loan.'

'Which you frittered away on God knows what.'

'That's because the project was shelved. I have to live, you know.'

'You get eighty grand a year from the directorships,' George reminded him. 'For which you do, let's face it, sod all.'

'That's not true. Give me a serious stake this time and I'll work my balls off.'

'I've heard that before. In any case, it could be years away, if it happens at all.'

Toby frowned. It wasn't like George to be so negative. 'You're still buying up the empty homes?'

'I've made offers to the executors,' George corrected him. 'Some of the survivors are undecided whether to stay or sell, but I've made it clear I'll arrange a quick cash purchase, if that's what they want.' He saw Toby's expression and looked aggrieved. 'It's the least I can do to help. Otherwise those properties might be virtually impossible to sell.'

'Exactly. No one will want to live in Chilton now. So why not go one better? Buy up the village and then demolish the place. Stick up a nice memorial and build a completely new town next door.'

He sat back, satisfied that he'd proved George wrong about not earning his directorships. This idea alone was worth a few million. But George seemed to think differently. He stared at Toby as if he'd just proposed moving the village to Neptune.

'Well, why not?' Toby tried to press home his point. 'You've said yourself, the place is full of ghosts. We just need the right PR to get the message across.'

'And what about the listed buildings? What about the twelfth-century church?'

Toby flapped his hands. 'You've ignored restrictions like that in the past. The point we have to make is that a new development would be in everyone's best interests.'

'You don't think the thirty-five-million-pound profit might strike anyone as offensive? The fact that our best interests happen to be rather more rewarding than anyone else's?'

Toby shrugged. 'If you're worried about public opinion, why are you trying to buy up the village?'

'To help the victims. I know it'll be misinterpreted, but that's a risk I'm willing to take. We just need to be patient, otherwise it will look as though Carl Forester did us a huge favour.'

Mentioning Forester seemed to suck some of the light from the room. Already the name had come to represent more than just the man himself. It was the byword for a tragedy. A media event.

'Well, maybe he did,' said Toby carefully. 'Is that so terrible to admit?'

George said nothing. He opened a drawer in his desk and took out a cardboard folder. He tossed it across the desk and glared at Toby.

'You'd better read this,' he said.

Julia said, 'What do you mean?'

'Maybe there's some way we can flush him out.' Rather than elaborating, Craig asked a question of his own. 'You know about Matheson's planning application?'

'You could hardly miss it, thanks to your father. It seemed like there was a story in the *Argus* every week.'

'Mmm. Dad could be an objectionable old sod, especially when he got the bit between his teeth.'

'You didn't agree with him, then?'

'I had mixed feelings. I doubt if he or the others would have cared if it had been happening in someone else's back yard. But for all their selfishness, it doesn't invalidate their argument. It's a beautiful place. Matheson shouldn't be allowed to dump housing estates all round it and walk away with twenty or thirty million quid.'

Julia gasped. 'You're kidding?'

'At least that much. He owns hundreds of acres around the village, so even if only a fraction gets developed he'll make a fortune. And if he uses his own construction company to build the homes he'll profit twice over.'

'That's shocking. I didn't realise there was so much money involved.'

'That's a conservative estimate, allowing for the downturn in the economy. The fact is, for years we've had a severe shortage of housing in the most affluent part of the country. For landowners and developers, the stakes have been raised to the point where all kinds of corruption become tempting. So you start off, perhaps falsifying a report here and there. You put pressure on councillors, planning officers, you offer bribes and inducements. But if the bribes don't work, maybe you have to use threats?' He paused, stared at his coffee, seeming to make a conscious effort to calm down.

Then he looked up at Julia. 'Once you get started down that road, where do you stop? We're living in a world where people will kill for the loose change in your pocket. What do you think someone would do for twenty million?'

It was a peculiar experience to read about such devastating violence, described so dispassionately. Toby would much rather have studied the report alone, away from his uncle's brooding presence. Glancing up, he saw George pouring himself another sherry.

'What's the latest on the Caplans' daughter?'

'No change.' George cleared his throat. 'I visited her earlier this week. Keith's sister is there every day. I've offered to cover the cost of a private clinic, but really they're doing all they can for her.'

'Getting very generous in your old age,' Toby muttered.

George grunted and waited for him to finish reading. Then he said, 'It's this Julia Trent that worries me.'

'I don't see why. The police clearly think she's delusional.'

'It could still attract some unwelcome attention, especially after that quote from Craig Walker.'

'I saw that. Are you going to sue him?'

'Don't be ridiculous. Philip Walker died a hero. The last thing I can afford is a slanging match with his son.' He picked up his sherry, swilled it round and looked at it with sudden distaste. 'He's asked to see me.'

'Craig?'

George nodded. 'Hopefully I can forestall any more bad publicity.'

'Do you want me to come along?'

A look of amusement warmed his uncle's face. 'I'm perfectly capable of dealing with him.'

Toby shrugged, biting back an urge to respond. George quickly grew morose again. 'Do you really see Carl Forester dreaming up something like this?'

'Who knows what his state of mind was like?' Toby waited a beat, then added quietly: 'The police obviously think losing his job was a factor.'

'I had no choice, after that business with Laura. And it was two years ago. Surely that wasn't sufficient provocation for . . . what he did?'

'We'll never know, will we?' Toby lifted the report. 'I haven't read this properly. Can I take a copy?'

George considered for a moment. 'Make sure you keep it safe. And don't show it to anyone.'

Toby nodded and switched on the photocopier. While it warmed up he poured himself another coffee.

'I know this has been very stressful,' he said. 'Why not take some time off? A couple of months in the Caribbean would do you the world of good. Leave things to me for a while.'

'I'll take a holiday when I'm good and ready,' George snapped. 'When I know the business is in safe hands.'

Toby felt his face heating up. 'If you'd let me liquidate my assets, I would never have had to borrow from someone like Vilner.'

'Rubbish,' George barked. 'You'd have squandered that money as well. Anyway, you can't unload shares when a business is struggling. It sends all the wrong signals.'

Toby said nothing. When his uncle was in one of these moods there was no sense arguing with him. He fed the report into the photocopier, a flash of light as each page gave birth to another. He allowed a reasonable interval to pass before he made another appeal.

'At least let me start on the paperwork. I could get the plans for the access road amended.'

George let out a sigh. 'You're prepared to knuckle down, are you?' he said. 'No return to the old habits?'

'I promise.'

There was still doubt on George's face, but at last he nodded. Toby suspected it was more to get rid of him than anything else: a tactic Toby had exploited successfully in the past.

'All right. But don't do anything that could jump up and bite us. We're not filing anything till we've got public opinion firmly on side.'

They shook hands on it, more like business acquaintances than family. George followed him downstairs and through the wide entrance hall. At the door Toby said, 'Give my regards to Vanessa,' with his customary lack of sincerity.

'I will,' said George in a matching tone.

Toby jogged to his car without looking back. He had a lot to consider, not least of which was his uncle's behaviour. He'd never seen the old man like this. Definitely losing the plot.

Thirty-Five

Julia absorbed what he'd said, then shook her head. 'That's quite a leap to make,' she said. 'You can't go accusing someone like George Matheson of mass murder.'

Craig shrugged. 'Actually, I already have.'

'What?'

'Someone asked me if I thought the application could ever be revived. I pointed out that George might be in a better position because of the massacre.'

'Someone?'

'A person I trusted,' he said. 'But she's also a journalist.'

'Oh.' Julia grimaced. 'What was Matheson's reaction?'

'Not a lot in public. But I received a nicely crafted letter from his solicitors, drawing my attention to the laws of libel and defamation.'

'I don't suppose you can blame him.' In the same conciliatory tone, she said, 'Just because he stands to benefit, it doesn't mean Matheson had anything to do with what happened. It could just be a dreadful coincidence.'

'And if I choose to disagree, I'm . . . what? A nutty conspiracy theorist?'

Julia grinned. 'I can't rule it out.'

'Okay.' Now he was grinning too. 'In that case, maybe we should find out one way or the other.'

'What?'

'George Matheson. I've arranged a meeting with him tomorrow.'

Julia felt her heart speed up. 'Tomorrow? And you want me to come?'

He held up his hands to placate her. 'Hey, I shouldn't have sprung it on you like that. Forget I mentioned it.'

Julia frowned. She lifted her coffee cup but it had gone cold. There was a film of grey scum on the surface.

'Time I was getting back,' she said.

He nodded. She stood up and put on her coat. He went to help, but she turned and shrugged it on herself. She picked up the walking stick and propped it under her arm like a baton. She wanted to make the return journey without using it.

A cold blast of air assaulted them as they stepped outside. The wind had strengthened, picking up grains of sand as it whipped over the beach. Julia shielded her face with her hand, and Craig muttered, 'Should have brought the car.'

'Sorry.'

'It's okay. I understand now why you were so wary of me.'

They set off in silence, then Julia said, 'What exactly did you mean about "flushing out" the second killer? You want to investigate what happened in Chilton?'

'Yes.'

'But how? We're not detectives.'

Her use of the plural wasn't lost on him. She cursed herself for the slip of the tongue.

'To start with, we talk to Matheson. And we find out more about Carl Forester.'

'And supposing we uncover evidence that someone else was involved? What then?'

'Turn it over to the police, of course. I'm not some kind of vigilante.'

'That isn't what I mean. We're looking for a man who took part in a killing spree, then calmly murdered his partner and made it look like suicide.' She looked him in the eye. 'So what will he do when he realises we're on his trail?'

Vanessa waited until she was sure Toby had gone. Then she waited a little longer, to see if George would come to her. He didn't.

It took whole minutes to get up from her chair and walk along the hall to his study. In the weeks since the last diagnosis – the *terminal* diagnosis – a strange separation had occurred. There was Vanessa; and there was Vanessa's body. Vanessa's body was an appalling creature, weak and pain-wracked and crumbling from within like a gutted building. It transformed the simplest of tasks into an extraordinary effort of will. It had nothing to do with *Vanessa*: the person, the lifeforce.

And yet, when the body finally expired, Vanessa the person would go with it. That didn't seem fair. Sometimes, at night, she screamed out her fury at the unfairness of it. She screamed until her eyes poured with tears and her throat burned and her chest throbbed.

But she never made a sound. Because George mustn't know how she felt.

Outwardly she remained stoic, composed, even brave. 'You're so *brave*,' her friends had said, right up until the last few months. Until she stopped seeing them.

George didn't dare use the B word. But then he hardly spoke to her at all.

The door to his study was heavy, with an antique porcelain door-knob. She needed both hands to twist it.

He looked up, genuine surprise on his face. He was at his desk, the report open in front of him. Something else as well, which he'd just slipped between the pages. A furtive glance to make sure it was hidden.

'Sorry,' he said. 'I meant to come and see you.'

'I'm not a cripple.' To prove it, she remained standing. She walked over to the photocopier and rested both hands on the lid. It was warm. She turned to George and he blanched, as if she could see inside him.

'I let him take a copy of the report.'

'Was that wise?'

'I told him to be discreet.'

Vanessa chuckled at the thought. 'And what did he make of it?'

'Dismissive. He's all gung-ho to prepare another application.'

'I take it you've not yet told him about Kendrick?'

'No.' His eyes narrowed. 'Do you think I should?'

'It's your business. You're entitled to do with it as you wish.'

George nodded slowly. 'But?'

'I mean it. Toby's as much a disappointment to me as he is to you. He ought to be fending for himself.'

George went on studying her. Still anticipating a barbed comment, an incisive criticism. It was one of the most enduring features of their long marriage, and she knew he had developed an almost masochistic attachment to them.

He closed the report and patted it reassuringly, along with whatever treasured document was concealed within it.

'I told him about Craig Walker. He asked if I wanted him to be there.'

Vanessa dipped her head to acknowledge the humour. 'You might consider having someone present. James Vilner, perhaps.'

George frowned. 'Why?'

'Walker's father was brutally murdered, and from what he said to the press it seems he blames you. His judgement is blunted by grief and anger. He'll need to vent that anger somehow.'

George looked dismissive. 'I doubt he's coming here to attack me.'

'Perhaps not. But Vilner's presence could achieve much more than any solicitor's letter. At a fraction of the cost.'

She had been ready for George to scoff, but instead he pursed his lips, which was his habitual and quite unconscious signal that he intended to appropriate someone else's idea.

'I'll give it some thought,' he said.

Which meant *yes*.

Thirty-Six

Just before they reached the hotel there was a gap in the dunes, allowing a glimpse of the sea. The tide was coming in, filling the deeper channels and racing across the sand from several directions at once. Julia thought of Craig's message, wiped smooth and gone for ever.

'You know, I think it's partly because he's still at large that I came here,' she said as they entered the car park. 'I'm hiding from him.'

'That's understandable,' said Craig. 'But remember how you felt when you locked yourself away at university. It doesn't work for ever.'

'No. I know. I'm just not sure if I'm ready right now.'

Craig unlocked the Golf and put his bag on the back seat. Julia glanced at the hotel. Against the winter sky, its lights blazed warm and enticing.

'The trouble is,' he said, 'we don't have a lot of time. That report's supposed to be confidential, but I reckon we've got a week at most before the media get their hands on it. Everything leaks eventually.'

Julia's face fell.

'Of course, there's a chance they'll overlook what you said,' Craig went on. 'But if they don't . . .'

'They'll eat me alive. That's what the police told me.'

Craig nodded. 'And once your allegations are made public, the danger you're talking about will exist regardless of what you do.' He waited a second. When she didn't speak he smiled and patted her arm. 'Anyway, you need to get inside. It's cold out here.'

He opened the driver's door and climbed in. Julia watched him reverse from the space and thought about the report, almost wishing it hadn't made any reference to her allegations. Then Craig wouldn't be here, and she wouldn't be facing this dilemma.

There was a flash of brake lights as he reached the pavement. She felt an odd gnawing in her stomach. Not fear, exactly. Indecision. Regret. Shame.

During interviews she was highly emotional.

'Wait!' she shouted. She took a couple of wobbly steps forward, fumbling with the stick and waving her hand until he spotted the movement in his wing mirror. He backed up alongside her and opened his window. She clutched the door handle and knelt down.

'All right. I'll come with you.'

The doubts began to appear almost the second she said goodbye. She still wasn't sure what to make of Craig. On one level he was perfectly friendly, but there had been moments when she had sensed a definite hostility in him.

She crept into the hotel like a teenager breaking her curfew, and saw with guilty relief that the lobby was deserted. She had barely reached the stairs when Kate burst into view and bore down on her with all the wounded ferocity of a hoodwinked parent.

'I thought you were popping outside to speak to him, not gallivanting off somewhere.'

Julia raised her hand in an appeal for mercy. 'It was hardly that. We went to the café. And I'm quite capable of looking after myself.'

'Really?' Kate glanced pointedly at the walking stick. 'So who is he? What does he want from you?'

'His name's Craig. He's the son of Philip Walker, one of the Chilton victims.'

At this, Kate's temper seemed to dissipate, but she continued to look troubled. 'And is he a journalist?'

'Yes, but nothing relevant to this.'

'I'm not so sure. That name sounds familiar.' She sighed, examining Julia's face as if for signs of wear and tear. 'I hope he's going to leave you alone now.'

Julia tried to look non-committal, but Kate saw through it immediately.

'You're supposed to be recuperating.'

'I've agreed to go somewhere tomorrow. Just for a few hours.'

Kate pursed her lips. In that moment, Julia was tempted to tell her all about the police report and the second killer. By now she knew Kate well enough to trust her, but then considered the reaction she was likely to get. It wasn't difficult to imagine Kate confining her to her room, or worse still, sending her back to hospital.

Having gambled on successfully persuading Julia to work with him, Craig had avoided a long return journey by booking a room at a B&B a couple of miles away on the Lydd road.

In contrast to the enticing photographs on its website, Seascape turned out to be a semi-detached house with a brown pebbledash exterior and moss on the roof. Inside, the decor was tired but clean. The owner was a woman of a certain age, widowed or divorced, with improbably big hair and make-up applied on an operatic scale. When he got to his room, the first thing Craig did was make sure the door locked from the inside.

The second thing he did was have a drink. He'd packed an overnight bag with just the essentials: a change of clothes, toiletries and a litre of Scotch. He had to use a plastic beaker from the bathroom, but that barely affected the flavour. He'd have swigged it from the bottle if need be.

It wasn't as full as he expected. Then he remembered having a few mouthfuls on the beach, while Julia was reading the report. At the time he'd been jittery about her decision. It had been a close call, but in the end he'd won her over. That was an achievement to celebrate.

While he drank, he allowed himself to feel a twinge of guilt, but no more than that. There was a lot at stake here, and it wasn't as though he'd lied to Julia. He just hadn't told her everything.

After a long, relaxing soak in the bath, Julia ate alone in the hotel dining room, reflecting on her encounter with Craig. Then she sat in the guests' lounge for a while, playing cards with a reticent young woman who was appearing as a witness at the Crown Court in Maidstone. In an hour they exchanged no more than a dozen words.

Kate pounced as she was about to call it a night. If anything, she looked even more worried than she had earlier.

'I've Googled him.'

'What?'

'Craig Walker. He might have been telling the truth about what he writes nowadays, but that's not what he used to do.'

'What do you mean?'

'He was an investigative reporter. A damn good one, by the look of it. Worked on quite a few cases involving organised crime.' Kate paused, and Julia couldn't understand why she looked quite so tense until she added: 'He had a bee in his bonnet about police corruption.'

'Ah.'

'I'm not criticising him for that,' Kate added quickly. 'I know full well that some police officers are corrupt. If someone brings that to light, all well and good. But it means you need to be careful. It's possible he has a completely different agenda to yours.'

It took several minutes of solemn assurances that her advice would be heeded, before Julia could finally extricate herself and return to her room. She now felt even more thankful that she hadn't mentioned the second killer, but also wondered if she ought to rethink her decision about tomorrow. The trouble was, she didn't have Craig's mobile number to call and cancel. There was no option but to wait and see how she felt in the morning.

It was ten o'clock when she got to bed. Sleep came easier than she expected, but it was fitful and troubled. Amid many disjointed dreams was one of startling clarity and impact, quite unlike any she'd had before.

It was a cold, clear night. She was on the beach at Camber Sands, the tide far out, foamy waves gleaming in the distance. In the centre of the beach the yew tree from Chilton's village green loomed over her. She approached it barefoot, feeling her toes sinking into the sand. The upper branches of the tree swayed gently. Maybe from a light breeze. Maybe not.

He was hiding. Waiting for her.

She carried a heavy iron bar. A poker, perhaps, or a crowbar. Its solidity lent her a courage she had no right to feel. Reaching the trunk of the tree, she paused a moment. She ran her hand over the smooth bark and the tree responded, its shiver of pleasure dislodging the intruder who had dared to conceal himself in its embrace.

The man in black dropped from the upper branches and landed on his back. He lay still, but she could see his chest rising and falling. His head was encased in the black helmet.

Then her perspective changed and she saw herself as if from a distance, slowly leaning over and lifting the visor. She gasped, stepped back, and she was inside herself again, reeling with a terrible knowledge.

She had seen his face. She knew who he was.

The first blow came almost as a surprise to her. It shattered his visor and sent shards of plastic flying across the beach. Fragments of bone, too, and a spray of blood that splattered her legs. The man let out a gurgling exclamation. Julia gripped the crowbar tighter, using both hands to bring it down with all her strength, again and again.

It went on until long after he was dead. She didn't cease until every bone was shattered, every organ pulped, every inch of him pummelled into dough, and blood and sand clung to her legs like treacle.

Then she stopped. Dropped the gore-slicked crowbar and stood, breathing hard, her muscles vibrating with energy. She heard the waves sucking on the sand, closer now. The tide would come in and cover this abomination, and when it retreated the world would be clean again. And safe.

She looked up and saw her parents, watching from an upper window of the hotel. The sad, solemn faces of ghosts. Seen through their eyes, she had resorted to a savagery that made her no better than the killer. It was clear from the tilt of her father's head that he was ashamed. *This isn't how we brought you up to behave.*

'No!' she screamed. She would rather die than suffer his disapproval.

Grabbing the crowbar, she took a few steps away from the body. A full moon lit up the sand as she carved out her message.

I'm not her, she wrote. Over and over, while the blood dried on her legs and sweat ran into her eyes and dripped from her nose on to the sand.

I'm not HER.

Telling herself she could make it true. She could turn back the past and become a different person.

She woke, drenched in sweat, and threw herself out of bed. Stood stock still in the middle of the room, the thudding of her heart eclipsing all the tiny noises of the hotel at night. The dream continued to parade in her head: eyes open or shut, it made no difference. All she could see was the body exploding under the barrage of blows. Her parents' terrible shame.

I'm not her.

Please, God.

I'm not her.

Thirty-Seven

Max Kendrick was always up early. Even after more than a decade of freedom he found prison hours the most natural routine. Illogical, perhaps, but if he lay in bed there was always a nagging sensation that he was missing out on something.

He was renting a large house in Berkshire, overlooking the Thames. Seven bedrooms and four bathrooms at twelve thousand pounds a month. Not cheap, but probably better than a hotel in the long term, given that he was housing half a dozen of his team.

It was an attractive, peaceful location. He liked having the river nearby, liked the plop and slosh of the water as pleasureboats drifted past. He liked the tall willow tree that hung out over the water as if straining for freedom. He imagined it would look spectacular in summer, dripping blossom like tears, but he had no idea if he'd be here to see it. He never stayed too long in the same place.

There was a small gym adjoining the master bedroom. He worked out on the machines for twenty minutes, then took a run, a mile or so each way along the exclusive private road. Two of the team accompanied him; at least one of them armed at all times. Probably not necessary, but another old habit he found hard to break.

On the way back, the place was coming to life. He nodded greetings to a professional golfer and the chairman of a FTSE100 company, while ignoring the platoon of ghostly Eastern Europeans who cooked and cleaned for them. It amused him to realise how seamlessly he'd made the transition to First World supremacy.

He found running useful. Something about the rhythm of pounding footsteps helped him to think. He had taken to business like a natural, but he was conscious that he lacked a proper education. To compensate he prided himself on thinking longer and harder than anyone else. Preparation was his watchword. Know everything: then you couldn't be outsmarted.

It was thorough research that had uncovered Toby Harman's gambling debts, and led him to James Vilner. He knew George Matheson had been furious when Vilner was appointed as Kendrick's go-between, but there was little George could do about it. Which made his request for Vilner's help today all the more intriguing. Matheson was meeting the dead campaigner's son, Craig Walker, and wanted Vilner present. No reason given.

When Kendrick got back to the house, Jacques was in the kitchen, nursing a tall mug of freshly brewed black coffee. Jacques hated running, or physical exertion of any kind. He stayed thin because he had no interest in food or alcohol. No vices at all, in fact, except killing.

They had met in August 1997, when Kendrick was one of ten high-risk prisoners transferred to Tortola in the British Virgin Islands to serve out the rest of a sentence for aggravated burglary. Volcanic eruptions had forced a closure of Montserrat's prison and destroyed its capital city, Plymouth.

By that time an even more momentous encounter had taken place; the one that was to transform Kendrick's life. It was Jacques who quickly recognised the potential of his plan, and suggested he set his sights much higher. From then on he had served as a faithful lieutenant. It was Jacques who'd willingly helped remove any of the obstacles in his path. And it was Jacques alone who knew his real identity.

'Refreshed by your run?' the little man scoffed.

'Will be when I've had a shower.'

185

'Shari was down here looking for you.'

Kendrick scowled. 'Why?'

Jacques assumed a hideous falsetto: 'Why does he bring me all the way to England if he don't wanna see me or be with me?'

'That's what she said?'

'That's what I made sense of. She was weepy and whispering.' Jacques smiled. 'She's scared of me.'

'She's right to be,' Kendrick muttered. He pondered for a minute. Got himself some grapefruit juice from the large American-style refrigerator. Jacques waited, puppy-like. Not exactly panting, but not far off it.

'It's time she went,' Kendrick said at last. 'I don't need the distraction.'

'Plenty of women over here if you want one.' Jacques sounded vaguely contemptuous of the idea.

'That's your repressed homosexuality talking,' Kendrick said, and Jacques laughed mirthlessly.

'I'll give her the news, then?'

'Nothing to tell. Just get someone to pack her bag, put her in a car and send her back.'

'Alive?'

Too late, Kendrick had tipped the carton to his lips. He spluttered juice from his nostrils and laughed.

'Yes. Alive.' He pinched his nose, then sniffed. 'If I wanted her dead, I'd have said so. Wouldn't I?'

Jacques looked slightly crestfallen. 'Always pays to ask.'

When Julia woke on Wednesday, she immediately thought about the nightmare. It was the first one where she had been the attacker, rather than the victim, although that gave her precious little comfort.

It was also the first dream where she had lifted his visor. She could clearly recall the powerful sensation that accompanied the sight of the killer's face, but no matter how hard she tried, she couldn't recreate that image in her mind. It was maddening and frightening, and it led her directly to her next thought.

She was about to spend the day with a man she hardly knew, and they were intending to pay a visit to George Matheson. And that, she realised with a start, almost certainly meant going back to Chilton. Just the thought of driving through the village made her fluttery with panic.

You've got to face it sometime, she told herself. And you've got to start trusting people again.

But not today, a skittish voice spoke up. Kate's right. You don't know anything about his motives. You could tell him it's too soon. You're not physically strong enough yet.

The warring voices continued while she showered, dressed and went down for breakfast. Just because Craig hadn't mentioned his investigative work, it didn't automatically follow that he was concealing it from her. On the other hand, she'd sensed a lot of pent-up anger. Although he'd said he wasn't a vigilante, she couldn't rule out that his objective was to make someone pay for his father's death.

Unless . . .

Her sudden intuition as to the reason for his hostility towards her was almost as shocking as last night's dream. She should have seen it straight away. The question now was: should she confront him, or try to ignore it?

She sat down at a table in the dining room. Reflecting on yesterday's conversation, she knew one fact was beyond debate: sooner or later a journalist was going to read the police report and sniff out allegations of a conspiracy. When that happened, there was no telling what the consequences would be.

Kate wandered into the dining room, holding a mug of tea in both hands. She perched on a chair opposite Julia and gave her a contrite smile. 'Sorry if I was a bit heavy with you last night.'

'That's all right. I know you've got my best interests at heart.'

'Are you going with him today?'

'I think I have to.'

'And I can't persuade you otherwise?'

'Sorry. No.'

Kate nodded slowly, as if she had guessed as much. Her name was called from the kitchen and she took a quick gulp of tea, then stood up.

'Just be careful, okay?'

Julia was in the lobby just before nine. The presence of a police car outside made her jump, until she saw they were here to collect the woman appearing as a witness.

Craig's Golf turned in a couple of minutes later. As she went outside, Julia realised it felt good to be doing something active. Scary but exhilarating, like the first day in a new job. The weather was beautiful for mid-February, almost springlike, with a clear blue sky and a light breeze.

She strode over to his car with a decisive, almost normal gait. She had decided to dispense with the walking stick altogether today. It wasn't about vanity, she told herself. It was about independence.

Craig looked relieved when she opened the passenger door and got in. 'You're definitely up for this?'

She nodded, then saw the weariness in his face. 'Rough night?'

'Not great.'

'I suppose it was a long drive over here?' she said, realising she had no idea where he lived.

Craig looked away, sheepishly, and put the car in gear. 'I stayed in a B&B down the road.'

'Oh,' she said, surprised.

'I booked a room on the off chance that you'd agree to this. Sorry. It was a bit presumptuous of me.'

'Mm,' she agreed, but resolved not to let it upset her. She owed him this one, she decided.

They settled into a pattern of alternating silence with small talk, starting neutral and easing towards the personal. She asked him about his journalism and he made light of it, claiming to write a lot of frothy nonsense.

'Surely you get to attend some big sporting events?'

'Sometimes. More often I'm stuck on a broken-down train at the arse-end of the country, on my way to watch a bunch of overpaid idiots hoofing a ball around a field in the pissing rain.'

She chuckled. 'I hope it pays well.'

'When you're freelance it can be patchy. Luckily my wife's an accountant. Partner in a large firm in Crawley.'

'Quite high-powered, then?'

'Oh yes,' said Craig, with a sardonic edge. 'She's climbing the corporate ladder, all right. Almost one of the boys.'

It was an odd comment, delivered with unmistakable bitterness, and it served to kill off the discussion for a while. They had reached Hastings, where even the sunshine and a glassy blue sea couldn't compensate for the poverty and neglect evident in the once-magnificent seafront buildings.

'Tell me about your teaching,' he said. 'I saw that thing on the local news.'

Julia smiled. While she was in hospital, a TV crew from the local station had visited her school and filmed touching get-well messages from her pupils. She'd watched a recording of it at the hotel and it had brought her to tears.

'They're a fantastic bunch. I can't wait to get back to work, hopefully after Easter.'

'Must be pretty stressful, though, controlling a whole class of kids?'

'Sometimes. But the children have so much energy, it seems to transfer itself. It's very invigorating.'

'I wouldn't have the patience,' he said. 'I find it hard enough with my two.'

'You've got children?' She registered the surprise in her voice and scolded herself. Why shouldn't he have children?

'Tom and Maddie,' he said. 'They're a handful sometimes, but great with it, of course.' A pause, during which his gaze grew distant and inexpressibly sad. Then he said, 'What about you? Do you have a partner?'

She made a dismissive gesture. 'I was with a guy, Peter, for nearly six years. He was head of English at a secondary school in Brighton. He'd always been very skilful at avoiding talk of marriage and babies, so last year I got sick of it and I put him on the spot.' She laughed. 'Basically he did a runner on me. Said he wasn't interested in settling down. It turned out he'd been looking into a teaching exchange programme. A few weeks later he buggered off to America, and that was that.'

'What a bastard.'

'Better to find out when I did. After that I had the classic rebound relationship. Met a guy called Steve at my local gym.' She gave a rueful chuckle. 'He visited me once in hospital. Tried to persuade me to sell my story to the papers, and then go travelling with the proceeds. I haven't spoken to him since.'

'Doesn't seem like much has gone right for you,' he said. 'I heard you lost your parents last year.'

Encouraged by the sympathy in his voice, she told him about finding their bodies, realising what had happened to them. Talking about it wasn't as difficult as she had feared.

'We still have the inquest to come, in a couple of months. And there's the house to clear.'

'If you need a hand with that, let me know. I'm in Chilton a lot of the time.'

'Are you?'

'Staying at my dad's place. The media attention wasn't fair on the kids. It also means I can keep an eye on the house.'

'How do you manage with the children?'

'Nina works from home some days. Her parents help out. And three times a week I collect them from school, then stay with them till Nina gets in.'

He sounded casual enough, but she had a feeling he was holding something back. It reminded her of Kate's warning about him, and for a few minutes she gazed pensively out of the window, unsure whether to say anything.

As if he sensed her unease, Craig became restless, tapping out little tunes on the steering wheel. Then he said, 'I have a small confession to make.'

She swallowed back a memory of her nightmare. 'Go on.'

'We're not actually seeing George until this afternoon. There's someone else I want to visit.'

'Who?'

'Carl's mother. Peggy Forester.'

The killer had received another message last night. Once again there was an implicit threat to betray him.

```
Craig Walker is asking questions. It's
possible he suspects a conspiracy.
He'll be at Chilton Manor tomorrow. Go over
everything you did and make sure you're
watertight. Can anyone link you to our half-
witted friend?
Remember: one slip-up and you're finished.
```

The situation was becoming intolerable. It only reinforced his view that he had to take control. Find some way to turn the tables on Decipio. And yet, he couldn't ignore the warning. Was he watertight?

The instant he asked himself the question, one word popped into his head.

Peggy.

Thirty-Eight

'Stop the car.'

'What?'

'I mean it. Stop the car.'

Craig muttered an objection, but he checked his mirrors and pulled in at the kerb. They were on the outskirts of Hastings, heading towards Bexhill. Julia opened her door a couple of inches before she felt Craig's hand on her arm.

'What are you doing?'

'I'll get a bus back to Camber.' She glared at him until he retracted his hand.

'Jesus, you're overreacting, aren't you?'

'Am I? What else haven't you told me, Mr Big Shot Investigative Reporter?'

He looked flabbergasted. 'Where did you get that from?'

'Kate, at the hotel. She used to be a police officer.'

He snorted. 'That makes sense. Okay, so I used to do some serious journalism, and now I don't. It's no big secret.'

'Kate thinks you might have ulterior motives. Perhaps you're just out to discredit the police.'

Craig looked disgusted. 'That bastard killed my dad, remember? All I want is to get the truth. If the trail leads to bent coppers, or anyone else for that matter . . . then so be it.' He spread his hands.

'I'm gonna go where the facts take me. If you don't want to come along, fine. But I happen to think you're owed the truth as well.' He reached down and pressed the button that released her seatbelt, then folded his arms and waited.

Julia pushed the door open a little further, but made no move to get out.

'Why didn't you tell me about Peggy?'

'I didn't want to load it all on you at once.'

'Because you knew I'd say no?'

He answered with a grunt. 'Probably. It was stupid of me. You can stay in the car if you want. I'll see her on my own.'

Julia nodded, then pulled the door shut. She felt cheated, but she was also conscious of a terrible fascination at the idea of meeting Peggy Forester.

'All right,' she said at last. 'But from now on, you're going to be straight with me, okay?'

Falcombe was two miles east of Chilton, just off the A275 between Lewes and Chailey. The oldest part of the village wasn't much bigger than its neighbour, but whereas Chilton had remained unspoilt, Falcombe had long since succumbed to the lure of expansion. Estates spread out like tree rings, from a cluster of post-war prefabs near the centre to insipid twenty-first-century boxes around the perimeter. The sight of the tightly packed homes gave Julia renewed appreciation for Philip Walker's crusade.

Peggy Forester lived in a council estate dating back to the Fifties, about a mile from the main road. Unlike the newer developments, it was a wide street with grass verges and generous front gardens. Unfortunately the houses, set well back from the road, were little more than drab brown pebbledash shelters.

Craig reduced his speed as they looked for number 88. Ignoring their right of way, a tatty old BMW emerged from a driveway and hurtled round a parked Land Rover, forcing Craig to brake sharply.

'What happened to manners?' he said.

Julia's murmur of assent turned into a groan as she counted off the properties. In a street of virtually identical homes, Peggy Forester's wasn't hard to miss. Sheets of hardboard had been nailed to every window, and another board covered the pane in the front door. Graffiti had been sprayed all over the wood, none of it complimentary about the occupant. The front garden was devoid of grass or shrubs, a dark bumpy landscape that Julia assumed was freshly turned soil.

She was wrong. The smell hit them the instant they opened the car doors.

'Oh, Jesus,' said Craig, pulling a handkerchief from his pocket and covering his mouth. 'What the hell is that?'

Julia was half out of the car, breathing in shallow gasps. She shook her head, her mouth clamped shut on rising bile.

The entire front garden was filled with dogshit. Dozens of turds, accumulated over several weeks. Some of them fresh and glistening, some dry and crumbling, some a mouldering paste. Scraps of plastic lay trapped in the muck, indicating that many people were bagging them up and then throwing them in the garden. There were also half a dozen little white bundles that Julia identified as soiled disposable nappies, planted in the excrement like obscene bulbs. A larger shape caught her eye, rotting and pulpy with a suggestion of fur. She pointed and made a questioning sound.

'Maybe a fox?' said Craig, twisting away in revulsion. 'We'll try round the back.'

They got in the car and sped off, Craig opening the windows once they were clear of the house.

'You don't seriously think she's living there?' Julia said.

'As far as I know.'

'That's appalling. No matter what Carl did, how can anyone treat his mother like that?'

'The tabloids love to stir up a frenzy, then they skip along to the next story. This is what they leave in their wake.'

He navigated a route that brought them roughly parallel to Forester's road. They parked outside another row of grim council houses.

'Are you sure you're up for this?' he said.

'I'll give it a try. How are we going to get in?'

'I don't know. There's usually a twitten or something.'

There was, but it was narrow, and overgrown with brambles and nettles. It took them a few minutes to pick their way to the point where they guessed they were level with Forester's back garden. It was bordered by a thick hedge, at least eight or nine feet high, that had obviously gone untended for years. Buried deep within it was a rusty iron gate. Craig reached out and tested it, then brushed the metal flakes from his hand.

'We can probably force it open.' He looked at Julia. 'Unless you'd rather go back to the car?'

She shook her head. 'Not now I've come this far. But you're going first.'

'Fair enough.' He began wrenching the gate back and forth, breaking off the foliage that blocked its path. Once he'd created a big enough gap, he knelt down and wriggled through. Julia watched him, unimpressed.

'I must be mad,' she muttered. 'What if she's got a dog?'

'No sign of one,' Craig called back. 'You'll be all right. There's plenty of room now.'

Her resolve wavered briefly as she crouched down, imagining how Kate would react if she could see her now. Turning sideways, she eased herself between the gate and the hedge in awkward crablike steps, wincing as a stray branch clawed at her hair.

On the other side Craig was waiting to help her up, and they both plucked leaves and twigs from their clothes. Peggy's back garden was a jungle of weeds and long grass. A crumbling concrete path led to the back door, which was half glazed and intact. There were no boards over the rear windows, and as Julia looked up she glimpsed movement in the kitchen.

They heard a lock turning, and the door opened. Carl Forester's mother was small and wiry, dressed in jogging pants and a faded grey sweatshirt. She had greying brown hair in wild curls and a mean face with a raw, mottled complexion. Julia could feel the hostility radiating from her.

'Get off my place! This is mine!' she yelled. Her voice was slurred and indistinct. She tottered as she spoke.

'Mrs Forester?' Craig took a couple of steps forward. The woman turned slightly, raising her arm. She was brandishing a bread knife.

'Leave me alone! Go away!'

Craig motioned to Julia to stay where she was, then dug in his pockets and produced a roll of notes.

'Mrs Forester, it's all right. I've brought the money you're owed.'

Her eyes narrowed suspiciously. 'Money?'

'From the newspaper. You remember they did an article about you.'

They could see her searching her memory. She looked confused, but slightly less suspicious. 'All fucking lies.'

'I know. The man who wrote it was fired.'

'Fucking should have been.'

'They still you owe you a fee,' Craig said, showing her the money. 'Here it is. A hundred pounds.'

Peggy Forester blinked a few times, her brain working so furiously they could almost hear the cogs turning. Then she put the knife on the draining board and nodded. Held out her hand.

'Give it here.'

Craig approached cautiously. 'We have to come in, I'm afraid. You need to sign a receipt.'

The woman eyed him, as if she didn't understand. Craig stopped a couple of feet from her. She thrust out her hand. 'Give it.'

'I can't do that, Mrs Forester. You have to sign for it.'

There was a stand-off for maybe thirty seconds. Craig held her gaze, showing no fear, offering no possibility of a compromise. Moving closer, Julia saw her face was a mass of broken blood vessels. Her eyes were milky and restless. Her hands shook as if under someone else's control.

Craig looked at his watch. He gave the tiniest of shrugs, turning to Julia as if preparing to depart.

A flash of panic showed in Peggy's eyes. 'Come on, then,' she said. 'Get it over with.'

The killer was either very lucky or very unlucky. He couldn't decide which. A few minutes either way could have made all the difference.

The VW Golf had passed him while he was still planning his approach. He watched them pull up outside her house. Saw the man get out and realised it must be Craig Walker. It took him slightly longer to identify the woman, and at first he couldn't believe it was really her. He didn't want to believe it.

He sat very still, controlling his reaction. He watched them recoil at the state of the garden. When they got back in their car he dared to think he'd had a lucky escape, but he didn't entirely believe it. They wouldn't give up this easily.

He got out and explored on foot. He soon found the overgrown path that ran along the back, and sure enough, he could hear them thrashing through the weeds. He moved back, well out of sight, and reflected on his luck. If he had acted perhaps ten, fifteen minutes earlier, there would be no one for them to talk to.

On the other hand, he might have left the house and walked straight into them. That would have been a catastrophe.

He returned to the car and drove it round the corner, parking at a safe distance from the Golf. He wanted to see them when they came out. Perhaps something in their body language would hint at what they'd discovered.

Peggy Forester stood back to let them enter, then shut and locked the back door. The kitchen was a small square room with hideous green units that might have been the originals from the Fifties. The floor was brown lino, cracked and split with age. There was a small Formica table and two chairs. A coffee mug and a half-empty bottle of supermarket-brand vodka sat on the table. An old saucer doubled as an ashtray, overflowing with butts.

The kitchen's inner door was shut, so they couldn't see any more of the house. Julia shivered. She felt claustrophobic and frightened. The room wasn't big enough for three adults, especially when one of them reeked of alcohol and had a knife within reach.

But Craig admired the room with the relaxed enthusiasm of an estate agent at a viewing. 'Nice kitchen,' he said without a trace of irony.

Peggy grunted. 'It's my place.' Then she turned her head and muttered, as if to someone standing behind her.

Julia exchanged a glance with Craig, whose eyes briefly widened. He indicated the chairs but Julia shook her head. She felt safer standing.

'Why don't you sit down, Peggy,' he said, taking the other seat for himself. 'Terrible mess out the front,' he added conversationally.

'Never go out there,' she said. 'Not safe.'

'You mean *you're* not safe?' Craig asked.

'Not safe anywhere. Only here. I don't go nowhere.'

Julia couldn't help shrinking back as Peggy crossed the room. Thankfully she'd left the knife on the draining board. She poured some vodka into the mug and slurped it down.

Craig produced a sheet of paper and smoothed it out on the table. It was filled with text and had two dotted lines at the bottom for a signatory and a witness.

'I don't suppose you get many visitors?' he said.

'Eh?'

'People coming to see you. Carl's friends, for instance. Do they visit you?'

Peggy's eyes narrowed hatefully, perhaps at the mention of her son's name, or perhaps because she'd deduced what Craig was doing. Her hands twisted together, working out her agitation. Her left leg was juddering to the same tempo as her hands.

'Don't see no one,' she said. 'Got my money?'

'Yes, a hundred pounds.'

She nodded hungrily.

Craig said, 'What if I gave you two hundred?'

She nodded again. 'Two hundred.'

'Yes, but I need you to tell me something. Something about Carl.'

'I don't know nothing. Told the police. That fucking bitch.' She tottered to her feet, searching for the knife. Craig gently took her arms, easing her back down.

'It's all right, Peggy. We're not the police.'

'Fucking police. Hate 'em.'

'I'm sure you do. I want to know about Carl's friend. The one who helped him on January nineteenth. Do you understand what I mean?'

Her eyes roved the room, anxious not to make contact with him. 'Didn't know him.'

'You didn't know the other man?'

'What other man?'

Craig exchanged a glance with Julia. The conversation had the rhythm of a comedy routine, but no one was laughing.

'Are you talking about Carl?' he asked, confused.

'Little bastard stole from me. Always thieving. Tried to make him learn. He was mine. You're allowed to hit 'em if they're yours. To make 'em learn.' She grabbed the mug and drank greedily. A dribble of alcohol ran down her chin and she caught it with her hand. Then she licked her palm like a child with an ice cream.

Craig suppressed a shudder. He turned to Julia: *What now?*

On impulse she said, 'Mrs Forester, did Carl have a motorbike?'

Peggy reacted as if she hadn't known Julia was in the room. She scrutinised her closely, deciding if she posed a threat.

'It wasn't his. Too nice for him. I said he must've stole it.'

Julia stared at Craig. Her heart was thumping so loudly she imagined he could hear it. She had to moisten her lips before she dared speak again.

'He stole a motorbike?'

'He said it was a lend. Giving it a ride.'

'Who lent it to him, can you remember?'

'Said it was secret. Thieving little bastard.'

'Why was it a secret?' asked Craig.

'Wasn't allowed to tell. Said he'd kill me.' She took another mouthful of neat vodka, swallowing it as though it were water.

Craig was frowning, trying to make sense of what she'd said. 'Carl threatened to kill you?'

She spat with disgust. Craig recoiled from the fine spray of vodka. 'Not Carl,' she said.

Julia understood. 'You mean the other man?' she said. 'Carl's friend would kill you. Is that what Carl told you?'

'Said he'd come here. In the night. Said he'd kill me.'

'And did you tell this to the police?' Craig asked.

Peggy addressed Julia as if she hadn't heard him. 'Fucking police. Saying I made him wrong. I stuck my knife in her.' Her eyes glittered with pleasure. 'Serves her right. Bitch copper.'

'Mrs Forester, what about the other man? Why did he tell Carl he'd kill you?'

''Cause he could. He could do anything, Carl said.' She raised the mug, then stopped and looked directly at Julia. 'Carl said he was the Devil.'

Thirty-Nine

In all the long months of planning and preparation, he'd only been unlucky twice. That was how he saw it. He hadn't made mistakes. He hadn't fucked up. He'd been unlucky.

The first incident, he'd dealt with it promptly and effectively. It was old news now. He barely gave it a thought.

The second incident, he'd needed to visit Forester at home. Some important last-minute instructions. He made sure the mother was out on one of her extended drinking sessions, but still he'd worn a suit and carried a briefcase. He had a cover story ready, in case Peggy walked in on them. Carl, dumbfuck that he was, couldn't see why one was necessary.

'So I don't have to kill her, remember?'

Just as he was finishing up she blundered in, pissed and incoherent and bleeding from the nose. She'd got into a fight with two men over a game of darts and been thrown out of the pub.

He introduced himself as an insurance salesman. Could he interest her in a life policy at a modest monthly premium? Peggy went ballistic, accusing him of trying to take advantage of her dimwitted son. At this, Carl had scowled angrily and said nothing.

After screaming at him for letting a stranger into the house, Peggy slapped her son's face hard enough to leave a handprint on his cheek, while Carl just stood there and took it. Too scared and stupid to fight back. The next time they met, Carl was sporting a black eye and a split lip. But he swore he'd kept to the story. And Peggy had swallowed it.

Even so, there was a slim chance she would remember him. If she did, she might be able to identify him. And that made her a threat.

He'd been there about fifteen minutes when he saw movement in his rear-view mirror. Walker and Trent emerged from the footpath and crossed the road towards their car. It was difficult to read their mood at this distance, but he thought the woman looked a bit shaky, a bit unsteady on her feet. In contrast, Walker seemed fired up, as though it had been a successful visit.

So what had Peggy given them?

He sat very still and waited until they had driven past. Then he made sure he had what he needed, and opened his door.

Time to find out.

They didn't talk much on the way back. Squeezing through the hedge, Craig tore his shirt and swore loudly enough to set a dog barking further down the block.

When he got in the car he looked uncharacteristically sombre. 'I've spent a lot of time thinking about what it would be like, meeting the mother of the man who killed my father. I thought I would hate her, but really I just felt sorry for her.'

'What was all that about a newspaper owing her money?'

'I made it up. I knew she'd be reluctant to talk.'

'You know she'll just spend it on booze.'

'Yeah, and do you know what?' he said. 'I don't blame her.' He started the car and pulled away. 'We'll get some lunch, shall we?'

She didn't argue, although the encounter with Peggy Forester had sapped her strength. She wanted to stand in the shower and scrub away every trace of the visit.

They decided on the Half Moon in Plumpton, tucked away on a quiet country road. It was the kind of place her parents had loved,

Julia thought sadly, thinking of all the major family occasions they'd celebrated with a meal in a cosy Sussex pub.

As she got out of the Golf, a sudden cramp in her stomach made her gasp. She doubled over, retching a couple of times. Craig hurried round to her and tentatively rubbed her back.

'Are you all right?'

'Fine,' she managed, still coughing. She straightened up, her vision distorted by tears, and forced a smile. 'Just need to rest for a while.'

'Do you want me to take you home?'

She shook her head, hoping he wouldn't see how tempted she was. 'Let's see how I feel after we've eaten.'

He went in the same way as Walker and the woman. There were no other options.

First he waited a minute or two, watching for movement at the neighbour's windows. He held a mobile phone to his ear in case anyone came along the path. When he'd decided it was clear, he took a pair of latex gloves from his pocket and put them on. He pushed open the gate and scurried towards the house, keeping low so Peggy wouldn't see him.

Pressed tight against the wall, he ducked beneath her kitchen window, then reached out and tapped lightly on the back door: the kind of noise a cat would make. Even if she didn't have a cat, she was bound to be curious.

He heard her muttering as she unlocked the door. As soon as it opened he sprang up and launched himself into the house, shoving Peggy in the chest. She stumbled backwards, yelping in surprise. A half-smoked cigarette fell from her mouth. She struck the table and fell to the floor. A bottle of vodka toppled over and began slopping out its contents. Perfect.

Peggy was still too shocked to scream, but he didn't have long. He pushed the door shut with his heel and grabbed her arms as she floundered, trying to grip the table and get to her feet. He kicked her in the stomach, just hard enough to knock the wind from her.

She made a groaning sound. Her head was flopping loosely on her neck, eyes wild and disorientated. She was drunk, he realised. She couldn't make sense of what was happening.

Even better.

He knelt on her chest and pinned her arms to the floor. Put his face close to hers and watched carefully as her eyes swam into focus. They were wide with incomprehension, but they contained no recognition. She didn't remember him. Maybe he was in the clear.

'Those visitors,' he said. 'What did they want?'

She blinked several times. 'Money,' she said, perhaps thinking he was here to steal from her. 'Hundred quid. You can have it.'

He shook his head. Pressed his knee harder. 'What did you tell them?'

'Nothing. Told 'em nothing.'

'You're lying. They asked you about Carl. Tell me.'

'They wanted to know about the bike. I said it wasn't his.'

'A bike?' For a second he was genuinely confused. 'What sort of bike?'

'Someone gave him a lend. Noisy fucking thing. Green, it was.'

Then it clicked. The Kawasaki. On one occasion he'd brought it down to try it out over the fields. He'd let Carl take it for a ride, and the stupid bastard had disappeared for nearly an hour. He claimed he'd just taken it round the country lanes, but he must have gone home and showed it to his mother. And now Walker and Julia Trent knew about it.

One slip-up and you're finished.

'No,' he said aloud. He wasn't going to let that happen.

Craig ordered a cheddar ploughman's and a pint of Harveys bitter; Julia had soup and sparkling water. She found a vacant table and sat down. Combined with last night's dream, Peggy Forester's reference to the Devil was resonating powerfully in her mind. When she lifted the visor, was it the shock of recognition that had caused her to recoil, or something far worse?

She jumped as Craig touched her arm. 'What's wrong?'

'Nothing,' she said. 'Just a silly idea.'

'What?'

She shook her head. She couldn't tell him. Instead she said, 'Even if Peggy told the police what she just told us, they'd still dismiss it. They'd assume it was Carl who threatened to kill her.'

'Maybe. But we're not the police. We know there was someone else involved, and Peggy Forester has just confirmed it.'

Julia pulled a face. 'I wouldn't go that far. Even if what she said is true, we're no closer to identifying who this man is.'

Craig grudgingly assented, then took a long drink of beer.

'Still, it gives us some leverage with Matheson, don't you think?'

Peggy Forester just stared at him. Sobering quickly, but still too befuddled to know what was going on.

He grabbed her arms and half lifted her, yanking her upright until she was on her knees. Then he used all his strength to slam her head against the edge of the table. She hit it high on the skull with a thick, heavy sound. Her eyes rolled up in her head and blood gushed from the wound. When he let go she dropped like a dead weight, collapsing into the puddle of vodka around the table.

He plucked up the cigarette, saw it was still alight. He turned and examined the room. The kitchen window was open a couple of inches. The ledge was thick with grime. It was home to a bottle of washing-up liquid and a small army of dead flies.

He removed the key from the back door, then returned his attention to Peggy. She was unconscious. Not dead. That was better, really, for his purposes. But the next bit was tricky. He needed her to stay unconscious. He needed to be sure.

The floor was obviously uneven, for the vodka had spread in an arc, a little finger jutting out towards the hallway. Careful not to tread in it, he reached over and picked up the bottle. He poured the rest of the alcohol over Peggy's shoulders and hair.

Then he stepped back as far as he could and tossed the cigarette on to her body. It landed in the crook of her neck, disappearing in the folds of her sweatshirt. He'd assumed it would ignite the alcohol with an almost clear flame, like a sambuca or a Christmas pudding. But nothing happened.

Shit. He'd have to rethink. Perhaps light a match.

And then he saw something which made him smile. A tendril of grey smoke emerged from the sweatshirt. Then another, slow and sinuous. Then several at the same time. Fascinated, he took a couple of steps closer. He could see little yellow flames blinking in and out of existence within her clothing. The sweatshirt was melting, turning black. And still Peggy lay immobile.

He realised he was going to have to stay and watch. Not just to make sure the fire took hold, but because it was so absorbing. How many times did you get the chance to see someone burned alive?

It took a few minutes for the fire to get going, and by then it had burned through to her skin. The vodka on the floor ignited, scorching the cheap linoleum and producing foul-smelling smoke. He retreated to the door, covering his mouth with his hand. It was almost time to leave.

He left the kitchen window open a fraction, partly to draw in oxygen for the fire. He took the key, stepped into the back garden and locked the door behind him. Then he slipped the key through the window and dropped it on to the ledge.

He retraced his route through the hedge and along the footpath. He was back at his car, sipping from a bottle of Evian, when he saw a plume of smoke rising over the rooftops.

It was another ten minutes before a fire engine thundered past. His car shook in its slipstream.

'Hurry up, lads,' he muttered. 'You'll miss the barbecue.'

Forty

They stretched lunch out to well over an hour, and by the time they left the pub Julia felt physically refreshed and in far better spirits. The jitters didn't set in until they were a mile or so out from Chilton, and it suddenly struck her that they were about to confront the man who might have masterminded the slaughter on 19 January.

'Tell me about George Matheson,' she said.

'The classic self-made man,' Craig said. 'Came from an ordinary middle-class family. Not academically brilliant, but very bright, very tough. They reckon you could never get one over on him. Had a lot of luck, as well. Moved into property at the right time, got out of equities before the stock market dived.'

'Good at reading the future, or inside knowledge?'

'Bit of both, I imagine. In interviews he's always boasting about his instinct. When he buys a company, he doesn't care about all the due diligence and formal paperwork. He visits the premises, talks to the staff on the shop floor. If he gets a good feel about the place, he'll buy it regardless of what the balance sheet says.'

'And it's always worked?'

'Not so much lately. There are rumours that he's overreached himself. He's sold off quite a few assets in the past few years, mainly to help prop up the core business, but there are signs that it hasn't worked.'

'Hence the planning application?'

Craig nodded. 'Twenty or thirty million in the coffers, I guess that's going to ease the financial pressure.'

Julia mulled it over. She knew they were both thinking the same thing. Was Matheson desperate enough to countenance mass murder for that money?

'What about his wife?'

'Vanessa. They've been married for thirty years. She comes from one of those old families with oodles of class but no money. He was the bit of rough who went out and made a fortune. She gave him the respectability and the contacts he needed on his way up.'

'Sounds like a good match.'

'By all accounts it's a pretty empty relationship these days,' said Craig. 'Whether he's got someone on the side, I've no idea.'

'Do they have children?'

'No. They tried for years, according to one article I read. But there was some kind of problem. Of course the fertility treatment wasn't as sophisticated as it is now.'

'That's sad.'

He gave her a sharp look. 'You feel sorry for him?'

'In that respect, yes.' She matched his disdain. 'We don't know he's done anything wrong. Let's not prejudge, eh?'

'All right,' he said. But he sounded a little grumpy, and once again she wondered if it was a mistake to get involved. Did she really have the appetite for this?

Tall wrought-iron gates barred their entrance to the property. Craig pulled up alongside an intercom and pressed the button. After a few seconds a gruff male voice said, 'Yes?'

'Craig Walker, to see George Matheson.'

There was a pause. The speaker clicked off and the gates began to move apart.

'Was that a servant, or the man himself?' Julia said, as they drove along a winding gravel drive.

'I'm not sure if he has any servants,' Craig said. 'Apparently they live quite frugally.'

'Really?' Frugal wasn't the word she'd use to describe the stunning white mansion gliding into view behind a screen of immaculately trimmed poplars.

Craig heard her intake of breath and said, 'Parts of it date back to the fifteenth century. Something like eighteen rooms, plus a pool, tennis court and a couple of acres of formal gardens.'

They parked next to a brand-new Jaguar saloon. Julia shut her eyes for a moment, steadying her nerves.

As she got out, George Matheson emerged on to the grand portico. He was taller than she'd expected, six feet or thereabouts, but a little stooped. He had thick grey hair and unruly eyebrows, framing strong features and a ruddy complexion. He looked more like a retired builder than a wealthy entrepreneur.

At first she was concentrating so hard on walking without any sign of impairment that she failed to register the confusion on Matheson's face. It was only when she reached the steps she saw him staring at her as though she were a ghost.

He looks terrified, she thought. But the insight did little to ease her own anxiety.

'This is Julia Trent,' said Craig as he walked up the steps.

'Yes. I, ah . . . yes.' George shook hands with Craig, then abruptly turned before Julia had time to offer her hand.

Leading them inside, he indicated where they could hang their coats and then strode across a vast entrance hall. The walls boasted a tasteful selection of oil paintings, mostly landscapes, some precious-looking urns and an imposing grandfather clock in the corner. Julia had a moment to admire the wide double staircase and galleried landing, before they entered an equally vast living room. This time the artwork was mostly watercolours and a few pencil drawings: all figurative, probably originals, probably very valuable.

Sensing movement in her peripheral vision, she turned to see a man in a black suit step away from one of the immense sash windows. He was about as tall as George, with a slender but powerful physique and close-cropped fair hair. He was good-looking in a slightly coarse way, with a large nose and well-defined cheekbones. His skin was taut but blotchy, with traces of acne scars beneath both ears. His eyes narrowed, emanating hostility.

'This is James Vilner,' said George. 'He's, uh, an associate of mine.'

Vilner nodded curtly, but he didn't say a word in greeting. He directed his gaze at each of them in turn, then resumed his position at the window. The sight of his broad back and apparent indifference sent a chill through her. The effect was somehow more intimidating than if he'd marched up and stood looking over their shoulders.

George indicated a haphazard selection of sofas and chairs, and asked if they wanted a drink.

'Just had lunch,' said Craig.

Julia also declined, and caught Matheson's relief. He kept snatching furtive glances at her, his eyes feasting on her body as if mentally undressing her. Not ogling her breasts, she realised. Trying to picture her wounds.

'You seem to have made a remarkable recovery,' he blurted when she caught him at it.

'Thank you.'

He turned his attention to Craig. 'And can I offer my condolences. As far as I'm concerned, your father's campaign was never personal. I bore him no ill will, and I'm sure he felt the same.'

Craig nodded slowly. 'I guess I owe you an apology, as well. What I said about the development was never intended to be made public.'

At first George looked gratified, then grimly amused. 'But you stand by your comments?'

'I'm here to see if you can change my mind.'

'And how would I do that?'

'Give me a cast-iron commitment that there'll be no second application. You'll guarantee the land around Chilton won't be developed under any circumstances.'

George gave a little bark of laughter, and shook his head regretfully. Julia glanced at Vilner, sensing that he had absorbed every word.

'That's asking the impossible,' George said, his gaze also flickering towards Vilner. 'No one can predict the future. It's quite feasible that, in time, opinions will change.'

'So you do intend to make a fresh application?'

'I don't necessarily intend anything of the sort,' George said. Julia thought she detected a degree of emphasis on the *I*, but Craig didn't seem to pick up on it.

'You know the police have completed the preliminary report?' he said.

George shook his head, but his eyes slid away. 'What's that got to do with anything?'

'It's a whitewash,' Craig declared. 'Julia wasn't shot by Carl Forester. There was another man there. Dressed in motorcycle leathers and a full-face helmet. He killed Carl and made it look like suicide. He got away before the police arrived.'

George's mouth tightened. There was another darting look at Vilner, and it struck Julia that perhaps George found the other man's presence just as unnerving as they did. But if so, why was he here?

Then she realised Vilner had turned and was staring right at her.

'Is this correct?' George asked.

Julia nodded. 'Yes.'

Vilner spoke for the first time. 'What did the police say?'

'They didn't . . . they thought—'

'That you'd imagined it?' George answered for her.

Her shoulders dropped and she turned away, determined not to let him rile her.

'We've just spoken to Peggy Forester,' said Craig, drawing their attention away from Julia. 'Carl had befriended someone, but he wouldn't tell his mother who. According to him, this friend said he'd kill her if she ever found out about him.'

'And Peggy confirmed the friend had a motorbike.'

George waited a second, then forced a laugh. 'And you regard that as proof of your theory? The woman's a hopeless alcoholic, isn't she?'

'She was lucid enough this morning,' said Craig.

Vilner took a few steps towards them. His eyes were still narrowed, unreadable. 'So what are you after, really?' he demanded.

George raised a hand to quieten him. 'Whatever it is, I don't think this meeting will achieve anything.'

Emboldened by the knowledge that Vilner could be held in check, Julia said, 'What happened at the farm?'

George looked taken aback. 'I beg your pardon?'

'The report mentions an incident, a couple of years ago. Carl assaulted the farmer's wife.'

'Laura Caplan, yes,' said George. He cleared his throat. 'Carl let himself into the house. He had a selection of her underwear spread out on the kitchen table. When Laura walked in she found him masturbating over them. Her daughter also witnessed it. They were very distressed.'

'He was sacked as a result?'

'Yes. Of course, the police told me they think it was a factor in . . . in what he did.' He shifted in his seat. 'Believe me, I've examined my conscience on many an occasion since then, and I'm absolutely certain I was right to fire him.'

'Why didn't the Caplans go to the police?'

'It was awkward. Carl had worked for me – and for them – for several years. For most of that time he'd been a satisfactory employee. We all agreed losing his job was punishment enough.'

'And I daresay you wanted to avoid the bad publicity?' Craig said.

'In fact, it was Laura Caplan who made the final decision. For Megan's sake.' He shut his eyes for a second. 'Not that it did either of them any good, ultimately.'

'How is Megan now?' Julia asked.

'On the Glasgow coma scale she scores seven, from which I understand she may survive and she may not. If she does, she may have serious brain damage, or she may not. We just don't know.'

As if that sombre note seemed a suitable place to conclude, he stood up. 'I understand how bitter you must both feel, but I'm afraid these allegations are ludicrous. I don't accept for a minute that Forester collaborated with anyone, and neither do the police.' To Julia, he added, 'I'm sure there's some other explanation for what you believe you saw.'

She didn't respond. Having kept her emotions in check for this long, she wasn't about to be goaded into tears. She got up and nodded at Craig to let it go. In her assessment the encounter had ended in a draw, which considering they were on hostile territory was a reasonably good result.

Walking to the door, she sensed Vilner's gaze on her, his stillness crowding the room like an oppressive weight. She felt her legs go weak and prayed they wouldn't buckle beneath her.

George accompanied them back across the hall. This time there were no handshakes, no pleasantries.

'It would be hypocritical of me to wish you luck,' he said as he opened the door. 'I can only say, I hope you know what you're doing.'

Forty-One

Julia felt little relief as the front door shut behind them. If anything, the crawling sensation of being watched intensified as she headed for the car. Checking behind her, she saw no one at the ground-floor windows.

Then she looked up, and gave a start.

'What is it?' said Craig.

She shook her head, spoke in a low voice. 'Upstairs window.'

Craig reached the Golf and took a casual glance at the house.

'Bloody hell.'

A ghostly figure stood at a window on the first floor. She wore a white gown and a sort of cowl over her hair. Her face was so pale it glowed, her dark eyes burning with intensity. She was staring straight at Julia, and when she saw them looking she gave no reaction. She didn't smile, or flinch, or turn away.

Julia got in the car and slammed her door shut. 'Who is that?'

'I think it's his wife. I saw her on 19 January.'

Julia shivered and hugged herself. 'At first I thought it was . . . I don't know. Not human.'

Craig grunted. He started the engine, then paused, his brow furrowed.

'*I hope you know what you're doing,*' he quoted. 'Does that sound like a threat to you?'

'Maybe, but right now I couldn't care less. I just want to get out of here.'

Vilner didn't wait for George to return to the drawing room, or whatever the hell it was called. He strode into the hall and caught George in a pose of utter despair, his forehead resting against the door as if he'd just tried to ram it.

'I'm leaving too,' Vilner said.

George sprang up, fighting a losing battle to conceal how stunned he was. Not the only losing battle in his life right now, Vilner suspected. By contrast, he thought he'd concealed his own reaction pretty well.

'You'll be briefing Kendrick?' George said.

'That's right.'

'I could make it worth your while to give him an abridged version.'

Vilner stared at him. A grin slowly lit up his face. 'Uh uh,' he said. 'I only back winners.'

George winced, exactly as if it had been a physical slap in the face. 'I wouldn't be so sure about that,' he said. 'It's a good offer, and I'm only making it once.'

'Don't waste your time, George,' a voice rang out. Thin and reedy, but projected with real determination. Vilner turned to see Vanessa Matheson at the top of the stairs. It was the first time he had seen her in the flesh, and she was nothing like the photos, most of which were years out of date. She looked terrifying: a gaunt spectre, so thin and light she was virtually floating above them. Her small black eyes drilled contempt right through him.

Vilner summoned a smile for her as he pulled the front door open. 'Good advice,' he said to George. 'I'd say you've got enough problems at the moment.'

He left without another word. Crossing the driveway, he reached for his mobile, then thought better of it. Phones were a risky form of communication, and mobiles were especially vulnerable. His conversation with Kendrick would have to wait.

Neither of them spoke as they drove along Hurst Lane. At the fork in the road Julia glanced along the track that led to the farm. There was a dark green Land Rover parked about a hundred yards away. She felt sure she'd seen it somewhere else today.

She considered mentioning it to Craig, but thought better of it. For one thing, it would initiate a conversation when what she craved was silence. And after being spooked by George's wife, she didn't want him to think she was paranoid.

They reached the village proper, where the day's contingent of tourists seemed to be packing up and leaving. It was almost four o'clock, the sun low in the sky, long shadows stretching like fingers across the green.

'I'm sorry you've got to drive me back,' Julia said, as Craig gave a slightly wistful glance at the Old Schoolhouse.

'It's the least I can do,' he said.

They followed a minibus past the shop and round the bend. Spotting a vacant parking bay outside her parents' cottage, Julia said, 'Can we stop a minute? I'd like to check on the house.'

'Sure.' Craig pulled in. 'Do you want me to come with you?'

Julia was searching her handbag for the right set of keys. It was tempting to say yes, but if she didn't find the courage to go in alone now, it would be even harder next time.

'No, I'll be fine.'

She got out of the car. Despite the fine weather, the temperature was rapidly falling. Could be in for a frost tonight, she thought, glancing at the row of cottages, their chimney pots and TV aerials silhouetted against an indigo sky. Light poured from the homes on each side, while the dark windows of her parents' house resembled missing teeth.

She slotted the key in the lock, picturing the night in December when she had found them dead. Her hand trembled until she got the better of it. She turned the key and thought: Peggy Forester's road.

That's where she had seen the Land Rover. Or one very like it.

She went inside and turned on the light. Waited a moment, just as she had done two months ago. The house felt empty, abandoned, but still she called, 'Hello?' As if her mother might call out from the kitchen – 'In here!' – and she'd go in to find Mum rolling pastry while her father fetched vegetables from the garden for the evening meal, and they could celebrate that nothing bad had happened because someone had found a way to roll back time . . .

Not going to happen.

She sniffed. The air felt stale and clammy. It was over a week since Neil had last checked on it, just before he returned to Cheshire. One of the neighbours had a key, but only for emergencies. In the living room the wallpaper was beginning to curl away from the corners, and she could smell the fusty, organic aroma of mould spores. If they didn't do something with the house soon it would be uninhabitable.

Before attempting the stairs, she rested for a minute. Without fully realising it, she had been putting on a front for Craig, and it was only now she appreciated how much it was taking out of her.

The next challenge was more emotional than physical: venturing into her parents' bedroom for the first time since their deaths. She could barely bring herself to look at the bed, but a large leatherbound diary on her father's bedside table caught her attention. For over forty years he had faithfully recorded the minutiae of his daily life, and there were whole boxes of them in the spare room, along with stacks of paperwork that would, sooner rather than later, need to be sorted out.

She picked up the diary and wiped dust off the cover with her elbow. She suddenly had a very clear recollection of herself as a child, going to kiss him goodnight as he sat at his desk. Sometimes she would read a little at his shoulder, frowning to make sense of his elegant squiggles, and once she had asked what he was doing. 'Capturing all the precious moments, so they're never forgotten,' he had told her. She had considered this, and asked, 'How do you know what's precious?'

Now she recalled his sad, wise reply: 'When enough years have passed, everything is precious.'

The Scotch was concealed in the rear footwell, behind the driver's seat. It sang to him the instant Julia went inside. He tried to ignore it, but held out for less than a minute.

One swig. Not even a full mouthful. That couldn't hurt. He'd had, what, a couple of pints at lunchtime? Still below the limit.

Craig wiped his mouth, savoured the burning in his throat, then found the Extra Strong Mints in the glove compartment and popped a couple into his mouth. Couldn't risk Julia smelling it on his breath.

He waited a couple more minutes, and was debating whether to have another sip when Julia emerged from the house. When she got in the car, he saw she was holding a diary.

She looked at him and sniffed. He thought he was busted, until he noticed the tears running down her face.

'You okay?' Without thinking, he reached out towards her. His fingers had almost touched her cheek when she twisted away. He withdrew his hand as though it had been burned.

'I'm fine.' She sniffed again. 'Why?'

'You're crying.'

She rubbed her cheeks, looking slightly incredulous, as though she hadn't been aware of it. Feeling embarrassed for her, he started the car and checked over his shoulder before pulling out. It had been a long, stressful day for both of them, but at least it was nearly over.

After Vilner left, George wearily climbed the stairs to join his wife. He was only fifty-six, but most of the time lately he felt about a hundred. He wondered if Toby was right. Perhaps he should take himself off to Antigua for a few months. To hell with the business, and Kendrick, and the rest of them. If it all fell apart while he was away, did it really matter? He had nothing left to prove, and scarcely anyone to prove it to.

Vanessa watched him approach. She was gripping the banister, shaking with the effort of remaining upright. Still she had this compulsion to push herself to the limit, no matter the toll it took on her. He didn't know whether to feel admiration or pity. He had tried both, and both had been met with scorn.

'How are you?'

'Dying,' she said. 'What's your excuse?'

He offered his arm, and she took it grudgingly. More and more now she was confined to her room, and he had arranged for private nurses to help care for her. Her doctor had suggested a hospice might be more comfortable for her last days or weeks, but Vanessa was adamant that she wanted to stay at home.

He helped her into bed, trying not to feel aggrieved by her intervention with Vilner. It was humiliating that she'd witnessed just how sordid his professional life had become.

Once she was settled, he sat beside her and recounted the visit, not sparing her any of the details. It felt surprisingly good to unburden himself: a sign that the bond between them, stretched thin by time and neglect, nonetheless remained. She was all he had left, and soon she would be gone.

'Vilner's presence has backfired,' he said. 'Now Kendrick will know exactly what type of trouble we're in.'

Vanessa ignored the veiled criticism of her decision. 'Do you believe their story?'

'That's hardly the point. Julia Trent believes it, and clearly she's convinced Walker. How much longer before other people start to fall for it?'

Her eyelids slipped shut, and she was silent for a long time. Perhaps mulling over the problem, or perhaps asleep. Reaching under the covers, he found her hand and wrapped it in his. It felt no bigger than a child's. The image brought tears to his eyes, imagining how it might have been to sit here as a father, reading a bedtime story in a room filled with toys and games instead of monitors and morphine.

Vanessa's eyes snapped open. She saw the tears and looked away, as if to spare him further indignity.

'If the allegations are true, do you think Kendrick had something to do with it?'

George sighed. 'I don't even want to think about that.'

'You'll have to warn Toby. It's not fair to leave him exposed.'

'But can he be trusted to keep his mouth shut?'

'You let him take a copy of the report,' she reminded him.

He considered a moment. He went to ask her a question, but her eyes had closed and the tone of her breathing had changed. This time she was asleep, and she needed it. She needed to be left alone.

Just go, a voice in his head urged him. Run away now. Before it all gets a lot worse.

But he knew he wouldn't.

Forty-Two

The drive back was slow and fraught. There was no easy route across country, and almost immediately they became entangled in a mix of school-run and early commuter traffic.

'Don't know why they call it the rush hour,' Craig grumbled. 'It starts at three and lasts till eight.'

'Overpopulation,' said Julia. The irony wasn't lost on either of them.

'He won't give up. A few years from now there'll be housing estates all round Chilton.'

'Don't be a pessimist.' She thought about George's comment: *I don't necessarily intend anything of the sort.* Had she detected the emphasis on *I*, or was it her imagination?

Craig said, 'What did you make of him?'

'I'm not sure. I think he already knew about the police report. His initial surprise was because *we've* got a copy, but he was faking his reaction to the content.'

'I thought so, too. I wonder how he got hold of it.'

'Same way you did, I suppose. A connection in the police.'

'That's a worrying thought,' Craig said.

'I didn't realise you were going to tell him about the second killer.'

'I wanted to see how he reacted.'

'He seemed genuinely upset when he was talking about the Caplans.

That would be quite a challenge to feign, if he was the one who killed them.'

Craig scowled. 'I'm not suggesting he did it himself. He'll have hired someone.'

'What? A hit man?'

'Yeah.'

'Then why involve Carl? Why not just get the hit man to kill everyone?'

'Because it raises too many unanswered questions. Sooner or later the police would discover that Matheson had the perfect motive. This way the answer was served to them on a plate. Some maladjusted loner with a grudge goes on the rampage and then kills himself. A nice tidy conclusion. No need to look any further. No need to think about who benefits.'

She considered this for a moment. She had a feeling they were thinking the same thing. Then Craig said, 'That other guy. Vilner.'

Julia gripped the diary close, worrying at a loose flap of leather in the corner. He sent her a look. Testing the water before he said it.

'Could it have been him?'

She didn't answer for a long time. They were approaching the small town of Battle. Ahead of them the traffic was slowing again, a chain of red lights flashing in the darkness.

'Maybe,' she said.

As they drove into Battle, Craig suggested they stop and grab a drink. He got the feeling Julia only agreed out of politeness.

They found a tea room still open on the High Street, close to the abbey. Craig ordered coffee and a bacon sandwich; Julia a pot of tea. When she got up to use the toilet, Craig asked if he could borrow her mobile. 'The person I'm calling is avoiding me,' he explained.

He looked up the number on his own phone and dialled it on Julia's. While it rang, he looked around the café. It was a small, tidy place, picturebook pretty and slightly twee, but exactly in keeping with its location. And it wasn't licensed, which was probably a good thing.

Abby picked up with an uncertain 'Hello?'

'You haven't been answering my calls.'

'Craig, I'm really sorry. I didn't—'

'I know, I know. Your editor talked you into it, you had no idea of the trouble it would cause, blah blah blah. That's not why I called. I need a favour.'

There was a pause while Abby registered that she'd been forgiven, albeit with strings attached. In the background he could hear soft music, then a woman's voice. He heard Abby draw away from the phone and mention his name.

'Okay,' she said to him. 'What is it?'

'Will you find out everything you can about a man called James Vilner? He's in his late thirties, supposedly some kind of businessman.'

'Supposedly?'

'If he's in business, it's likely to be of the illegal variety.' He gave her a brief description. 'He has a Northern accent, but I imagine he's based in London or the South East.'

'And what's your interest in him?'

Craig smiled to himself. He didn't have to tell her, but he knew the truth would be a great motivator. 'He's an associate of George Matheson's.'

Another pause. When Abby spoke, she made a bad job of concealing her interest. 'Can I use what I find?'

'I wouldn't expect anything else.'

Abby winced. 'I suppose I deserve that. I'll get started on it tonight.'

The killer saw them park and set off on foot. He was glad of the chance to stop and regroup. He could see all manner of opportunities opening up, but to exploit them fully he had to do some preparation.

He drove back to the petrol station he'd just passed and bought fuel. Then he returned to the car park and pulled up in sight of

Walker's Golf. There was a supermarket adjoining the car park. It took him less than five minutes to buy what he needed.

He drank some water and ate a cheese and pickle sandwich. The bread was dry and the cheese was sweaty, but he didn't care. He had brought chocolate as well. He needed calories. There was still a lot to do. He felt tired but elated. It had been a long and busy day, but an extremely productive one.

While he waited, he listened to the radio. Top story on the local news was a serious fire at the home of 'Chilton spree killer Carl Forester'. Unconfirmed reports of a body found in the gutted building, though no word yet as to its identity.

When the bulletin ended, the DJ and his sidekick took it upon themselves to speculate further. A tragic accident, they surmised. Or suicide. Peggy Forester was a lonely woman, an alcoholic, despised by the whole community. Who could blame her if she had taken her own life?

The killer listened and laughed. Listened and laughed.

They were in the café twenty minutes or so. Craig told her he'd asked his journalist friend to make some checks on James Vilner, which she agreed was a good idea. After that they said very little. Just kept exchanging tired smiles.

Walking back to the car, he called his wife. Unconsciously Julia drifted to the other side of the pavement, giving him a little more privacy. At first he sounded cold and stilted, then his whole body and tone was transformed, and she guessed the phone had been passed to his children. There was something heart-rending about the way he pumped so much vitality and affection into his voice, as if that could compensate for his absence.

Then Nina again. Craig kept nodding and saying, 'Yes. Yes.' Julia guessed he was being harangued about something. Finally he said, 'No, I haven't forgotten tomorrow. I'll be there.'

He slipped the phone into his jacket. 'Nina's away on business tomorrow night, so I'm staying over.'

'I'll bet your children can't wait till you're back for good.'

He said something she couldn't decipher, then shook his head and turned away. It took a couple of seconds for the truth to dawn on her.

'Oh God. I'm so slow on the uptake.' She laid a tentative hand on his shoulder.

'My fault,' he said. 'We've separated. That's the real reason I'm at my dad's.'

'With everything you've been through, it must have put a lot of strain on the marriage.'

He gave a sarcastic laugh. 'That, and the fact she was screwing someone else.'

'Oh.' She looked down. 'I'm sorry.'

'It happens, doesn't it? Probably my fault as much as hers.'

They reached the Golf. Away from the streetlights, the sky was studded with stars. Craig unlocked, but made no move to get in. They stared at each other across the roof of the car.

'So what does Nina think about all this?'

'What? My quest to find the truth?' He let out a hollow laugh. 'She thinks I'm on a fool's errand. And I'm starting to wonder if she's right.'

'You're not suggesting we should give up?'

'I don't know. You should, perhaps.' He shrugged, then examined her face as if seeing it for the first time. 'You look even worse than I feel.'

Julia smiled. 'You say the nicest things.'

There was a moment's silence, both of them suddenly a little self-conscious. Then Julia shook her head. Opened her door.

'Come on, we're both exhausted. Let's get going.'

The traffic thinned out as they moved east, into more remote countryside, then turned south towards the coast. Julia found her eyes growing heavy. Several times she jerked awake as her head bumped against the window.

It was nearly six-thirty when the Golf turned into the hotel car park. The farewell was hurried and slightly awkward. No definite statement of intent or arrangements for the future; merely an exchange of mobile numbers and an agreement to speak again soon.

'Thanks for coming with me,' Craig said, but there was more disappointment than gratitude in his voice, as if her presence had in some way fallen short of his expectations.

Is that it? Julia found herself asking as she got out of the car. She felt an odd sense of loss, a sense that something worthwhile had been abandoned too early, without a struggle. Even though she had far more doubts about a Matheson conspiracy than Craig, it still saddened her to think their quest for the truth might be over almost before it had begun.

Forty-Three

Craig was aware of conflicting emotions as he watched Julia disappear into the hotel. Disappointment that the day had ended on such an unsatisfactory note, and also frustration that Julia hadn't embraced his theories about the massacre. Considering he was just about the only person who believed in her – and not to mention that he had very good reason to resent her – he thought she might have been a little more appreciative of his support.

And yet, in spite of that, he also felt despondent at the thought of her walking away from the investigation. It was perplexing. He'd been quite prepared to carry the fight alone before Julia had entered the picture. Why should it be any different now?

Almost without thinking, he reached for the bottle in the footwell. With the coffee and a sandwich in his system, another mouthful wouldn't do any harm. He glanced at the hotel, made sure no one was looking, and tipped the bottle back once, then again. The giddy hit of energy was desperately welcome.

He turned left out of the car park. By now the roads were almost deserted, whereas back home in Crawley it would still be gridlock. He found himself wondering if he could convince Nina to move out this way, then remembered that they had separated. If things stayed as they were, he could live anywhere he wanted.

Alone.

The flare of headlights in his rear-view mirror jolted his attention back to the road. A car was suddenly riding on his bumper, then it swerved across the centre line and raced past. It was high and square, some sort of jeep. Must be doing at least seventy.

'Boy racer,' he muttered in disgust, forgetting that Nina often levelled the same charge at him. He watched as the driver feathered the brakes on a tight left-hand bend and disappeared from sight. Glancing at the dashboard, he saw his own speed was around forty miles an hour: well below the limit.

He accelerated slightly, but was careful to stay within the bounds of his visibility. There was no street lighting out here. The road ahead was a pale narrow ribbon, twisting and turning across the featureless landscape. Darkness pressed against his windows, making him feel isolated and exposed.

This is all a mistake, he decided, experiencing a sudden longing for light and warmth and family. He should be at home, working to save his marriage, not chasing round the country trying to prove some ridiculous theory.

Once again, Kate was lying in wait. Knowing how exhausted she looked, Julia was expecting to be scolded for overdoing it. Instead Kate's first words were: 'Peggy Forester's dead.'

'What? She can't—' Julia just stopped herself from blurting out: *We visited her this morning.*

'There was a fire at her house,' Kate went on. 'They found a body inside. Too badly burned to identify, but they think it's her. Good riddance, I say.'

'When was this?'

'Sometime this afternoon. Why?'

Julia shook her head. 'No reason.'

Now came the appraisal. Kate frowned. 'Do you want me to call a doctor?'

'What?'

'You look like you're about to flake out. The way you're going, you'll end up back in hospital. Or worse,' she added darkly.

Julia was too weary to argue. 'I'll get an early night.'

She made it to the stairs and gripped the banister, stifling the pain because Kate was still watching. A throbbing headache had started up, and her vision swam in and out of focus. Kate's right, she told herself. I do need to see a doctor.

Somehow she made it to her room, where she dropped her father's diary on the bed and collapsed next to it, staring at the battered cover but seeing something quite different.

The grimy, claustrophobic kitchen. The vodka. The cigarettes. Peggy's inebriation and erratic behaviour. Accident or suicide. It had to be one or the other, didn't it?

But that idea niggled at her, along with something else. Something she couldn't pin down.

Coincidence. Wasn't it a terrible coincidence? It also meant they were probably the last people to see her alive. That in itself had all kinds of implications, but right now she was too tired to work out what they were. Her last memory was of kicking off her shoes, shuffling a little to get comfortable and closing her eyes, telling herself she would just rest for a minute or two.

Once Craig started thinking about Tom and Maddie, he couldn't stop. He knew he was becoming maudlin and sentimental, but fears about their safety kept crowding in. Today he'd met Matheson and James Vilner. He'd seen the nature of the people he was up against. What was he playing at?

There was a right-hand bend ahead, a couple of hundred yards away. He couldn't see the angle yet, but it looked to be tight. There was a large, unlit building on the inside corner, obscuring his view of any oncoming traffic. A barn, he guessed, probably a store for winter feed. There was a fence running along the perimeter to his right, and some distant ghostly blobs that might have been sheep or cattle.

The fields to his left were unfenced, but separated from the road by a ditch. His headlights picked out tall reeds and the dark shimmer of water.

He was less than a hundred yards away, shifting to third gear, when the car burst into view. A familiar shape: high and square, some sort of jeep. And coming right at him. Straddling the centre line, it straightened out of the corner but made no effort to move over. It was gaining speed, its main beams high and blinding, filling his windscreen with light.

Craig reacted on pure instinct. Wrenched the steering hard left and sent the Golf bumping across the narrow verge. He stamped on the brake, but the wheels had already lost traction on the wet grass. The bonnet tipped forward and he felt a choking pain across his torso as the seatbelt reeled him in. His head smashed against the side window and he blacked out.

Forty-Four

Julia was woken by noise: loud, urgent, indistinct. Her mind scrambled to process the sounds. While still emerging from sleep she'd heard smashing glass, thumping feet, and screams. She'd heard people screaming.

Now she was awake, and people were still screaming. She could hear running, doors slamming, and over it all an alarm was blaring, high-pitched and insistent, drilling through her brain. She had a feeling it was still early in the evening, that she hadn't slept long. She felt groggy and nauseous and confused. If it was a dream, why hadn't the noises stopped?

If it wasn't a dream, what was it?

None of it made sense until she pulled in a breath and felt the tickle of smoke in her nostrils.

There was a fire. She had to get out.

But when she went to act on that impulse, nothing happened. It felt as though a fast-acting concrete had been poured on to her body. She tried frantically to make her limbs obey. She could feel her muscles tense and relax, tense and relax, but it did no good. She couldn't move. She was going to lie here, conscious but immobile, and burn to death.

Craig was cold. Freezing cold. Icy water seeping through his jeans. Something warmer trickling in his hair.

He opened his eyes to utter darkness. He thought he'd gone blind. Quelling a rush of panic, he blinked a few times and moved his head. It hurt. There was a powerful throbbing just above his right ear. A hot tearing pain at the base of his skull, as though someone had tried to rip his head off.

Gradually his vision adjusted to the dark. The first thing he saw was the spent airbag, draped over the steering wheel like a monstrous condom. The Golf had nosedived into the ditch, and all the front windows had shattered. He was in muddy water up to his waist, chips of glass sprinkled on the surface like diamonds.

He flexed his leg muscles, tentatively lifting and twisting his feet. To his relief, he didn't seem to have any broken bones. He tried turning the ignition off, but the steering column must have distorted, jamming the key. He had to settle for wrenching the rest of the keys free. His other hand plunged into the water and groped for the seatbelt catch. He felt his ribs protest as the belt released and his body pitched forward. He grabbed the doorframe and swore as grains of glass punctured his skin.

Next he tried opening the door. It moved a couple of inches, then jammed. Either it had met resistance in the ditch, or the frame was buckled. Using his elbow to sweep the frame clear of glass, he levered himself into a crouching position on the seat. As he did the car shifted slightly, sliding a few inches deeper into the muddy water. With a sudden irrational vision of the whole car going under, he reached out of the driver's window, gripped the roof and hauled himself up and out. He left a wet muddy smear across the roof as he pulled himself over the back of the car and then half jumped, half fell on to the grassy bank.

He lay still for a minute, gasping for breath, tears in his eyes, cold and wet and hurting in a dozen places, but more grateful to be alive than he would have thought possible. He pressed his face into the grass and inhaled its sweet aroma and the rich loamy scent of the soil beneath.

Then he became aware of a low vibrating rumble through the earth. Seconds later headlights speared the darkness. A car. He was about to jump to his feet and flag it down when self-preservation kicked in. He had two very good reasons to stay hidden.

Firstly, the car that forced him off the road had followed him from the hotel, overtaken at high speed, then turned round and driven back towards him. It might still be in the area.

The second reason lay in pieces in the flooded footwell. When he licked his lips he could taste a hint of Scotch. Maybe not enough in his bloodstream to get him disqualified, but he couldn't take the chance.

He waited for the car to pass, the rasp of its tyres taking an age to recede. Then he got to his feet and did his best to check himself over.

He was a mess. Jeans and most of his jacket soaked. Mud everywhere. Blood in his hair and on his face. His right palm dotted with small incisions, now throbbing even more urgently than his head wound. He patted his pockets and found his wallet and phone intact. The phone still worked, but there was no signal.

'Who am I gonna call?' he asked himself.

He turned and examined the ditch. In darkness the car was almost impossible to see. It was pitched at such an angle that dipped headlights would miss the reflectors at close range, so there was a good chance it wouldn't be discovered until morning.

He set off back the way he'd come, feet squelching on the road, pumping his arms to try and generate some warmth. There was a small chain of lights in the distance, one of which must be Julia's hotel. He figured he'd driven a couple of miles on a meandering route. In a dead straight line it was probably a lot less, but going cross-country in the dark presented its own hazards: ditches, fences, animals.

After a couple of hundred yards he reached a layby and sat down. A sporty hatchback screamed past, pumping bass from its speakers like a gigantic heart. He glimpsed three or four kids who looked scarcely old enough to drive. One of them gleefully gave him the finger. Craig laughed.

He took off his shoes, wrung out his socks and put them back on. It didn't make a lot of difference, but he felt better for it. Gazing along the road, he noticed a sign with an arrow indicating a footpath. There were symbols for parking, toilets and the sea, along with the words: '1 Mile.'

A mile to the coast, then he'd turn left and head along the beach to the hotel. He looked at his watch, which had also survived intact. It was seven o'clock. He pictured Julia warm and relaxed as she sat down to dinner. He started fantasising about a hot bath and a mug of coffee.

The path was uneven and overgrown with weeds. He had to pick his way carefully, but his eyes were now accustomed to the dark, and he found he could see quite well. The sky was clear and full of stars, the sea a faint silvery glimmer on the horizon.

Then a bright yellow-orange flare caught his attention. It was coming from the western end of the chain of lights. It seemed to grow and fade in strength, with a pulsing, sinuous movement. The sky above it had grown hazy, blotting out the stars. That's when he put it together. He started to run.

Forty-Five

Someone was shouting her name. Julia tried to respond, but the sound that emerged was too weak to be heard over the alarm. In despair she shut her eyes and let her body go limp, and as she did a kind of nervous spasm caused her leg to move. She flexed it, and managed to swing one foot off the bed.

From the hall, Kate called her name again, her voice tight with fear and desperation. There was an urgent thumping on her door.

'Julia? Are you in there? Wake up!'

'I'm here,' Julia croaked, desperately afraid that Kate would give up and leave her. 'I'm coming.'

Regaining command of her body, she made a tremendous effort to raise herself, first on to her elbows, and then virtually slithered off the bed. She could feel control of her muscles gradually returning, and she was able to get upright. She felt woozy and disorientated, and there was an uncomfortable dull ache in her abdomen, but at least she could move.

Thank God she was still dressed, she thought. There was no way she would be capable of putting clothes on in a hurry. Glancing back at the bed, she noticed her father's diary and picked it up, then stumbled towards the door. Kate was shouting and knocking again.

Julia unlocked the door and was almost bowled over as Kate burst in. The air behind her was murky with smoke. The whole building seemed to be vibrating with the commotion of raised voices, thumping footsteps and the muffled roar of the fire.

'Come on,' Kate said, grabbing her arm and pulling her out of the room. There was no time for explanation. Julia did her best to run, one hand cupping her mouth to reduce the effect of the foul, choking air.

With Kate virtually propping her up, she descended the stairs into thicker smoke, billowing from the front doorway and the residents' lounge. A figure backed out of the room, holding a fire extinguisher. It was Sandy, the chef. She turned towards them, her face bright red, tears streaming from her eyes. She shook her head.

'No good. It's spreading too quickly.' From inside the room they heard two small explosions. Bottles of spirits igniting.

'Upstairs is clear,' Kate shouted. 'Just get out.'

Sandy nodded, gesturing towards the kitchens. 'That way.'

Kate took the lead, still holding on to Julia, with Sandy close behind. Although Julia's legs felt stronger now, the pain in her abdomen was growing more intense. Her eyes were smarting and her heart felt like it was beating at an unnatural rhythm. They hurried through the kitchens and saw a couple of other guests just ahead of them.

The cold night air was a fabulous shock, like plunging into a pool. There were about a dozen women grouped on the lawn, some doubled over, some crying and hugging each other, some just standing in a daze. There was a loud crash and flames leapt towards the French doors which led out to the garden.

'Get back!' Kate shouted. She and Sandy began ushering people to the bottom of the garden. Julia could hear her muttering as she did a head count.

'Best to head for the beach,' she said. 'Then along the path to the road. The fire brigade are on their way.'

'What happened?' Julia asked. 'Was it an electrical fault?'

There was another crash from the building, and at the same time the alarm abruptly cut out. Julia glanced back and saw smoke pouring from an upstairs window. Sandy saw it too, and looked heartbroken.

'Brick through the window,' she said, 'followed by a Molotov cocktail. One in the lounge, one through the front door. Bloody miracle they didn't hit anyone.'

They reached the gate, everyone trying to file through without panicking. Someone stumbled, and there was a shriek. 'It's all right,' Kate shouted. 'Just follow me.'

Once they were through the gate, Julia insisted she could walk unaided. While Kate went off to check on the other guests, Julia rested for a moment and wiped her eyes. She felt much more alert now, but the nagging pain had spread to her lower back and kidneys. Trying not to dwell on it, she followed the line of guests around the perimeter of the grounds. Smoke poured into the sky, and tiny fragments of ash rained down on them. The sea lay off to her left, dark and almost silent, just a faint slurp against the sand.

The hotel had been firebombed. That was crazy. Why the hell would—

Then she thought of Peggy Forester, burned to death within hours of their visit.

Reaching the footpath that ran between the beach and the road, she heard sirens approaching. There was a small crowd of spectators on the pavement, watching the fire from a safe distance. When they spotted the line of evacuees, a few came forward to help. Julia saw one man remove his coat and offer it to a woman wearing only a thin dress.

The first fire engine drove past, braking hard as it reached the hotel. A second appliance was just behind it. Almost everyone turned to look, and there were a few muted shouts and cheers. Then Julia noticed one of the spectators had kept his back to the road. He was watching the guests file towards him. Too far away to see clearly, but he was wearing dark clothes. His face was obscured by something. He'd turned his collar up, or perhaps had a scarf wrapped around his mouth.

Despite the distance, Julia knew the moment his gaze settled on her. She felt it in every nerve ending, and as he broke away from the crowd and hurried towards her, she recognised the set of his body: fast, powerful, determined. Exactly the way he had moved when he strode into sight from Hurst Lane.

It was him. The second killer. Coming for her.

Julia turned and ran.

Her only option was west, towards the dunes at the back of the beach. The killer had blocked her path to the north. The tide was too close to go south, and the burning hotel was to the east.

A cautionary voice told her she shouldn't be doing this. In her current condition just walking was a struggle, let alone running. But it had been an instinctive decision, made without any rational thought. Too late to change her mind now.

It got darker and colder as she climbed the dunes. The sand was loose and deep, and after just fifteen or twenty strides she was exhausted. Marram grass whipped at her bare feet, and a discarded Coke can sliced the skin on her little toe. Risking a look behind her, she saw a vague black shape reach the path and pause, scanning the beach.

Julia threw herself down, dropping the diary. Spotting a deeper hollow about ten feet away, she crawled towards it, grabbing clumps of grass and wriggling on her belly. She was acutely aware of how isolated she was, but knew that staying in the crowd wouldn't have protected her if the killer was armed. At least this way she wasn't putting other people in danger.

Any more than she had already, she thought grimly.

Reaching the hollow, she curled up, paddling with her feet and hands to dig herself into the sand. It was freezing cold, and she began to shiver. The pain in her lower back was spreading through her body like icy water, a sensation accompanied by a haunting image of internal bleeding. She fought off the idea that she might escape from the killer, only to fall unconscious and perish alone in the sand.

She lay on her side, her sight of the dunes now restricted to just a few yards. Sounds drifted across the beach as if from another world: sirens, doors slamming, the crackle and spit of the hungry fire.

And then something closer. Much closer.

Heavy footsteps on the sand.

She pressed herself into the hollow, trying to merge with the land. She stopped breathing. Above her the sky opened like a vast dome filled with stars, each one impossibly cold and remote. She felt a wave of vertigo, a feeling that she might tip forward and be pitched into the void.

A few grains of sand fell on her face. She heard an exhalation, angry and frustrated. He was right above her, perhaps only a couple of feet away, but the shape of the dune meant he couldn't see her.

He must have gone out on to the beach and circled round. That meant he'd guessed her route. Outmanoeuvred her. One more step and she was dead.

She shut her eyes and waited. Her lungs felt as though they would burst. Her head swam with the effort of not breathing, not moving, not jumping to her feet and begging him to finish her off: anything to break the unbearable tension of not knowing if she would live or die.

There was another angry sigh. Another dusting of sand on her eyes and her lips.

Then something snarled, low and menacing and very close.

Forty-Six

It was a dog. Julia could hear it panting. She thought she could smell it, too, a warm wet odour, with a tang of the sea.

The dog growled again. This time she placed it. Across to her right, a few feet away.

A man's voice cried, 'Billy! C'mere, now!'

But the dog held its ground. It went on snarling, and it sounded like it meant business. She heard the rustle of movement from above, the killer reacting to this new threat.

'Billy! Heel!'

The dog gave an answering yelp, but instead of running back to its owner, it took another couple of steps towards her. She could see it now, a lean black shape against the sand, lowering its head as if preparing to attack.

Craig had once prided himself on his fitness, but it had been a few years since he'd exercised on a serious basis. One of his knees started protesting within the first mile or so, and a stitch set in that left him gasping as much as panting. Every time he felt his resolve weakening, he glanced up and focused on the leaping flames. He had to know where the fire was. He had to know Julia was all right.

He heard the sirens as the fire engines passed on the coast road.

Smoke was pouring into the sky, and he prayed that wherever it was, the occupants had escaped in time.

When he got to the beach he found running on the compacted sand much easier on his joints, and he was even able to pick up his speed a little. Despite the burn in his lungs, he felt almost euphoric, as if the ordeal he'd been through had only made him stronger and more focused.

He was a couple of hundred yards away when he saw beyond doubt that it was the hotel. Despite the valiant efforts of the firefighters, the building was being consumed by flames. He knew at once that in one sense he was too late: Julia's fate had already been decided. Either she had got out in time or she hadn't. If she hadn't, there was no way she could survive.

That realisation brought him up short. He leaned over, breathing hard, and spat on to the sand. It was as his heart rate slowed that he became aware of a man's voice, just ahead of him, calling for something. Then he heard barking and saw a dog, up on the dunes. He was about to dismiss it and run on when he spotted something else, a dark shape just beyond the dog that moved slightly, revealing a flash of pale skin.

Quite abruptly, the dog stopped barking, turned and looked at its owner, then ran back towards the beach. Julia waited a few seconds, too scared to move, before cautiously raising her head. Now she could see two figures on the beach. The dog was again growling, but its owner moved in and grabbed its collar. The other figure, instead of hanging back, seemed to be moving in her direction.

Her heart pumped furiously, but she knew she couldn't run any more. She was confused. How had the killer managed to get back down to the beach so quickly, and without the dog sensing it?

Something else bothered her. Even in the darkness, the outline and movement seemed familiar. Not just familiar, she realised. Miraculous.

She called out, as best she could, and tried to sit up. She had to make sure he had noticed her. By now she could see his face, dirty and dishevelled and full of worry. Somehow he didn't look quite right, and she wondered if perhaps he was merely a hallucination, in which case she would probably just fall back and freeze to death in the sand.

His relief at seeing her was so great that at first he didn't stop to wonder what she was doing here. As he reached her, he saw her eyes roll up and she passed out. He knelt down and made sure she was breathing, checked her airways and felt for her pulse. Her skin felt dangerously cold. He eased his hands underneath her and gently began lifting her up. As he did, she moaned and opened her eyes.

'It's okay,' he murmured. 'Take it easy.'

He had her upright when suddenly she wriggled out of his grasp.

'My diary!'

'What?'

She twisted, pointing at something in the shadows. When he was sure she wouldn't collapse, Craig let go of her and searched until he found the diary lying in the sand. Turning back, he saw that Julia's whole body was trembling uncontrollably. Without a word he opened his arms and she fell into his embrace. He held her tight, her tears dampening his neck as she nuzzled into it.

'He was here, Craig,' she said. 'He came to kill me.'

Moving slowly, they made their way over to the road. The crowd of onlookers had grown. There were police cars and ambulances parked at the kerb. Most of the guests were wrapped in blankets and borrowed coats. The fire crews were up on ladders, spraying water from three different vantage points, but it looked like a lost cause.

Julia told Craig what she knew about the firebombing, how she'd spotted the killer and hid from him in the dunes. She thought he might doubt the story, but there wasn't a trace of disbelief in his face.

'He ran me off the road. I think he'd overtaken me a minute earlier, which means he'd followed me from the hotel.'

'So he knew where I was staying?'

'I guess so. After dealing with me, he must have come back here and started the fire.'

'That's not all,' she said. She told him about Peggy Forester. 'The news report was suggesting an accident, or maybe suicide.'

'You think he was there this morning, the same time as us?'

She nodded. 'Did you get a look at the car?'

'Not really. It was a four-wheel drive. A Land Rover, maybe.'

'There was one parked in Hurst Lane. I think I saw it in Falcombe as well.'

The conversation was interrupted by Kate, who ran towards them, holding a blanket. There was a second when her relief was tempered by a suspicious glance at Craig, but she seemed prepared to put aside her misgivings. She wrapped the blanket around Julia, then embraced her.

'What happened to you? I couldn't find you anywhere.'

'I went on to the beach to get some fresh air,' Julia said. Staring over Kate's shoulder, she saw Craig give a rueful nod: endorsing the lie.

They broke apart, and Kate grabbed her hand. 'Come on. We need to get you checked over.'

Julia allowed the other woman to lead her to an ambulance. While she was explaining Julia's medical history to a paramedic, there was a small commotion within the crowd. One of the hotel guests was ushered to a waiting police car and bundled inside, then driven off at high speed. Julia realised it was the woman she had played cards with.

'The police think she might have been the target,' Kate confided. 'She's giving evidence at a trial for heroin smuggling.'

Julia made the right noises of concern and sympathy, and once more exchanged a meaningful glance with Craig. Kate left her in the paramedic's charge and plunged back into the crowd. Julia was helped into the ambulance and lay down on a stretcher. After a thorough examination, the paramedic decided her blood pressure was slightly low, and recommended further tests at hospital.

Then he turned to Craig. 'Are you the next of kin?'

Craig was just a fraction too late to answer, but the paramedic shook his head. 'Doesn't matter. That cut on your head needs looking at, anyway.'

Before they left, the paramedic was called away to treat a firefighter for smoke inhalation. As soon as they were alone, Craig moved close to Julia and spoke quietly.

'It looks like the police have jumped to the wrong conclusion. The question is whether we can risk putting them right.'

'What do you mean?'

'First, we know they don't believe in the idea of a second killer. Secondly, if we make a statement alleging we were followed here, then we should really admit to visiting Peggy Forester. And aside from the killer, I bet we were the last people to see her alive.'

Julia looked doubtful. 'But would they really suspect us . . . ?'

'She's Carl's mother. Carl murdered my dad and tried to murder you. Frankly, I can't think of a better motive for wanting her dead.'

Julia sighed, realising how credible that might seem, compared to their own allegations.

'As for what happened here tonight, what can you really tell them? A man followed you along the path, and you ran away from him. Did you see him clearly? Can you describe him?'

She shook her head. 'I didn't imagine it,' she said, her voice wavering.

'Hey. I know that.' He took her hand. 'He drove me into a ditch, remember? I'm just saying there isn't a lot we can prove at the moment. Certainly not enough to get the police interested. All we risk doing is putting ourselves in the frame for Peggy's death.'

Julia had to agree. 'So we're on our own?'

'I'm afraid so. But at least tonight he's come out into the open. We know he exists, and he's shown us what he can do. We really only have one choice now, don't we?'

Julia saw the cold anger in his eyes. She heard movement outside the ambulance, the paramedic returning, and quickly nodded.

'We fight back,' she said.

PART THREE

Forty-Seven

Vanessa was awake by 6 a.m. Most nights now she slept only fitfully, woken by poor circulation and delirious visions of death. Often there was a pressing need to urinate, and although she had accepted the humiliation of incontinence protection, there were many times when she could not bring herself to use it. Better to suffer the discomfort of getting up and struggling to the en suite bathroom.

Afterwards she decided against returning to bed. The room was too hot, and her skin felt slick with sweat. In small bird-like steps she moved to the window and drew the curtains back, intending to let in some fresh air.

A grey, misty dawn cast an ethereal light over the countryside. The sky above the Downs was pale and clear, promising another unseasonably warm day. Vanessa watched birds circling high overhead and heard the distant competing cries of gulls and crows. It was only when he moved that she noticed George in the garden.

He was at the far end of the lawn, sitting on the bench that overlooked the terraced area leading down to the tennis court. At the top of the steps was a large stone plinth forming the base of a tiered fountain. The centrepiece of the top tier was a delicately carved figurine of an angel. As Vanessa watched, George leaned forward and almost toppled on to the path in front of it.

He remained on his knees, not moving. She imagined the cold seeping into his ageing joints, but if he was aware of it he gave no sign. He was dressed in the same trousers and sweater as the night before, and she wondered if he had slept at all.

Then, to her astonishment, she saw him clasp his hands together and dip his head in prayer. She had to say it to herself before she could believe it.

He's praying to the stone angel.

It brought a smile to her face, but never one to soften her own stone heart. She whispered to the glass: 'You won't bring her back.'

Seven o'clock, and Julia was lying in bed, staring at the ceiling of her flat in Lewes. After nearly four weeks away, the surroundings felt both comforting but slightly unfamiliar. When she'd finally got to bed she thought she might sleep for days, and yet just five hours later she was awake and reflecting on what she had said to Craig.

We fight back.

Now, with the clarity that daylight brought, much of that confidence had evaporated. Instead she felt an irrational conviction that the killer was untouchable.

After a swift journey in the ambulance, she and Craig had spent the evening in the Conquest Hospital in St Leonards. While Craig waited in A&E to have his cuts cleaned and dressed, Julia underwent a thorough range of tests, including a CT scan, and her heart rate and blood pressure were monitored over several hours. Finally she was seen by a disarmingly handsome young doctor whose upbeat conclusion didn't preclude him from delivering a severe rebuke.

'You've had a remarkably lucky escape,' he told her, 'and not just from the fire. There's a lot of messed-up tissue in there.' He poked a long finger in the direction of her belly. 'Unless you let it heal properly, there's a chance the whole caboodle will rupture like a bag of rotten tomatoes.' He smiled at the expression on her face. 'I'm resorting to such unpleasant imagery precisely because it's more likely to lodge in your mind. Now, repeat after me.' He intoned in a slow, exaggerated voice: 'Walking is good, but walk slowly. Don't run.'

Feeling about seven years old, Julia repeated, 'Walk slowly. Don't run.'

'No jumping, climbing or heavy lifting.'

'No jumping, climbing or heavy lifting.'

'I will adopt a lifestyle appropriate to a sensible young woman recovering from a serious gunshot wound.'

'No,' said Julia. 'That's just too condescending.'

The doctor laughed. 'Yeah, I was pushing it a bit, but you get the point, don't you?'

It was nearly midnight before she was able to leave. She was touched to find Craig waiting for her, and even more gratified when he insisted they take a taxi back to Lewes.

'But it'll cost a fortune,' she said. 'Surely there are still trains running?'

'You're not getting a train after what you've been through, and neither am I.'

After hushed negotiations at the taxi rank, and a quick detour to a cashpoint, they drove home in relative comfort. Sitting together on the back seat, sharing an exhausted, intimate silence, there was a moment when Julia was tempted to raise the one thorny issue that remained between them. She was still debating how to broach the subject when she fell asleep, and she didn't awake until they reached the Cuilfail tunnel on the approach to Lewes. She opened her eyes to find Craig watching her, a gentle smile on his face, and knew she couldn't mention it now.

Her flat was one of six in a double-fronted Edwardian villa in a narrow road behind the castle. When the taxi pulled up, Craig insisted on seeing her safely inside. Her main set of keys had been left in the hotel, but fortunately one of her neighbours kept a spare set. Even more fortunately, she didn't resent being woken by Julia.

Craig followed her up the stairs and waited while she unlocked her door. 'You sure you're going to be all right? You're welcome to the spare room at my dad's place.'

'I have to get used to living here again at some point. Might as well be tonight.'

Craig didn't look happy about it, but finally relented. 'I guess there's no reason to assume the killer has your address, but don't answer the door to strangers. Don't let anyone in here.'

'Craig, I've lived on my own for years. I know the score.'

'Yeah. Sorry. But ring me if you need anything.'

His farewell was accompanied by a kiss on the cheek, and Julia was struck by the contrast with the last time they'd parted; how morose she had felt that their journey together might have ended.

Once inside she had gone straight to bed. Her sleep was deep and dreamless, and she'd woken this morning with the feeling that she was entering a new phase of her life. The fire at the hotel had interrupted her recuperation, but also served as a warning that she had to take the whole process more seriously from now on.

In the meantime, the day stretched ahead of her with the promise of nothing more than simple domestic chores. After so long away from her home, it was a blissful prospect.

At seven-thirty she made coffee – black, because there was no milk – and took it back to bed. After a little more daydreaming she picked up the diary, which she'd kept with her like a talisman at the hospital, careful never to let it out of her sight. She was aware of a reluctance to intrude on her father's privacy, and at first she could only skim the pages, as if this way she was merely skipping lightly through her parents' lives, rather than trampling all over them.

Until a name stopped her dead. Left her gripping the diary, staring at it in disbelief.

Carl Forester.

It appeared in the second week of August. Earlier entries had revealed her father fretting over the conifer trees in the back garden. They'd grown too high and become unmanageable. The publican at the Green Man recommended Forester, described by her father as *a local chap, from Falcombe, willing to do odd jobs*.

Feeling a tightness in her chest, she turned the page to the following week. She spotted the name again, in the entry for 17 August.

Carl Forester here this afternoon. Cut the conifers by eight or nine feet. I should be able to handle them from now on. Charged £30 cash. Seems a good deal. A nice enough lad, but very quiet. Possibly not 'all there'.

She read it half a dozen times before it sank in. Then she shut the diary, unable to face any more.

Carl Forester had known her parents. He had been in their house. He'd probably been offered endless drinks while he was working. Perhaps he'd eaten their biscuits or some home-made cake.

She had an image of him standing in their garden, his spiky hair wet with sweat. A glass of lemonade in one hand, perhaps a chainsaw in the other. Her father doing his best to make conversation, perhaps pointing out the rose bushes or the shed he'd so proudly assembled.

At any moment Carl could have snapped. He could have killed them. Was the rage already building? Was he harbouring fantasies about unleashing death on the village?

She lay back on the bed and tried to make sense of it. She knew her response was irrational, but to discover her parents had had a seemingly innocent encounter with Forester, with the man who had tried to kill her, affected her in ways she couldn't explain.

She closed her eyes and a rush of images ran through her mind. The chase across the village green. The second killer striding towards Forester. Carl's whoop of celebration as the two men exchanged a high five.

Then she remembered something that made her sit up with a jolt. The whoop. The sound he'd made.

And she knew she had to go back to Chilton.

Forty-Eight

Three or four times a week DI Sullivan ate breakfast at a transport café on the A3, a few miles from his home in New Malden. It was his cardinal rule that these breakfasts were consumed without interruption, so any and all incoming calls were ignored for the duration of the meal. On Thursday morning this proved hugely beneficial.

Only when he'd wiped the plate with the last piece of toast, drained his mug of tea and wiped a blob of ketchup from his shirt did he pick up his phone. There was a short, terse message from Craig Walker, wanting to arrange a meeting. The hint of a demand irked Sullivan, so he decided to make Craig wait.

First he rang George Matheson and gave him the inside track on the fire at Peggy Forester's place. The body they'd recovered from the ruins was almost definitely hers.

'What about the cause?'

'There's not much left for forensics to work with, but it's about fifty–fifty between accident or foul play. Some evidence of an accelerant in the kitchen, but it was probably the booze she was always chucking down her throat.'

'That's interesting,' George said. 'Have you identified any recent visitors to the house?'

Sullivan's antenna twitched. 'Sounds like you know something.'

'Craig Walker was there yesterday morning. Along with Julia Trent.'

'I'll check, but I don't think they've come forward.' He whistled. 'Do you think they topped her?'

'I wouldn't like to say,' George quickly added. 'Obviously I'm telling you this in an unofficial capacity.'

'Of course. Do you want to make it official?'

'I'm not sure if that's altogether wise.'

'Could be more useful to sit on it for now.'

George cleared his throat. 'Well, yes. That was my thinking.'

Sullivan barely ended the call before a cackle of laughter burst out. Talk about lucky. He pulled at his mouth a couple of times, trying to form a solemn expression for his next conversation.

Craig must have been getting his kids ready for school. There was a girl whingeing in the background.

'What's this about a meeting?' Sullivan said.

'We need to discuss my investigation.'

'What's that got to do with me? I gave you the report and the address of the hotel. That's me done.' He stopped there, careful not to over-play his disinterest.

'I think you'll want to hear this.' Craig sounded subdued, hard to make out above the whining girl. Sullivan wondered why he didn't just give her a slap.

'All right,' he said. 'I can spare you half an hour this afternoon.'

Julia had several misgivings about going out so soon, but justified it on the basis that she wasn't breaking her pledge to the doctor. She didn't intend to do any running, jumping or anything else. And he hadn't said she mustn't drive.

Leaving the flat, she was half convinced her Mini wouldn't start, although a friend who lived locally had been keeping an eye on it for her. The handbrake was a bit sticky, but the car started on the third attempt. Apart from religiously checking her mirror for signs of someone following, it was a wonderful feeling to be driving again: another big step towards regaining her independence.

She was in Chilton at just after eight. The good weather was holding, and by the time she parked outside the church it was probably fifteen degrees warmer than it had been on 19 January. Certainly mild enough for just a cotton top and a light jacket.

Aside from that, there were some disturbing similarities with the morning of the massacre. No one in sight, and little sound apart from the coarse cry of the rooks. Her muscles kept flexing as she crossed the green, her body willing her to jump in the car and drive away.

A couple of For Sale boards had gone up in Arundel Crescent. At number two the trap window in the upstairs bedroom was open, just as it had been on 19 January. As she reached the front door Julia heard thumping inside, then a clamour of voices. She rang the doorbell, wondering if it stood any chance of being heard.

After a few seconds an internal door banged shut, muffling the noise. There was the rattle of a chain, and the front door opened a few inches. A man peered out.

'Gordon Jones?'

'Who wants to know?'

'My name's Julia Trent. I wonder if I could speak to your wife?'

He scrutinised her carefully. 'You were here, on the nineteenth?'

'Yes.'

Removing the safety chain, he opened the door and seemed to relax. He was in his forties, Julia guessed, with thin limbs but a large torso. He had grey hair and a thick moustache that aged him by at least five years. His forehead was creased into a permanent frown.

There was another loud bang from inside the house. Gordon turned and shouted, 'Stop fighting! You've got ten minutes to get ready.'

Julia offered a sympathetic smile. 'I need to talk to your wife.'

'She doesn't live here now.' His voice was flat, as though all the emotion had been wrung from him long ago. 'She had a . . . a nervous breakdown. I tried to help her. We all did. But she insisted on moving out. She was worried the children might be taken away from her.'

A piercing shriek was followed by raucous laughter. Gordon flinched.

'I have a childminder while I'm at work, and my mother helps out when she can. But it's not the same.'

'How often does she visit?'

'She doesn't. It's too upsetting.' He pushed a hand through his hair and let out a juddering sigh. 'That bastard ruined a lot of lives. Sometimes I wish he hadn't shot himself. I'd like to . . .' He trailed off, his gaze focusing on a different future. Then he snapped back to the present. 'I'll get you the address.'

When he opened the living-room door, Julia glimpsed two small boys wrestling on the floor. An older girl danced round them, pumping her fists and chanting: 'Fight, fight, fight!'

Gordon returned with a notepad and pen. 'It's a rented flat in Brighton,' he said as he wrote it out.

'You go to see her?'

'Once or twice a week.' Almost shamefully, he added, 'She never answers the door.'

'Why not? You didn't do anything wrong.'

'I was away, the day it happened. On a damn stag weekend, of all things. I don't think she'll ever forgive me for making her cope on her own. That's my role, isn't it? Husband and father. I'm supposed to protect my family.'

But nothing happened to them, Julia almost said. She knew Alice's response had nothing to do with what was logical or rational. Gordon probably knew it too.

A sob escaped his throat. Embarrassed, he tore the page from the notebook and held it out. 'Tell her we miss her,' he said. 'Tell her to come home.'

The buzz of his intercom woke him at some ungodly hour. Toby ignored it, but then his mobile rang. His business phone, which narrowed the range of callers somewhat.

Swearing, he threw back the covers and rubbed his eyes. After checking the mobile's display, he swore again and got up to answer the intercom. A familiar voice growled, 'You've got about thirty seconds to make yourself decent.'

He pulled on jogging pants and a t-shirt, and was taming his hair with water when Vilner rapped on the door. Toby lived in a sixth-floor apartment in Chelsea Harbour, which cost a straight million five years ago but had already appreciated by nearly fifty per cent.

He opened the door. Vilner was alone, looking fresh and relaxed and dangerously cheerful. He was wearing jeans and a suede jacket over a white shirt. He grinned when he saw Toby.

'Not a morning person, then?'

'No. What do you want?'

'Coffee would be good, for starters.'

Toby scowled, but didn't argue. Vilner followed him into the living room, where he made a show of admiring the apartment. Drawn by the view, he wandered over to the balcony doors and looked out at the marina and the Thames beyond. Toby went into the adjoining kitchen, put the kettle on and found an old jar of instant coffee. He wasn't going to brew fresh for Vilner. When he returned to the living room, Vilner let out a long whistle.

'So this is how you rich boys live? Bit bloody different from where I grew up.'

'You know, I'm surprised you can walk with the size of the chip on your shoulder.'

A flash of anger from Vilner, then a grudging smile. His eyes roved the room and settled on one of the few things that looked out of place. A little pile of paper on the floor.

'As it happens, I had a very modest start in life,' Toby said quickly. 'My mother never had any money. My aunt and uncle offered help, but she didn't always take it.'

'Why's that?' Vilner was ambling towards the document.

'They didn't approve of her lifestyle. There were always conditions attached. Sometimes she wouldn't meet them.'

'So you lost out as a result?' Vilner leaned over and examined the title page.

'Not really,' Toby said, adding smugly: 'Not once they put me in boarding school.'

But Vilner wasn't listening. He knelt a little awkwardly and picked up the report. The report Toby had sworn not to show to anyone else.

'Where'd you get this?'

'George. Someone leaked it to him.'

Vilner wore a triumphant smile. 'You won't mind if I have a look?'

'Go ahead.' There was nothing he could have done, Toby told himself. He made the coffee and brought it out. Vilner was leafing through the report.

'Craig Walker's seen this,' he said. 'Him and Julia Trent were at your uncle's yesterday.'

Before Toby could put on a poker face, it was too late. Vilner tutted. 'Oh dear. I don't think our Toby's in the loop any more.'

Toby sipped his coffee, and grimaced. The question he wanted to ask was, *What were you doing there?* But instead he said, 'What did they want?'

'A guarantee there won't be a second application.'

'I hope George didn't give it to them. He's agreed I could get started on preliminary work for the development.'

Vilner exuded a vague sense of pity as he searched Toby's face, as though looking for something he already knew was absent. It made Toby uneasy.

'I know my uncle's getting worked up about this,' he said, keen to break the silence. 'But I don't see the problem myself. I think we'll be fine.'

'Well, that's a comfort,' said Vilner with a dry insincerity. Still holding the report, he set his coffee down and wandered out of the room as if this were his own apartment.

'Where are you going?'

'Having a look round.'

Toby felt a sense of dread as he followed Vilner into the spare bedroom, which was used as an office. There was a large pinboard on the wall, covered in architectural drawings and site plans and an artist's impression of the finished development in sumptuous watercolours. There was also a double-page spread from the *Daily Express*, showing a photograph of Carl Forester as a mischievous gap-toothed schoolboy beneath the headline: THE MAN WHO KILLED A VILLAGE.

Vilner stood and examined the board, the blond stubble on his chin glittering under the recessed lights. He tutted, shaking his head. Just as Toby went to ask what was wrong, Vilner dropped the report and grabbed the front of his t-shirt. His other hand was now holding a pistol.

That's why he was wearing a loose shirt, Toby thought. *That's why he couldn't kneel properly.*

Vilner slammed him against the wall. Toby groaned and tried to protest, but Vilner forced the gun into his mouth, drawing blood that mingled with the oily taste of the metal.

'I'm getting sick of this,' Vilner growled. 'You. George. All these different fucking agendas, and I reckon at the top of every one it says: screw Vilner.'

Toby did his best to shake his head. Not true.

'You owe me over a quarter of a million quid. You promised me a contract worth a million or more. But I'm starting to think I'm being sold a pup.'

His pressure on the gun eased up a little. Enough for Toby to splutter and say, 'You're not. I swear it. No one's trying to rip you off.'

'Then sell this place. Pay me what you owe.'

'I can't.' Toby swallowed blood. 'It's in George's name.'

Vilner shook his head. 'You useless fucking parasite.'

'The development,' Toby said, hating the way it came out as little more than a gargle. 'It'll be worth the wait.'

'Yeah? Well, you'd better make bloody sure it happens. Otherwise

I'll find another way to get what I'm owed. The messy, painful way. You understand?'

Toby nodded. Vilner stepped back, swept up the report and marched out of the room. Toby waited until the front door slammed shut before sinking to the floor and covering his face with his hands.

Forty-Nine

As she crossed the green, Julia's gaze was fixed on the grass ahead. She wasn't aware of anyone nearby until someone said, 'Miss Trent?'

She started, almost dropping the note, and found George Matheson beside her. Registering her alarm, he stepped back. 'Sorry. I didn't mean to startle you.'

She said nothing. Her heart was beating wildly; her body clammy with panic. To her relief, a man emerged from one of the homes in the crescent. She wasn't alone. She had witnesses.

George's face was creased with anxiety. A sheen in his eyes suggested recent tears. While she regained her composure, he studied the floral tributes heaped around the tree.

'Isn't it peculiar how grief has to be paraded these days? I've always found it rather off-putting, but there's no doubting the sincerity.'

Julia said coolly, 'I suppose we each do what's best for us.'

'Absolutely.' He nodded towards the crescent. 'I take it that wasn't a social visit?'

'I wanted to see Alice Jones.'

'Still determined to unearth a conspiracy?'

Stung by his derision, she said, 'I have my own reason to speak to her.'

He waited for an explanation, but she was determined not to supply it.

'You've heard about Peggy Forester?' he said.

'The fire? Yes. It's a terrible tragedy.'

'I imagine the police might take a more cynical view.'

'What do you mean by that?'

'You and Mr Walker visited her yesterday. Surely you've offered to make a statement?'

His confidence demolished any hope that she could lie. Instead she responded with a challenge. 'No, we haven't yet. Why? Do you think we killed her?'

George let the question hang in the air. While she waited, Julia decided to say nothing about the firebombing at the hotel. Better to see if he already knew.

Eventually he conceded the point. 'All right. It may have been no more than an unfortunate accident.'

'Or maybe someone didn't like what she told us.'

'That Carl once borrowed a motorbike from a friend? I hardly think that constitutes a threat to anyone.' His tone softened as he gestured at the green around them. 'Isn't it possible you were mistaken about a second killer? In such a stressful situation, your state of mind must have been . . .'

'Deranged?' She let out a laugh.

He dipped his head in apology. 'That was insensitive of me. And please don't feel I'm being unsympathetic. I admire the way you've coped with your ordeal. And I know what it's like to lose a loved one.' He gestured in the direction of her parents' cottage. 'Will you keep the house, do you think?'

Thrown by the change of subject, she faltered. 'I, er, I haven't decided yet.'

'If you want to sell, I'm willing to pay the market value in cash. No surveys or quibbles.'

She gaped at him, staggered that he could be so blatant.

'It's an offer open to all the residents,' he went on. 'Oh, I know some of them will attribute the murkiest of motives to it. Craig Walker certainly will. But this has nothing to do with the development. I simply want to help in any way I can.'

'And if I say no?'

He spread his arms. 'Your prerogative. I'm making the offer because the massacre may have a detrimental effect on values.'

Julia nodded. She hated to admit it, but it was possible his intentions were genuine.

'I'll bear it in mind,' she said. 'I still have their effects to clear out.'

'Another harrowing task.' Looking wistful, he said, 'I remember when my mother died, sorting through her papers and getting an entirely new perspective on her life.'

His sympathetic tone invited Julia to confide in him. 'I've been reading my father's diary,' she said. 'It turns out my parents knew Carl Forester. He cut down some trees for them last summer.'

'I believe he did casual work for a lot of people round here.'

'It was just such a shock, seeing his name. Knowing he'd been inside their house.'

'You're wondering how it didn't seem obvious to them, what he was capable of?'

'Yes. I suppose that's it.'

He expelled a long, heartfelt sigh. 'It's scant consolation, but I've done much the same thing myself.'

Craig made it from Chilton to Crawley by seven-thirty, via two taxis and a train. He'd shaved, showered and was wearing clean clothes, but when Nina opened the door her first words were: 'What the hell's happened to you?'

His hand had risen to the cut on his head. There was a nasty lump, but it was concealed by his hair. Maybe something showed in his eyes.

He gave her a brief update, making light of the accident. He didn't mention the second killer, or the fact that he'd been drinking. Nina's only comment about Peggy Forester was: 'Serves her right. She belongs in hell, doesn't she?'

Craig gave a half-hearted shrug, which earned him a dirty look. Nina thought he was disagreeing out of spite. She picked up her travel case and said goodbye to Tom and Maddie.

'Where is it again?' he asked.

'Manchester. I'll be back in time to collect the kids tomorrow afternoon.'

He accompanied her to the front door, the unasked question writhing in his head like a trapped bird. *Is Bruce going with you?*

She didn't kiss him. Didn't even say goodbye.

After speaking to DI Sullivan, he walked the children to school, then popped into a bakery and bought croissants for breakfast. He had several hours before he was due to meet the policeman, and in the meantime he had to notify a claim for the damaged Golf and sort out a replacement car.

Abby Clark rang while he was walking back. 'Got that bio you wanted. And you were right.'

It took him a second to remember the favour he had asked. 'Vilner?'

'A decidedly shady character. Be careful how you tread there.'

'What's his connection to George Matheson?'

'Seems to be a link with George's nephew, Toby Harman. Gambling debts, from what I can make out. Among his other talents, Vilner does a lucrative line in moneylending.'

'George's nephew owes money to Vilner?'

'A lot. And I suspect neither he nor George are all that flush with cash at the moment. It seems Vilner was set to provide site security for the housing development, no doubt using the same thugs he employs for debt collection and door staff.'

'So he's counting on the planning application going through?'

'They all are,' said Abby. 'And there's another name I've picked up. A man called Kendrick. He's from Trinidad, apparently.'

'Where does he fit into this?'

'No idea. So far I haven't found anyone who knows him. But I'm starting to get that special tingly feeling. You remember that?'

He snorted. 'Yeah. Just about.'

'I'll go on digging, let you know when I find something.'

Fifty

Alice's flat was in a purpose-built block on a hill to the west of London Road, not far from the Withdean sports stadium. As Julia got out of the car a train thundered past, concealed by a bank of trees, and she realised the flats backed on to the main railway line. That aside, it was a peaceful, pleasant spot. An ideal refuge, Julia thought.

The block was divided into four flats on two floors. There was a glazed front door with an intercom for visitors. She pressed the buzzer, imagining how wretched Gordon Jones must feel each time he stood here. Through the glass she could see a bland communal hallway and a steep flight of steps to the upper flats.

A minute passed with no response. Julia pressed the buzzer again, and a door opened at the end of the hall. A shadow appeared but came no further.

Julia crouched down and pushed her hand into the letter box, lifting the flap up. 'Alice? Is that you? I'm Julia Trent. I don't know if you—'

'Are you alone?' a voice hissed.

'Yes.'

'Do you swear?'

'Yes. Of course.'

A pause, then the shadow moved closer. Although she'd only glimpsed her face in January, Julia thought she had a pretty good idea of what Alice looked like. Seeing her now, Julia's first reaction was that the wrong tenant had answered. This woman looked about fifty, wrapped in a faded pink dressing gown, her face etched with worry lines, her hair more grey than brown. It was only when they made eye contact that Julia recognised her.

'Did Gordon send you?'

Julia nodded. 'You don't seem surprised.'

'I knew you'd come one day,' said Alice with weary resignation. She led Julia along a narrow hallway that had a vaguely institutional feel to it: plain magnolia walls, a tiled floor and an overpowering smell of industrial detergent.

Alice's flat was equally functional, clearly a product of the buy-to-let craze of recent years. Julia entered a good-sized living room that could have come from a daytime makeover show: cheap laminate flooring and a fake fireplace with a seashore theme. There was little sign that Alice had done anything to personalise it. No ornaments or photographs. Not even pictures of her children.

'I never thought you'd survive,' Alice said. She sank on to a pale fabric sofa. Julia noticed a pillow and a duvet neatly stacked on the floor and wondered what was wrong with the bedroom.

She sat at the other end of the sofa. 'What do you mean?'

'I watched them putting you into the helicopter. It was like they were holding a smashed china doll. You were bundled up, but you looked broken inside. They were trying to keep all the pieces so they could glue you back together.'

'I hadn't considered it like that,' Julia admitted. She noticed Alice's eyes were glittering with an unnatural fervour. The pitch of her voice rose and fell as she spoke. At times it was unnervingly high, but Alice didn't seem to be aware of it.

'I almost wish you hadn't,' she added, with no trace of rancour. 'It wasn't our destiny to survive. He should have killed you, and then me. He should have finished the job.' Her laugh sounded like plates of metal grinding together.

'I don't agree,' said Julia. 'I think your destiny is what you make it. I'm proud I came through this. And you should be too.'

'What do I have to be proud of? I was hiding in the corner like a timid little mouse. My children were—' She choked up. 'My children were braver than me.'

'You kept them safe. You did the right thing.'

Alice's eyes narrowed. 'You mean you didn't want me to open the door and let you in?'

'Would it make you feel better if I said I hated you for it?'

'Do you?'

Julia shrugged. 'I don't know. Chances are, I'd never have made it anyway.'

Alice shook her head as if unconvinced, mumbling something under her breath. Julia sighed. She could see now why Gordon had been so despairing.

'You were at the window when Carl chased me out of the church-yard. You told the police you didn't see anything after that.'

Alice turned and found Julia staring at her. She tried to look away but the intensity of Julia's gaze seemed to hold her spellbound.

Julia said, 'I told them there was another man involved. He killed Carl and then shot me. But when Carl first greeted the other man, he made a noise. He whooped.' She hesitated, took a deep breath. 'Your bedroom window was open. The little trap window at the top. You must have heard him.'

A fleeting look of relief, but Julia didn't stop to reflect on it. She leaned closer, her eyes locked on Alice's, daring her to break free. Daring her to lie.

'Please,' she said. 'Tell me what you heard.'

Alice swallowed. Her body was rigid, vibrating with tension. Julia could feel it through the sofa.

'I'm a terrible person,' Alice said at last. 'I lied to the police. I lied to everyone.' She began to weep. 'I don't deserve to be alive.'

* * *

Vanessa spent most of her day in the largest of the first-floor bedrooms. As well as the bed and a wardrobe, there were two easy chairs and a desk. George had also thought to add a TV and music system, a kettle and a small fridge. When Vanessa first saw what he'd done, she said, 'It's like some ghastly motel room. Did you include a trouser press as well?'

When he returned from his walk in the village, she was resting in the armchair, a folded *Telegraph* on the table alongside an untouched cup of tea, her laptop closed at her feet like a sleeping pet.

He made himself a cup and sat in the armchair opposite, stirring his spoon slowly so as not to wake her. There was a tiny clink as he put it down, and he turned back to find her eyes wide open and watching him. The shock made him slop some tea into his lap. He plucked at his trousers, wincing at the heat.

'Careful,' Vanessa said, nodding at his groin. 'You might need it again one day.'

He grunted, unsure how to respond. After taking a sip of tea, he said, 'I've just seen Julia Trent in the village.' He ran through the conversation, recounting Julia's intention to find Alice Jones, and her discovery that Carl had worked for her parents. 'I offered to buy the cottage,' he admitted.

'Pointless,' Vanessa said. 'She'll see it for what it is. Another tactic.'

George said nothing. In her final weeks he'd vowed not to rise to the bait.

'What about Peggy Forester?' Vanessa asked.

'She was very defensive about their visit. They haven't told the police they were there.'

Vanessa's eyes lit up. 'That's worth knowing.'

'I'm not sure it has any real value. Not unless I'm prepared to use it.'

'Aren't you?'

George sighed. 'I don't know. I've a feeling it may be counter-productive. Better for us all if the fire was purely an accident.'

Vanessa regarded him sadly. 'Oh, George, I do believe you're losing your nerve.'

'It won't do you any good,' Alice said. 'I can't get involved.'

'What do you mean?'

Alice responded with another question. 'You know why I'm here? Why I had to leave my children?'

'Gordon said you had a breakdown.'

'It was a bit more than that.' She gave another grating laugh. 'Our neighbours, the Grangers, actually slept through the whole damn thing.'

Julia nodded. She remembered reading it in the police report.

'About a week later I happened to see Brian in the crescent. He was in a foul mood because his car had been damaged on 19 January. He thought one of the emergency vehicles scraped it, but the insurance company was denying liability. He went on and on about it, as if that was the only important thing that happened.'

Alice shook her head. 'I just went ballistic. I had some shopping with me. I took out a bottle of wine and hurled it through his living-room window.'

Julia gasped. 'Was anyone inside?'

'His wife, but she was upstairs, luckily. Then I went indoors, opened another bottle of wine and drank most of it straight down. Then I swallowed two packets of paracetamol. It was only because the Grangers called the police that they found me in time.' She shook her head, as if trying to dislodge the memory. 'After that, there was no chance anyone would trust me with the kids.'

'I'm very sorry,' Julia said. 'Weren't you offered help?'

'Oh, yes. All sorts of fancy counselling. They thought I had post-traumatic whatever it is.'

'PTSD. It's nothing to be ashamed of.'

'Maybe not in your case. All I did was run and hide. I don't deserve any help.'

She hunched over, her head tipping almost to her knees. She covered her face with her hands and her body shook with silent tears. Julia watched helplessly for a moment, then shifted closer and laid her hand on Alice's back, rubbing it gently.

'You don't have to go on suffering like this.'

'Yes I do,' said Alice. 'Because it's not PTSD or anything like that. It's guilt.'

And now Julia understood. She knew why Alice had come here. Why she had chosen to run and hide all over again.

'You heard him, didn't you? The second killer.'

There was a long silence. Then, in a whisper, Alice said, 'I saw him.'

Julia said nothing. She was aware of a heavy weight in her stomach. Eventually Alice straightened up, uncovered her face. Her eyes were raw with pain.

'I heard something that didn't make sense. I waited a bit, then decided to have another look. You must have been up in the tree by that stage. I saw him, a man in motorcycle leathers. He was standing over Carl, holding the gun.'

'This was after he'd shot Carl?'

'Yes. I didn't know if it was good news or not, so I waited till I heard the police siren.'

'Why didn't you tell them?' said Julia, trying to keep the exasperation from her voice.

'When they took my statement, nobody asked me about him. They were all talking as though Carl had shot himself. I already felt like a coward for not trying to help you. I thought . . . if I told them, they'd probably just laugh at me.'

Julia could only nod sadly. Recalling the scepticism that had greeted her own statement, there was a good chance Alice was right.

'And that's why you're here, isn't it?'

'I'm so scared,' Alice said. 'I'm so scared he'll track me down.'

Julia took her hand. 'Hiding's not the answer. I felt exactly the same, but it didn't work.' She paused, debating how much to disclose. Alice sensed it and gave her a questioning look.

'The hotel where I was staying was firebombed.'

Alice gasped. 'Was it him?'

'I think so.'

'And the police? Do they agree with you?'

There was a knowing look on Alice's face, a strength born of cynicism. Julia suspected she was pursuing a hopeless cause, but felt compelled to go on trying.

'We should both go to them. With two of us, there's a better chance of convincing them.'

Alice was defiant. 'What if the killer finds out? What if he targets my children?'

Julia sighed. In her heart she knew Alice was right.

'Your husband thinks it's his fault,' she said. 'He misses you terribly.'

'I can't tell him,' Alice said. 'I have to carry this alone. They're safer this way.'

'What about when the killer's caught?'

'He won't be. How can they catch him if they don't even know he exists?'

'Exactly. That's why you have to come forward.'

'It's catch-22,' said Alice bitterly. She pulled her hand free of Julia's. 'And you shouldn't be stirring up trouble. You should just forget it ever happened.'

'I can't do that,' Julia said.

'Then you're a fool,' Alice declared. 'Because he'll come after you again. And this time he'll kill you.'

Fifty-One

When the phone rang George was in his study, brooding on his wife's advice. Putting Walker and Trent in the frame for Peggy Forester's death might well neutralise the threat they posed to him, but there was also a danger it could backfire. For one thing, the media might choose to portray them as vigilante heroes, which would only increase the potential audience for their conspiracy theories.

His gloom deepened the instant he recognised Toby's voice.

'Vilner. We should pay him off. Whatever it takes. Just get rid of him.'

George smiled at the use of the word 'we'. 'What's brought this on?'

'He's a loose cannon. It was a mistake to offer him the security contract. I accept that now.'

'You still haven't told me what's happened.'

'He came here this morning. He was . . . aggressive. Unstable.'

Toby fell silent, but George waited, sensing there was more to come.

'He took my copy of the report.'

George swore under his breath. 'Did he say what he was going to do with it?'

'Not specifically. But it's leverage.'

Kendrick, thought George, nearly saying it aloud. He wasn't ready to break the news to Toby just yet.

'What makes you think he'll be bought off?'

'Everyone has their price,' Toby said.

George snorted. *And what makes you think I can afford it?* But he didn't say that either. Knowing Toby's cavalier attitude to money, it would have little effect.

'I realise I have no right to ask you,' Toby added. 'But if something's not done now, we all stand to lose out.'

'I'll consider it, although I wouldn't be terribly optimistic. Vilner's no fool. Exploiting weakness is what he's good at.'

It was a deliberate dig at Toby, and his nephew knew it. For once there was no protest, no retaliation, just a meek, conciliatory, 'Thank you.'

George put the phone down, almost wishing Toby had lost his temper. In the heat of an altercation he might have found it easier to deliver the bad news about Kendrick. He also saw how discharging Toby's debts could be regarded as a fair way to conclude their relationship. Severance pay.

As ever when his problems threatened to overwhelm him, he unlocked his desk and took out the photograph he kept hidden at the bottom of the drawer. He placed it on the desk and tenderly stroked his finger across the perfect, beautiful face.

One o'clock, and Sullivan was ensconced in a quiet corner of a comfortable boozer on the edge of Ashdown Forest, polishing off a meat pie and leafing through the *Daily Mail*. He considered buying a third pint but decided to wait and let Walker get it for him.

Craig was predictably punctual, stalking into the pub a moment later. He spotted Sullivan, who lifted his empty glass and mouthed, 'IPA.'

'It's your bloody round,' Craig said when he returned with the drinks. He didn't slop any this time, Sullivan noticed.

'Least you can do after dragging me out here,' he said, raising his glass. 'So what have you got that's so interesting?'

Perhaps he misjudged the tone, because at first Craig looked reluctant to speak.

'Julia Trent told me about the second gunman. I don't know why her allegations weren't taken more seriously.'

'Because there was no evidence found at the scene, and no one else saw him.'

'But the report basically implied she was a headcase. I don't think she is.'

'She was given a rough ride, I'll grant you that.'

'So you accept she's telling the truth?'

Sullivan merely shrugged, lifting his glass to help conceal his growing excitement.

'We have other proof he exists,' said Craig. 'He firebombed Julia's hotel last night, and he ran my car off the road.'

When Sullivan remained silent, Craig's frustration showed. 'I'm not making this up, for Christ's sake. I think the same man might have murdered Peggy Forester.'

'Peggy Forester?' Sullivan repeated thoughtfully. 'Why do you say that?'

Craig faltered. 'Well . . . the fire at her house.'

'Do you possess information suggesting it was started deliberately?'

The formal language clearly spooked Craig. He sat back, struggling to rein in his emotions. 'I've just told you what happened to us yesterday. This isn't just coincidence, or paranoia. Surely you can see that?'

'Oh, I'm open to the idea of another killer,' Sullivan said. 'Though I'm not sure how many of my colleagues would be.'

Craig's relief was palpable. 'So you will make some inquiries?'

'What makes you think I'm not already working on it?'

'What do you mean?'

Sullivan drank, then exhaled cheerfully. 'Okay. You've read the report. Let's say there was another killer. You need a strong motive. There was a real grudge against the Caplans, for a start. And who did the Caplans work for?'

'Matheson,' said Craig, before realising it was a rhetorical question.

'Yep. Plus it was Matheson's gun they stole, and some of Matheson's opponents were the victims. So maybe . . .' He grinned, spotting a tiny light of comprehension in Craig's eyes. 'Maybe it was someone looking to throw doubt on George Matheson. Someone who wants the housing development stopped once and for all.'

He gulped another mouthful of beer. Craig was staring at him, all the colour drained from his face.

'Maybe someone who, for good measure, tried to coerce a serving police officer into revealing inside information, and then targeted a vulnerable witness.'

Craig finally found his voice. 'That's fucking ridiculous.'

'Is it? How do I know you didn't set this hotel on fire, then drive your car into a ditch? Any witnesses to your accident?'

'It was a quiet country road.'

Sullivan shrugged: point proven. For a moment Craig looked like he might lash out. Instead he gritted his teeth and said, 'Carl Forester killed my father.'

'Yeah. Well, according to you and Julia, this other gunman *killed Carl.*'

Craig threw up his hands, as though it was too absurd to merit a response.

Sullivan went on. 'And now you're saying he also killed Peggy Forester.'

'Oh, come on. What are you playing at?'

'Do you know where she lives?'

Craig's gaze slid away. 'Falcombe somewhere.'

'Ever been there?'

'Hey, if you're going to accuse me, you'd better do it by the book. Arrest, caution, legal representation.'

'Ooh, that sounds like a guilty man talking.' Sullivan laughed, beckoning Craig to calm down. 'We're just having a friendly chat.'

'Bullshit. You've got your own agenda here.'

'I'll ask you again. Have you ever been inside Peggy Forester's house? Did you talk to her at any time before her death?'

Craig jumped to his feet. 'You can't really believe I killed her?' He raised his fists, and Sullivan tensed, clutching his beer glass in case he needed to ram it into Craig's face. Purely in self-defence, of course.

But Craig must have seen the folly of his actions, and perhaps also sensed Sullivan itching to retaliate. He kicked his chair back and stormed out.

The Berkshire house came with a study, but it wasn't big enough for Kendrick. He had converted one of the bedrooms instead, adding several desks and upgrading the internet connection to the highest bandwidth available. Jacques was an accomplished programmer and also the designated security expert: he saw to it that the house was swept for listening devices once a week. Kendrick had gained enough advantages from industrial espionage to appreciate its importance, and he was determined never to become a victim of it.

He was doodling on a notepad while reading a document on screen when the call came through. He listened, grim-faced, before saying just three words.

'Okay. Do it.'

He put the phone down and stared blankly at the display. He felt the faintest of tremors as he reflected on the order he'd just given. Not fear, exactly. More like uncertainty. But that was bad enough. This wasn't a decision that could be reversed.

Glancing at the notepad, he saw he'd drawn a number of inter-secting circles around a single word, written in capitals and given a shadow effect. He smiled. He hadn't even been aware of writing it.

Decipio.

Fifty-Two

Craig was back in Chilton by three o'clock, still feeling sick to his stomach. He almost expected to find the police at the Old Schoolhouse, waiting to arrest him. Their absence gave him no comfort. If, as he suspected, Sullivan intended to keep this to himself for his own amusement or gain, the implications were even worse.

He had only himself to blame for the mess he was in. He should have guessed Sullivan wouldn't take him at face value. He wondered if the detective had been playing with him from the start. Perhaps he'd only given him the report in order to lure him into a trap.

When Julia rang, he still hadn't got his thoughts clear. As he picked up the phone he decided to say nothing about the meeting. He was already worried that she didn't fully trust him. The last thing he wanted was to create more doubt, especially after last night's events had seemed to bring them closer.

Julia sounded every bit as tired and dispirited as he did. 'We made a big mistake. We should have gone to the police and told them everything.'

'Why?'

'We forgot that George Matheson knows about our visit to Peggy Forester. I saw him this morning—'

'You saw Matheson?' Without meaning to, he'd snapped at her.

'Yes. I bumped into him in Chilton.' Julia sounded mystified by his tone.

'And did you ask him where his friend Vilner was last night?'

'No. I didn't think of that. Actually, he seemed quite upset. Look, Craig, don't bite my head off. I'm only telling you what happened.'

'Sorry. What were you doing back there so soon?'

She began telling him about an entry in her father's diary which mentioned Carl Forester, and her decision to go to Chilton to speak to Alice Jones. Craig's attention drifted, only snapping back when she said, 'George offered to buy the cottage.'

'What? The cheeky bastard!' He thought of the meeting on Wednesday, and Julia's hunch that George had also got his hands on the police report. And today, the way Sullivan kept pressing him to say if he'd visited Peggy Forester, as though he already knew the answer. He groaned.

Julia halted mid-flow. 'What?'

'Just had a thought about George's mole in the police.'

'Go on.'

'I'll tell you when I know for sure. What were you saying?'

Julia described her visit to Alice's flat. 'She's in a terrible state, torturing herself over what happened.'

'She hid upstairs with her kids. Nothing wrong with that.'

A long pause. Craig even wondered if the connection had been broken. He pressed the phone to his ear and caught Julia's fretful sigh.

'She saw the killer.'

'What?'

'Alice saw him, standing by Carl's body.' She laughed bitterly. 'At least it means I didn't imagine it.'

'No, it's great news,' said Craig. He couldn't understand why she sounded so defeated.

'The trouble is, she point-blank refuses to go to the police. She thinks it's too dangerous to speak out.'

Craig groaned. 'She doesn't have a fraction of your courage.'

'I don't have three children to protect.'

'What about if we just tell the police ourselves?'

'She says she'll deny it, and accuse me of harassing her. We have to face it, Craig. We're on our own with this.'

'Maybe, but we're making progress, I'm sure of that. Look, can we meet up and discuss where we go from here?'

She agreed more readily than he expected. 'I'm coming to Chilton tomorrow, to make a start on clearing out the cottage. Say, ten o'clock at my parents' place?'

'Great.' Ending the call, Craig reminded her to take care, before reflecting that he would have done well to follow that advice when he became involved with Sullivan.

The killer spent a restless evening, thinking about what he had done and what was still to do. Already he was savouring the moment of Decipio's unmasking, the moment when the tables would be turned. Just a day or two away, he hoped.

In the meantime there had been another curt exchange of messages, and Decipio had warned him of a new threat.

When asked if he'd played a part in Peggy Forester's death, his reply was carefully noncommittal. He had no intention of supplying any more of the rope that could hang him. He understood now how naive and trusting he had been, and he was furious with himself.

It was a severe disappointment that both Craig Walker and Julia Trent had emerged unscathed on Wednesday night. Worse still, it didn't seem to have scared them off. Trent was poking around, trying to cause trouble, and it was scant consolation that so far no one else seemed remotely convinced by her story.

In his darker moments he was prey to a queasy conviction that his whole grand scheme was unravelling. That no matter what he did, no matter how bold or resourceful his actions, some tiny snagging detail always remained to catch him unawares. Even something as trivial, as innocuous, as a *fucking diary*.

Fifty-Three

Julia woke on Friday feeling stronger and more refreshed than she had for weeks. Perhaps it was just the effect of a full night in her own bed, or perhaps evidence that she'd recovered from Wednesday's exertions; whatever the reason, it provided a welcome antidote to an otherwise bleak predicament.

Yesterday, after returning from her frustrating visit to Alice Jones, she had occupied herself with mundane chores: shopping, housework, catching up on her mail, while also taking plenty of rest. Once or twice she had picked up her father's diary, but couldn't quite bring herself to read on. In the evening she phoned her brother and some friends to let them know she was back home. It felt like a significant announcement: normal life was about to resume.

Nevertheless, she felt some trepidation as she drove to Chilton. It was difficult not to think about the last time she'd intended to begin the clear-out, or to dwell on everything that had happened in the weeks since then. Without fully acknowledging it to herself, she timed her journey to arrive at ten o'clock so that Craig could accompany her.

It was another mild day, this time with heavy skies and a fresh wind. Julia had to park in the village itself, and as she pulled up Craig emerged from the Old Schoolhouse. He was wearing a thin v-neck sweater over a white t-shirt. It was the first time she'd seen him without a jacket, and she couldn't help noticing how broad his shoulders were. Probably a good job, for it looked like he was carrying the weight of the world on them.

Their greeting was a little awkward. A moment's hesitation, then he kissed her cheek. 'Nobody followed you here?'

She shook her head. 'No. I kept checking.'

'Good. Sounds silly, but we really should take these precautions until the killer is caught.'

Julia nodded, but couldn't help recalling Alice's bitter retort: *How can they catch him if they don't even know he exists?*

As if he'd read her mind, Craig said, 'I can't believe Alice Jones won't help us. Do you think we could get her husband to persuade her?'

'I doubt if she'd listen to him any more than she listened to me.'

Craig sighed. 'And what about Matheson? Is he going to dump us in it over the visit to Peggy Forester?'

'I'm not sure. He seemed to be on a bit of a charm offensive yesterday, but that might change. What was your theory about his police contact?'

Craig looked decidedly evasive. 'Still working on it.'

Julia waited a moment, frowning. 'Okay.' They reached the row of cottages and she found the front-door key. 'Did you get your claim sorted out?'

'The Golf's being recovered today, allegedly. They won't give me a courtesy car until they know if it's repairable, so I've hired one.'

Julia put the key in the lock and then froze. 'Did you hear that?'

'What?'

'Sounded like something inside.'

Not *something*, she realised. *Someone*.

The lock jammed for a second. The door swung open just as another, sharper noise rang out: urgent footsteps clattering on the kitchen floor. The back door banged open, and as Craig pushed past her, Julia glimpsed a dark figure fleeing towards the rear fence. The same dark figure who had hunted her in the dunes on Wednesday night.

Craig ran through the house in pursuit. For a second Julia was transfixed by terror and confusion. Then she came jolting back to life. She couldn't let Craig go it alone. This was her fight, too.

By the time she reached the door Craig was attempting to climb the barbed-wire fence at the bottom of the garden. The fence backed on to a field of dark soil where some kind of winter crop was just emerging. The field rose in a gentle incline for about a hundred yards and the killer was more than halfway up, anonymous in a baseball cap and black coat.

'Wait here,' Craig shouted.

'No.' She joined him at the fence, slightly breathless but otherwise okay. No pain. Craig saw the steely determination in her face and said nothing more. He pressed down on the wire and helped her climb over.

The killer crested the ridge and disappeared from sight. Craig set off after him, Julia lagging behind almost immediately. He was nearly at the top when Julia hit a loose clod of earth and felt her ankle give way. She cried out as she fell, causing Craig to hesitate. He turned and ran back to her.

'What's happened?'

'Twisted my ankle. I'm all right.' She reached out and let him help her up.

'You should have stayed at the house,' he said, then flinched at the ferocity of the look she gave him.

Holding on to his arm, she hobbled the last few yards to the top of the ridge. From here the field dropped away towards a line of oaks next to a stream which marked the eastern perimeter of George Matheson's land. The killer had vanished.

'Bugger!' said Craig. Julia wasn't sure if part of his resentment was that she had slowed him down.

'If he's in the trees, he could have gone either way. We won't catch him.'

'Was it the same man you saw in Camber?'

She nodded. Now that the immediate danger was past, the adrenalin dissipating, she could feel her legs starting to tremble. There was a peculiar coldness spreading through her body, turning every muscle to jelly.

'He must have been lying in wait for you,' Craig said.

Julia tried to respond but her throat had closed. She noticed the clouds had turned black and the sky white, like a photographic negative. She heard Alice, booming out of the air like the voice of God: *He'll come after you again. And this time he'll kill you.*

'What did you say?' Craig asked, but she wasn't aware that she'd spoken. Perhaps he had heard Alice too.

Then he leapt at her, and in her last moment of consciousness she understood that Craig must be the second killer. It had all been a terrible deception.

Fifty-Four

The killer ran, thinking of 19 January, thinking of the risks he had taken, but trying not to dwell on his failure. He had been in the cottage almost an hour. The place was cold and neglected, and with a bit of luck he might have completed his search without being disturbed. Instead, the bitch had turned up with Walker in tow.

He hadn't found anything incriminating, but it was of little consolation. Once again he'd risked exposure, identification, even capture, and gained nothing in return. At the back of his mind a shrill voice warned that the situation was slipping away from him. But he wouldn't listen to it.

Once he was deep in the trees, he made sure he was no longer being pursued, then rested for a few minutes. Instead of dwelling on another wasted effort, he thought about something more inspiring: the embryonic flames licking at Peggy Forester's body. *That* was the true measure of his abilities.

He had considered setting the cottage alight, but rejected the idea. As far as he knew, the police hadn't yet linked the fires at the hotel and Peggy Forester's, but another one might well attract suspicion.

His car was about half a mile away, parked in a beauty spot on the outskirts of Falcombe. When he reached it, he sat inside and spent a while considering his options. He could return home now. Or while he was down here, he could force the issue.

Julia regained consciousness just as Craig staggered to a halt, pondering how to get her over the fence. His breathing was laboured and he was very flushed.

'I'm okay,' she said. 'You can put me down.'

'Sure?'

'Yes. Before you have a hernia.'

Craig gratefully lowered her to the ground. He kept a hand against her back, and she gripped his shoulder until she was sure she could stay upright.

'What happened?' she said.

'You fainted. Just keeled right over.'

That's why you grabbed me, she thought, with a frisson of guilty relief. How could she have imagined Craig was the killer? It was a silly idea, completely illogical, but it persisted in a corner of her mind, a little warning light that wouldn't be extinguished.

He helped her over the fence and they went back indoors. He insisted on sitting her down on the kitchen floor and soaked a towel in water. While she dabbed her face and neck, he went to check the rest of the house.

He was upstairs when she was gripped by a painful coughing fit that left her feeling hot and woozy. There was a nasty metallic taste in her mouth, and when she got up and spat into the sink, the sight of blood nearly made her pass out again. Hearing Craig's footsteps on the stairs, she quickly ran the tap and rinsed it away, then pretended to be washing her hands.

'The only room that looks disturbed is the back bedroom. Paperwork all over the floor.' He frowned, walked past her and inspected the door. 'I wonder how he got in?'

'Mum and Dad kept a spare key under the back step.'

'But how would he have known that?'

'Everyone round here does it.'

'I suppose,' he agreed. 'Do we call the police, or not?'

She shrugged. She didn't want him to notice she was still gripping the sink to stay upright. 'If nothing was taken, we could spend hours giving statements, and what will it achieve? Even if we tell them everything, they won't believe us.'

'Yeah,' he said wearily. 'You're probably right.'

Julia thought again of Alice's warning. *He'll come after you again. And this time he'll kill you.*

'He can't have been lying in wait,' she said. 'How would he have known I was coming here?' Looking at Craig, a thought popped into her head. It was mean, and unworthy, but she couldn't stop it.

You knew.

'No,' she said, as if rebuking her own devious imagination. 'He must have been looking for something.'

'But the house has been empty for weeks,' Craig said. 'Why now?'

'It must be connected to what we're doing. Talking to Peggy Forester, Matheson, Alice Jones. All this activity, and somehow there must be a link to this house. To my—'

'What?'

'It's the diaries,' she said, and a little of her spirit seemed to leak out with the words. 'I told George Matheson about the diaries.'

It was eleven o'clock when the buzzer sounded, announcing a visitor. George checked the monitor by the door, then pressed the button to open the gates. Since speaking to his nephew the day before, he'd given a lot of thought to what approach he should take with Vilner, or indeed whether to contact him at all. Now that decision was moot.

He opened the front door as the Range Rover drew up. Vilner got out and stood still for a moment, seemingly oblivious to George's presence in the doorway. Instead he gazed in the direction of the village, then turned and swaggered towards the house. There was an intensity in his face that George hadn't seen before. When they first made eye contact it was all George could do not to recoil. He was tempted to slam the door in Vilner's face, or at least call up to Vanessa to alert her, but saw how feeble he would look.

'I don't recall arranging a meeting,' he said.

'You didn't,' said Vilner, nimbly climbing the steps and brushing past George. 'It's time we got a few things understood.'

Fifty-Five

Bernard Trent had been a hoarder. That much was evident when Julia and Craig examined the back bedroom more carefully. The wardrobe had been ransacked, the clothes ripped off the rail and piled in the corner. Nine or ten cardboard boxes had been tipped upside down, spilling out not just three dozen diaries but also half a lifetime's worth of bills, receipts, warranties and instruction manuals.

A glossy brochure for a Philips music centre caught Julia's eye. She remembered how as a child she'd accidentally broken the Perspex cover over the turntable. Her father had been set to explode until he saw she was inconsolable. He had tried telling her it didn't matter, that the turntable would function just as well without the lid, but she'd been perceptive enough to appreciate that he was bitterly upset, and aware that her brother wouldn't have escaped punishment so easily.

She sniffed. Wiped her nose and said, 'Let's get started.'

They spent a few minutes tidying up, scooping the various documents into piles. Much of it was obviously undisturbed, but some of the diaries had been opened and then discarded. Julia sat cross-legged on the floor and picked up a couple of volumes. Craig followed suit, sitting with his back to the bed. For a time they read in a companionable silence, no sound but for the whisper of paper on paper. It struck Julia that in any other circumstances she would have felt uncomfortable letting a stranger look at such personal documents.

Craig was first to grow restless. 'What did you say to George, exactly?'

Julia gazed at the wall, losing focus as she thought back to the previous morning. 'That I'd read Dad's diary and discovered Carl did some work in the garden last summer.'

'And?'

'That was it, really. We talked about Carl, about the fact that no one could have predicted what he was going to do.'

'Did he ask any questions? Anything about the diaries?'

'No. He didn't seem particularly interested in them.'

'So maybe it's just a coincidence?'

'I don't believe in coincidences. Not any more.'

'No. Me neither.' He turned a page, then sighed. 'Riveting stuff, isn't it?'

It felt disloyal to agree, but she couldn't help smiling. 'Dad looked into self-publishing a memoir, but Mum dissuaded him. Said it would cost too much.'

'He should have stuck it online and called it a blog. The publishers would have been beating a path to his door.'

Silence for another minute or two. He shut the diary and tossed it on to the pile. 'Hang on. Where's the one you had on Wednesday?'

She looked up at him. 'Back at my flat.'

'That's the one that mentions Carl?'

'Yes.'

'And there's nothing else that seems significant?'

'I only read as far as August.' She tutted. 'I'm so stupid.'

'We didn't know it was important until half an hour ago.' He got to his feet. 'Come on. We'll take these back with us.'

Vilner strode towards the drawing room where two days before they had listened to Julia Trent's allegations. George had little choice but to follow.

'I saw Toby,' Vilner said. He chose a delicate Queen Anne chair that seemed overwhelmed by his muscular frame. Leaning back, legs splayed, his posture radiated power and dominance: a tactic George had himself used many times.

'I know. He said you threatened him.'

'I warned him not to try and stitch me up,' Vilner said bluntly. 'I'm giving the same warning to you.'

George absorbed the comment, hoping to look unperturbed. 'That's why you're here?'

'That's one reason.' He paused a beat. 'This offer you made, to buy my silence? I talked to Kendrick, but I didn't tell him everything. I wanted a bit more background before I mentioned Julia Trent. Then I read the police report—'

'You stole the police report,' George cut in.

'So did you.' Vilner's gaze hardened. 'You weren't going to tell me about it, were you? That's got me wondering what else you're hiding.'

'I don't answer to you.'

'No, but like it or not, you're stuck with me.' His eyes glittered. 'I'm on the team, and so far I've had a raw deal. That's got to change.'

'In what way?'

'Two options,' Vilner said, pointing his fingers horizontally like a child making a gun. 'If you're keeping the business, I'm willing to wait for the contract, but in the meantime I want a sign of your appreciation. Two hundred grand in cash, right now.'

George's cheeks bulged with indignation. 'That's almost as much as the original debt.'

'When the risks increase, so do the rewards.'

'I can't lay my hands on that amount of money,' George said. 'It's tied up in long-term assets.'

Vilner wore a knowing smile. 'You mean shares? Property? Like Toby's apartment?'

'Yes.'

'Then turf him out and sell up.' He paused to let the suggestion take root. 'Option two. If you sell the business to Kendrick, where does that leave me?'

'I imagine Kendrick will retain your services. He seems quite content to employ you now.'

'That's only to spite you, George, as you well know.'

'You think he'll dump you when you've served your purpose?'

'Who knows? Hope for the best, expect the worst,' Vilner said. 'I want a cast-iron guarantee that I'll benefit from any sale. That means a stake in the holding company.'

George spluttered again. 'You want a share of what I've taken years to build up? A business I've sweated blood to make successful?'

'I don't care if you sweated your mother's milk. You need my co-operation, and you need my silence. For that, I want ten per cent.'

'Ten per cent?' George exploded. 'You must be mad.'

Vilner got to his feet, not quickly or angrily, but with a calm determination that made George go cold.

'It's a simple enough choice,' Vilner said. 'You give me ten per cent, or you lose everything.'

Julia wasn't really expecting to find anything in the diary. She was half convinced there must be some other reason for the intruder, perhaps related to her presence there. But certainly nothing to do with her parents.

Back at her flat, Craig asked if she felt strong enough to read it, then indicated the kitchen. 'How about if I make us an early lunch?'

Julia nodded. 'A sandwich would be nice. There's ham, cheese, tomatoes.'

She left him to it and fetched the diary from the bedroom. She sat down on the sofa and asked herself, *I'm not afraid, am I?* Taking a deep breath, she quickly skimmed the entries up to the day when Carl Forester's name first appeared. Then she read on, telling herself there was nothing to fear.

The remainder of August was uneventful, though Bernard did mention how he and Lisa had sat outside one warm evening. *So much more light now the conifers are lower.*

The next two months were in a similar vein. A spell of bad weather had him raging.

Forecast wrong as usual. Walked to Ditchling and got soaked. £10 for a taxi back – I ought to invoice the Met Office!

The entry for 25 November was much longer than most. There was a jagged look to the writing; heavy indentations as though he'd pressed harder than usual. He was angry when he wrote this, Julia knew at once. But that wasn't the only reason it stood out.

Carl's name seemed to leap off the page. She stopped reading and looked up. Craig was clattering in the kitchen, opening cupboards and drawers.

'Got any pickle?'

'Top right, next to the oven.'

She looked back at the diary. Took a deep breath and read the entry for 25 November.

Cool, overcast day. Quite pleasant. Had the usual walk this afternoon, but Lisa felt tired so we decided to cut back through the woods north of the farm. We heard a strange noise and thought it was kids mucking about. I left Lisa and went to investigate. I found a clearing with two men setting up targets on the trees. One had a shotgun. It turned out to be Carl Forester, the lad who cut our conifers. The other was a nasty bit of work, with an extremely threatening manner. He marched up and accused me of trespassing on private land. I argued that villagers have always been entitled to walk in these woods. Lisa heard the commotion and called me away. Very unpleasant. I still wonder if I should have gone to the police, but talking to Lisa afterwards she's not certain that Matheson allows access to the woods any more. All in all it cast quite a shadow over the day.

Craig came in with the sandwiches. She looked up and he reacted to the change in her face.

'You've found something, haven't you?'

'He saw them,' Julia said. 'Carl and the other killer. Dad saw them both.'

Fifty-Six

When Toby recognised the Range Rover outside Chilton Manor, his first impulse was to turn round and drive back home. After yesterday's conversation, he hadn't expected his uncle to speak to Vilner so quickly, if at all. For a moment he was torn with indecision. He didn't want to blunder into their meeting, but nor did he want a wasted journey.

He parked around the far side of the house and let himself in via the old servants' entrance. He had possessed keys to the house since his teens, when he had lived mostly with his aunt and uncle during holidays from school and then university. Since then he'd been permitted, if not exactly welcome, to come and go as he pleased. His aunt in particular seemed to resent it when he turned up unannounced, and in the past year or so he had drastically curbed his visits.

There was a chance Vanessa was here now, but he thought it unlikely. She and George had lived separate lives for as long as Toby could remember, and she had always preferred the house in London. Even so, he kept his movements stealthy as he passed through the scullery and into the huge, bare kitchen. He was stung by the folly of his uncle's existence. Used properly, with an army of servants, the manor could be a sumptuous home. The way George lived he might as well be a miserly pensioner cooped up in a bungalow.

Pausing in the hall, he could hear voices in the drawing room. He

295

hurried upstairs to George's office. Knocked gently, just in case, and opened the door.

His uncle's desk was unusually tidy. Toby had the impression there wasn't much work done in here any more. He conducted a quick search of the room on the long shot that he might find something of value, but both the desk drawers and filing cabinet were locked. Resisting the urge to kick something, he let himself out.

He was easing the door shut when he heard a noise at the end of the hall. A burst of music from a TV or a radio. He frowned, listened again to be sure he wasn't imagining it. The music gave way to the drone of conversation. Someone changing channels.

He moved quietly along the hall, alert to any movement on the stairs. He'd only been a minute or two in George's office. If the meeting downstairs had ended, Toby was sure he'd have heard them coming out.

The sound originated from one of the unused bedrooms. He waited a second, feeling oddly indignant. Who the hell was it?

Taking a deep breath, he opened the door and marched in as if he had every right to be there, then stopped in shock at the sight that greeted him.

It was a vision from a nightmare: a hideous spindly creature rearing up in bed, eyes like dark buttons set deep in a raggedy skull, bony arms clawing the air in outrage. It turned those terrible eyes on him and spat with disgust.

'Get out! Get out!'

Craig sat down next to her and read the entry himself. It seemed to take an age before he turned to Julia.

'He saw them practising with the shotgun.' He let out a sigh. 'If only he'd gone to the police. The whole massacre might have been averted.'

Julia was stunned by his comment. 'That's not fair. Dad couldn't have known what they were planning.'

Craig at least had the decency to look abashed. 'You're right. I'm sorry.'

He took the diary from her and read it again. His frown grew deeper. 'Look at this. *He marched up and accused me of trespassing on private land.*'

'It's George Matheson's land.'

'Yeah. So maybe they had his permission?'

'Maybe.'

'*An extremely threatening manner,*' Craig quoted again. 'Sounds like a pretty good description of Vilner.'

Julia nodded. In the gloomy silence that followed, Craig devoured his sandwich in several bites, his brow creased in a thoughtful frown. Julia picked up the diary, and steeling herself, read on through November and into December.

Finally she reached the last entry, made the day before they died.

Weather atrocious again, and more on the way. A quiet day at home. Started Our Man in Havana *by Graham Greene – superb! Watched* Countdown *– managed two 6-letter words. Lisa not feeling well. Coming down with flu, she thinks. I haven't been feeling all that bright myself. Hope we both shake it off before Christmas.*

And that was it. Her father's last words. Julia closed the diary and set it down. She could feel tears itching to come, but something was holding them back. Something lurking in her mind: a thought, a question, darting in and out of the shadows.

She remembered what she had learned in the wake of the tragedy, how the symptoms of carbon monoxide poisoning could often be mistaken for a cold or flu. When Dad wrote this, the boiler was already playing up. And the bad weather meant they'd closed the windows, probably keeping internal doors shut, too. Intensifying the concentration of CO.

Another scurrying question, but this time she caught it.

What if the boiler hadn't malfunctioned?

What if the boiler had been sabotaged?

Craig put his plate down, a sudden look of horror on his face. Maybe it was telepathy, or maybe just coincidence. Either way, they had the same idea at the same time.

'If your dad saw them, you don't think . . . ?'

He couldn't quite bring himself to say it aloud, but Julia could.

'He killed them, didn't he? He killed my parents.'

Toby recoiled in horror. The creature went on hissing at him. 'Don't look at me!'

Something about the voice was familiar. He looked closer, and understood . . .

'Vanessa?'

'What are you doing here?' She twisted away from him, clutching her blanket, dragging it up to conceal her body. Her skin was thin and yellowed like parchment, but her eyes held the remnants of the woman he knew.

'What's happened to you?'

Cringing beneath her blanket, she snarled, 'What do you think?'

She's dying, he thought. It was a stunning revelation, and right then he couldn't say how he felt about it. They had been on little more than civil terms for many years, but once, in the aftermath of his mother's untimely death from a drug overdose, they had been considerably more than that.

Vanessa had been beautiful then, in her way. A thin, icy beauty. His head swam at the memory of the moment when her distant sympathy became something else. He recalled the sureness of her fingers, the press and pull of her soft, expert mouth.

'Why didn't you say anything?'

'It's private.'

He checked over his shoulder to make sure the noise hadn't alerted his uncle, then shut the door and moved to a chair at the foot of the bed. He sat patiently until Vanessa released the blanket. There was pain in her eyes, and in her voice.

'I'll be gone soon. You might as well know.'

'I'm sorry.' He wasn't sure if that was true, but thought he should say it anyway.

His aunt looked irritated. She attempted to moisten her lips with her tongue, then reached for the water by her bed. He got it for her, and as he placed the glass in her hand her fingers brushed against his. Her skin was dry and scaly.

'Vilner's here,' she said.

'I know. I came upstairs to avoid him.'

She sipped the water. Afterwards her voice regained a little of its power. 'Do you know why?'

'I'm hoping it's to negotiate a deal.' He told her about his conversation with George. Her lips formed a caustic smile.

'You won't buy him off now,' she said. 'Vilner's scented blood. My bet is that he's playing each side against the other.'

She took another sip of water, the glass trembling in her hand. She wasn't making much sense, and he wondered just how lucid she was. Probably dosed up with morphine. But he was sufficiently intrigued to let her continue. Better to hear her out, then evaluate it later.

But Vanessa closed her eyes, seeming to forget all about him. He waited a long minute, then prompted her with, 'Each side?'

Her eyes opened, regarding him with what seemed like pity. 'Of course,' she said. 'You don't know about Kendrick.'

He frowned. Shifted closer to the bed. He could feel his heart racing. It wasn't just the look in her eyes; it was the way she spoke. Sad and yet thrilled, as if she'd been granted the opportunity to pronounce a terminal diagnosis on someone else for a change.

He stuttered a little as he spoke. 'Who-who's Kendrick?' Then another interminable wait for her to respond.

'Kendrick is buying the business.'

Toby thought he had misheard. 'What did you say?'

'George is selling up,' said Vanessa. 'And you're not part of the deal.'

Fifty-Seven

It was like losing them all over again. Julia felt blank. Anaesthetised. When she spoke, it was a shock to hear the words come out. It sounded like no one she knew.

'Do we go to the police?'

'I doubt they'll be able to find evidence of foul play.'

'They might at least take the idea of a second killer seriously.'

Craig looked at his watch. 'We should have reported the break-in straight away. Then there's the question of Peggy Forester. As soon as we admit to seeing her, they're going to take a very close look at us.'

Julia was still smarting from Craig's suggestion that her father could have prevented the massacre; now his slightly condescending tone only increased her irritation.

'Don't forget the hotel fire,' she said acidly. 'Not to mention your car accident.'

He frowned. 'What are you getting at?'

'Well, you weren't straight with me about your past, or about seeing Peggy Forester. I'm starting to wonder what else you've been holding back.'

'He drove straight at me,' he said angrily. 'The car ended up in a ditch. When I found you on the beach, my clothes were soaked, remember? I had cuts on my hand and my head. I didn't bloody invent it.'

'I'm not saying it didn't happen,' she countered. 'But how am I to know if the killer caused it, or something else?'

Now he looked mystified. 'Like what?'

'You tell me. Maybe you weren't concentrating.' She met his eye, wanting to measure his reaction very carefully. 'Maybe you'd been drinking.'

When she was alone again, Vanessa rested back on the bed and assessed the situation. She had never seen Toby so shocked, so furious, but to his credit he'd kept his temper in check. She'd cautioned that he would gain nothing from confronting George while he was angry. She half expected him to ignore the advice, but he had left quietly, without announcing his presence in the house. Soon Vilner would leave too, and perhaps George would update her on their meeting.

Then again, perhaps he wouldn't.

While she waited, she reflected on how easy it was to light a touch paper, but how difficult to predict the consequences. Perhaps, when he came up to see her, she would tell George what she had done.

Then again, perhaps she wouldn't.

The accusation seemed to deflate him. Craig's shoulders dropped. His gaze turned inward, dark with self-loathing.

'You're right,' he said quietly. 'I haven't been honest with you.'

He stood up and walked to the window, as if he needed to put some physical distance between them before he could explain. Julia waited, still angry and now a tiny bit afraid of what he might reveal.

'Years ago, I had quite a serious drink problem. It started when I was doing the investigative work. Stress of the job, I suppose. I was missing deadlines, picking fights with people, generally behaving like a twat. The turning point came when I had a run-in with the police.'

Julia thought of Kate's warning about him. 'What happened?'

'I had a good lead about a bent copper. A senior detective in the Met, taking backhanders from some major villains. I was putting the story together when I got a visit from his sergeant. He was adamant that his boss was completely straight, that someone was trying to fit him up. He appealed to me to let it go. He was very plausible, very friendly, with only the merest hint of a threat. I told him I'd consider it.'

He turned away from her. 'The next day I got pulled over and breathalysed. I was way over the limit, ended up with a year's ban.'

'You think it was down to this sergeant?'

'I never knew for sure. But I took the coward's way out and drop-ped the story. After that I had no stomach for my job. The kids were little, and Nina was threatening to kick me out. I managed to stop drinking and make a new start, and after that I didn't touch a drop for years.'

He turned back to her. 'Then Dad was killed, and I found out about Nina's affair, and I hit the bottle again.'

Julia nodded. 'I thought I could smell it in the car.'

'I had a mouthful of Scotch when we stopped at your parents' cottage. A bit more when I dropped you off . . .' He shrugged. 'But the accident happened just as I described it. Alcohol wasn't a factor.'

'It must have been on your mind when we discussed whether to go to the police?'

'Yeah, I suppose it was, although my main concern was how they'd view our visit to Peggy Forester.'

He sounded genuine enough, but Julia had reached the point where she was no longer sure of anything.

'Did you ever find out what happened to the policeman?'

'The senior one was definitely bent, but he retired early and skipped off to Spain. Never faced justice. His faithful sergeant is now a detect-ive inspector, working here in Sussex.' Craig laughed. 'And if you think that sounds like a disaster, wait till you hear about the mess I'm in now.'

George felt drained by his encounter with Vilner. Again he thought of Toby's suggestion on Tuesday. Pack a case, jump on a plane to Antigua. Leave it all behind: Vilner, Kendrick . . . Vanessa.

No. He couldn't leave Vanessa behind.

When he looked in on her, she was sound asleep. That was good. He could spare her the details of his encounter with Vilner. No sense burdening her.

Ten per cent was an outrageous demand. Vilner didn't have the evidence to justify it, but he knew, as George did, that the media wouldn't give a damn about evidence or the lack of it. Neither would Craig Walker, come to that.

He wondered if that was part of Vilner's game plan. Use Craig and Julia Trent as his mouthpiece, enabling him to stay in the background. That's how I would do it, he thought. Join forces with my enemy's enemy.

That got him wondering if he should employ a similar tactic. In admitting that he'd kept information back from Kendrick, Vilner had made a serious error. No doubt he assumed George wouldn't rat on him to Kendrick, for fear of weakening his own position. But George knew that when the problems were stacking up, you dealt with them one at a time. You prioritised. First defuse Vilner's threat, then worry about where it leaves you with Kendrick.

But it was a big step, not to be taken lightly.

Sleep on it, he decided at last. Speak to Kendrick tomorrow.

Julia decided she needed coffee. Refusing Craig's offer to make it for her, she went into the kitchen. Craig followed and hovered tentatively in the doorway.

'His name is Sullivan,' he said. 'I spotted him in one of the news broadcasts. Figured he owed me a favour.'

'That's how you got the report?'

'And the address of your hotel,' he admitted glumly. 'But it was a risky strategy from the start. I saw him yesterday, and told him what had happened this week. I thought it would convince him that there was a second killer. It turned out he didn't need convincing.'

Julia, rinsing the cafetière under the tap, stopped what she was doing. 'He agrees there was a second killer?'

'Yes. But he thinks it's me,' Craig said. Blunt and bitter.

Julia couldn't quite mask her shock. She opened a drawer, took out a dishcloth and began drying the cafetière. Of course he wasn't the killer. She saw the killer this morning, in her parents' house. Craig had been right behind her. He couldn't be in two places at once.

Unless there was more than one person involved . . .

Her train of thought must have been obvious to Craig. He said, 'It's not me. If you believe nothing else I've said, you must believe that.'

Julia didn't feel ready to comment. 'But you think Sullivan is George's inside man?'

'It would explain a lot. He's exactly the kind of lowlife who'd end up on Matheson's payroll.'

He said nothing more, just leaned against the doorframe and watched as she spooned coffee into the cafetière. His presence didn't make her uneasy, as she might have expected, and she realised her gut instinct was to believe him. Then she thought of the other terrible insight she'd had about him, and decided now was as good a time as any to confront him.

'You resent me, don't you?' she said. 'You wish Carl had killed me outside the village shop.'

Toby was steaming with rage on his way back to London, and that rage was reflected in his driving. He chopped in and out of lanes, tail-gated the cars in front, and in Streatham he jumped a queue by moving into the opposite carriageway and driving through a pedestrian crossing on the wrong side of the road. He raced away to a barrage of horns and flashing headlights, and knew he was perilously close to doing something he would regret.

On one level he could appreciate the need to calm down, but at the same time he'd never before had to contend with such devastating betrayal. He tried persuading himself that Vanessa was confused, that somehow she had misinterpreted the situation, but in his heart he didn't believe it. He knew how his uncle operated. Time and again George had made deals and not said a word until the papers were signed, even though, as a director, Toby should have been entitled to prior knowledge.

So this latest revelation couldn't be dismissed. George was intent on selling the business from under his nose. Giving away his birthright.

Toby had to prevent it, somehow. He had to find a way to fight back.

And he would.

Fifty-Eight

'It was Sullivan who first planted the idea in my head,' Craig said. 'The first time we met up, he told me Dad was shot twice. He said Carl had gone back to . . . finish the job.' He swallowed. 'He was taunting me that Dad only died because of you.'

'I suppose it's true,' said Julia. Feeling the prickle of tears, she kept her back to him so he wouldn't see them. The kettle boiled, and she poured hot water into the cafetière.

'I'm very proud of him,' said Craig. 'I'm proud he helped to save you. And I know it's totally irrational, but part of me does feel bitter about it. If you hadn't gone running across the green, if you hadn't *needed* saving, he might be alive today. And I've found that hard to deal with.'

'It wasn't exactly easy for me,' Julia reminded him. 'You don't have a monopoly on grief. Or regret.'

She poured the coffee and quickly set the cafetière down. Put a hand over her mouth as tears ran down her cheeks. Her shoulders twitched with each silent sob. She heard Craig take a step into the kitchen.

'It was never personal,' he said, 'And once I met you I realised what a stupid notion it was. My father did absolutely the right thing.'

She felt his hands gently grip her arms and turn her to face him. There were tears in his eyes and a sorrow on his face that matched hers. Dismissing the last of her doubts, she stepped into his embrace. The feel of his body, his strength and his warmth, made her heart beat faster.

They stood like this for a long time, then parted just enough to look into each other's eyes. Julia felt her cheeks reddening, a slow bloom of heat that didn't stop at her face but spread deliciously through her body. He reached out and cupped the back of her head, pulled her close and guided her mouth towards his, their eyes still locked together, solemn and scared and hungry.

She'd always thought all that stuff about fireworks was a lot of nonsense, the type of thing you only found in romantic fiction. But after so much time on her own, after so many difficult weeks without any real intimacy or affection, the first touch of his lips against hers was like an explosion. It felt like breaking into sunshine after a year in a freezer. It made her feel complete when she hadn't even known she was broken.

It was a perfect moment. One of those all too rare occasions when he acted without any thought whatsoever. He simply did what he felt was right.

A perfect moment, and it ended with a phone call. His mobile, bleeping from inside his jacket.

They broke apart, both a little awed and embarrassed. Craig fumbled for the phone, read the display and felt his stomach contract. Even as he took a step backwards, Julia read his expression and busied herself with the coffee.

'Nina?'

'Craig. The police are here.'

Her words blasted the air from his lungs. *The killer had targeted his family.*

'Are the kids all right?'

'They're fine. I picked them up from school.' There was a rustle of movement down the line, and when she spoke next her voice was lower, almost a whisper. 'The police want to talk to you about Abby Clark. She's gone missing.'

'But I talked to her yesterday morning.'

'That's what Abby's friend told them. She seems to think Abby was working on something for you.'

Another shock, this one even greater. He glanced at Julia and saw her looking in his direction, reacting to the horror on his face. He was still reeling when Nina said, 'Where are you?'

'Chilton.' He answered too quickly, the lie automatic. Easier than explaining the truth.

'No, you're not. I rang there first.' A beat of silence. Then she hissed: 'You're with her, aren't you? Julia Trent?'

'Nina, listen, this isn't—'

'Well, that didn't take you long, did it? After all the bullshit you gave me.'

'It's not like that.' He looked at Julia again. 'Tell the police I'll be there as soon as I can.'

'What's happened?' said Julia. Inside her emotions were in turmoil. She didn't know whether to feel relieved or disappointed that the kiss had been interrupted.

'Abby's gone missing. The police want to interview me.'

'There might be a perfectly innocent explanation.'

He gave her a sharp look. 'Remember what we said about coincidence? Besides, Abby's a journalist. She's never incommunicado. No. This is because of me, because of what I asked her to do.'

'You don't know that,' she said, but he was in no mood to be placated.

'If she thinks she's on to a big story, she'll take risks. When she rang yesterday she was really excited. Not just about Vilner. She mentioned someone else.' He searched his memory. 'Kendrick, I think she said.'

'Who's he?'

'No idea. That's what she was trying to find out.' Again he was lost to her, gazing into the middle distance.

'Why did you lie to Nina?'

'I don't know,' he said grimly. 'Yet another disaster.' By 'another' she couldn't help wondering if he meant the intimacy they had shared.

She accompanied him to the front door, where he gave her a quick, impersonal peck on the cheek.

'Be extra careful, won't you? There's no telling what he'll do next.'

She nodded. Watching him hurry away, Julia felt a sudden conviction that she would never see him again, and the fleeting vision of happiness she had experienced this afternoon crumbled like a castle built from dry, brittle sand.

Fifty-Nine

It was a cold, clear night. She stood beneath a dazzling moon, the whole universe suspended above her. She was back on the beach at Camber, but there was no tree. No man in black. Kate's hotel was dark, deserted.

She turned her back on the land, towards the shore. But there was no shore. For as far as she could see there was only sand, rocks, seaweed. Abandoned boats tilted at rest on the seafloor. Fish glittering silver like distant reflected stars, twitching and flopping helplessly on dry land.

She was alone. Utterly alone.

She wobbled and nearly fell. The beach was shifting, trembling beneath her, the vibrations running into her feet and through her bones, threatening to shake her to pieces. She clutched her belly in panic. Looked up and saw a line of white froth gleaming in the darkness, the horizon rushing towards her.

A tsunami. A giant wave, boiling and foaming like a living thing, growing more immense with every second, fast and powerful and hungry, pummelling the ground beneath her feet. She had to run. She had to run *now*.

But she couldn't run. She couldn't move at all.

She shut her eyes and waited for the wave.

* * *

Julia woke, heart hammering. Took in her surroundings and settled back with a long sigh. Of all the bad dreams she'd had since the massacre, none had provoked a sensation of such absolute desolation. Loneliness on a cosmic scale.

It wasn't too difficult to guess what had prompted it. Last night, after waiting hours to hear from Craig, she had sent him a text. He phoned a few minutes later, apologetic but also weary and distracted. He had told the police what little he knew about Abby's enquiries. Vilner's name seemed to be familiar to them, but Kendrick's drew a blank. He'd also mentioned his theories about the massacre, but the police had been openly sceptical. They were more interested in whether Craig had been having a relationship with Abby, a possibility suggested by her current partner.

'Why did she think that?' Julia had asked.

'No idea. We got on pretty well. Flirted a bit. But that was all.'

His breezy denial made her wonder how he would describe what had happened between them. It also struck her that she only had his version of his marital problems. Perhaps the reality was more complicated.

Even more unwelcome was the possibility that Abby's fate was connected to their own enquiries. She pictured George Matheson, standing with her on the village green. His grief had seemed so genuine, his sympathy heartfelt, and yet all the time he must have been glorying in the deception. He'd participated in an act of mass murder and now he was covering his tracks with the same ruthless efficiency. She didn't want to believe it, but the evidence was becoming too strong to ignore.

The phone rang, making her jump. She glanced at the bedside clock: just after eight on a Saturday morning. It must be Craig.

But it was a woman's voice. 'Julia? It's Alice here. Alice Jones.'

'Oh.' Julia passed the receiver to her other ear. 'Are you all right?'

'I thought I should warn you. It's partly because of you that I've made this decision. I hope you'll forgive me if it's not quite what you suggested, but it's really the only option left.'

'Alice, slow down,' said Julia. 'I don't understand.'

'I haven't got much time. I just want you to be careful.'

'Has someone threatened you?' Julia hadn't given Alice's address to anyone, and she was sure no one had followed her to Brighton. How had they found her?

But Alice laughed her strange, off-key little laugh. 'No. That's why I'm taking this option, to be free of those worries.'

'Then what?' said Julia, so baffled she wondered if she was still dreaming.

'The *media*,' Alice said. 'It's going to hit you like a tidal wave.'

The phrase made Julia go cold. She grabbed the mattress and squeezed it to make sure it existed. She really was here, at home. Safe.

'I have to go now,' Alice said. 'I'm truly sorry. Goodbye.'

The line went dead. Julia immediately dialled 1471, but knew it would be hopeless. *We do not have the caller's number*.

She sat on the edge of her bed and stared at the carpet, wondering how it was that she might have convinced an unstable woman to commit suicide.

Craig was up first, at around eight o'clock. Since the massacre he'd found it difficult to sleep late, particularly on Saturdays. And after the grilling he'd got from the police the day before, he'd spent most of the night awake, trying to mediate between his many competing worries.

Creeping downstairs, he saw the envelope on the mat and knew immediately it brought bad news. The post wouldn't be delivered for another couple of hours yet.

It was a plain brown A4 envelope, hand delivered and bearing only his name in a standard typeface, printed on an inkjet or laser printer. He took it into the kitchen and put it on the worktop, then quietly shut the door and made coffee. It was a futile exercise in denial. The envelope lay like a predator, his heart thudding like a trip hammer at the thought of what it might contain.

Only the fear that Nina might walk in gave him the impetus to pick it up. With shaking hands he prised the flap open and turned the envelope on its side, shaking loose the contents.

A single sheet of heavy-duty A4 paper. Text on one side, a photograph on the other. The text was in the same neat font, in the very centre of the sheet. It said:

`Don't talk to the police. We will know.`

The photograph was of Tom and Maddie, with Nina, hurrying along a busy road. There were parked cars in the foreground and a low building in the background with a chain-link fence around it.

Nina collecting the kids from school. Taken recently, probably a long-range shot with a zoom lens. But what made him light-headed with terror was the way the picture had been pierced by a pin or perhaps the nib of a pen, not once but four times.

Four neat little holes, obliterating the eyes of his children.

A coughing fit sent Julia to the bathroom. Once again she spat blood into the basin, shockingly bright against the white ceramic. She knew she shouldn't ignore it, but also felt unwilling to waste her day in a hospital waiting room. Perhaps if it hadn't improved by Monday . . .

Rinsing her mouth, she remembered that Gordon Jones's note had included a phone number along with the address. She rang and discovered the number belonged to the other ground-floor flat. The woman who answered said there was a problem getting Alice's phone connected, and she had agreed to pass on messages.

'Will you fetch her for me?' Julia asked. 'It's urgent.'

'Oh, she's not here, love. She went yesterday. Doesn't look like she's coming back, neither.'

'Did she say where she was going?'

'Not a word. I only know because the landlord was round here last night. Shame she didn't say goodbye.' The woman sniffed. 'Still, mustn't judge. She's had her share of problems, that one.'

Julia thanked her and put the phone down. She spent a restless half-hour tidying up, making tea she hardly drank and toast she didn't eat. All the time imagining Alice calmly preparing to end her life.

She thought about her warning: the media descending on her. Had Alice written some kind of note, confessing that she'd seen the second killer?

Julia's heart twisted with fear and guilt. Those three boisterous children didn't deserve to lose their mother. But what could she do?

Finally she overcame her reluctance to call Craig. She rang his father's number, then his mobile, but there was no answer. She would have to try his home number.

It was Nina who answered, just as Julia knew it would be. She sounded harassed and short-tempered.

'Is Craig there?'

'He's gone out. Who is this?'

'Julia Trent.'

Nina made a noise, a mixture of disgust and contempt. 'Don't you think you've done enough damage with this ridiculous story about the massacre? Leave my husband alone and keep your mad theories to yourself. You're nothing but trouble.'

She slammed the phone down. Julia slumped back in her seat, feeling physically winded. The dream had been a terrible premonition. She was completely alone.

Alone in the path of the wave.

Sixty

George had barely slept all night. Vanessa woke in distress at four in the morning, bleeding heavily. The doctor came out and judged her too frail to be moved to hospital. When he emerged from her room, his face was grave.

'It won't be long now,' he told George. 'You need to prepare for the end.'

George had nodded. Much later it struck him that he was preparing for the end in more ways than the doctor could have imagined.

By then it was seven o'clock. He went for a walk around the grounds, enjoying the serenity of a world not yet fully awake. The air was crisp and cold and brilliantly clear, the sky unblemished but for a few slow dissolving vapour trails. He tried to imagine himself into Vanessa's dwindling existence, forced to confront the knowledge that soon these glorious mornings would continue without her.

Then he reflected that his own existence was none too glorious at the moment.

It soon got worse. George had eaten a meagre breakfast and was sitting at Vanessa's bedside when Terry Sullivan rang.

'The shit's hit the fan,' the policeman told him. 'You know there was a witness called Alice Jones, hiding up in her bedroom?'

George grunted non-committally. He didn't want Sullivan to know he'd pored over every word of the report.

'Turns out she's been telling us a load of porkies. That or she's totally flipped.'

'What?' said George. He could feel a chill creeping up his spine.

'She's now claiming Julia Trent was right. There *was* a second killer.'

'She's made a statement to that effect?'

A bark of laughter from Sullivan. 'If only.'

George grimaced as he guessed it. 'The media?'

'Yep. Shacked up with the cheapest, tawdriest tabloid of the lot. And you know why it was them rather than us? She says we can't guarantee her safety. Part of the deal is that they've got her and her family in a secure location, and they're going to keep them there for as long as it takes.'

'As long as it takes?' George repeated, buying himself time to think. Beside him, Vanessa stirred, opening her eyes.

'Till the killer's caught. Which every right-thinking tosspot who reads this rag will say is only fair and reasonable. Meanwhile the other papers will compete for the privilege of ripping us to shreds, accusing us of incompetence, corruption, you name it.' He let out a heavy sigh. 'The fallout's going to be horrendous.'

'How did you find out? I assume the story hasn't been printed yet?'

'No. They like to give us a bit of advance warning. Often it's thinly disguised blackmail. They'll go easy on the force if we agree to co-operate.'

'And will you?'

'That's a decision for the top brass. Word is, they're shitting bricks about it.'

'So what will you do? Renew the investigation?'

'I can't see we've any choice.'

Vanessa gave him a questioning glance. George smiled and shook his head, as if to say, *It's nothing*. She closed her eyes again.

'Of course, she could have cooked this up just to line her pockets,' Sullivan went on. 'Wouldn't surprise me if her and that Trent woman are in it together.'

'It's a possibility,' George agreed. He thought of his encounter with Julia on Wednesday. She had seemed determined to speak to Alice Jones: it looked like she'd succeeded.

'Even so, it's gonna bring a lot of heat down on you, especially if they link it to Craig Walker's allegations.'

An uneasy pause. Sullivan clearly laying the groundwork for something, George guessed. Or perhaps waiting for him to make the suggestion.

'We do still have the fact that they visited Peggy Forester.'

Sullivan cackled. 'Yeah. Your trump card, hopefully. I'll have to try and work out the best strategy for using it.' Another pause, loaded with significance. This time George knew exactly what was coming.

'We also need to talk about my remuneration. The stuff I've done up to now, that was a favour, but we're moving into high-risk territory. If I'm gonna stick my neck out for you, there's got to be something in it for me.'

George faked a laugh. 'Absolutely. Why don't you call in sometime this weekend and we'll put some figures together?'

Vanessa had turned her head away from him. Her eyes were still shut, but whether she was conscious he couldn't say. After ending the call, he took a moment to order his thoughts. It actually required no time at all to assess the situation. He could sum it up in three words.

It's falling apart.

The moment she saw the house in Arundel Crescent, Julia knew it was a wasted journey. Every window was closed, and a dull reflected light shone from the glass. There was no hint of sound or movement inside.

Still she knocked and waited. She cupped her hands and peered through the lower bay window. The living room looked reasonably tidy, a few toys scattered here and there. A glass of water stood on the window ledge, stale with bubbles.

Above her the crows circled like black rags. Their cries took her back to 19 January, and it struck her that each time she returned here she felt *more* affected, rather than less, as though the village wasn't done with her yet.

Finally she wrote a note: *Gordon, I'm worried about Alice. Please call me.* She signed her name, added her contact numbers and slipped it through the letter box.

It was just after ten in the morning, and much warmer than it had been in January. Back at the flat she'd heard a weather forecast that warned of an imminent change: storm-force winds and torrential rain. In a spot of banter, the news presenter had said, 'Oh well, I suppose we can't complain,' and the forecaster had merrily agreed. 'Our luck had to run out sometime.'

That phrase came back to her now, as she returned to her car. It wasn't particularly comforting, but at least it was an improvement on Nina Walker's parting shot.

You're nothing but trouble.

The doctor had suggested Vanessa should have a private nurse on hand for most of the day, and as soon as she arrived George took the opportunity to retire to his office. He allowed himself a small sherry and contemplated what action to take.

Vilner was still the immediate concern. Before the policeman's call, George had virtually decided to go ahead and tell Kendrick that Vilner was cheating him. It was a risk, of course, but the news from Sullivan made it clear he was facing calamity on several fronts. To stand any chance of defeating his enemies, he needed to assess their strengths and weaknesses, test their alliances.

But first he rang Toby to tell him of yesterday's encounter with Vilner. It was a brief, disingenuous conversation. He gave the impression that the meeting had been arranged as a direct consequence of

Toby's request. He said he'd opened negotiations with Vilner, but warned it was likely to be a long and difficult process. In the meantime he ordered Toby to keep his head down and his mouth shut. And he wanted no further work on the second application.

'But you said I could do it,' Toby complained.

'And now I'm saying you cannot.' He tried to outline the possible fallout from the Alice Jones story, but Toby went on protesting, trying to find a way round it, until finally George lost his temper. 'Just do as you're told for once,' he roared. 'I'm in enough of a mess right now, without your childish bloody whingeing.'

He slammed the phone down, the anger hot in his veins. Just what he needed to take on Kendrick. A quick gulp of sherry, then he grabbed the phone up again.

Sixty-One

Nine-thirty, and Sullivan found himself waiting like a jilted lover amid the teeming mass of humanity on the concourse at Victoria Station. Impatient shoppers and tourists barged past as if he'd chosen that precise spot purely to inconvenience them. He'd been loitering long enough to draw the attention of a couple of transport police. He let them get within a couple of yards before flashing his warrant card. One of them scowled as he turned away; the other had the decency to blush.

'Fucking clothes hangers,' he muttered, not caring if they heard.

He'd been summoned to an urgent conference at Scotland Yard to debate the potential fallout from Alice Jones's revelations. The thought of a Saturday wasted on hot air and management speak filled him with gloom, and there wasn't even the prospect of a game of buzz-word bingo with a few like-minded colleagues. More and more now-adays the senior officers were young, clean-cut college boys – and girls – with settled home lives and delicate sensibilities, immaculate in their political correctness.

Still, ironic to think he would be better apprised of the situation than anyone else there. He had no intention of sharing any of that knowledge, however. First he had to decide how it could be used most profitably, and at the least risk to himself.

Fucking with Craig's head had lost some of its appeal, especially

320

now Alice Jones had given him an opportunity to secure a decent payday from George. But her allegations, combined with Craig's, also made him uncomfortable. At the back of his mind lingered the fear that there was something a whole lot bigger going on here, something he would be wise to avoid.

He looked at his watch again. When Craig rang this morning, asking for an urgent meeting, Sullivan half hoped to discourage him by stipulating Victoria Station, but Craig had immediately agreed. Sullivan spotted him now, threading his way through a party of tourists dragging suitcases towards the Gatwick-bound train.

Dispensing with a greeting, Sullivan barked, 'You've got two minutes, max.'

'That's long enough,' Craig said, handing him an envelope. 'Have a look, but don't flash it around.'

Slightly wary, Sullivan opened the envelope and took a peek at the contents. He frowned. 'Your kids?'

'Yeah. There's a message on the other side.'

Sullivan read it, then silently thanked his maker that he'd agreed to this meeting. Being the good actor he was, he affected disdain.

'All this proves is that someone doesn't like you.'

Craig's face darkened with fury. 'Someone like you, for instance?' Before Sullivan could respond, he added, 'Don't try to deny you're in Matheson's pocket. I won't believe you. But did you know this is the kind of thing he'll stoop to, or are you part of that as well?'

'I'm part of nothing,' Sullivan growled. 'I dunno what the fuck you're talking about. You got any proof it was George that sent it?'

A few passersby must have heard the aggression in his voice, for suddenly the space around them grew larger. Sullivan glanced round, concerned only that the uniforms were well out of earshot.

'A journalist friend of mine was investigating the massacre,' Craig said. 'Now she's gone missing. I've come to London to find out what's happened to her.'

Sullivan was mystified. This was something he knew nothing about.

At the same time he realised Craig wouldn't yet know about Alice Jones.

'Tell me her name. I'll see what I can find out.'

Craig looked dubious, but gave him the details, and the name of the Met officer in charge of the case. He ended by saying, 'All that crap on Thursday about me being the second killer. This had better put an end to it.'

Sullivan handed the envelope back. He grinned. 'You never really struck me as a mass murderer, shame to say.'

'Good. And if it is Matheson who's behind this, you can tell him he won't get away with it. No one threatens my kids. No one.'

'Hey,' Sullivan said. 'I know you're angry, but I won't say this again. I am not part of this. I'm as much in the dark as you are.'

Craig stared at him, his eyes narrow with suspicion. Finally he sighed. 'Then God help both of us.'

The phone call changed everything. The killer saw immediately how it could be exploited. This would fit perfectly into his plans.

The net was closing. No point denying it, or pretending it wasn't happening. But that was okay. He was smarter than the people who were looking for him. Smarter and more devious and, most importantly, more ruthless. He was still one step ahead, and Alice Jones had just put him further in front.

The existence of the second killer couldn't be disputed for much longer. Even without physical evidence, the combination of witness accounts and media pressure would soon convince the police to take it seriously. And once the killer's *existence* had been accepted, all that mattered then was his *identity*.

What he had to do was give them someone else. Someone plausible. Someone with a clear, undeniable motive.

Like greed, for instance.

And viewed like that, there could be only one possible candidate.

* * *

Julia drove back to Lewes, haunted by the dream and the terrible sense of desolation as her body crumpled in the face of the tsunami. Alice's fate remained heavy on her conscience. The desire to share her burden created an almost physical ache, but the only possible candidate was Craig. And he was out of bounds.

Back at the flat, she checked her phone. Someone had called twenty minutes before, but withheld the number. That only added to her despair.

She ate a bar of chocolate and slumped on the sofa for an hour, watching some God-awful excuse for Saturday-morning TV. This is ridiculous, she thought at last. Sitting around all day would send her insane.

On impulse, she decided some gentle exercise would do her good. She found her gym bag and packed a towel and a one-piece swimsuit. With the weight she'd lost, it probably wouldn't be a great fit, and some of her scars might be visible. Did she really want people staring at her?

Then she thought, *Sod it*. She was past caring. Let them look.

She was almost out of the door when the phone rang.

George concluded his conversation with Kendrick, feeling like a starving man who'd crawled into a den of wolves in search of meat. But it was too late now. The deck was shuffled, the cards would fall as they landed.

He returned to Vanessa's room. The nurse raised a finger to her mouth: *Don't wake her*. George gazed at his wife's pygmy form beneath the sheets. Even though it was barely an hour since he'd left her, she seemed yet more diminished, as if her intention was to depart the world via a process of miniaturisation, becoming smaller and smaller until finally she vanished altogether.

He smiled at the thought. If only it were that benign.

The nurse had unplugged the phone extension, so as not to disturb her. George didn't realise until he felt the buzz of his mobile. He read the display and felt his heart tighten.

He listened, incredulously, to the first glimmer of positive news in what felt like a lifetime. 'You're sure?' he said. 'There's no doubt at all. She is waking?'

Now the caller grew more sombre, more guarded. Adopting the same tone, George said, 'There's a long way to go, of course. But it's cause for hope, at least. Thank you. Thank you so much.'

He finished the call and gave a start when Vanessa said, 'What's happened?'

Her eyes were open, her brow creased with concern. It was only then he registered the tears on his cheeks. He brushed them away with his fists.

'Nothing,' he lied. 'It's nothing.'

Let it be Alice, Julia thought, or failing that, Craig: apologising for Nina's tirade.

But it was a male voice, educated and polite with just a touch of the Estuary wide boy. A combination that Julia instinctively knew meant trouble.

'Julia Trent? My name's Guy Fisher. I'm calling about Alice Jones.'

'What's happened? Is she all right?'

He sounded perplexed. 'Good as gold. Why?'

'She called me this morning. It sounded like . . .' Now she felt ridiculous. 'I got the impression she might harm herself.'

'No, she's safe and sound. Done herself a very nice deal with us.'

Julia was frowning, relieved but confused, until it clicked. 'You're a journalist?'

'Yeah, though I can't divulge which paper. All top secret at the moment. Can't have our rivals getting wind of it and beating us to print.'

Now Alice's garbled conversation made sense: *It's not quite what you suggested.*

'A tabloid, I suppose?'

'One of the biggest and best,' Fisher shot back. She could hear the grin in his voice.

'What has she told you?'

'The works. It's explosive stuff.' He snorted. 'But I don't have to tell you that. Bloody scandalous, the police ignoring what you said about the other gunman. Thanks to their incompetence we've got a mass murderer still on the loose.'

She opened her mouth to explain that it wasn't so simple, then stopped herself. That was precisely what he was angling for.

'Don't worry,' he said. 'Alice is safe and sound with hubby and the kids, and we're gonna keep them that way till this guy is behind bars.' He sounded ridiculously proud about it. 'But this isn't just about her. You're a big part of the story. A much bigger part, to be honest. And that's where it gets a little tricky.'

'What do you mean?'

'This is a lot of money we're shelling out. You appreciate we have to make sure we're not being sold a pup. Part of the deal with Alice is that we talk to you, strictly off the record . . .' A hopeful pause. 'Unless you want to sign up as well?'

'I'll pass on that for now,' she said. 'Go on.'

'All right, off the record it is. We need to run through Alice's state-ment, make sure what she's given us is kosher. You're the only one who can corroborate it.'

'And if I say no?'

Fisher sucked air between his teeth. 'It could jeopardise the deal. I'm not saying it will. But it does make round-the-clock protection a bit harder to authorise.'

Bastard, she thought. Using Alice's safety to coerce her into helping.

He added, 'Alice assured us you'd be willing to help. She said you were a really decent person. The fact you were worried about her proves that.'

Julia sighed. 'What would I have to do?'

'Just meet up and go through the statement. It'll take twenty minutes, half an hour at most. I'll bring a disclaimer, forbidding us to quote directly from you.' He hesitated. 'Unless you want to reconsider? I can give you the name of a good PR firm if you want to get some advice first.'

'No,' said Julia firmly. 'I'll do this for Alice, but that's all.'

'Fair enough. We're on a tight timeframe, though. Can we meet this evening?'

'I suppose so.' And immediately thought: *I don't want you in my flat.*

'You're in Lewes, aren't you?' he said. She could hear the tap of a keyboard. 'Is the Hamsey Arms any good?'

'That's fine.'

'Great. Probably the earliest I can get down there and still meet my deadline is seven o'clock. That okay?'

She agreed reluctantly. 'How will I recognise you?'

'Easy. I'm drop-dead gorgeous.' More laughter, all from him. 'Nah, I'll be the guy still working his butt off. You won't miss me.'

She put the phone down in a temper. To think she'd worried herself sick about Alice committing suicide, and instead the woman had hawked her story to the gutter press. She snatched up her bag and slammed the door behind her.

Sixty-Two

Heading south, Vilner felt faintly queasy. This was his third visit to Chilton in four days, and potentially the most important one. He still wasn't sure if he was doing the right thing, but he'd weighed it up as best he could and decided it was worth a punt.

He drove carefully, observing the speed limits and traffic signals. He couldn't risk getting pulled over with some of the gear he had on him. When Kendrick phoned him, he ignored it. He wanted to delay the conversation until after this was done. By then he'd know exactly what he was facing.

The meeting might get unpleasant, so he had prepared carefully. For one thing, he was more than an hour early. He'd borrowed an anonymous two-year-old Volvo, which he parked in the village. He wore a dark grey suit and cashmere overcoat. The weather was turning, and there were only a handful of people around, mainly sightseers by the look of them. Vilner attracted barely a glance as he took a briefcase from the boot and crossed the road into Hurst Lane.

The trees were straining in the wind, as though they wanted to be somewhere else. The sound was like a hundred human voices crying a lament. Leaves and twigs fell all around him, and he felt a brief nostalgic longing for the noise and smell of traffic, the buzz of the crowd.

As he walked, he didn't think too much about what lay ahead. Instead he thought about the woman.

Julia timed her swim about right. In the early afternoon the indoor pool was at its quietest, and she easily ignored a few prurient glances. She intended to be long gone by three o'clock, when an inflatable assault course was floated out on the water and hordes of local children materialised to play on it.

In the course of a dozen unhurried laps her anger melted away and left her far more forgiving of Alice's decision. Unlike the police, a newspaper would have few qualms about providing protection on the basis of what might be spurious allegations. They appreciated the pure news value of the story, never mind its veracity.

For a woman torn by an agonising separation from her family, it must have seemed like the perfect answer. And in a roundabout way it might achieve what Julia wanted: a renewed police investigation. The only thing that rankled was the way Alice had volunteered her assistance, although Julia suspected that was more the reporter's doing.

The pool was part of a leisure centre, with large windows along two of the outside walls. Each time she rested, she gazed up at a slice of sky above the cliffs that overlooked the town. Now she watched a finger of grey cloud slowly gliding across the blue, like a bruise spreading on clear skin.

She shivered. It was time to go.

She dried off and dressed in a cold, poky cubicle that brought to mind her school days: damp clothes and teasing and towel snaps. As she walked out through the lobby, the automatic doors opened and a gust of wind buffeted her. The woman at the desk gasped. 'My goodness, it's blowing out there.'

Julia nodded, glad she'd brought her car, but wishing she didn't have to go out again this evening.

It took her only a couple of minutes to drive home, but longer to find a vacant parking space in the busy streets near the castle. As she got out of the car, the sun was finally extinguished by cloud and a whole different season seemed to take hold. No rain yet, but there was a vicious edge to the wind, something almost malicious as it whipped up from nowhere and subsided just as quickly. She hurried back to her flat, litter and dry leaves skittering in her wake. More than once she turned, convinced there was someone behind her.

Her name was Louise, and she'd recently started work at a pub in Crouch End part-owned by Vilner. She was twenty-five, petite and pretty, with large liquid eyes and an alluring gap between her front teeth. From what he'd gathered, she had spent a few years travelling and working abroad, returning to the UK when a relationship ended.

What impressed him was that she wasn't intimidated by him the way most people were. She looked him in the eye, and when he tried out a bit of sarcasm she came right back at him. They'd had one date so far, concluded with no more than a prim goodnight kiss, but he'd sensed a real chemistry between them. Tonight he was taking her to a favourite restaurant of his, out in Amersham, and then, with any luck, back to his place for a nightcap.

That was later. First, there was this.

The house looked cold, empty, abandoned. Vilner waited in the lane, hidden by trees, and watched for five long minutes. The wind swirled over the roof, rattling the tiles and keening round the chimney pots. A crushed can blew across the yard and snagged in the hedge. In one of the outbuildings a loose plank drummed against something metal. Lots of noise to distract and deter him, but at last he was satisfied.

He made a full circuit of the building, examining the windows and doors, frequently pausing to listen. He knew the place was unoccupied, but there were curtains and blinds drawn everywhere, so he couldn't scope out the interior. The back door was just as solid as the front. It didn't give a fraction when he tried the handle.

He returned to the front door. There were two locks: a straight-forward cylinder at the top and a mortice deadlock below it. He opened the briefcase and took out an electric pick gun. In prison he'd learned the basics of lock picking, and over the years he'd developed his skills with a traditional set of hand tools, but once mastered the electric picks were much quicker and less obtrusive.

Today his luck was in: the mortice hadn't been used. It took him less than a minute to overcome the cylinder, and the door sprang open. He lifted the briefcase over the threshold and shut the door behind him. A gust of wind boomed in the chimney breast. The roof timbers creaked like a ship in a storm.

He could see the room to his left was empty, furrows in the carpet where furniture had once stood. He knelt to put the pick away, and take out his gun. Flipping the briefcase lid, he caught a flash of movement from the room to his right. Something coming in fast and heavy. No time to use the gun. All he could do was twist sideways and ride with the blow, but it wasn't enough.

His last conscious thought was, *Not lucky at all.*

There had been another recent call, number withheld, but no messages. Nothing from Craig.

She fretted for more than an hour before finally deciding she had to warn him. Unwilling to risk another confrontation with Nina, she tried his mobile and got the answering service. She quickly composed a message.

'Craig, it's Julia. I thought I should warn you, Alice Jones has sold her story. The journalist wants me to corroborate it, so I've agreed to a meeting this evening. I'll ring you when I get back, probably around eight. If you get a chance, ring me and we can discuss how much I should reveal.' She swallowed, thinking: *But we're not allowed to speak to each other.*

Less than a minute after she put the phone down, it rang again. Either Craig was responding to her message, or Nina had intercepted it and was about to scream at her.

But it was neither. A woman with a cultured but slightly abrasive Scottish accent said, 'Am I speaking with Julia Trent?'

'Yes.'

'Julia, my name is Sheila Naughton. I believe you're aware there's a major new exclusive being prepared, and I wondered if you'd care to add your own comments to—'

'No, thank you. I have nothing to say.'

Julia put the receiver down and held it there, as if restraining a small animal. Within ten seconds it rang again. She lifted the receiver and cut the call. Another ten seconds and it rang again. She pulled the line plug from the socket.

Clearly Guy Fisher had failed to keep the story under wraps.

The onslaught had begun.

Vilner was thirteen again, conning money from a nonce in a Gents near Sovereign Street. Too late he realised he'd been set up for an ambush. A second man stepped from a cubicle and shoved him off his feet. His head hit the grimy tiled floor and he passed out. When he came to he was lying face down in a puddle of stale piss, one of the men tugging on his jeans while the other knelt over him, stroking his cock and breathlessly explaining where he was going to put it.

In a sudden frenzy Vilner kicked backwards and caught the first man in the face, then reared up and grabbed the other one by the balls, wrenching them as hard as he could. Slippery from the wet tiles, he wriggled through a flurry of blows and managed to get away. Bursting into the twilight of a winter afternoon, he sprinted towards the safety of the Christmas shopping crowds on Briggate, and the intoxicating blend of terror and elation felt just as vivid upon recollection a quarter of a century later as it had at the time. For a moment he was truly superhuman, capable of anything.

Then he opened his eyes and saw he wasn't in Leeds. He wasn't thirteen any more. And he wasn't about to fight his way to freedom.

This time the ache from his head wound was eclipsed by a pain in both arms so excruciating he could hardly breathe. He blinked furiously to clear his vision, but even when he'd stared at them for what seemed like an eternity, he still couldn't make sense of what he saw.

His hands were missing.

Sixty-Three

Craig didn't look at his mobile until he was on the train back to Sussex, at the end of a long and harrowing day. When the buffet trolley approached, he thought he'd never in his life wanted a beer as much as he did now. It took all his willpower to shake his head and watch the trolley pass.

He listened to Julia's message and checked the time. It was gone six-thirty, probably already too late to call her. In any case, he was in no mood to discuss Alice Jones and her tabloid exclusive. Abby Clark was dead, and it was his fault.

After his meeting with Sullivan, he'd gone to see Abby's partner, Marie. His visit had several purposes: to offer her some support, to find out if she knew anything else that could help find Abby, and to assure her that he and Abby had never had an affair. He'd been there an hour or so, sharing tea and sympathy, when the police arrived with the news they'd been dreading. The body of a woman, believed to be Abby, had been recovered from the Thames.

Until that point, Marie had made a supreme effort to hold herself together. Now she disintegrated in front of his eyes. When the police officer asked if she was able to identify the body, Craig offered to accompany her. In a private moment at the mortuary, he learned that the cause of death wasn't yet confirmed. There was evidence of violent trauma, but it wasn't clear if this had been inflicted by an assailant, or whether she had collided with something in the water. The post mortem should tell them more.

He returned to Marie's flat, and sat with her while she made a succession of difficult calls to Abby's family and friends. It wasn't until he walked back to the tube station, emotionally drained and boiling with fury, that he allowed himself to say the words in his head: Abby had been murdered.

He was equally convinced the killer was either James Vilner, or the other man, Kendrick. One or both of them had engineered the Chilton massacre, almost certainly on behalf of George Matheson. Abby had died because of the favour she had done for Craig. Because she'd come too close to the truth.

That in itself was almost impossible to bear. What made it even worse was that he couldn't prove any of it.

Vilner stared. His vision blurred again and instinctively he tried lifting his arms, but they wouldn't move. He blinked and stared, blinked and stared, but no matter how many times he did it the result was always the same. Both his hands were gone.

'You've never taken me seriously, have you?' said a voice. He realised there was someone in the room with him. He forced his head up and made out a pair of workman's overalls, splattered with what looked like red paint.

'Best to demonstrate from the start that I don't go in for half measures,' the man went on. 'Though what I did in Chilton should have made that clear.'

The man waited, perhaps expecting a response, but Vilner's brain wouldn't process the words. They reached him like someone shouting through a waterfall; just static flooding his skull. He couldn't believe he'd been so thoroughly outplayed. He thought he'd come here early enough to anticipate a trap, but his opponent was earlier still.

He looked back at himself. He was slumped in a half-sitting position on the floor of what had once been the farmhouse's dining room.

Instead of carpet below him, there was a thick layer of plastic sheeting, the type builders put down when laying foundations to prevent damp penetration. The sheeting ran the entire width of the room and was taped to the walls at a height of about two feet. The only other things he could see were a couple of large buckets, a roll of heavy-duty plastic bags and a DeWalt Alligator saw with the same red paint along the blades.

He opened his mouth to speak but vomited instead, an acidic gruel which dropped on to his chest and pooled in his lap. He stared at it for a moment, then back at his arms, which ended in stumps covered in crude white dressings. There were thick tourniquets around both wrists.

The man saw him studying them and said, 'I applied those before the surgery. After all, it's no fun if you bleed to death this early on.'

The torrent of pain must have let up slightly, for Vilner made sense of the phrase *bleed to death*. He was struck by a thought: *How will I drive Louise tonight if I don't have any hands?*

His lips formed a smile of profound disbelief, and he began to cry.

Sixty-Four

The Hamsey Arms was a long low building on the outskirts of Cooksbridge, just north of Lewes. To reach it, Julia had to drive along a dark, thickly wooded stretch of road. By now the wind had risen to gale force, an almost relentless howl audible over the sound of her engine. She could feel the tyres bumping over debris in the road. Her headlights picked out trees writhing in the wind. She'd already heard reports of blocked roads and railway lines, and the storm was forecast to get worse as the evening went on.

The main bar faced out towards the road. The well-lit interior looked cosy and welcoming as she turned into the car park. The fact she'd arrived in one piece filled her with relief, as did the sight of eight or ten other cars: she wasn't the only one crazy enough to venture out on a night like this. There was a small garden at the front, with picnic tables and planters made from beer barrels. A couple of the tables had overturned, and it looked like the planters would be next.

Just as she switched off the ignition, a single fat raindrop exploded on the windscreen and ran down the glass. Then another. Then it was as if someone had tipped an enormous tank of water upside down. The sudden deluge pounded on the roof and made the sound of the wind almost insignificant.

She turned up the collar of her coat, as if that would make a difference, and prepared for a soaking. When she opened the door, the wind nearly tore it from her grasp. She got out, slammed the door and locked it, then hurried as fast as she dared towards the pub.

She entered the bar on a rush of wind and rain. Bottles and glasses rattled in the draught, and there was nervous laughter. A dozen or so faces turned to stare, then gradually looked away. The main group was a family gathering, taking up several tables festooned with gift-wrapping and party novelties. A rather imperious elderly lady sat at one end, wearing a paper crown. There were about fifteen people with her, including several excited children.

Julia tidied her hair, wiped rain from her face, undid her coat. Then she looked up, scanning the bar, and just as it occurred to her that the weather might have caused him to delay or even cancel their meeting, she spotted him.

The train was packed with Saturday shoppers and a fair number of football fans. Craig found himself squashed into a window seat beside an obscenely overweight man who reeked of beer and body odour. Keeping his breathing as shallow as possible, he planted his face against the window, his reflection pale and anxious in the darkness.

He'd learned from Marie that Abby's laptop was missing, along with her treasured Blackberry. When asked, the police officer wasn't sure if these items had been recovered, but he thought it extremely unlikely. So did Craig. Which meant no one knew exactly how far her enquiries had progressed.

Now he went back over their conversation on Thursday morning. She knew virtually nothing about Kendrick, other than that he was from Trinidad. What she'd learned about Vilner had confirmed Craig's suspicions. Vilner had got on board the Matheson gravy train as a result of money he was owed. What had she said? Gambling debts run up by George's nephew. Toby someone. Harman?

He flinched as a volley of raindrops rattled on the window. The man next to him shifted, pressing further into his space. Craig tried to ignore the discomfort. Something in the conversation was snagging right at the back of his mind, but he couldn't see it. Couldn't force it into the light.

The train rumbled and shook, and he glimpsed leaves swirling past. He thought about his father's lawn, always kept so tidy, and idly wondered at what age a man developed the patience to sweep his garden after every storm. He thought about the creep he'd caught taking photographs of the front door.

He thought about Julia, how they read her father's diary and shared a maelstrom of emotions that led first to a passionate disagreement and then, quite unexpectedly, to a different kind of passion.

A loud snore from his fellow passenger jolted Craig from his reverie, leaving an infuriating conviction that this insight, whatever it was, had been tantalisingly close.

Personal space. Something about personal space.

Guy Fisher wasn't quite what she'd expected. The voice on the phone had been assured, even cocky, but the man sitting alone at a corner table looked geeky and the very opposite of drop-dead gorgeous. It made her wonder how often he'd impressed someone who heard his voice, only for them to be disappointed when they met him in the flesh.

On the other hand, there was little doubt it was him. He was virtually the only customer sitting alone, and he was the only one tapping away on a laptop. There was paper all over the table, and a briefcase standing upright on the seat next to him.

He looked fairly young, late twenties or early thirties, and wore a blue shirt under a black Armani bomber jacket. She could see the bulge of a serious beer belly pressing against the table. He had brown hair, slicked back with gel or mousse, and he wore glasses with square lenses that did him no favours. Something about his almost wooden focus on the laptop reminded her of that puppet from a 1960s TV show. What was he called?

She cleared her throat as she reached him. He didn't acknowledge her, but went on typing as if he couldn't possibly interrupt himself mid-flow. She waited, deciding she would count to five and then walk out.

On three he looked up, almost surprised, as if he hadn't really expected her to show up. 'Miss Trent? I'm Guy Fisher. Take a seat.' His rubbery lips formed an ingratiating smile, and she had to suppress a giggle.

Joe 90, she thought. That's who he looks like.

She took off her coat before sitting down. As her back arched she saw his gaze dart towards her breasts, searching for the outline of her nipples through the shirt. She folded her arms and looked him in the eye.

'It's good of you to come,' he said, closing the laptop. He gathered up the paperwork and shuffled it into some sort of order. She noticed a glass by his side, containing an inch of what looked like Coke, and wondered if he was going to buy her a drink. Not that she really wanted one, but in the circumstances it was only polite to offer. She had a feeling politeness was just one of the social skills he lacked.

'With you in a second,' he said. He lifted the briefcase on to the table, put the laptop away, then began hunting through the papers again.

A cheer went up across the room. Julia turned to see a waitress emerge from the kitchens, holding a birthday cake ablaze with candles. When the old woman saw it she smiled benevolently. The adults were applauding, while the children knelt on their seats and chanted, 'Gran-ny! Gran-ny!'

'Ahh. Isn't that sweet?' Fisher gave her a sickly grin. He placed the papers in an upper pocket in the briefcase, then began to slide the case around. 'This is what you need to see.'

A ferocious gust of wind shook the building and the lights in the bar flickered on and off. Julia glanced at the window and saw her reflection strobing in the glass: here*gone*here*gone*. Fisher turned the briefcase so the upper half was facing out towards the room. His right hand was resting inside it.

'Here we are,' he said.

He was holding a black pistol.

Sixty-Five

Another gust of wind, and a loud crash from outside. One of the children screamed and clutched her father. The lights flickered again, but stayed on. There were ominous groans from the drinkers at the bar.

The man sitting opposite her ignored it all. He stared at her through his ridiculous glasses, and she understood that they were simply part of his disguise, along with the Estuary voice and the slicked-back hair and the paunch. He wasn't a journalist, here to verify Alice Jones's story.

He was the second killer.

He watched her closely. His smile was hideous, no warmth or light in his eyes.

'I take it you've worked out who I am?'

'Yes.' The sound of her own voice surprised her. She hadn't expected it to function. She certainly didn't expect it to sound so calm.

'Good. Now this is where you have to be very sensible. Otherwise a lot of people will get hurt.' He nodded towards the bar. 'Take a look around.'

Julia did as she was told. The family party was singing 'Happy Birthday'. The old woman sat through it, her face illuminated by the candles, her smile a little forced, as if she would really rather be at home with her feet up. The other customers were watching them, or talking to each other, or busy eating and drinking.

No one had noticed anything wrong. No one else knew there was an armed man in the pub.

'I'm not going to kill you,' he said. 'But we need to go somewhere, and we need to do it quietly. If there's any fuss, the first thing I'll do is shoot you in the leg, so you can't get away. Okay?'

She nodded dumbly.

'The next thing I'll do is shoot the bar staff, because they're most likely to try and phone for help. Then I'll shoot a few of the customers to create a panic.' He made a show of assessing the best contenders. 'The old woman, probably. And at least one of the kids. I'll aim for their faces. It'll be messy, and it may not kill them straight away. While they're screaming, everyone else will be too traumatised to react. They certainly won't stop us leaving. Am I getting my message across?'

He smiled again. He could have been running through the itinerary for a perfect evening out.

'Yes,' she said through gritted teeth.

'Great. We're going to stand up like a couple of good friends and walk out without so much as a word. That old lady and her delightful family get to remember this occasion the way they should.' He smirked. 'All right?'

Julia said nothing. Reluctantly she met his eye and nodded.

'Well done.' He glanced around, then shut the briefcase and stood it upright on the table. No urgency. No fumbling. His voice had remained steady the whole time, she realised. No emotion when he talked about shooting a child in the face.

'The gun will be concealed by the case,' he said quietly, 'but I'm still holding it. Remember that. Don't get it into your head that you're going to play the hero.'

He stood up and ushered her towards the door. She felt as though she'd been hypnotised. Her body seemed to respond to his commands without any conscious input from her brain. She walked like a robot, her movements stiff and unnatural. Surely someone will notice, she thought. Surely someone will stop us.

But no one did.

He led her across the car park, towards a silver Renault Laguna. He must have pressed a key fob, for the lights flashed and there was a bleep as the car unlocked.

'Round the back,' he said, shouting to be heard above the storm. In the corner of the car park a couple of fence panels had blown down, and now the wind was lifting loose slats, trying to tear them free. Julia had a second to think about making a run for it, then she felt him bump against her and knew she'd never do it in time.

She still felt numb, disbelieving, but that worked in her favour. It held the worst of the fear at bay, allowed her mind to clear a little. If she couldn't run, what *could* she do?

He'd let her put her coat back on, though the rain was pelting her hair and running down her neck. She wore her handbag over her shoulder. It wasn't large, or particularly expensive. A neat rectangle of black leather, bought on holiday in Greece a couple of years ago for thirty or forty euros. Neat, compact, unobtrusive.

Right now it was the most precious thing she owned.

He directed her to stand behind the car while he opened the door and slung the briefcase on to the back seat. Then he opened the boot and gestured at it.

'Get in.'

Julia didn't protest. Afterwards she wondered if she should have. Maybe that would have made him less suspicious.

Instead she complied, quickly and meekly, climbing in without assistance, folding herself into the space by turning on her side and drawing up her knees, the handbag trapped awkwardly beneath her body, where he couldn't see it.

'Have a pleasant journey,' he said, and shut the boot with a heavy whump.

As soon as it closed, Julia wriggled until she could reach her handbag and pull it clear of her body. She was in complete darkness. The boot smelled of chemical cleaner. The rain was drumming on the bodywork above her.

She returned to a foetal position and held the handbag in both hands. Felt for the strap and turned it upright before opening the zip. Then she put one hand inside and carefully probed the contents until her fingers closed around the beautiful smooth weight that was her mobile phone.

The killer was opening the driver's door when he felt a vibration in his pocket. It was the phone he had taken from Vilner, and he was intrigued to see who would be calling. He pulled the phone out and dropped into the driver's seat. At the same time a little firework seemed to go off in his head, a spray of bright light that bloomed into the letters of one simple word.

Phone.

She felt him climb into the car. Heard his door close, just as a comforting electronic glow lit up the boot compartment. A strong signal, and plenty of battery strength. Julia felt a flood of gratitude and promised never to curse this wonderful invention ever again.

Then she felt the car rock on its suspension, and knew the killer had realised his mistake.

He opened the boot just in time to see her thumb pressing out a number. She tried to turn away from him, shielding the phone with her body. He punched her in the head with savage force. The blow knocked her against the back seats and she passed out. He delved for the phone and read the display.

Calling . . . 999

He disconnected the call and slipped the phone into his pocket. Grabbed her handbag and slammed the boot shut. That was close. Too fucking close.

Back in the car, he took off his fake glasses and removed the padding under his shirt. He wiped his face, then picked up Vilner's phone again. *One missed call*, it said. He found the number and stared at the name in the display.

Then he started the engine. It wasn't yet seven-thirty, on one of the longest, most demanding days of his life, and there was still a lot to do. But phase one was complete.

Mission accomplished.

Sixty-Six

Craig took a taxi home from the station, the driver regaling him with accounts of ships run aground and motorway pile-ups caused by the storm. It made him wonder if he should stay over in Crawley. He could sleep in the spare room and leave early tomorrow.

Now he knew the fate that had befallen Abby, the threat to his children seemed even more potent. It made him consider whether it was wise to go on living apart from them. At the very least he ought to tell Nina about the photograph, but equally he feared her reaction. She, like any sensible person, would probably insist that he stop investigating the massacre, whereas Craig was inclined to do the opposite: confront his enemy head on. But first he needed to be sure who that enemy was.

Stopping at a junction, the car rocked on its suspension as if pushed by unseen hands. The windscreen wipers were slashing back and forth, but had little effect on the torrent of water falling on the car. The driver peered over his steering wheel at traffic lights that were barely more than smudges of colour in the darkness.

'Filthy weather,' he muttered. 'Any other night I'd knock off early, but I can't miss a Saturday.'

'Hard to imagine anyone going clubbing.'

'Oh, they will.' The driver snorted. 'And wearing next to nothing, too.'

Craig had his key ready when he got out of the taxi, but even the short dash to the front door left him drenched. In the hall he took off his coat and paused, registering the unnatural stillness: it caused a moment of utter, debilitating panic. He was too late.

Then he heard footsteps on the stairs and Nina came down, wearing a bathrobe. Her toenails looked newly painted, and her hair was wrapped in a towel.

'Where are the kids?'

'Mum and Dad's,' said Nina. 'They're sleeping over.'

'Oh.' His relief that they were safe was mixed with disappointment at not seeing them. He might as well brave the weather and go back to Chilton.

Nina stepped forward, coming close enough to touch. Her robe was open, revealing plenty of cleavage, her breasts damp and flushed and glistening. He could smell body lotion and feel the heat radiating from her skin.

'Stay here tonight,' she said. 'I'll cook a meal. We can talk.'

'Maybe,' he said, his stomach churning as he pictured her in bed with Bruce Abbott. Then he thought of the kiss he'd shared with Julia, the desire he had felt. Last night he'd endured a barrage of accusations from Nina after stupidly lying to her on the phone, but judging by her mood now, perhaps she had accepted his denials.

It struck him that she hadn't asked about Abby. He stepped sideways, easing away from her. 'I need to change out of these clothes.'

Nina bravely ignored his lack of enthusiasm. 'Why not have a shower?'

She's going to suggest we make love, he thought, turning towards the stairs so she wouldn't see his face. 'Anyone rung?' he called back.

'Yes,' said Nina, with evident displeasure. 'Lots of reporters, wanting to speak to you. They wouldn't tell me why. I took their numbers.'

He grunted. Probably wanting his reaction to the Alice Jones story. He decided he'd wait to hear from Julia before he went back to them.

Upstairs, he stripped off and decided a shower was a good idea. He stood under the hot spray, slightly worried Nina would seek to join him. If the timing hadn't been so dreadful, he might have welcomed her suggestion to discuss their predicament over a meal, calmly, intelligently, like proper grown-ups. But he couldn't imagine doing it right now. Not with Abby dead, and his kids unwitting pawns in the game, and the second killer still out there—

And not when you're in love with Julia, a quiet voice shamed him.

He sighed. Just being here, having a shower, sent the wrong signals. He couldn't pretend to be interested in reconciliation, but nor could he humiliate her by appearing to encourage an advance. He should have said something straight away, the moment she stepped into his personal space.

And then he had it, all at once. Dad's garden. The intruder. Julia reading her father's diary.

Not personal space.

Territory.

Vilner's phone rang again. The killer was well away from the pub, making good progress. The atrocious driving conditions had slowed him a little, but on the upside the roads were virtually deserted.

He pulled into a layby, glancing warily at a stand of trees looming over the car. He could hear them creaking as they swayed. The rain flew at the windows in horizontal waves, like someone tossing buckets of water at the car. He picked up the phone and answered with a cheery, 'Hello!'

'Vilner?' A slightly mystified voice. Hard to make out any detail with the storm raging around him, but it was male, with some sort of unusual accent.

'He's not here,' the killer said, having to shout.

'Who is this?'

'You'll find out soon enough. For now all you need to know is that Vilner is no longer on the scene. You'll be dealing with me, and only with me. Is that clear?'

A long silence followed. Whether it was shock, or anger, or incredulity, the killer had no idea.

He ended the call.

Craig ran into the bedroom, ignoring the fact that he was soaking wet. He wiped his hand on the bed and picked up his phone. Rang Julia's mobile. It was switched off. He rang her home number. No answer.

He tried her mobile again, returning to the bathroom to grab a towel. While he dried, he replayed her message.

Craig, it's Julia. I thought I should warn you, Alice Jones has sold her story. The journalist wants me to corroborate it, so I've agreed to a meeting this evening. I'll ring you when I get back, probably around eight. If you get a chance, ring me and we can discuss how much I should reveal.

Dressing quickly, he tried her number one more time, then hurried downstairs. Nina heard the urgency and came out of the kitchen, frowning.

'Where are the numbers?' he called.

'What?'

'The reporters that rang you. Where are their numbers?'

Something in her face changed. Her voice was harder when she said, 'What's happened?'

'I don't know yet.' He grabbed his shoes and began putting them on.

'You're not going out in this weather?'

'I might have to.'

She sighed in a way that suggested she was trying very hard not to scream, and stomped back into the kitchen. Craig laced his shoes and ran through his idea once again, testing it for flaws.

Julia's father had encountered Carl and the other killer, practising in woodland owned by George Matheson. When challenged, the killer had accused Julia's father of trespassing on private land.

Craig remembered how he had reacted when he found the souvenir hunter in his father's garden. He'd said, 'Get the fuck off *my* property.' Not because he stood to inherit the house, but because the family connection gave him a sense of ownership.

Now he asked himself: what if the killer's attitude was borne from the same instinct? That the reason he'd been so arrogant was because he considered the woods belonged to him.

Because he was related to George Matheson.

He thought of the nephew, Toby, forced to offer Vilner a contract after running up gambling debts. He felt a tingle of excitement. Under scrutiny, the idea didn't fall apart. But he also felt a much stronger current of fear. Because the one person whose opinion he valued wasn't answering her phone. And he had no idea where she was.

Sixty-Seven

Kendrick put the phone down. He looked at Jacques, just back from a futile expedition to find James Vilner. Jacques immediately saw something was wrong.

'If I'm not mistaken,' Kendrick said, 'that was a declaration of war.'

Jacques looked confused. 'From Vilner?'

Kendrick shook his head. 'I suspect Vilner was the first casualty.' He gazed at the floor, all kinds of scenarios running through his mind. 'No. From Toby.'

'Toby's got Vilner?' Jacques sounded more shocked than surprised.

'We should have guessed when the emails stopped. He's obviously decided to go it alone.'

'What do you think he's planning?'

Kendrick shrugged. 'I don't know, but it's time to find out.'

'I just went past Chelsea,' Jacques said wearily. 'I could have checked the fucking apartment.'

'I don't think he'll be there, but send a couple of men. The rest of us will be going to Sussex. We're paying a visit to Uncle George.'

Jacques gave a greedy smile. 'I'll get the guns and the radios.'

Kendrick nodded, then turned towards the window. Having grown up with hurricanes, he'd barely paid attention to the storm raging outside, but now he listened to the howling wind, and grew thoughtful.

'Do we have a chainsaw in the garage?'

'I think so.'

'Good. Bring that as well.'

There were half a dozen names on the list Nina gave him. Craig recognised most of them. The first three had obviously been on fishing expeditions. They were vague about the story they were proposing to write, as though they'd heard something was in the offing and wanted to see what he knew about it. He told them he knew nothing.

The fourth was a Scottish woman, Sheila Naughton. She admitted Alice Jones had come to her with an exclusive about the Chilton massacre. Before she could ask him to comment, Craig jumped in with his own question.

'Have you spoken to Julia Trent about this?'

Naughton was taken aback, but admitted she had. 'I talked to her briefly this afternoon.'

'You didn't arrange to meet her, or get a colleague to meet her?'

'No. She put the phone down on me.' Exasperation quickly turned to curiosity. 'Why?'

'It doesn't matter,' Craig said, and ended the call.

But it did matter. It meant Julia had gone to meet an impostor.

Nina was the other side of the room, radiating tension and hostility, all thoughts of reconciliation apparently long gone. 'Well?'

'Julia's missing. I need to find her.'

Nina shook her head, as if Craig were guilty of some terrible lapse of judgement. 'I told her to stay out of our lives. Maybe she's—'

Craig cut her short. 'You did what?'

Nina threw up her hands in despair. 'She's the problem, Craig. Egging you on with this ridiculous obsession. I'm offering you a chance to mend our relationship, and all you care about is running off into the night to find that bloody woman.'

Craig was almost breathless with shock. It took him a few seconds before he could speak. 'When? When did you tell her that?'

Nina reddened, sensing she was now on the back foot. 'This morning. She rang after you'd gone out.'

Craig stared at her for a moment, feeling utterly betrayed, then strode into the hall. Nina followed, hesitating in the doorway. She watched him putting on his coat, her eyes shining with tears.

'You're overreacting,' she told him. 'She'll turn up somewhere.'

'Yeah, that's right,' Craig said. 'She might turn up the way Abby Clark turned up. Dead.'

He opened the front door and slammed it shut behind him.

Julia's head cleared slowly. The heat from the exhaust became painful, forcing her to curl up even tighter. She could hear little apart from the barrage of rain on the bodywork, the hiss of tyres on wet roads, the rumble of passing vehicles.

In the darkness she tried to assess her injury. She was cut just above her right ear. She didn't think it was deep, although the blood was matted and sticky in her hair. She had a thumping headache, but other than that she felt okay.

Grimly she reflected on how she had been deceived. He'd sounded so plausible on the phone. What he told her about Alice going to the media made perfect sense after the call she'd had from Alice herself. And the other caller, the Scottish woman, had also referred to it.

That part must be true, she deduced. Alice really had gone to a newspaper, probably the one which employed the Scottish woman, and the killer had been tipped off. It was perhaps no more than pure chance that he had reached her before the genuine journalist.

She cursed. If she'd spoken to the woman first, she wouldn't be in this predicament. After the near miss at Kate's hotel, and again at her parents' cottage, he had finally got her. But who was he?

Not James Vilner. She and Craig had got that wrong. She wondered what else they'd got wrong. Then she thought about Craig. If not for Nina's outburst this morning, she probably would have asked him to accompany her this evening. And then what . . . ?

It was pointless to speculate. It was done now, and it had to be faced. She tried to dredge up the courage she'd found on 19 January. *Every second she stayed alive was a tiny victory*. Wasn't that what she had told herself?

She said it again now. Said it over and over. But somehow it was different this time. Deep down, she didn't believe it.

She believed she was going to die.

Sixty-Eight

Just as he'd predicted to anyone who would listen, the meeting at Scotland Yard achieved nothing. 'A six-hour wank session,' were his exact words, and by the time he got home Sullivan's mood had only worsened. Half his weekend already wasted, and now it was blowing such a gale that even a stroll to his local pub didn't hold much appeal.

And despite spending much of the day tuning out the conference while he pondered his own problems, he still hadn't formed a viable plan to resolve them. During the breaks he'd made some calls and discovered that Craig's journo buddy wasn't missing any more: she'd been fished out of the Thames.

That was very bad news, and not just for her. It was getting much harder to disregard what Craig had been telling him. There was some-thing big and bad going on here, almost certainly connected to the massacre, and as he saw it, only one person could give him the answers he needed.

It would be easier to do by phone, and because he'd had a long day and it was such shitty weather, Sullivan was sorely tempted. But it would be very unwise. With the stakes so high, only face-to-face contact would suffice.

The other factor, which he thought less likely all the time but couldn't quite abandon completely, was that he might persuade George to cough up some cash while he was there. For if he had to summarise his game plan right now, it basically amounted to *take the money and run*.

It took him less than twenty minutes to reach the farm. The biggest challenge wasn't negotiating the narrow, storm-lashed roads. It was controlling his excitement. In one day he'd outwitted his two most dangerous opponents, and now he had both at his mercy.

Answering Vilner's phone had been a slightly impetuous act. Probably not sensible to goad this man Kendrick when he knew so little about him. Still, posing as a journalist had been a stroke of pure genius. He had George to thank for warning him about Alice Jones. It provided the perfect opportunity to lure Julia into a trap, safely away from her home and the protection of her friends and neighbours.

Later he would return to the pub and dispose of her car. Before that, there were many other tasks to complete. Some would be easy, some extremely challenging. He was determined to enjoy them all, especially the chance to make Julia suffer. Pay her back for the worry she'd caused him, all the extra work she had forced him to do.

He pulled up outside the farmhouse. The path had turned into a sea of mud. The wind was screaming through the trees, and it looked as though one of the outbuildings had lost part of its roof. He had a sense that he was poised on the brink of a supreme triumph, his destiny about to be fulfilled. It seemed quite apt that a storm should be laid on in his honour.

The car went through a series of sharp turns. Julia had to brace her shoulders and feet against the sides of the boot to stop herself being thrown about. A couple of minutes later she felt the car bumping over an uneven surface. When it came to a stop, she had only a few seconds to prepare for what lay ahead. She made a conscious decision not to do anything rash. She felt weak and disorientated, in no state to take him on.

He opened the boot. Rain blew in over her face and she blinked, struggling to clear her vision as he loomed over her. He had discarded the glasses; he looked younger and thinner, but no less threatening. She could see in his eyes the arrogance of the man who had shot Carl Forester at point blank range. The man who had tried to kill her not once, but twice.

'Out!' he shouted, and stood back, pointing the gun at her.

She got to her knees and managed to climb out of the car. At first she was surprised by the rural setting, but when she saw the old redbrick farmhouse and the ramshackle outbuildings she had the first inkling of where they were.

He slammed the boot and marched her towards the house. A couple of times she stumbled on the muddy path, and in response he jabbed her with the gun.

'Is this the farm?' she said when they got to the house. Without answering, he bundled her inside. The internal doors were shut and the hallway felt cramped and cold. There was an unpleasant smell in the air. Something familiar. Something that reminded her of Chilton's church on 19 January. Before she could identify it, a far more powerful thought overwhelmed her.

'You killed my parents.'

He examined her closely. 'Why do you say that?'

'My father saw you with Carl, out in the woods. He put it in his diary.' She could feel control of her voice slipping away, her throat closing up. 'That's what you were looking for yesterday morning. The diary.'

He smiled. 'Quite the detective, aren't you?'

'George Matheson must have told you about it,' Julia said. 'He was the only one who knew.'

The killer tipped his head slightly, as if conceding the point. 'They were a loose end,' he said. 'They had to be dealt with.'

It took her a few seconds to comprehend that he was referring to her parents. He was admitting it. She shook her head, tears welling in her eyes.

'Who are you?'

But he didn't answer. He grabbed her arm, opened the door to her right and thrust her into a scene straight from hell.

At first she thought it was a pool, a shimmery blue surface, and the man trussed up in the centre seemed to be floating adrift on it. By her side there was a bucket containing some sort of pink, fleshy creature. A starfish? The gleam of metal confused her and she looked closer. It was a signet ring.

Her bile rising, she looked again at the man lying prisoner and recognised James Vilner. She saw the bandages dark with blood where his hands should have been, and knew then why the smell had reminded her of the church.

'Oh my God.'

Her legs collapsed but the killer caught her, lowered her until she was sitting against the wall. The plastic sheeting was cool and slippery. Blood had pooled and dried in its creases. She rested her head back and shut her eyes. This would go away if she wished it hard enough. It would all go away.

The killer removed her coat and picked up a roll of packing tape. He pulled her hands behind her back and bound her wrists together. While he worked, Vilner began to stir. He was lying sideways on, his legs tied with nylon cord. His head flopped in her direction, and his eyes fluttered open. He regarded her with an expression she'd seen on children suffering at the mercy of playground bullies: *Why me?*

The killer noticed and said, 'I believe you've met Mr Vilner here.'

'What have you done to him?'

'He won't answer my questions.'

There was a noise from Vilner, an objection. 'Fucking . . . madman,' he said. His voice was a hoarse whisper.

'You just have to admit it,' the killer said. Satisfied that Julia was securely bound, he moved across to Vilner and used the nylon cord to pull him into a sitting position. Vilner let out a howl of agony, his arms hanging uselessly at his sides.

'Go on, then,' the killer said. 'Tell me. Why did Carl run into the village?'

'I don't know.'

'Where did he get the gun? You gave it to him, didn't you? You're Decipio?' The killer casually tapped one of the stumps, and Julia saw fresh blood bloom through the bandages. This time Vilner made no sound. He gritted his teeth and gave his tormentor a look of such pure malevolence that even Julia flinched.

'I don't know . . . what you're talking about.'

'Very well. Was it Kendrick who tried to set me up?'

Julia frowned. Kendrick was the name that Abby had given to Craig. She had no idea who or what Decipio was, and it seemed that neither did Vilner.

The killer hunched forward and set to work, doing something to Vilner's leg. Vilner jerked and kicked, but the killer swatted the other wrist to subdue him. When he moved aside, Julia could see he'd tied a tourniquet around Vilner's left ankle.

He picked up a large twin-bladed electric saw, caked with blood.

'Please,' Julia cried. 'He's told you he doesn't know. You must believe him.'

The killer ignored her. He brought the saw down and stopped an inch from Vilner's foot. Vilner stared at it and went rigid, the veins standing out at his temples, sweat beading on his forehead and upper lip. He began to talk rapidly, his dry lips smacking together between each sentence.

'Kendrick's buying the company. From your uncle. Didn't want you involved. Neither of them. Kendrick's using the massacre to force a lower price. He got me to be go-between, to piss George off. He knows about your debts. And the contract you offered me.'

'But if I'm cut out of the deal, you won't get the contract.'

'Kendrick promised me a nice commission either way. Fucking scary, the way he operates. You're nuts . . . if you think you'll get away with this.'

'Why should Kendrick care what happens to you? You were quite prepared to double-cross him.'

Vilner grinned. 'I just hedged my bets. So much shit happening. So many secret agendas.'

'And that's why you tried blackmailing my uncle? That's why you barged into my apartment and threatened me *with a gun*?' His voice rose to a screech on the last three words. The blade moved closer and Julia screamed at him to stop, but the sudden shrill whine of the saw made her appeal meaningless.

James Vilner was going to die, but he felt no fear.

For several hours he'd been drifting in and out of consciousness, until he hardly knew the difference any more. He'd had all kinds of visitors: his mother and father, holding hands like newly-weds. Several of his lovers, standing shyly in a line. The first man he'd killed. He greeted them all. Made peace with them all.

Now there was a woman in the room. She was familiar, but he couldn't quite place her. She was attractive enough to be Louise, the girl he was dating, so that's who she became. He was particularly glad to see her.

The others were his past. Louise was his future.

He watched Toby bring the electric saw down on his right ankle and he felt strangely calm. He knew there was pain, but it was like watching an explosion from behind bombproof glass. It couldn't reach him.

There wasn't much blood. Afterwards Toby picked up the foot, still in its brown boot, and dropped it into a bucket. The woman went white and vomited, and for the first time it occurred to Vilner that maybe she wasn't a hallucination.

Toby said something to her, then turned back to Vilner. He looked like a child denied his favourite treat.

'Just confess, and all this will be over. You're Decipio, aren't you? You sent Carl into the village?'

Vilner shook his head. Afterwards the room drifted lazily back into place.

'Tell me.' Toby showed him the gun in his hand. He aimed it at Vilner's chest and said, 'Speak to me, you bastard.'

Vilner made a momentous effort, sucking up all the little strength that remained and forcing it out in three tiny words.

'*Let her go.*'

Toby shook his head, leaning close enough to embrace him. 'Wrong answer.'

Vilner felt the muzzle against his chest and knew this was the end. Ignoring Toby, he gazed instead at the woman. Weeping, she met his eye and he smiled, recognising a rare courage. He prayed she had a better chance than him.

Not Louise, he thought, as the pressure on the trigger nudged the barrel a little closer to his heart. *Julia.*

Sixty-Nine

Craig drove to Lewes first. It was a frustrating journey, all the more so when it proved fruitless. Julia's car was nowhere in sight, and she didn't answer her doorbell. He managed to rouse one of her neighbours, who let him into the building, and together they stood at Julia's door, knocking and calling for several minutes.

He returned to his car, musing over what he knew. He was satisfied Sheila Naughton had told the truth. Perhaps one of her rivals had got wind of the story, and was fooling Julia for his or her own purposes, but Craig didn't think so. Julia had been deceived by someone with far more sinister motives.

If it was the second killer, and the killer was Toby Harman, he had somehow acquired enough inside knowledge to appear convincing. It was evident from what little the other reporters knew that the story had been kept tightly under wraps. So how had he known about Alice?

It was now gone eight o'clock. The rain had eased off slightly, but the wind was as ferocious as ever. The radio had reported an overturned lorry on an exposed section of the A27 near Lancing, and there were trees down across the South East. Driving into the wind, Craig had to press the accelerator to the floor just to do thirty or forty miles an hour.

He decided to head for Chilton. If nothing else, he could check out her parents' cottage. If she wasn't there, he really only had one option left.

On the B2112 a fallen branch had partially blocked the road. Craig swerved round it and had a brief flashback to his accident on Wednesday night. Thank God he'd stayed sober tonight.

He pulled up by the cottage, got out and hammered on the door. While he was waiting, a roof tile shattered in the road a few feet from his hire car. A curtain twitched next door and he glimpsed a pale face, staring at him as though he was mad.

Perhaps I am, he thought. Anyone with a scrap of sense was indoors. He jumped back in the car and drove along the High Street. Something came flying at him out of the darkness and splattered against the windscreen: a sodden bouquet of flowers. The floral tributes had been blasted all across the green, and the pond was frothing like a miniature sea. Only the yew tree seemed immune, the slow nod and sway of its huge limbs managing to convey a kind of dignity.

Hurst Lane was full of debris, but by now Craig had ceased caring what happened to the car. He skidded to a halt at the entrance to Chilton Manor.

'It's Craig Walker,' he yelled. 'Let me in.'

No answer, but the gates began to move apart in sluggish jerks. As soon as the gap was wide enough he floored the accelerator and raced along the driveway, feeling slightly disconcerted that George had let him in so willingly.

A security light illuminated his way up the steps. George Matheson opened the door, looking a decade older than the last time Craig saw him. He was unshaven, his hair untidy, and he wore a saggy cream cardigan. He had the demeanour of a bewildered old man with nothing ahead of him but loneliness and death.

In contrast, Craig was fast and strong and angry. He wanted answers and he was determined to get them. He barged into the house and saw George recoil, as if expecting to be assaulted.

'What have you done to her?' he demanded.

Vilner was dead. At the final moment it was almost a relief to know his torment was ended. The suffering he'd experienced would be forever seared in Julia's memory. The dig and spit of the saw on bone. The stench of blood and burning flesh. The boom of the gunshot and the sick dizzy silence that followed, as though even the storm had been cowed into retreat.

Toby sat back on the plastic. His posture relaxed, and he turned to face her, tired but elated, his mouth half open, his wet tongue lolling like a dog's. She felt his gaze on her skin, burning through her clothes, and knew he had rape on his mind. She had to distract him.

'Vilner was telling you the truth,' she said. 'There's no way he could have lied to you. He's not who you think he is.' *And you're not who we thought you were*. She and Craig had got it wrong, and for that she might end up paying with her life.

'You're Toby Harman?' she said. 'George's nephew?'

He nodded, still staring at her body, a preoccupied smile on his face.

'Why did you kill my parents?'

Now he met her eye. 'Like you said, they saw us in the woods.'

'So you sabotaged the boiler?'

The pain in her voice seemed to fire his enthusiasm, as if she had enquired about an unusual hobby.

'It was an interesting challenge. I went in several times when they were out, to look at the system and see how to block the flue. Then I let myself in after they'd gone to bed and put the heating on. The first night one of them must have woken up and turned it off. So I had to go in again the next night.' A smile bloomed in his eyes. 'The next night, they didn't wake up.'

She shut her eyes. She could feel something deep inside her curl up and die. She wanted to collapse with grief, or scream and sob out her pain, but she forced herself to stay in control. There was something she wanted even more than that. More than anything. That's what she had to concentrate on.

When she opened her eyes he had edged closer. He was curious, waiting to be entertained. She remembered her mantra: *Every second she stayed alive . . .*

'Why kill them before the massacre? Why not let Carl do it for you?'

'He was unreliable.' From the way he scowled, Julia knew she'd hit on a sore point. It provoked an understanding so powerful that she gasped.

'It was a mistake, wasn't it?'

'What?' He blinked rapidly, like a nervous tic.

'The massacre. You didn't plan it at all.' She reached back to the moment when the second killer marched on to the green, recalling how at first his determination had seemed to offer hope. He'd been angry when he said: *What the hell are you doing with that?* Then the abrupt change of mood: the high five, Carl's whoop of celebration. That was Toby wisely playing along, until he could get hold of the gun.

'He got away from you. He wasn't supposed to be in the village at all.'

The accusation carried a physical force, changing the dynamic between them. She saw the truth in Toby's eyes, and drew strength from it.

'But you couldn't stop him, because he had the handgun. I didn't understand what you meant at the time, but you were asking him about the Walther.' She dredged up all the contempt she could muster. 'Those people died because Carl went crazy and you were just too cowardly, too weak to stop him?'

He moved with astonishing speed, hitting her in the face. An open-handed blow, but delivered with a lot of strength. She hit the back of her head on the wall and cried out. She could taste blood in her mouth. One of her teeth had come loose.

Taking her by the arm, he dragged her up and into the hall. The wind bellowed overhead and there was a distant crash, like a cry for help. The whole house shook, and for a moment she wondered if perhaps they weren't alone. When she spoke, she couldn't keep the fear from her voice.

'Where are we going?'

'Upstairs,' he snarled. 'To the bedroom.'

Seventy

Craig repeated the question. 'What have you done to her?'

Quickly regaining his composure, George was equally forthright. 'I've no idea what you mean. How dare you come barging in here.'

'Julia's gone missing. Just like Abby Clark.'

'Who the hell is Abby Clark?'

'Don't give me that.'

George sighed. 'Let's discuss this like grown men, shall we?'

Reluctantly, Craig followed him into the sitting room. The curtains weren't yet drawn, and the security light revealed a glittering torrent of rain falling almost horizontally. While Craig described Julia's message and his attempts to contact her, George poured himself a brandy. The sight of it caused a pang of longing, but when offered a drink, Craig shook his head. The exterior light snapped off and the tumult beyond the house ceased to exist.

'Let me see if I understand you,' George said, settling into an armchair. 'You believe Julia was enticed to a meeting with someone posing as a journalist?'

'It's the second killer. But to do it, he had to know about Alice Jones.' He paused a moment. 'You have a police insider, don't you? DI Sullivan.'

George couldn't close down his reaction quickly enough: he flinched.

'I'll take that as a yes. He gave you a copy of the report.'

'What of it?' said George. 'The report was leaked to you as well. It doesn't make either of us complicit in the massacre.'

A fair point, which Craig chose to ignore. 'Did Sullivan tell you what Alice Jones was doing?'

George stared morosely into his glass, as though fearing what it would cost to answer truthfully. 'He rang me this morning.'

Before or after I saw him? Craig wondered. He said, 'And who did you tell?'

George gave him a sharp look. 'You really think she's been kidnapped by the other gunman? Carl's conspirator?'

Craig nodded. 'I'm glad you agree there was a second killer.'

'I thought it was ludicrous at first. But now . . . I accept it's a possibility.'

'And if the massacre wasn't just Carl venting his rage, what do you suppose was the real motive?'

George shook his head, as if this was further than he could go. Craig kept up the pressure. 'Your nephew, where does he live?'

'Toby? He has an apartment in London. Why?'

'He owes money to Vilner?'

George's face clouded with shame. 'Gambling debts. That's how Vilner ingratiated himself in our affairs.'

'So Toby needs the development to go ahead, even more than you do?'

'We've been over this ground before,' said George wearily. 'It's a matter of debate whether the massacre has helped or hindered the application. More importantly, I don't believe anyone would commit murder on that scale just to smooth the way for a housing development. Certainly not my nephew.'

'Not even with millions at stake?'

'No.' George sounded emphatic, but Craig saw doubt in his eyes.

'Where does Kendrick fit into all this?'

'What do you know about Kendrick?'

'Very little. Abby Clarke, a friend of mine, was investigating him. The police recovered her body from the Thames this morning. And I've had an anonymous threat that my children will be harmed if I talk to the police.'

George blanched. 'I told you,' he said. 'I tried to warn you of the risks you were taking.'

Craig stood up. 'Is that an admission of guilt?'

'Absolutely not. But when you pry into matters that don't concern you, there's no telling what the consequences will be. Your friend might have stumbled on something quite unrelated.'

'What is Kendrick, then? A criminal?'

'What is Kendrick?' George repeated softly. 'You might well ask. On the surface he's a businessman from Trinidad. He inherited his father's empire, such as it was, and made a great success of it. I wouldn't be surprised if some of his tactics were rather . . . unorthodox.' His eyes lost focus as he looked inward, and shuddered.

'What does he want with you?' Craig asked.

There was a strange sound, something between a cough and a laugh, and it took Craig a moment to realise it hadn't issued from George. He turned to see a spectral figure in the doorway, gripping a walking stick. This was the face at the upstairs window on Wednesday afternoon, and Julia had been right. At first glance it didn't look quite human.

George followed his gaze and gasped, half rising to his feet. But it was left to Vanessa Matheson to answer Craig's question.

'He wants everything.'

He made her climb the stairs ahead of him, jabbing the gun in her back when she faltered. With her hands bound behind her, Julia had to work hard not to stumble.

Rather than contemplate what he might do to her, she thought about the admissions she had forced from him. Ultimately it might be of no help, but she wanted to know. She wanted to understand.

On the landing she stopped, taking in the worn carpet and faded wallpaper. Yellowing gloss paint on the skirting and doorframes. There was something sad about this house. Unloved.

'You came here first,' she murmured.

'What?'

'Both of you. It's what happened here that mattered.'

Once again she'd hit home. He marched her into a small room, bare except for a single bed and a small table, and threw her face-down on the mattress. For a second her head was enveloped by an old pillow, damp and mildewed. Julia thought of poor Megan, smothered while she slept, and in a panic twisted her head to one side.

'The murders here were different. Laura Caplan was sexually assaulted.'

'That was Carl,' Toby snapped. He sat astride her, facing towards her feet, and took out the roll of tape. The bed protested under their combined weight. When he leaned forward to tie her ankles, she could feel he was aroused. He pushed down, grinding his erection against her buttocks.

'But you wanted them dead,' Julia said, not caring that she was antagonising him. She had nothing to lose now.

He wound the tape around her ankles, air snorting from his nostrils as he worked. Staring at the floor, Julia noticed a discarded pair of men's jeans and felt a tiny flare of hope.

'Why?' she persisted. 'What was so important about the Caplans?'

He finished tying her feet, still writhing on top of her, and let out a little groan of pleasure. Then he got off and knelt beside her. He put his face very close to hers, and gave her an answer she would never have expected.

'Their daughter.'

Seventy-One

They came in three Jeeps. Three Grand Cherokees in midnight blue. Kendrick was in the lead car. Halfway along Chilton Way he signalled them to a halt. Before he opened his door, a man in the back seat jumped out and put up an umbrella, only to have it torn from his grasp by the wind.

'Forget it.' Kendrick marched back to the third vehicle in line and motioned the passenger to open his window. He indicated the trees at the side of the road.

'You two stay here. Cut down a tree and block the road. If anyone comes along, tell them you've called the fire brigade. It'll buy us some time.'

There was a plan to follow. An excellent plan. So far it had worked like a dream. If he didn't get control of himself, he might throw it away. But he couldn't resist.

Julia was appalled. 'Megan Caplan? You killed them because of Megan?'

Toby nodded. He rolled Julia on to her back. If she had gathered what was on his mind, she did well to conceal it.

'My uncle was having an affair with Laura Caplan. That's why he reacted so badly when they caught Carl wanking over her underwear. My aunt is terminally ill. George was waiting for her to die, then

Laura was going to divorce Keith, who was a boring skinflint, and move in with her lover.'

As he spoke, he realised he was rubbing himself through his trousers. His hand sprung away, and then he remembered: he could do whatever he liked now. His mouth felt dry and he swallowed, then moistened his lips with his tongue.

'Megan was going to be made his sole heir. Cutting me out.'

'But Megan's still alive.'

'In a deep coma. I'll deal with her when I have to.'

He fumbled with the buttons of her shirt. She let out a whimper, which only served to heighten his pleasure. Her stomach muscles clenched beneath his fingers. He could have just ripped the shirt open, but it felt better to do it slowly. Erotically.

'How do you know all this? Did you confront George?'

He heard the emotion in her voice and smiled. 'Of course not.'

He reached the last button and allowed his hand to brush over her breasts. She tried to shrink away but had nowhere to go.

'Someone else told you?'

'I received an email, warning me what George was planning. I was faced with losing everything. I had to find a way to stop him. It was bad enough that the first application had been turned down. I was in debt to Vilner. I was desperate. I needed to get rid of the Caplans. Then I thought of Carl.'

Breathless, he drew back her shirt. The sight made him light-headed. It wasn't because she was slim and well toned, or because her breasts were visible through the gauzy material of the bra. What thrilled him were her scars. The legacy of 19 January.

His legacy.

'Carl was the perfect candidate,' he said. 'I pretended to bump into him one day in Falcombe. He remembered me from the summers I spent down here, when I was at university. I got him pissed, then started coming down here regularly. We'd go to pubs where no one knew us, and I set about indoctrinating him.'

He reached out and traced his finger along the ridge of red skin that ran vertically from just below her sternum and disappeared into her jeans. He pictured her on the operating table, the surgeons elbow-deep in blood, living organs slippery in their hands.

'I kept talking about Laura Caplan, what a bitch she was. How she used to laugh at him, telling everyone how inadequate he was. I convinced him his whole life had been destroyed by that one incident in her kitchen, and pretty soon he was steaming for revenge. Of course, it helped that he was already a headcase. I just had to wind him up and point him in the right direction.'

'It was your idea to steal your uncle's shotgun?'

Toby nodded. 'We made it look like a break-in, but I'd deactivated the alarm the night before. George just assumed he'd forgotten to set it.'

'And what about everyone else Carl killed?'

'I don't know why he did that. I was upstairs, dealing with Megan. I heard him go outside and followed him down the lane. I couldn't call out in case someone heard me. Then I saw him pull the pistol and shoot the man in the pub garden. After that, I had no choice but to wait and see what happened.'

He stopped, unhappy with the direction they were taking. His erection softened. Her body had lost a little of its allure, which was probably a good thing.

'You were in the lane when I found the postman?'

'Yes. I watched him going round the village. I couldn't risk showing myself, but I couldn't let him be taken alive either. When he chased you on to the green I saw my chance.' He laughed. 'I finished him off, just as I'd intended to do back at the farmhouse. I thought I'd finished you off, too.'

'And you've achieved nothing,' Julia said.

'I wouldn't say that. A lot of the protesters are dead. The Caplans are out of the picture. So is Vilner, now.'

'All these lives destroyed, and you're not a penny richer.'

He dismissed her scorn. 'I will be, once George is dead.'

'You'll kill your uncle?'

Toby stood up, proud that his self-control hadn't deserted him. Observing Julia's pathetic show of defiance, he understood how she'd survived the fall from the tree. She never knew when she was beaten.

'First he's going to come here and shoot you, before tragically taking his own life.' He grinned. 'The mystery of the second killer will be laid to rest at last.'

He took a look around, satisfied himself she was secure here. This was the only room that could be locked with a key. He was at the door when she threw a last desperate question.

'But what if Carl killed the others for someone else?'

He stopped, irritated. 'What?'

'This Decipio you mentioned?'

'That was Vilner.'

'No it wasn't. You don't know who it is.'

Her words rang in his head as he strode out. He slammed the door and turned the key in the lock. The wind roared around the house and rain pounded the roof, but despite the noise he still heard her shouting as he descended the stairs.

'You don't know who he is. But he knows you.'

Julia kept her eyes tightly shut while a long minute passed, trying to blot out the storm, listening for proof that he was leaving. Finally she heard it: the faint muffled thud of the front door closing.

He had gone to Chilton Manor to get his uncle. That meant she had a little time. Half an hour, perhaps. Was that long enough? The voices in her head wouldn't agree on anything.

You can't afford to delay, the first one said.

You have to be sure he's gone, the other cautioned.

And of course, they were both right. So she waited. But only for another minute or so.

Then she swung her legs round, and used her stomach muscles to propel herself into a sitting position. She slid off the bed, landing on the floor with a thump. She waited, her heart pounding like a kettle drum. If Toby was bluffing, he'd have heard that. He would be up here any moment.

More agonising seconds passed, but he didn't appear. Julia let out a sigh of relief and shuffled on her bottom until she was sitting with her back to the crumpled pair of jeans. Her fingers stretched as far as the tape would allow, probing the cold denim until finally, with a small prayer of thanks to Keith Caplan, she made contact with the smooth leather belt.

She smiled. *Every second she stayed alive . . .*

Seventy-Two

It seemed to take an age for Vanessa to enter the room. Both George and Craig offered help, but she waved them away. She was similarly dismissive when George implored her to go back to her bed.

'No,' she said. 'I want to know what's going on.'

The two men stared at each other. Craig cleared his throat and said, 'I need to speak to your nephew. Julia Trent has gone missing.'

Vanessa made it to a high-backed chair and shuffled round, positioning herself above it. Craig had to fight the impulse to guide her down; the furious determination in her face told him it wouldn't be welcome. At close range her skin was impossibly thin and translucent, as if at any moment it might rupture like worn fabric.

'I don't see the connection,' she said.

'Craig believes . . .' George began, and then faltered.

'I think Toby was involved in the massacre,' Craig said, his own voice a little unsteady. Despite her frailty, or perhaps in part because of it, Vanessa carried an air of haughty command. Neither man spoke as she descended, gingerly, and finally sat, pulling the folds of her dressing gown around her.

'Involved how?' she said.

'The other gunman that Julia described,' George explained. 'With Alice Jones coming forward, we probably have to accept—'

'You suspect that was Toby?' Vanessa broke in. Craig felt a hot flush of embarrassment. The mere presence of this elderly, dying woman in the room made his accusations seem offensive, indecent, even implausible.

'He believes I also had something to do with it,' George added.

Vanessa's gaze snapped from her husband to Craig. 'I rather think not,' she said, as if humouring a small boy. Then back to George, her eyes like burning coals. 'Didn't you tell him?'

George twitched. 'Tell him what?'

'About Laura,' said Vanessa, producing a crumpled photograph from her pocket. She tossed it on to the floor and sneered. 'About the woman you loved.'

Julia knew exactly how she would free herself. She had it all worked out in her head, but real life was stubbornly refusing to play along.

The belt had a thick buckle made of polished steel. The pin in the centre of the buckle was about an inch and an half long, with a tiny rounded head. Providing she could apply sufficient force, she reckoned it was sharp enough to puncture the tape binding her hands.

At first she tried spearing the tape by propping the pin upright and then forcing her wrists down on it. The problem was that the pin kept slipping sideways. Because she was working blind, her hands tied behind her back, she couldn't tell if she had it positioned correctly before she pushed down. She wasted a lot of time and energy and ended up tearful and frustrated.

It wasn't going to work, she thought. She couldn't count on having more than half an hour. She'd wasted ten or fifteen minutes of that already. Despair was like a crouching predator, waiting for its moment. She fought every urge to surrender to it.

Then she had an inspiration. Bring her hands round in front.

She fell on to her side and pulled her knees up to her chin. Thanked God for the weight she'd lost in the past couple of months. Even so, it was a struggle to slide her arms over her buttocks. The pressure caused the tape to bite into the skin around her wrists. She felt a tearing sensation in her shoulders and gritted her teeth. She had to make this work.

With a cry of pain and victory, she wrenched her hands into the space behind her knees. Rested for a moment. *You're halfway there*, she told herself. Now she just had to loop her hands over her feet.

She drew her legs in as tightly as she could, knees pressing against her chin, and stretched her arms to their limit, scraping her wrists down across her ankles. But it did no good. The way her feet were bound together, there simply wasn't enough clearance. One foot at a time it would have been easy, but like this it was impossible. Truly impossible.

'Shitting shitting shit!' she shouted. The seconds ticking away felt like a march of ants across her skin. She'd heard what Toby was planning to do when he returned. She had a very simple choice: escape or die.

Craig picked up the photograph. It was obviously a couple of years old, taken one summer during the harvest. A pretty girl with light brown hair was perched on a hay bale, beaming at the camera while George stood next to her, his arm suspended in mid-air as if he'd intended an embrace but lost his nerve at the last moment.

'George wouldn't have harmed the Caplans,' Vanessa told him. 'Not Laura or that little brat, anyway.'

The words were delivered with an unsettling mix of amusement and bitterness. Craig thought back to the doubts Julia had expressed about George's involvement. She'd described how upset he became when he talked about the Caplans, saying she didn't think he could have faked his reaction.

George wore an expression of absolute horror. He waved his hands in agitation, stumbling over his words. 'No, you're wrong. Vanessa, please, darling—'

'Don't use that term on me. I meant nothing to you, all those years you were sneaking off to see her. Insulting me, humiliating me, screwing that common little whore right under my nose.'

George became distraught, shaking his head, trying to make himself heard. 'This isn't the right time. Let me take you back upstairs.'

'I'm staying here.'

'But I have so much to explain. I can't do it like this. Please, Vanessa.' Tears welled in his eyes, and for a moment Craig thought he was going to prostrate himself and beg for her forgiveness.

'Listen,' he said, 'Julia's still missing, and this isn't going to help her.'

The Mathesons regarded him as if they had forgotten he was there.

'I may have made a big mistake,' he went on, 'but it would put my mind at ease if I could speak to Toby. Could you phone him for me?'

George cast an anxious glance at his wife, then nodded. He went over to the phone on the wall. Craig was aware of Vanessa shuffling unhappily in her seat. He wished she had never joined them. Rubbing a sudden fatigue from his eyes, he realised he'd reached the end of the line. He had no idea where to find Julia. No idea if he should go after Toby, or Vilner, or Kendrick.

He didn't look up until he heard George, in a puzzled voice, say, 'The phone's dead. Must be the storm.'

Then Vanessa said, 'Please leave us now. We have a lot to discuss.'

Craig stood up, intending to comply. Desperate to salvage something from this wasted journey, he said, 'Can you give me Toby's number? And his address. I'll go and see him if I have to.'

Then someone in the doorway said, 'That won't be necessary.'

Vanessa saw him first, then Craig. George was still grasping the phone, as if he couldn't decide what to do with it. His puzzlement grew as he registered the astonishment on their faces, and only then did he turn towards the door.

'Toby!'

It was George who confirmed his identity, but Craig already knew. He read it in the man's dangerous, almost feral presence. Clad in dark clothes, Toby's hair was plastered to his head and his shoes were clotted with mud, but his eyes were alert and predatory. He exuded an odour of blood and death that stilled the air in the room and for a moment robbed Craig of all thought except one: Julia was dead.

'Where is she?' he shouted. It was a gut reaction, but it got the response he wanted. Toby's eyes narrowed in acknowledgement, just as dazzling beams of light cut through the room.

Craig launched himself towards Toby. He heard Vanessa scream, 'Run!' and as he passed her he felt a slap on his thigh far more powerful than anything a desperately ill woman could muster. By now Toby was turning, acting on his aunt's advice. Craig tried to follow but his right leg gave out beneath him and he stumbled, crashing into a small table. He looked down and saw blood streaming from a slit in his trousers. In his periphery he registered Vanessa thrusting forward and just managed to dodge clear as the blade slashed down again.

George cried out and moved to restrain her, but she was already collapsing back in her chair, a craft knife gripped in her thin, trembling hand. Clutching his leg, Craig was dimly aware of a door slamming as Toby made his escape, followed almost immediately by a loud, urgent thudding on the front door.

Police, he thought. *Thank Christ the police are here.*

Seventy-Three

Desperation forced her to compromise. If she couldn't bring her hands in front of her, she'd have to leave them where they were. It didn't mean they were useless.

She got hold of the belt, then lay still and thought about it. The way her hands were now, she couldn't straighten her body. That meant there was no point trying to stand up. But by rocking on her spine she was able to build enough momentum to move into a sitting position.

Now her hands were visible between her knees. From this position she could get enough leverage on the buckle to work at the tape holding her ankles. She lined up the pin against the centre of the tape and pushed down on it. The tape bulged but held.

She pushed harder. Felt the tape resist, resist . . . and then split. The pin burst through.

She used the buckle like a gutting knife, dragging it upwards through the tape. Once half had been cut, the other half separated easily. Her feet were free. She looked at them in amazement. She couldn't quite believe she'd done it.

But there was no time to reflect on her achievement. She slipped first one and then the other foot through her arms. Now her hands were in front of her. She sat cross-legged and wedged the belt buckle between her feet, using her toes to prop the pin upright.

She worked intently. The pain and fear receded. She threw all her attention on the task in front of her, oblivious to concepts like survival and freedom and escape. Forgot about passing time. The only thing that mattered was *now*.

It wasn't the police.

While George went to the door, Craig stretched his leg out straight and examined the wound. The cut was about three inches long, but not too deep. He ripped his jeans open further and pressed down on the cut to stem the bleeding. Vanessa's malevolent gaze prickled the hairs on his neck.

'Why did you help him?' Craig asked her.

'Fuck off,' she snarled.

George came back in, pressed between two huge men in dark coats. Other men followed, filling the room with menace and testosterone. There were six of them in all, their leader distinguished not so much by his mixed-race complexion and slimmer frame, but by his un-mistakable aura of power. Even Vanessa seemed to baulk at the sight of him.

'What's been happening here?' he said, to no one in particular.

George babbled something about needing to treat the wound, but as he moved towards Craig strong hands pulled him back.

'Sit down, George,' the man said. He peered at Craig's leg. 'It's not serious.'

'You're Kendrick?' Craig said, with a lot more assurance than he felt.

'Well done.' He turned to Vanessa, noted the knife in her hand, and tutted. 'You'd like to explain?'

She ignored the question. Kendrick took a step towards her and she spat at him. Nothing came out except air, but it made him recoil, and Craig sensed a fearsome rage, barely held in check.

George intervened. 'Toby was here,' he said quickly.

Kendrick spun to face him. 'I thought so. Where's he hiding out?'

George considered for a moment. 'I don't know. The farmhouse, possibly. It's only a couple of hundred yards from here.'

'I know where it is,' Kendrick said.

He directed a sharp look at Craig, who'd been about to mention Julia. Then he thought of Abby Clark's fate and clamped his mouth shut.

Kendrick addressed a thin, weasly-looking man who had stepped into view from behind a couple of the heavies.

'Jacques, go and check it out. Take Barrett. Let me know when you find him.'

The weasel disappeared, accompanied by one of the men. Four left, including Kendrick, who settled in the chair Craig had recently vacated and beckoned for George to sit also. Craig remained on the floor, holding his leg. He could feel the blood congealing, sticking to his hand.

Kendrick acted as if there was no hurry. He plucked at his trousers, wriggled himself comfortable. He was wearing a heavy overcoat and calfskin gloves. He pressed his hands together and rested them against his mouth like a child saying his bedtime prayers. Only then did his gaze settle on Vanessa.

'It's time you explained yourself, woman.'

She met his eye with a cool contempt. She looked relaxed, at ease with herself. There was a palpable sense of pleasure that, despite such powerful company, she was once more the centre of attention.

In contrast, George was vibrating with tension. 'Tell me you didn't have anything to do with it,' he pleaded.

'She was going to take my place,' she said. 'Her and her little brat.'

'Megan,' said George, sounding broken-hearted.

'Toby's not up to much. But he's family.' Vanessa's dark eyes glittered with malice. Her voice scratched like dry straw dragged through a pipe. 'He's *my* family. And you were going to pass over him in favour of that bitch. It was my duty to warn him. I had every right, given how you treated me. I told him to find a way to stop it.'

She said something else, but no one heard her because of the noise George made as he fainted and slipped from his chair.

In the end she pushed so hard, the belt burst through the tape and jabbed her wrist. Blood sprang from the wound, but Julia hardly noticed it. She tore the tape apart and stood up, rubbing life back into her arms. Then she buttoned her shirt, repulsed by the memory of his touch, but relieved that he'd gone no further.

She tested the door, indulging a faint hope that it had somehow failed to lock properly, but it was secure. She rattled the handle a couple of times, then examined the room for something to use as a ram. The only contender was the bedside table.

The door was composed of a solid frame with six rectangular panels. The panels felt relatively flimsy to the touch, and so it proved. Gripping a leg of the table in both hands, she swung it like a baseball bat at the middle section. Shards of wood flew from the panels, and a dent appeared in the central strut. Another four blows and there was a hole big enough to climb through.

She hurried downstairs on legs wobbling from the adrenalin rush. Outside the storm was howling. It took a few seconds to summon the courage to enter the living room, where she snatched up her coat without looking too closely at Vilner's mutilated corpse.

Back in the hall she noticed there was a phone on a shelf by the door. She picked it up but it was dead. Probably disconnected after the massacre.

Her next unwelcome discovery was that the front door wouldn't open. Toby must have used the deadlock, which meant it couldn't be opened without a key.

She didn't know it at the time, but it saved her life. The door rattled and shook, and she realised it wasn't from the wind. For a moment she stood transfixed, unable to comprehend that she had failed. She'd thrown away her best hope of survival.

The door shuddered under a massive impact, and only then did

Julia come to her senses. She turned and dashed into the kitchen as a second blow reverberated through the house and the door burst open.

No one else went to George's aid, so Craig did it, dragging his leg across the carpet. George was already coming round, his eyes flickering like a dying bulb. Craig helped him sit up, feeling almost as stupefied as the older man.

If Vanessa was in any way disturbed by her husband's reaction, she gave no sign of it. Instead there was a gleam of satisfaction in her eyes.

'You planned the massacre?' he asked her.

'No. I sent Toby an anonymous message, suggesting he do something about the Caplans, to preserve his inheritance. It was his decision to use Carl.'

'You didn't help organise it?'

'No.' She snorted with disdain. 'I rather wish I had.'

Craig shook his head, still unable to believe that this . . . this shadow of a woman had presided over the murders.

'Bit of a shock, isn't it?' Kendrick's tone was one of mock gravity. He seemed to be thoroughly enjoying the revelations.

'What about the gun?' George asked Vanessa. 'The Walther with the silencer?'

Vanessa shook her head. 'No idea. Ask Toby.'

'We will,' said Craig.

'Or ask *him*,' Vanessa said. 'The half-caste.'

Kendrick chuckled. 'Quite a mouth you have,' he said. 'I don't know how you stayed married to her all this time, George. Not when you had young Laura Caplan waiting in the wings.'

George refused to acknowledge Kendrick. 'We never set out to deceive you,' he told his wife. 'Please believe that.'

'Be quiet, George,' Vanessa said. 'It's far too late.' Imperious as ever, she grasped her walking stick and tried to stand up. 'I'd like you all to go now,' she declared. 'It's my desire to die in peace.'

Kendrick rose and gave a little bow. 'Let me help you.'

'No,' said Vanessa, but Kendrick ignored her. He blocked her path and grabbed the hand that held the knife, crushing her wrist until she released it. That was when Craig understood why Kendrick hadn't removed his gloves.

With his other hand, Kendrick clasped Vanessa's throat. It was so swift, so effective, no one had a chance of saving her. Craig started to move but felt a gun at his neck, one of the heavies standing over him. George could do nothing but stare, a wild, almost delirious look on his face, as though his hold on reality had already broken.

Vanessa can't have weighed much more than sixty pounds. Kendrick lifted her, squeezing harder all the time, until she was fully upright. Then he lifted her higher. Her feet came off the floor. Her eyes bulged. She let out a low gurgling moan, swatting her arms, kicking her legs uselessly in mid-air, writhing and fighting like a mangy street cat until the moment when the light vanished from her eyes and she wilted, dangling from his grasp like a rag doll, broken and loved by no one.

Kendrick went on holding her for a few more seconds, as if he had something to prove, then he opened his hand and let her lifeless body drop to the floor in a messy heap of skin and bones.

Seventy-Four

Toby had driven to the house, but the arrival of the man he assumed was Kendrick meant he couldn't get back to his car. Instead he had to detour through the manor grounds and run back to the farm. Beyond the imperative to survive, there was only one thing on his mind. Vanessa had helped him escape by attacking Craig. Despite all their differences over the years, she had sacrificed herself in order to save him.

Vanessa was Decipio.

It was obvious, now he thought about it. Even the contemptuous tone of her emails was entirely in character, and yet he'd never once suspected her. Neither had George, judging by his reaction.

Toby couldn't help marvelling at how expertly he'd been played. Vilner had gone to his death protesting he knew nothing about the massacre, and it turned out he'd probably been telling the truth.

Vanessa had her own selfish reasons for wanting the Caplans destroyed, but she'd skilfully convinced Toby he was doing it for his own benefit. And thanks to George, in the weeks since the massacre she'd had an unwitting source of information. That was how Decipio had known what Craig and Julia were up to.

If only she'd revealed her identity, he thought. They might have made a far more effective team that way.

And how ironic she had saved him, considering that tonight he had intended to kill her, before forcing George to write a suicide note confessing to his part in the massacre. Except Craig fucking Walker had been there, and then Kendrick and his thugs had turned up. He shouldn't have answered Vilner's phone earlier, he told himself. Goading Kendrick had been a serious error.

He reached the house and was about to go inside when his panic abruptly vanished. His tactical brain regained control, a small voice urging him to wait a second. Urging him to *think*.

Kendrick's men would come after him. The farmhouse was the obvious hiding place. Glaringly obvious.

He made a detour and found shelter in one of the outbuildings with only seconds to spare. Light washed over the yard as a big Jeep Cherokee pulled up and two men got out. Both were carrying guns.

Toby watched, delighted that a combination of foresight and good luck had once again delivered him from peril. If he had a regret, it was that he would be denied the pleasure of taking Julia's life.

On the other hand, at least it would save him a job.

Julia hid behind the kitchen door and frantically looked round for a weapon. At the back of her mind a question surfaced: why had Toby broken the door down?

Then she heard voices in the hall. Two men. For a single glorious moment she imagined they were here to rescue her, but an instinct for self-preservation stopped her from calling out. Instead she kept quiet, and listened.

When they found Vilner, a man with a strong Essex accent exclaimed, 'Look at the fucking state of him. Kendrick's gonna do his nut.'

The other man spoke with a Caribbean lilt. He sounded remarkably sanguine about the discovery. 'I don't think he'll be shedding many tears over Vilner.'

'So where the fuck is Toby?'

'I don't know. Check the house.'

Julia froze. The back door was fifteen feet away, bolted at the top and bottom. She'd never unlock it in time. Instead she shrank back against the wall as heavy footsteps approached. A muscular form leaned into the room, scanned it and retreated. She heard the creak of the stairs, and the squawk of a two-way radio.

'It's Jacques,' said the Caribbean voice. 'We're at the farmhouse. Vilner's dead. No sign of Toby yet.'

A shout from upstairs interrupted him. Conscious that she wouldn't get a better opportunity, Julia crept forward and waited for the second man to climb the stairs. She peered into the hall and saw the front door hanging drunkenly on a single hinge. That had to be the better option, she decided. But she would have to move fast: something she wasn't supposed to do, or worse still, might not be capable of doing.

There was no choice. She took a deep breath and ran.

Kendrick stood at the window, staring into the night. The wind was raging harder than ever, and with each gust the lights flickered. Craig eyed the door, trying to assess the likelihood of escape should they be plunged into darkness.

No one restrained him when he eased himself up and sat on a chair. His leg had stopped bleeding but was starting to throb. He tried to help George, but the older man shrugged him off, remaining slumped on the floor. His dull, uncomprehending gaze wouldn't be diverted from his wife's body.

'She helped him,' he said. 'She helped him kill Laura.'

Craig nodded grimly. Remembering what Vanessa had said, his mouth went dry at the thought of the question he had to ask Kendrick.

'You knew what they were doing, didn't you?'

Kendrick turned, studying him as one might study an exotic animal, slightly unsure of its ability to bite or sting.

'I knew about Toby,' he said. 'Vanessa's involvement was a surprise.'

'When did you find out?'

'Right at the start. We quickly identified Toby as a potential weakness, someone we could exploit. As standard practice, we searched his apartment and put a keylogger program in his computer. Vanessa contacted him using an anonymous email account, warning him of the threat to his inheritance.' There was some grudging admiration in his voice. 'We monitored their communications and learned that he planned to use Carl Forester.'

'And you did nothing to stop him?' Even as he spoke, Craig cursed the naivety of his question. 'Of course you didn't. You went one step further. You recruited Carl yourself.'

Kendrick's smile acknowledged the truth. There was an electronic bleep from within his coat. Turning back to the window, he produced a heavy-duty walkie-talkie and said, 'Kendrick.'

Urgent chatter down the line, but the only words Craig heard clearly were: 'Vilner's dead'. He didn't know whether to feel shocked or relieved. Was Julia there as well? Was she safe?

Kendrick said, 'Keep looking,' and listened again. There was an exclamation, clear enough for Craig to recognise Jacques's voice.

'Someone here,' he shouted. 'A woman.'

Then all they heard was the blast of a gun.

Toby, crouching by the Jeep, was astonished to see Julia run from the house. Somehow she had freed herself and got away from them. Didn't she ever give up?

A moment later there were angry shouts, followed by the flash and boom of gunfire. The front door splintered, and grit and stones flew up from the yard. Wild shots, fired as one of the men ran downstairs, judging by the trajectory.

He watched Julia pass, her face creased with pain. There was an uneven rhythm to her movement that suggested she wouldn't get far. Catching her would be easy, he decided. If nothing else, she could be useful as a bargaining chip. An insurance policy.

His plans might be in tatters, but it didn't mean he was out of the game. This was the time to show his real ability. Time to improvise.

* * *

'Who is it?' Kendrick demanded. When an answer wasn't forthcoming, the man closest to Craig raised his gun and took the safety off.

'Who?' Kendrick said again.

Craig glanced at George, whose eyes were a silent plea: *Tell him.*

'Julia Trent.'

Understanding dawned on Kendrick's face. 'Toby kidnapped her, along with Vilner?'

'I think so.' Craig couldn't resist a smile. 'Does that mean she's escaped?'

Kendrick turned away, ignoring Craig, and barked orders at his men. 'Moss, stay here. You two, go and help Jacques with the search. Find them both and bring them back here. If anyone gets in the way, kill them.'

The two men trooped out, leaving just the one nearest Craig. He was about forty, well over six feet tall, a vast slab of muscle and quite obviously no stranger to violence. Craig knew these were almost certainly the men who had followed and photographed his children, the men who had killed Abby and thrown her body in the Thames. If he was going to take them on, he would have to choose his moment carefully.

He thought about Julia. She was still alive. Still fighting. No matter what happened here, he would take comfort from that.

'Come on,' said Jacques. He was first to the Jeep, and climbed into the passenger seat. Barrett made to follow, but hesitated as he opened the door.

'Shouldn't we go after her on foot?'

'No. This is quicker.'

Barrett nodded. He knew better than to question Jacques twice. He put his gun away and got in, the vehicle rocking as his bulk tipped it to one side.

'Who the fuck is she?' he said.

'Don't know. But she's a witness. We have to stop her reaching the village.'

390

Barrett turned the ignition and the engine fired up with a much rougher noise than usual. Before he could comment on it, he was aware of Jacques flinging himself against the dashboard in a spray of blood and gore. A dark figure rose in the rear footwell, no more than a shadow falling across his face before he heard but barely felt the first of the two shots that killed him.

Seventy-Five

Julia was halfway along the lane before reluctantly she dropped her pace. She could ignore the twinges in her ankles and legs, but not the tearing pain in her abdomen. It was similar to a stitch, but far more intense. She thought of the doctor's instructions on Wednesday night. *Walk slowly. Don't run.* She almost laughed.

Don't get kidnapped. Don't end up fleeing for your life.

The village first appeared as a distant scattering of lights, warm and welcoming. A lull in the wind nearly pulled her off balance, and in the sudden eerie silence she heard the vibration of a heavy vehicle, moving fast over rough ground. She turned, saw the flash of headlights and threw herself towards the verge.

She expected to fall into a prickly but yielding hedge. Instead her shoulder struck something solid. A wooden gate. In desperation she hauled herself up and slithered over, falling out of sight just as the Jeep rumbled past.

Squinting at the ghostly forms of plants and bushes, she sought out the contours of the building and finally understood where fate had directed her.

The Old Schoolhouse.

*   *   *

It took Toby less than a minute to pull the dead bodies from the Jeep. There was blood all over the driver's seat and steering wheel, but this was no time to be squeamish.

The big 4x4 was unfamiliar. He stalled it once as he made a three-point turn, then stamped on the accelerator and was nearly pitched out of his seat when the front wheels bounced over the rutted track.

He felt sure Julia would be heading for the village. Setting off after her, he had a flashback to 19 January, when he'd watched helplessly as Carl went loping along the lane with the shotgun on his back and a newly acquired pistol in his hand. Although Toby had been horrified by the unexpected turn of events, hadn't he secretly exulted in the devastation that Carl was sure to leave in his wake?

The answer was yes. He had felt it then, and he felt it again now, as he rolled into Chilton and drew up between the green and the church. There was no one in sight. Then he saw something that made him smile. The BT box had been vandalised, just as it had been in January. Kendrick had made sure the phones were cut off.

Toby imagined the mindset of the remaining residents. In the midst of a ferocious storm, finding their phones were dead, would anyone really open their door to an unexpected caller? After everything they'd been through, would they want to help a stranger in trouble?

'No,' he said aloud. No chance at all.

So where had she gone?

'Vanessa was right, wasn't she?' said Craig. 'You supplied Carl with the handgun, the silencer. Was the massacre your idea? Did you send him into the village?'

'Those are not questions you should ask,' Kendrick warned him.

'But it achieved what you wanted?'

Kendrick's snort was answer enough.

'So why are you here now?' Craig said.

'Because Toby fucked up, and so did Vilner. They've made a mess which I'll have to clear up.'

'You'll never get away with this.'

Kendrick laughed, and said cryptically, 'I know the man I am, and I think I will.' His radio squawked. This time he didn't bother turning away. Craig heard every word.

'Yes?'

'We're at the farmhouse. Jacques and Barrett are dead, and the Jeep's gone. I reckon we just missed him.'

'He won't have got past the roadblock,' Kendrick said. 'Load the bodies into your car, then go and find him.'

Craig kept his expression neutral. Kendrick's face was flushed with anger. He threw himself down on a sofa and glowered at the ceiling. The wind pushed at the windows with a low groaning sound, and the lights dimmed for a second or two. Craig tensed, ready to spring, but the lights recovered.

Having Toby on the loose was a mixed blessing. It was keeping Kendrick preoccupied, and probably the reason he and George were still alive. On the other hand, he was desperately afraid for Julia. How much longer could she stay out of Toby's reach?

Julia bent low and hurried across the garden. Broken tiles littered the lawn. The TV aerial was hanging by its cable, halfway down the roof. The back door was locked, and a quick search of the surrounding area revealed no obvious hiding place for a key. She considered knocking, but the house was dark and clearly unoccupied. Craig must be in Crawley, safe at home with his wife and his children. He probably hadn't even realised Julia was missing yet.

She searched for a fragment of tile to break a pane of glass in the door. She waited for a strong gust of wind to mask the noise, and tried to cover her hand with her sleeve. The glass shattered on her first attempt, and at the same time another tile slid from the roof and exploded right at her feet. Her yelp of alarm was snatched away and lost in the night.

She reached in and felt for the latch. As the door swung open she was aware of an approaching engine. She ducked inside and knelt on the kitchen floor as another big four-wheel drive went past. A vivid spasm of pain shot through her stomach and made her curl up tight. Bright spots danced in front of her eyes, and nausea rose in her chest.

It was nearly a minute before it subsided enough for her to stand up. As she did, a wave of vertigo sent her clinging to the kitchen units, the roaring gale completing the illusion that she was on the deck of a ship, pitching through the ocean. She was desperate to lie down, desperate to close her eyes and blot out her predicament. But she couldn't. Not until she had called the police, at least.

Thankfully there was a phone sitting on the worktop, ghostly pale against the dark granite. She shuffled along and picked it up. Listened for a dialling tone, but there was only silence. She stared at the blank display and had a flashback to a young mother, curled protectively over the body of her son. Blood on white-blond hair.

They had done it again. Isolated the village. Cut her off from help. And at that thought, something in her gave way, just as it had done in January. The first thread of sanity, perhaps. Then, she had kept fighting, but it was different this time. Her stomach was in agony. She was cold, terrified, exhausted. She couldn't fight any more.

Several loud bangs came from outside, faintly audible through the droning wind. They barely registered in her consciousness. She dropped the phone and stumbled into the hall. Groped for the light switch and turned it on. She climbed the stairs as if in a dream. She didn't care where she was going. She didn't care about anything. As far as she was concerned, she might as well already be dead.

Seventy-Six

Sullivan's foreboding grew with every mile, with every blocked or flooded road. After passing a dozen accidents and abandoned cars, he pulled in just past Handcross Hill, seriously doubting the wisdom of his journey. He tried phoning George but couldn't get through. Having come this far, he decided reluctantly to press on.

Turning off the B2112, it was no great surprise when his headlights picked out a fallen tree across the road. He pulled up behind a Jeep and swore to himself. Spotting a large figure at the wheel, Sullivan wondered if between them they might be able to move the tree far enough to get past.

He got out of the car, the rain pelting his face and soaking through his shirt. The wind tore at his parka, which no longer zipped up over his belly. Pressing it together, he hurried over to the Jeep. The driver was a white man, about thirty, with cropped dark hair and a tough suspicious face. He opened his window a couple of inches. 'Tree's down, mate.'

Yeah, thanks for that, Einstein. 'Don't suppose you've got a tow rope?' Sullivan said. 'Or better still, a chainsaw?'

He was joking, but the man did a weird double take. It was a look Sullivan had seen a thousand times in his career: the involuntary twitch of a guilty man.

'Nah, mate,' he said. 'I'd turn round if I were you.'

But Sullivan was already moving towards the tree. Almost immediately he noticed the shape was wrong. The trunk ended in a clean line. It had been cut.

His hand automatically reached for his warrant card. Time to get some sense out of this joker, he thought. Turning back, the Jeep's door opened and Sullivan cautioned himself to play it cool. In his younger days a suspect who resisted arrest could expect a good kicking, but out here there was no help at hand, and this bloke looked pretty useful.

'Go on,' the man growled. 'Piss off out of here.'

'Hey,' said Sullivan, instantly forgetting his own advice. 'You don't talk to me like that.'

He produced the warrant card, but the other man seemed unconcerned. He turned his back on Sullivan and strode towards the policeman's car.

'Hey!' Sullivan yelled, furious at being ignored. He started after him, and as he drew alongside the Jeep a second man appeared from his hiding place on the far side of the vehicle. He was holding a gun.

For such a large man, Sullivan was remarkably quick to react. He ducked and threw himself towards the trees, but he didn't stand a chance. The bullet struck him in the back, just above his kidneys. The impact propelled him on to the verge, where he stumbled and fell, rolling to a rest in a muddy, bramble-filled ditch.

Toby couldn't remember when he had last felt so supreme, so magnificent. He only wished there was time to stand back and contemplate his brilliance.

Anticipating that Kendrick would send more men, Toby parked the Jeep in plain sight at the southern end of the High Street, close to the shop. He got out and ran across the green, trampling over sodden bouquets, and took shelter under the yew tree. Resting against its trunk, he had the unsettling impression that he was in the presence of something not just alive, but sentient. The bark felt as warm as flesh, and seemed almost to be trembling. Just the wind, he told himself.

Within seconds another Jeep emerged from Hurst Lane. Toby quickly checked his gun. It was a Croatian-made nine-millimetre automatic pistol with a fifteen-round magazine. He'd bought it with the help of an acquaintance, a City banker who supplemented his already lavish income with cocaine dealing. Toby never actually made contact with the vendor, and his banker friend had every reason to keep quiet about the transaction. About as secure as he could hope for.

Just as he expected, the other Jeep stopped as soon as the headlights picked out the vehicle he'd commandeered. Two men got out, warily inspecting the village. Both kept their hands inside their jackets, concealing their guns from anyone who might be watching.

Toby had deliberately parked badly, angling the Jeep so the front tyre was half up on the kerb, and he'd left the door open a fraction. It was a subliminal message that told of abandonment, of a hasty escape on foot. And that was exactly how the two men responded to it.

They might look the part, Toby thought, but they weren't very bright. For a start they didn't split up. Side by side they walked towards the Jeep, glancing round once or twice in a half-hearted way.

Toby crept silently over the grass. One of the men cupped his hands and peered through the back window, while his partner made for the driver's door. Toby took him out first, shooting from about ten feet away. He had ample time to close in on the second man, who was caught on the turn and shot twice in the chest. He died instantly, but the first one was bucking on the ground, trying to speak with a mouth full of blood. Toby finished him off with a head shot.

Then he stood very still. Waited and listened. He could hear trees crashing together and loose fence panels banging and what sounded like a metal dustbin trapped in an alley, clattering back and forth. And over it all the wind continued to howl and scream. Against all this, the gunshots were insignificant. Toby almost felt disappointed when no lights came on, no doors opened.

This is how Carl must have felt, he realised. The whole village at his mercy. House after house of unwitting victims. It made him reconsider the motive for the massacre. Maybe there wasn't any mystery to uncover. Maybe Carl had done it just for the sheer hell of it.

Then one of his observations caught in his mind and wouldn't be dislodged. *No lights came on.*

He turned a full circle, checking every house in sight, and when he reached Hurst Lane he gave a joyful smile.

The Old Schoolhouse had been in darkness a moment ago. Now there was a light on upstairs.

Perfect.

A few more minutes ticked by. Craig tried to look relaxed, resting his head against the seat and surveying the room with half-closed eyes. George was still on the floor, a couple of feet away to his left. He had begun to weep silently, and did nothing to check the tears rolling down his cheeks. From time to time Kendrick shot him a disgusted look.

The other man in the room, Moss, was standing just behind him, to Craig's right. Still alert, watchful. Still holding the gun loosely at his side.

Craig sighed. The odds weren't good. He hadn't yet seen evidence that Kendrick was armed, but it seemed likely that he would be. So he went on waiting, but he knew it was a foolish strategy. Two against two offered a better chance than anything they'd get when the other men returned.

And when they came back, either with or without Toby, he felt sure that would be it.

He studied Kendrick. For the first time there was tension visible in his face. His jaw kept clenching and unclenching, and the veins at his temple stood out like worm trails on a sandy beach. His fingers performed busy trills along the arm of the sofa.

Craig reflected on the questions he'd asked earlier, and wondered if he should press him some more. Kendrick had virtually admitted to piggybacking on Toby and Vanessa's plan. If not for him, the only victims on 19 January would have been the Caplans. Instead Kendrick had persuaded Carl to continue his murderous spree. But why? Had he thought it would help him gain control of George's empire?

He was about to ask when Kendrick jumped to his feet, as if responding to some unseen signal. Craig felt the blood drain from his face, a queasy rush of adrenalin in his stomach.

But nothing happened. Kendrick paced up and down the room a couple of times, peering furiously out of the windows with a manner that suggested he felt the whole outside world was failing him. He produced the walkie-talkie and pressed the call button.

'Lloyd? Are you there?'

No response. Craig noticed Moss shifting uneasily. Probably not used to seeing his boss this rattled.

'Lloyd?' Kendrick shouted. 'Answer me. What's happening?'

There was an electronic burp, and then Craig heard a voice say, 'This is Parvez. We had a visitor. He wouldn't take a hint, so I had to do him.' A pause. 'Turns out he's filth. A Detective Inspector Sullivan.'

'Shit,' said Kendrick quietly. 'All right. Clear the fucking tree and turn round. We'll be there in ten.'

'Sounds like you're in trouble,' Craig said, disguising the dread he felt. The mention of any other police officer would have lifted his spirits, signalling that help was on its way. But Sullivan had almost certainly been coming here in a private capacity. The only saving grace was that Kendrick might not know that.

'Your men have seen sense and run away,' he went on. 'Why don't you follow their example?'

'Shut your mouth,' Kendrick ordered. But he looked shaken by the taunt, because neither of them believed for a moment that the men had fled.

It was much worse than that.

'Ten minutes,' Kendrick said to Moss. 'Then we kill them and cut our losses.'

Upstairs, Julia drifted into the nearest room and turned on the light. Finding herself in a study, she was taken by the possibility that there might be a different phone up here. She could try the police again.

There *was* a phone, on the desk, but of course it was dead too.

She sighed. Not thinking clearly.

There was an ornate captain's chair behind the desk. Julia sat down in it and leaned forward, crossing her arms and resting her head on them. For a few blissful moments she could deny the world's existence. The pain in her abdomen gradually receded, and she realised she felt absurdly tired, even sleepy.

The wind blew hard at the house. The light went out, then came back on. She jerked upright, the way you do when you doze off on a train or a bus. Outside, the broken TV aerial dragged over the tiles like fingernails on a blackboard. Julia shivered and stood up, needing action, needing to do something decisive.

Her attention was caught by the many framed photographs on the wall. Formal portraits from Philip Walker's long and evidently distinguished career. Poignant photos of a doting grandfather in carefully staged horseplay with Tom and Maddie. Even a couple with Craig as a young man: one on his graduation day, the other taken on an exotic palm-fringed beach.

And next to that, a slight oddity. A framed copy of a newspaper story, with the headline:

ATTORNEY GENERAL CATCHES THIEF

In a brave show of public duty, a member of Montserrat's Government apprehended a violent burglar late on Tuesday night. Philip Walker, who is currently one year into his term as

Attorney General, had been visiting friends when he spotted Robert Meade fleeing from a villa in Mayfield Road, Olveston. Local man Meade, 29, was found to have stolen cash and jewellery from the property. Following his arrest, officers from the Royal Montserrat Police Force discovered the householder, 53-year-old Errol Herbert, unconscious with serious head injuries. He was airlifted to Antigua for medical treatment and is in a stable condition. Mr Walker was hailed as a hero. 'Without his action, Mr Herbert would almost certainly have died,' said one officer.

The text was accompanied by two pictures. One was a photograph of Philip, taken at least ten years ago. The other was a grainy head-shot of the arrested man, who was of mixed race. His pale eyes glared at the camera with brutal indifference. That Philip Walker had tackled such a man helped explain why, years later, he had given his life to save her from Carl Forester.

Her thoughts were cut short by a noise from downstairs. Broken glass crunching underfoot on the kitchen floor.

There was someone in the house.

Seventy-Seven

She froze, listening for another sound, another clue. But the wind and the loose aerial made it impossible to hear clearly. There was only one way to be sure.

First she needed a weapon. In the top drawer of the desk she found a letter opener with a mother-of-pearl handle and a long thin blade. Gripping it at shoulder height, she crept across the room and on to the landing. She paused, hardly daring to breathe. The house shifted and groaned. The TV aerial rattled.

Still she waited, paralysed. A gust of wind was followed by the clink of glass hitting the floor, and she wondered if that was all she'd just heard. A piece of glass falling from the doorframe.

The warring voices were back. One said: *No, that was a different sound.* The other said: *Either way, you have to check. You can't stay here.*

If it was him, Toby, then he was here for a reason. He was here because he knew *she* was here. So hiding wouldn't get her anywhere. Trying to climb out of an upstairs window would leave her fatally exposed to an attack. And bearing in mind what he'd done in Camber, he could simply start a fire and kill her that way.

No. There was only one option. The one she had so recklessly proposed to Craig as they waited in the ambulance on Wednesday night.

Fight back.

* * *

She kept low, crouching awkwardly as she descended, one stair at a time, testing each tread as though negotiating a minefield. The hall edged into sight, revealing several open doors. All the rooms were dark. No sign of anyone lying in wait, but that didn't mean no one was there.

She reached the bottom stair and jabbed the knife as if shadow-boxing. The hall was empty, all the way to the front door in one direction and the kitchen in the other. The doors in between led variously to a cloakroom, a dining room and a living room.

Just as in the farmhouse, the open door was the better bet. From here it seemed an impossible distance away, standing like a prize at the end of a tunnel filled with unimaginable danger.

But a minute or two had now passed, and there had been no other suspicious noise, no movement. Maybe she had imagined it. Maybe it had just been the wind.

Then she heard him.

He breathed out.

He was in the living room. Very close. Perhaps hiding behind the door.

But he didn't react. He didn't spring out and attack her.

He couldn't see her, she realised. He must be relying on sound alone, and she'd come downstairs too quietly to be heard. If she could walk along the hall without making any noise . . .

It was a tough challenge, tiptoeing slowly when every nerve in her body was screaming at her to run. Her resolve lasted only until she got to the kitchen, saw it was empty and knew she had at least a few seconds' advantage while he got out from behind the door. She would just have to make those seconds count.

She ran across the kitchen, distantly noting that she could hear nothing from the hall. He was too slow to react, she thought. Ha! She made it to the back door and was about to burst into the cold raging night when suddenly he stepped into her path.

She jerked to a halt, slithering on the broken glass. It was impossible, but he was standing right in front of her, close enough that she could taste his rancid breath in her face. He held the gun in one hand and in the other a two-way radio, a radio he had taken from Kendrick's men. She guessed there must be another radio, set to the same channel, behind the living-room door. It had worked perfectly. It had flushed her out.

So this is it, she thought. This is where it ends.

He thought so too. 'Give up,' he said. Not a demand, or a request. A statement. A statement of the obvious.

No. She wasn't sure if she said the word aloud, or just thought it. He was aiming the gun at her, but some reckless intuition told her he wouldn't shoot. He wasn't done with her yet.

She turned fast, twisting on the balls of her feet, and at the same time hurled the letter opener like a spear. He flinched away but it caught him on the cheekbone. A line of blood materialised from nowhere and cascaded down his face.

She moved fast, but Toby was faster. As soon as he saw she wasn't intimidated by the gun, his hand dropped and he jumped forward, knowing he couldn't let her get the advantage. She was too unpredictable. Too fucking resourceful.

The cut on his face didn't hurt yet, but it pissed him off. If it had been on target it might have killed him. Blinded him, at least.

He hated her for that. He added it to all the other reasons for hating her. It fuelled him, made him more determined. He got to her while she was still on the threshold, still turning. He dropped the radio but kept hold of the gun. One free hand should be enough.

He was on her before she could move. Wrapped his arms around her, jamming the gun into her stomach. His other arm reached over her shoulder, locking around her neck.

'Give up,' he said again. 'Or Kendrick will kill Craig.'

For a bluff, it was pure genius. Totally instinctive. He had no idea he'd say it till the words came out of his mouth.

And it worked. All her resistance ceased. He almost heard the *whoosh* as the fight drained out of her.

Thank Christ for that.

Too slow. Too stupid. Not thinking clearly.

She had run right into his trap. Now he had her, literally in his grasp. She was aware of everything as if in slow motion: her mouth opening, drawing in a breath to scream. Adrenalin pumping furiously into her bloodstream, muscles primed for fight or flight. Some primordial imperative told her to run: get upstairs, create some distance and a chance to regroup . . .

A smarter section of her brain knew better. You can't move forward. Even if he doesn't shoot, he'll tighten his grip and crush your windpipe.

'Give up,' she heard him say. 'Or Kendrick will kill Craig.'

In that moment she wrestled control of her instinct and let herself go limp. She released a breath and with it some of the tension. She felt his body close in on her, but the hand around her neck relaxed. He thought she had surrendered.

She threw herself against him with all her weight. Drove both her elbows into his stomach. Whipped her head back and connected with his face. A loud crack as bone gave way to bone.

He screamed a guttural scream. His arms fell away and he stumbled. She heard a thud and didn't register it, but he had dropped the gun. It made no difference. By then she was moving, running across the kitchen, towards the only weapon she could see.

His nose was broken. The pain was atrocious. It felt like she'd driven a burning hot spike into his sinuses. There was a flap of skin hanging loose on his cheek. Blood pouring down his face. Only his fury kept him moving. The thought of what he'd do to her once he got her away from here.

He'd been so clever, planting the other radio inside the house. And now he was being denied the reward that his ingenuity deserved. His resentment was accompanied by a much darker thought: one he'd been struggling to deny for weeks.

It was over. From the moment he learned Julia was alive, he was finished. As soon as she'd reappeared with Walker, bleating about a second killer, he should have cut and run. And now it was too late.

No. He had to stay focused. *You can still do this*, he told himself. *You've seen off four of Kendrick's men. You can deal with this bitch.*

Stupidly, she didn't try to run upstairs. She stayed in the kitchen, and that meant he could easily catch her.

She reached the worktop next to the fridge. No knife block, thank God. There were probably knives somewhere, but she wouldn't have time to reach them. Another second and he'd slam into her from behind. Maybe trap her hand in a drawer and crush her fingers. He'd enjoy that.

He was two feet away. A foot. Close enough to smell her sweat and fear. Now she was turning. Probably about to beg for another chance. Well, she could forget that. He'd suffered enough at her hands. Now it was her turn.

Seventy-Eight

She could feel him close behind her, right on her heels. Not even enough distance to turn and fight properly.

This had to work.

She knew Craig was living in his father's house at the moment, but he obviously wasn't doing much cooking. The kitchen looked more like something from a show home. No dirty dishes on the unit in front of her. No spice racks or mug trees or egg holders. No knives. No clutter. Just a brushed-steel toaster and a matching kettle.

The kettle was modern, high-tech. Shaped like a tall jug, resting on a detachable base which plugged into the mains. It had a vertical strip of transparent plastic to show the water level. It was half full.

She grabbed it in desperation. Her stomach was protesting again, a terrible splitting sensation that could only mean something was seriously wrong. There was no way she could get upstairs. No way she could outrun him.

As she lifted the kettle clear of the base she realised how heavy it was. A solid, expensive piece of kit.

Good.

She could feel Toby closing on her. He was going to ram her, crush her against the units. She didn't even have time to turn properly. She just spun her upper body and brought the kettle round in front of

408

her, swung it over and down like a tennis serve, aiming for the point where she hoped his head would be.

At the moment of contact she thought of the dream. She was on the beach at Camber Sands and the killer had fallen from the tree. She'd beaten him to death with a poker or a crowbar.

Only it wasn't a poker, or a crowbar. It was an ordinary domestic kettle. And she didn't beat him over and over. She hit him twice.

But the result was the same.

His own momentum contributed to the force of the blow, like a man running into a wall. The kettle landed on the top of his head and she saw his skull crack. The sound it made was unlike anything she'd ever heard. It entered her ears and seemed to trickle through her body like an infection, a chilling nausea.

Toby came to an abrupt stop. His eyes rolled up in his head and his legs gave way.

She hit him again as he dropped. She didn't know why. Perhaps in response to some vestigial echo of her dream. Even as she did it, there was a voice telling her it was unnecessary. Sadistic, even.

Well, maybe I'm entitled, she thought. Maybe he owes me this one.

He lay at her feet, not moving. There was so much blood on his face, she couldn't tell if his eyes were open or shut. The back of his head was oozing dark, clotted blood. Blood mixed with something else. She didn't want to think about what it might be.

She was pressed against the kitchen units. Trapped. She couldn't move without stepping over him. She stayed like that for a long time, still holding the kettle, the water inside sloshing because she was shaking so hard.

Gradually the shock subsided. You have to move, she told herself. It's not over yet.

She stared at the kettle as if seeing it for the first time. Blood and hair had adhered to the underside. She set it down on the unit and looked at the body once more. Watching it for movement.

Holding the worktop for balance, she brought her right knee up and extended her foot over the body. She had an image of his hand whipping out, grabbing her ankle. She could feel her nerves jangling like a fire alarm, a wailing inside her head that made it an effort to think or breathe or move.

She planted her right foot on the far side of his body, then repeated the move with her left leg. A big exaggerated motion, her knee arching high, like some absurd mime artist.

When she was finally standing clear she felt drained, as though she'd just run a marathon. She gave the body one final glance, then left the kitchen, stumbled through the hall and into the cloakroom. She grabbed the sink as she felt herself blacking out. Possibly she did, for her next memory was of climbing to her feet, running cold water over her wrists while she looked in the mirror and a killer stared implacably back at her.

For a moment her parents were standing behind her, just as they had stood on the terrace in her dream, regarding her with quiet shame.

'I'm not her,' she whispered. But she knew it was a lie.

The last words he ever spoke floated back to her.

Kendrick will kill Craig.

Could she believe him? What would make Toby say that?

She knew Kendrick was here, in the village. It wasn't impossible that Craig was here too. Perhaps . . .

Perhaps he had come looking for her. Perhaps he hadn't given up.

She sighed. She faced herself in the mirror and made a conscious decision: she would ignore the pain in her stomach until she knew that Craig was safe.

If he hadn't given up, neither could she.

Seventy-Nine

Ten minutes, Kendrick had said. And then they would be dead.

Craig believed him. He found himself counting the seconds, knowing he had to act now or he might never see his children again.

With two minutes to go, the lights went out again. This time they didn't come back on.

Kendrick had just made another attempt to contact his men. The pair he'd sent after Toby weren't responding. Now, when the room went dark, he reacted as if they were under attack. Craig saw him draw a gun and fire several times, wild panicky shots directed at the driveway outside. There was a loud crash as one of the big windows shattered.

The guard, Moss, gave a shout of alarm and moved towards his boss. In the confusion Craig dived forward and threw all his weight into a tackle, trying to bring him down while also wrestling the gun from his hand.

He failed on both points. Moss was simply too strong. He was knocked off balance, but he didn't fall. For Craig it was like hurling himself at a brick wall. He grappled with the man's wrist, but Moss jerked his elbow back and caught Craig in the chest, knocking the air from his lungs. He was driven backwards by the blow, and in the darkness saw Moss turning, trying to aim the gun in his direction.

Then something flew past his head, and there was a loud thud.

The big man groaned and fell back, and as he did the gun went off. Craig also dropped to the floor, expecting another shot, but none came. Instead he could hear Moss breathing in painful gasps and swearing quietly.

Then a controlled voice said, 'Stay there, Craig. Move and you're dead.'

It came from less than three feet away. Craig was lying awkwardly on the floor, one of his legs caught beneath a chair. He wasn't in a position to get up quickly, even if he wanted to. His rebellion had failed.

As his eyes adjusted to the dark, Craig risked moving his head slightly. George was on his knees, facing Craig. Kendrick stood behind him, the gun against George's skull. It was a classic execution pose, but far from looking defeated, George's eyes were blazing with determination. Like Craig, he had been biding his time.

Kendrick said, 'Moss, are you all right?'

'Fucker threw something at me,' Moss growled. His voice was tight with pain. Craig turned, saw the dark gleam of blood on the big man's forehead. There was a broken ashtray on the floor next to him, but Moss was more concerned about his leg, clutching his calf with both hands. 'Gun went off as I fell,' he said. 'Caught my fucking leg.'

Kendrick sighed. 'Can you walk?'

'I don't know, boss.'

'Well, you're gonna have to. We're getting out of here.'

Then another voice shouted, 'Drop your gun.'

Kendrick turned towards the sound, his mouth forming an incredulous smile. From his position on the floor, Craig couldn't see the person who had just entered the room. But he recognised the voice, and for a moment thought he must be dreaming.

The power failure nearly killed her. She was approaching the grounds of Chilton Manor when a ferocious gust of wind was accompanied by a loud rending sound from the field to her right. Without consciously understanding what it was, Julia surged forward. The pylon toppled slowly, colliding with a tree and then landing in the field. At the same time she had the impression of a dark cable whipping through the air above her head.

Flinging herself down on the opposite verge, she saw a bright flash of lightning just feet away. There was a harsh burning smell in the air, and she understood it wasn't lightning. It was the live wire sparking as it hit the ground.

She lay on the wet grass, watching for another strike. The pain in her stomach was back with a vengeance, but she had no choice but to ignore it. She hadn't made it this far just to end up electrocuted in a freak accident.

At the next lull in the wind she got up and dashed clear of the cable's reach. Clutching her belly as she ran, she reached the manor gates and found little more than two twisted heaps of metal. Kendrick must have rammed right through them.

Seconds later she spotted Craig's car, destroying her last faint hope that Toby had been bluffing. On the approach to the house, she noticed one of the living-room windows was shattered. She could dimly make out shadows moving inside. Praying she wasn't too late, she struggled up the steps and found the front door was open.

Crossing the hall, a spasm of pain almost caused her to black out. It felt like someone was pouring hot tar into her stomach. She blinked away tears and checked the gun in her hand. After taking it from Toby, she had gone into the garden and fired into the air. If the moment came to use it in anger, she wanted to know she could pull the trigger.

Now that moment was here.

She stepped into the doorway and took aim.

'Drop your gun,' she ordered.

Eighty

She moved further into the room. Close enough to see who she was aiming at, but not so close that he could spring at her.

She recognised him straight away. He turned his head and looked at her in amazement. He glanced at the gun in her hand, then back up, studying her face. A quick, professional assessment. Would she have the guts to shoot?

'Toby's dead,' she told him, by way of an answer. 'I killed him.'

He gave the merest nod of his head, almost a congratulation. 'And my men?'

'Toby killed them.'

'Well, well. Quite a mess to clear up.'

Keeping her eyes locked on him, she called out, 'Craig? Are you all right?'

'I'm here,' said a voice from the floor. 'I'm okay. So is George. He's kneeling in front of Kendrick.'

'I can see him,' Julia said. 'Is there anyone else?'

'One of Kendrick's guys. He's on the floor near me. He's wounded, but he has a gun.'

'And he'll use it,' said Kendrick. 'He'll shoot Craig, and I'll shoot George, unless you put your gun down right now.'

'Don't listen to him,' Craig said. 'He was involved in the massacre.

Toby's only targets were the Caplans. It was Kendrick who persuaded Carl to murder the others.'

'I know,' said Julia. 'And I know why.'

Kendrick was still smiling, still radiating confidence. 'You don't know anything. Give me that gun and I might, just might, let you live.'

Now George spoke up. 'He's bluffing. Shoot him now. Don't worry about me. Shoot him.'

Julia's finger tightened on the trigger. Deep down she knew George was right. Her best chance of survival was to fire now, while Kendrick had his own weapon aimed at George. But in that scenario George was also likely to die. Kendrick knew it, and he was banking on the assumption that she wasn't capable of such ruthlessness.

'I know your real name,' Julia said. 'And I know who your target was.'

Kendrick's expression changed. There was a little more respect in his voice when he answered. 'In that case, you'll know how easily I can walk away from this.'

'Can you? Give up all your power and wealth?'

'I can get it again. It's easily acquired, if you have the right qualities.'

'I don't understand,' said Craig. 'Is this man Kendrick or not?'

'That's what he calls himself,' Julia said. 'His real name is Robert Meade. Isn't that right? Robert Meade, from the island of Montserrat.'

Craig could hear what Julia was saying, but none of it made much sense. That didn't matter, so long as she kept on talking. While everyone concentrated on her, Craig was slowly inching his way across the carpet.

Moss was still in a sitting position, but he had leaned to one side, resting against a sofa. Once or twice he'd shut his eyes for a few seconds. He hadn't yet let go of his injured leg, which meant his gun must be lying on the floor nearby. Craig kept shuffling closer, his hands feeling for the gun while he looked from Kendrick to Julia and tried to follow the conversation.

So Kendrick wasn't his real name? George appeared equally confused by this revelation. He was saying something when Julia's last sentence finally penetrated.

Robert Meade, from the island of Montserrat.

Craig knew that name. He'd read it somewhere. He had heard it spoken. Someone had told him about a man called Robert Meade.

'Oh no,' he gasped. 'No.'

Julia said, 'I'm sorry, Craig. You shouldn't have to find out like this.'

'My father?' Craig said.

Julia wasn't sure if the question was directed at her, or at Kendrick, who was now staring at Craig. Julia took a sly step closer, improving her line of fire.

'But Kendrick's from Trinidad,' George said. 'I researched him. He comes from a good family.'

Kendrick chuckled. 'Stolen identity, George. I met the real Max Kendrick in prison, more than ten years ago. The guards thought it was hilarious that we looked so alike. We could have been twins. Kendrick had run off when he was a teenager. The day he told me his family hadn't seen him for years, I came up with the idea of impersonating him, helping myself to some of their fortune. It was Jacques who convinced me to play a long game, and that way I got everything.'

George let out what might have been a sob. Kendrick sadistically prodded him with the gun. Craig saw Moss's eyes were closed and shifted another couple of inches.

'I left prison knowing everything about his life, all kinds of details that would convince his parents. He was released a couple of months later. Jacques got rid of him for me, and pretty soon I was living the high life in Trinidad, back in the bosom of my estranged family.'

'They accepted you?' Julia asked, remembering the malevolent gaze from the newspaper cutting.

'I think they had their doubts, especially the mother. But they were so glad to have their wayward son back, they believed what they wanted to believe. It's human nature, isn't it, George?' Again he jabbed him with the gun. 'By that time the old man was dying. And I made sure "Mummy" followed soon after.'

'And my father knew the truth?' Craig said.

'He would have done. He was the one who got me locked away in the first place.' He chuckled. 'When I came over here I hadn't given him a thought in years. It wasn't until we started due diligence that I found out about the campaign to stop the Chilton development. And who should be leading it but good old Philip Walker. Probably the only man in Britain who could look at me and know I wasn't really Max Kendrick.'

Craig felt a surge of fury. He opened his mouth to speak, but at the same time his fingers touched cold metal. He eased back a little further.

'There was no way I wanted to abandon the deal, so he had to be removed. Discovering that Toby was plotting to kill the Caplans gave me a perfect opportunity.'

'But why so many deaths?' Julia asked.

'It's an imprecise science,' Kendrick said, his eyes sparkling with humour. 'Carl wasn't exactly stable. All we told him was to make sure it didn't look like Walker was the only target. Even then he nearly bungled it. Luckily Walker came out, trying to be a hero again.' Another chuckle. 'Of course, we had the protection of knowing that even if a conspiracy came to light, it would be Toby, and possibly the Mathesons, who took the fall.'

'And you killed Abby Clark, didn't you?' Craig demanded.

'I take my privacy very seriously,' Kendrick said. 'She tried contacting one or two people in Trinidad, and I decided that was a little too close for comfort.'

George suddenly jerked forward, and for a second Julia thought he had been hit. Then he shouted, 'Shoot him, for God's sake. Shoot!'

The words emerged in a strange elongated stream, as if through a funnel, and although Julia knew it was the right thing to do, her body refused to obey. A black gauze was wrapping itself round her, pulling her down, and as she fell she heard gunfire, three shots from two different guns, and told herself that if this was dying, it really wasn't so bad.

Craig had to angle his shot high to be sure of missing George. He aimed at Kendrick's head just as Kendrick fired first at Julia, then in Craig's direction. He was moving at the same time, and even as Craig shut his eyes and felt hot blood hit his face he knew his own shot had missed.

He opened his eyes, amazed to find himself still alive, just in time to see Kendrick leaping through the window. Moss was lying dead beside him, and George was on his hands and knees, vomiting on to the carpet. There was no sign of Julia.

Kicking a chair away, Craig got to his feet and blundered across the room. He made out the shape of her body, face-down on the floor. He screamed her name into the darkness but she didn't respond. He dropped beside her and gently lifted her arm. There was no blood visible on her, no obvious wound, but it wasn't until he found a pulse that he let out a jagged breath and dared to believe it could be all right.

Eighty-One

She woke in a gloomy dawn to the patter of rain on the roof. Then the sun broke through and the birds began their raucous celebration of the coming day. Julia lay and listened to them, realising with a kind of awe that not only was she alive, but that for the first time in many days she had a genuine expectation of life, of recovery, of happiness.

Although Kendrick had fired in her direction, it had been way off target, partly because by then she had already collapsed. She had Craig to thank for her survival. It was he who decided her need for medical attention took priority over chasing Kendrick.

Together with George, he had carried her out to his car and driven like a maniac to the nearest A&E, in Haywards Heath. There she underwent an emergency operation to stem internal bleeding. She was also diagnosed with pneumonia, and spent the next two weeks in hospital.

As word of the events spread, the media attention became even more rabid than the first time around. Julia had to be kept under a strict guard: her only regular visitors were her brother and his wife, and Craig, who had needed two dozen stitches to repair the knife wound in his thigh.

It was Craig who updated her on the police investigation. Nothing had been seen of Kendrick, although the two men with whom he was thought to have escaped were later found dead, their Jeep abandoned in an industrial estate in Folkestone. The police believed this was a ploy, designed to suggest he had left the country by this route. Craig's police contact, DI Sullivan, was also found outside the village with a gunshot wound to the spine, and it was still doubtful as to whether he would walk again.

Kendrick's ruthlessness was confirmed when the police told Craig they thought he'd deliberately killed Moss, so as not to leave a witness who could reveal his whereabouts. It was several days before they traced his rented house in Berkshire, by which time it had been gutted by fire. There was no saying how long Kendrick had stayed there, or what he might have taken with him when he fled.

After that, the trail went cold. Julia understood now what he'd meant when he said how easily he could walk away. For a man who'd spent more than a decade inhabiting a false identity, it wouldn't trouble him to slip on a new one and resume his life somewhere else.

For Craig and Julia, that left one important question. Did he remain a threat to them?

The senior detective, when he was finally permitted to speak to Julia, took a fairly dismissive attitude. 'He's long gone, I'm sure of it. There's really no need to spend your whole life looking over your shoulder.'

Julia couldn't see quite as much reason to be confident, but in some ways it was irrelevant. There was no question of the police providing them with protection. She and Craig – and George as well, for that matter – would simply have to take their chances.

She was discharged from hospital on the understanding that she would spend a long period of convalescence at the Old Schoolhouse, under Craig's care. This time she intended to follow her doctor's recommendations to the letter.

First there was the media to contend with. Craig's advice was not to hide from them. 'They're like hunters,' he told her. 'It's the thrill of the chase that gets them going. Make yourself available and they'll lose interest a lot sooner.'

And so it proved. She gave several print interviews, made one TV appearance, and then she was left alone. The world had moved on to newer, fresher tragedies.

Returning to Chilton wasn't nearly as traumatic as she expected. She arrived back on a grey, nondescript morning at the beginning of March. An almost palpable air of exhaustion hung over the village, but unlike before there was no sense of menace, no feeling of unfinished business. Entering the house, she had insisted on going into the kitchen, seeing for herself the room where Toby had perished.

Where she had killed him.

She had stood a moment, waiting to see what ghosts might appear, but there was nothing. Just weariness, and a satisfaction that it was all over at last.

All over, but for one conversation.

It took place on her third day after leaving hospital. First she talked it over with Craig, and sensed a marked reluctance on his part. She knew he feared the effect it would have on her recovery. For her sake and for his own, he was trying to focus remorselessly on the future. He'd also made it clear he wanted that future to include a relationship between the two of them, an idea which grew more appealing with each passing day.

She spotted him from the window and left the house. It was a warm, sunny morning. After the second wave of forensic investigation, the clean-up had removed all the remaining flowers and wreaths, signalling an end to mourning and a slow return to normality. Now, apart from some trees lost to the storm, the village looked exactly as it had done before 19 January.

On the green, the great yew still dominated. George Matheson waited beneath it, gazing into the middle distance. He saw her and turned, offering an uncertain smile.

It seemed to take them both by surprise when they embraced. While still holding her, he said, 'I'm very sorry for what they did.'

They broke apart, and Julia nodded. 'You don't have to apologise. I know you had nothing to do with it.'

He seemed gratified, but still let out a heavy sigh. 'I don't think I'll ever come to terms with the scale of Vanessa's betrayal.'

'I remember that morning when we met here,' Julia said. 'I told you about my parents and you seemed so sympathetic, so genuinely upset about the massacre. I couldn't bear to think you were faking that grief.' She swallowed heavily. 'And now I know you weren't.'

'No doubt Craig told you what happened at the house. You know what drove Vanessa to do it?'

Julia nodded. 'Your affair with Laura Caplan.'

George gave a funny little laugh. He turned away from the tree and walked towards the pond. Julia fell into step beside him. The sight of a Royal Mail van driving up the High Street caused a momentary flutter of nerves, reminding her of how it had all started.

'How's Megan?' she said.

His face immediately brightened. 'She's making progress. Not talking yet, but she responds to stimulation. She squeezes my hand. Sometimes she smiles.'

Julia faltered. Her mouth felt very dry. He gave her an inquisitive glance, his face benign, as if he knew what was to come and wouldn't be offended.

'Is Megan your daughter?'

His expression didn't change. No surprise, no shock or anger. But he shook his head just the same, leaving Julia confused.

'I'm afraid the truth is even more tragic,' he said. 'I'm her grandfather.'

Julia felt too stunned to respond. She stopped by the edge of the pond, stared at the murky brown water and tried to make sense of this revelation.

'When I employed Keith, I had no idea,' George went on. 'Laura didn't say anything to me for years. Too frightened that I might reject her, she told me later. She was the result of a very brief relationship I had in my early twenties. I knew nothing at all about the pregnancy. Laura didn't find out about me until her mother died. By then she was married to Keith. When they saw the farm job advertised, Laura thought it would be a perfect opportunity to . . . well, observe me from afar, I suppose.'

'When did she tell you?' Julia asked.

'About two years ago. After the incident with Carl. Keith hadn't been particularly sympathetic. We were discussing it one day when suddenly she came out with it.' He shrugged. 'After that, we spent more and more time together, usually when Vanessa was in London. We were rather secretive, because Laura wasn't sure how Keith would react to the news. Their marriage was already in trouble.'

'Why not let Vanessa know the truth?' As she spoke, Julia remembered something Craig had told her. 'She couldn't have children.'

George frowned. 'That's right. We'd tried everything that was possible at the time, to no avail. It made her feel terribly inadequate, and I think over the years it ate away at her. Finding out that I had a daughter would have been a devastating blow. I was still agonising over how to break the news when the cancer was diagnosed.'

He sniffed, turned away from her for a moment. 'I was a dreadful coward,' he said. 'I decided it was best to say nothing. Once Vanessa had passed away, I'd intended to give Laura the financial support to leave Keith, and I wanted to pay for Megan's education.'

He stopped as a sob escaped him. Julia stepped closer, taking his hand and pressing it between her own. He looked at her with a face crumpled with grief, tears wet on his cheeks.

'It was an appalling mistake, and it cost so many lives. If it weren't for Megan, I don't think I'd have the will to go on.'

Julia said nothing. A noise behind her made her turn. Craig had emerged from the Old Schoolhouse and was walking towards her, looking concerned. She waved him away.

George blew his nose and recovered his composure. He looked at his watch and nodded to himself, as if he had said more than enough. But before they parted, Julia had one more question.

'What about the village?'

He shrugged. 'Nothing stays the same for ever. I can't guarantee that Chilton won't fall to the developers . . .' He rested a hand on her shoulder, gripping it tightly for a moment. 'But it won't happen while I draw breath.'

He kissed her on both cheeks, and wished her well. Julia watched him walk across the green and disappear into Hurst Lane. Then she turned and joined Craig by the yew tree. His expression hadn't altered.

'This just arrived,' he said.

He handed her a postcard showing a spectacular volcanic eruption on the island of Montserrat. She turned it over and read the back. It was addressed to her, care of the Old Schoolhouse. The handwriting was neat, square, unfamiliar. The message was short and sweet.

> *One day our paths will cross again.*
> *Until then . . . stay alive for me.*
> *Be lucky.*

Her laughter caught Craig unawares. He stared at her as if she'd lost her senses.

'What are you going to do?'

Julia gave him the card back. She looked up at the broad, graceful branches of the tree that had sheltered her and saved her life. Far above, she could see aircraft trails criss-crossing a milky-blue sky. A whole world carrying on as normal.

'I'm going to take his advice,' she said.

Acknowledgements

For their help with research into police procedures, telecommunications and medical matters, I'd like to thank Supt Steve Voice, Tony Deakin, Simon Cude, Dawn Hayes, Natasha Butt and Mr S Waquar Yusuf. I must stress that certain liberties were taken for the sake of the story, so responsibility for any errors or inaccuracies lies firmly with the author.

I owe a huge debt of gratitude to everyone at Janklow & Nesbit UK, particularly my agent, Tif Loehnis, as well as Rebecca Folland, Kirsty Gordon and Jenny McVeigh. At Preface/Random House I'd like to thank Trevor Dolby, Stephen Dumughn, Holly Roberts, Mari Roberts, Ben Wright and most of all my editor, the incomparable Rosie de Courcy: her faith, guidance and support played a crucial part in seeing this project to fruition.

Thanks to all my friends and family, especially my parents and parents-in-law, whose help over the past few years has been invaluable. Thanks also to Claire Burrell, Tracy Brown, Adrian Magson, Sheila Quigley, Nick Stone, Mike Paterson, Hugh Dickens and the late Bob Medland.

Special love and thanks to James and Emily for their patience and inspiration. And to my wife, Niki, who endured all the years of rejection alongside me, without ever losing faith that one day this would happen.

Now read an extract from
Tom Bale's second novel

TERROR'S REACH

Coming soon from Preface

One

They sent the first man in at midday. His job couldn't have been more straightforward. All he had to do was sit on the beach. Watch, listen, wait, and not be too obvious about it.

The target was Terror's Reach, a stunning accident of geography nestled within the dazzling surroundings of Chichester harbour. Officially designated as an area of outstanding natural beauty, it had a material wealth of corresponding splendour. One small island: five homes, nine residents and combined assets of well over a billion pounds. There for the taking.

But the remote location posed its own challenges. The options for reconnaissance were limited, long-term surveillance all but impossible. There was no passing traffic, no way to go unnoticed. The super rich are rightly paranoid about strangers in their neighbourhood. Anyone seen loitering on the island was liable to be challenged or reported to the police.

The solution involved a gamble, but with limited risk. The good weather helped: made their stratagem both plausible and appealing. As a result, there was some competition to be assigned the role.

Gough was pleased to be chosen. He knew this was regarded as just about the easiest gig of the lot, but it also carried serious responsibility. As first man in, his actions had a direct bearing on the whole operation. Get it wrong, and he was in big trouble.

He was under no illusions about the kind of people he was working for. If he screwed up, they would probably kill him. Simple as that.

Two in the afternoon: siesta time. With the temperature pushing ninety, any sensible person would be glad of the chance to lie in the shade and have a doze. But Jaden, at six years old, didn't see it in those terms. Bursting with restless energy, he had no intention of taking a nap, and he was making his feelings known to his mother.

Joe Clayton was aware of the protests coming from the other end of the garden, but he wasn't really listening to them. He was sitting on the broad stone terrace, finishing a lunch of cold meats and salad.

'I want to go to the beach.'

'Not now, Jaden. Sofia has to sleep, and so should you.'

'I'm not tired. Sofia's a baby. I'm six.'

'Well, go in the pool then. But only for a few minutes.'

'I don't want to go in the pool. I want to go to the beach.'

'It's too hot. And I have to stay here and watch Sofia.'

'I can go on my own.'

'No, Jaden.'

'It's not fair. You don't let me do anything.'

There was a tiny thud, followed by a louder cracking sound. Joe looked up and saw something skidding across the grass. The boy had thrown one of his cars to the ground. It must have ricocheted, hit another toy and possibly broken it.

Jaden glowered at the tiny die-cast models, furious with his mother, with himself, with the whole world. Joe found he could easily reach back and remember how it felt to be that powerless; the terrible aching frustration of childhood.

'I hate it here,' Jaden shouted. 'I wish we still lived with Nanny and Grandad.'

Joe winced on Cassie's behalf. He had already decided to intervene when he heard a first floor window thrown open. A voice roared: 'Cassie! Do something about that boy!'

The window slammed shut. On the lawn, Jaden scooped up the broken toy and fled to his refuge: a sun-proof beach tent that was variously a cave, a fire station and an enemy camp. His mother called after him in a more gentle, reassuring tone, but Jaden ignored her.

Maybe it was the heat making everyone so fractious, Joe thought. Not that Valentin Nasenko ever had much patience with his stepson. Little wonder the boy missed life with his grandparents.

Joe drained his glass of water, sliding the remains of several ice cubes into his mouth. He crunched them as he stood up. His chair scraped noisily on the stone, and he almost expected another angry tirade from above. When Valentin was busy, he demanded peace and quiet. *And what Valentin Nasenko wanted* . . .

Joe had been working for the Nasenkos for a little over nine months. He'd met them the previous September on the Greek island of Naxos. Having concluded a summer-long stint as a deckhand on various luxury yachts, he was helping out at a bar in Naxos town, owned by a former Australian surf champion.

Valentin's principal advisor, Barry McWhirter, had been in the bar when a fight broke out between rival football fans during a televised Champions League game. Impressed by Joe's adroit handling of the mini-riot than ensued, McWhirter invited Joe to meet Nasenko. One of his security team had resigned at short notice, and Valentin wanted an extra body to watch over his wife and newborn daughter for a three-week cruise around the Aegean.

At first Joe had been reluctant. The thought of babysitting a young mother and her child didn't hold much appeal for him, but inevitably the money on offer made the decision for him. One thousand euros a week, available in cash if he wanted it.

Cassie Nasenko had seemed equally unhappy with the arrangement. She rarely made eye contact and was constantly ill at ease in his company. When she deigned to speak to him, it was with the kind of haughty manner a Victorian duchess might employ to address her lowliest scullery maid.

The situation didn't improve when Joe overheard her singing some cheesy ballad and quipped that, with a bit more practice, she might make a decent karaoke singer. He later discovered that at the age of seventeen Cassie had reached the final stages of a TV talent competition, and had gone on to enjoy a brief but successful career as a pop singer.

It wasn't until the third week that she grew accustomed to his presence, and he came to see that what he'd perceived as arrogance was actually shyness. She was from an ordinary, lower-middle-class background, very similar to his own, and she still hadn't come to terms with the idea of having staff at her beck and call.

When the cruise ended it was Cassie, rather than Valentin, who suggested Joe should stay on the team. Joe suspected it was largely because of Jaden, Cassie's son from a short-lived relationship with an actor in a teen soap. Jaden was a quiet, troubled little boy, but Joe seemed to have struck up a rapport with him in a way that few others had.

Returning to the UK posed another dilemma. In many ways he was in no hurry to go back, and yet he couldn't deny his fascination with the idea: a feeling akin to the desire to touch a naked flame. It was there constantly in his dreams, when the past could be effortlessly unrolled and reworked. Joe had often troubled over the *if* and *how* and *when* of his return, always careful to avoid the remaining question: *What then?*

The answer, as it turned out, was simple. Just go to work and get through the day. Go to work and never think about where you might be instead.

Joe descended the half dozen steps from the terrace. The middle section of the garden was effectively a large playpen, a neat square of lawn fenced off for safety from the swimming pool and the jetty beyond.

It was littered with trikes and footballs and Jaden's current favourite diversion: a giant game of Connect 4 that was taller than he was.

Cassie Nasenko was sitting on a picnic blanket, staring pensively in the direction of Jaden's hideaway. Next to her, ten-month-old Sofia was stripped to her nappy and fast asleep beneath a large white parasol, her pudgy white limbs contrasting with her mother's deep tan.

Cassie was a small, slight woman with an almost boyish figure: narrow hips, bony shoulders and thin arms. At first glance she could have been mistaken for a teenager, rather than a woman of twenty-five, a wife and mother of two children.

Throughout the present heatwave, unseasonable even for June, she'd maintained a uniform of flip-flops, denim shorts and cotton shirts, knotted at the waist, with a bikini in place of underwear. Her sun-bleached brown hair was tied up in a ponytail, her green eyes clear and bright against the tan. A sprinkle of freckles over her nose gave her a pretty, tomboyish look.

At Joe's approach, she put on a brave smile. Close up, he was struck by how weary she looked. He knew Sofia often kept her up at night; the baby was teething at the moment, and having a bad time of it.

He said, 'I'll take him to the beach if you want.'

'I don't like giving in to him when he's had a strop.'

'No. But for a quiet life.' He nodded towards the house. 'Just this once.'

'All right. But only for ten minutes or so. Then he really has to get out of the sun.'

'You okay if I have a swim while I'm there?'

'Fine,' she said. 'But keep an eye on him. He's behaving like a little monster at the moment.'

'He's a good kid at heart,' Joe said. 'I'm sure he didn't mean what he said about living here.'

She looked him a little sharply, as though he might have over-stepped the mark.

'No,' she said. 'I think he meant every word.'

Two

Terror's Reach had captivated Joe from the moment he first set eyes on it. He was unfamiliar with the area, and had imagined Chichester harbour to be a man-made construction, with a sea wall and all the accoutrements of a commercial port: quays and cranes and slipways; maybe a yacht marina.

In fact, it was a vast natural harbour, straddling the counties of Hampshire and West Sussex. Eleven square miles of water in a tidal basin of mud flats and salt marsh. There were three main channels and countless other inlets, creeks and waterways around half a dozen peninsulas of varying size and shape.

The Reach was a small island on the eastern side of the harbour, once joined to the mainland by a narrow causeway, accessible on foot at low tide. Its name derived from a Victorian working boat, the *Terror*, which had sailed around Chichester harbour, transporting oyster catches from larger offshore vessels. The Reach marked the furthest southerly point on its route.

Although uninhabited until the 1890s, the island's sheltered coves and woods had been used by smugglers for centuries. When coastal erosion finally destroyed the causeway in the mid 1930s, a chain ferry was installed, jointly funded by the residents and by the War Office, which had acquired two thirds of the five hundred acre island for use as a training camp.

The ferry was superceded in the sixties by the construction of a road bridge, and while the Ministry of Defence still maintained the training camp, its lack of use in recent years had led to fevered speculation about its future. In the meantime, the only private dwellings were spread in a graceful arc on the south-western corner, with views out to sea and across the bay towards Hayling Island.

Originally there had been eleven relatively modest houses, but in the past two decades all but one had been demolished and replaced by much larger, architect-designed mansions. Now there were just five in total, with an average value of four million apiece, making property on the Reach almost as expensive as that in the more famous resort of Sandbanks, about seventy miles to the west.

It was sheer perfection, if not exactly perfection on his own terms. In the first few weeks he'd spent every spare moment exploring his new home, and it had brought him up short when he first caught himself thinking of it in that way. This felt like home, or at least the nearest thing to a home that he could hope for.

Jaden's whole demeanour was transformed once he stepped through the gate at the bottom of the garden. It was like he'd been granted an unexpected release from prison. His shoulders lifted and he grinned, whooping with pleasure as he broke away from Joe's grasp and tore off along the timber decking.

'Not too fast,' Joe said, breaking into a jog to keep up.

The decking was about five feet wide, forming a communal walkway that ran for some three hundred yards along the rear of the properties. Each home had a private jetty that branched out from the decking and extended fifty or sixty feet over the water, though today there was only a couple of small craft moored here. For most of its length there was no fence or safety rail on the seaward side of the deck, so Joe had to watch that Jaden didn't trip and fall in.

Nevertheless, he couldn't help admiring the boy's daredevil streak, perhaps because he recalled a similar quality in himself at that age.

It meant Jaden was already straining for independence at every opportunity, and angrily protesting whenever limits were imposed on him, to his mother's continual exasperation and despair.

Joe could appreciate both sides of view. To a restless, energetic six-year-old, the island must have seemed like a personal adventure playground, bursting with the potential for excitement. And in many ways, the Reach was the safest place imaginable in which to grow up. Only a handful of residents. Minimal traffic. No strangers passing through.

But Cassie, like many parents where their first-born was involved, saw danger lurking around every corner. Reasonable enough, given her husband's wealth. It was why Joe had been employed, after all. For weeks Jaden had been pleading to be allowed to go to the beach on his own, and Cassie had steadfastly refused.

Valentin's property was furthest from the beach, so they had to pass the other four homes. Three of the four were imposing buildings in vastly different styles: mock-Georgian, ultra-modern and faux-Gothic. The gardens were a little more uniform in design: all terraced, with a mixture of lawns and paved areas. Most had swimming pools; some had fountains and summerhouses. All were scandalously under-appreciated, in Joe's opinion.

It was Friday afternoon, a truly glorious summer's day, and yet there was no one outside, no one enjoying the weather or savouring the view. They didn't see a single resident until they reached the last house, owned by a retired couple named Donald and Angela Weaver. Theirs was the only remaining original property, and even though it had a substantial ground floor extension it was modest in comparison to its neighbours.

Donald Weaver was just visible amidst the mass of sweet peppers and tomato plants in his greenhouse, a small red watering can bobbing around in mid-air as if of its own accord. Jaden spotted him first, broke his stride to call and wave, but there was no response. Either Donald didn't notice him, or just couldn't be bothered to acknowledge the boy. Joe had a feeling it was the latter.

A few yards beyond the Weavers' home, the decking ended at a tall gate, marked with a warning on the opposite side: 'RESIDENTS ONLY'. In case anyone should ignore the sign, one of the residents, Robert Felton, had paid to install a simple combination lock, as well as adding a few yards of fencing to prevent anyone from simply climbing around the gate. It hadn't been a universally popular addition, but as owner of two of the island's five properties, Felton's wishes often tended to prevail, much to Valentin's annoyance.

Jaden had already fumbled the gate open by the time Joe caught up with him. They stepped down on to a short path of earth and gravel, fringed by wild grasses, bleached almost white by the sun. Less than ten yards away was the narrow shingle beach that ran along the island's southern shore, facing the open sea.

It was a beautiful, solitary location, mostly ignored by the residents, and little known to the outside world. Visitors weren't prohibited on the Reach, but nor were they encouraged. There were no parking areas, and the asphalt road gave way to a narrow track of beaten earth for the last thirty yards between the Weavers' home and the beach. In the way of further deterrents, nettles and brambles had been allowed to encroach on the path, and a sign marked 'PRIVATE PROPERTY' had been erected – illegally – by Robert Felton.

Today, however, those deterrents had failed.

There was a stranger on the island.

Gough heard them before he saw them, but only by a second or two. He didn't have time to react, and he was professional enough to know that sudden movements attract suspicion. So do furtive ones, in a situation like this. Better not to move at all.

He ignored them for a moment, then realised it would be unnatural to show no curiosity. So he turned and gave them a glance. A man and a boy, dressed for the beach. The man had a couple of towels rolled up under his arm.

They were from the Nasenko house, he thought. The kid was the wife's bastard offspring: nothing to do with Nasenko.

The man was a bodyguard. Had to be.

Gough made eye contact with him, registered the man's surprise, and maybe something else. Something harsher. To counteract it he gave the sort of quick nod that said: *Hello*, but also: *Yeah, I'm here, too. Get over it.*

Then he went back to ignoring them, knowing simple politeness demanded they ignore him in turn. He gripped his fishing rod and stared at the sea and worked very hard not to glance at the rucksack by his side. But he was acutely aware of what it contained.

If they left him alone, all well and good.

If they didn't, there was always the gun.

THE POWER OF READING

Visit the Random House website and get connected with information on all our books and authors

EXTRACTS from our recently published books and selected backlist titles

COMPETITIONS AND PRIZE DRAWS Win signed books, audiobooks and more

AUTHOR EVENTS Find out which of our authors are on tour and where you can meet them

LATEST NEWS on bestsellers, awards and new publications

MINISITES with exclusive special features dedicated to our authors and their titles

READING GROUPS Reading guides, special features and a the information you need for your reading group

LISTEN to extracts from the latest audiobook publications

WATCH video clips of interviews and readings with our authors

RANDOM HOUSE INFORMATION including advice for writers, job vacancies and all your general queries answered

Come home to Random House

www.rbooks.co.uk